Joy Dettman was born in country Victoria and spent her early years in towns on either side of the Murray River. She is an award-winning writer of short stories, the complete collection of which, *Diamonds in the Mud*, was published in 2007, as well as the highly acclaimed novels *Mallawindy*, *Jacaranda Blue*, *Goose Girl*, *Yesterday's Dust*, *The Seventh Day*, *Henry's Daughter*, *One Sunday*, *Pearl in a Cage*, *Thorn on the Rose*, *Wind in the Wires* and *Ripples on a Pond*. *Moth to the Flame* is Joy's third novel in her Woody Creek series.

Also by Joy Dettman

Mallawindy
Jacaranda Blue
Goose Girl
Yesterday's Dust
The Seventh Day
Henry's Daughter
One Sunday
Diamonds in the Mud

Woody Creek series
Pearl in a Cage
Thorn on the Rose
Wind in the Wires
Ripples on a Pond

Joy Dettman

MOTH TO THE FLAME

PAN

First published 2011 in Macmillan by Pan Macmillan Australia Pty Limited
This Pan edition published 2012 by Pan Macmillan Australia Pty Limited
1 Market Street, Sydney

National Library of Australia Cataloguing-in-Publication data:

Dettman, Joy.

Moth to the flame / Joy Dettman.

9781742610818 (pbk.)

Woody creek series; no. 3.

A823.3

Typeset in 12.5/16 pt Adobe Garamond by Post Pre-press Group
Printed by IVE

For Hannah and Dallas

PREVIOUSLY IN
THORN ON THE ROSE

Characters, in order of importance:

Gertrude Foote, retired town midwife, mother of **Amber Morrison**, grandmother of **Jenny** and **Sissy Morrison**.

Vern Hooper, father of **Lorna**, **Margaret** and **Jim**. **Vern**, mill owner, farmer, leading Woody Creek citizen, is also **Gertrude's** half-cousin and long-term lover.

Margot, **Georgie** and **Jimmy Morrison**, Jenny's illegitimate children. **Margot** is the daughter of **Bernie** or **Macka Macdonald**, conceived when a drunken prank turned to rape. **Georgie** is the daughter of **Laurie Morgan**, the redheaded water-pistol bandit who looked like Clark Gable. **Jimmy** is the son of **Jim Hooper**.

Cara Jeanette, Jenny's guilty secret. Her father may have been any one of five drunken American sailors. **Myrtle Norris**, a childless Sydney landlady, is no longer childless.

J.C. — Juliana Conti, the stranger buried beneath a small grey tombstone in Woody Creek's cemetery, and **Jenny's** birth mother.

Archie Foote, **Gertrude's** philandering husband and **Jenny's** natural father.

Maisy and **George Macdonald**, parents of eight daughters and hell-raising identical twin sons, **Bernie** and **Macka**.

Harry Hall, married to **Elsie**, a light-skinned Aboriginal woman raised since the age of twelve by **Gertrude**. The Halls have several children. **Joey Hall**, **Elsie's** son, born when she was twelve.

Charlie White, town grocer, and his daughter, **Hilda**.

Mr and **Miss Blunt**, town drapers.

Mr Foster, Woody Creek's postmaster.

Constable Denham.

Raymond King, a giant, stuttering youth who disappeared from Woody Creek fifteen years ago. Returns on a motorbike for his sister's funeral.

Jenny Morrison, born to a foreign woman who died before Gertrude Foote, the town midwife, learned her name, was adopted by Norman Morrison, a strange but gentle man, and his mentally unstable wife, Amber. At fourteen years old, with a wonderful life before her, Jenny is raped and gives birth to a daughter, Margot. She refuses to acknowledge the child, and flees Woody Creek to escape the marriage arranged by Amber and her rapists' father. Four months later, Jenny returns, with an expensive new wardrobe and a secret. Warned by Norman that she must make no attempt to contact her mother and sister, Jenny finds refuge with her always dependable granny, Gertrude. Within days, Jenny tells Gertrude she must return to the city.

'It's happened again,' she admits. 'But it's all right this time. I've got the name of a doctor who can fix it.'

'Fix it?' Gertrude replies. 'Murder is my name for it. Butchery, carnage, war on the innocent . . .'

The infant, Georgie, is born on the night of a storm. Once Jenny sees that baby's tiny hands, miniatures of her own, she can't give her away to strangers.

Jenny's sister, Sissy, has pursued Jim Hooper for years, and in 1940 they announce their engagement. Jim was always like a big brother to Jenny. He's the only boy in town who still treats her like Jenny, and with whom she can be the girl she used to be. Their friendship becomes something more. Six weeks before the wedding to Sissy, Jim has a change of heart and joins the army. Eight months later, Jenny's third child, Jimmy, Jim Hooper's son, is born, and, once again, Jenny flees the town, this time to Sydney and to Jim. He wants to meet his son before he is sent overseas.

Jim buys Jenny a wedding ring. He tells her she has to marry him, if just for Jimmy's sake. She is eighteen and requires parental permission to wed. She promises to marry him on her twenty-first birthday. Jim Hooper leaves Australia to fight the Japanese, and Jenny makes a life for herself in Sydney as Mrs Jenny Hooper, mother of one.

As a child, Jenny was hailed as Woody Creek's little songbird. By 1942, she is known as the girl who went off the rails — but not so in Sydney, an enormous, anonymous place. She finds work there with a band, singing at clubs and parties, finally living her childhood dream, her past wiped away. Happy, in love, working hard, caring for Jimmy, living an exemplary life, Jenny waits for Jim to return and for the promised happily ever after.

In 1943, Jim is listed as *missing in action*. The news comes in a telegram from Gertrude to the boarding house where Jenny and Jimmy are living with their landlady, Myrtle Norris. Jenny wears Jim's ring but she is not his wife. Once again, life begins to fall apart for Jenny, and in November of 1944 she returns to Woody Creek, leaving a part of her behind with Myrtle; a secret she must keep forever from Gertrude.

Gertrude never changes, nor does life on her fifteen-acre property. But Jenny has been changed by her two years in Sydney; and Margot and Georgie have grown. Jenny has difficulty enough settling back into a life of hard labour and no luxuries, without Vern Hooper and his daughters making things more difficult by trying to take Jimmy from her. Vern is determined to raise his only grandson in the Hooper household.

In 1945, Jenny and her father, Norman, are reconciled, the war ends and the army boys start coming home.

Ray King, a nervous stuttering boy who disappeared from Woody Creek fifteen years ago, returns for his sister's funeral. He tells Gertrude he is a widower, that he has a house in Melbourne. He tells Jenny he loves her. Each weekend he rides the many miles to court her.

'I've got three kids, Ray. I can't marry anyone,' Jenny says, but Ray persists.

Is this Jenny's chance to begin life again?

Sissy has found her own way out of Woody Creek. She spends her life as a guest in the homes of Norman's many relatives. Amber, who has lived for Sissy, lived through Sissy, is a lost woman. She is also a violent woman, unstable for most of her married life, wedded to a man she loathes. She murders Norman while he is sleeping.

Jenny, so recently reconciled with Norman, must now deal with his loss. And if that is not enough, Archie Foote, Gertrude's philandering husband, arrives in town for the funeral. He's close to eighty, has no grandfatherly inclinations, but is perhaps ready for fatherhood. Two daughters were born to him: Amber and Jenny. He played no positive role in Amber's life, but since sighting Jenny on stage as a nine year old, he has been obsessed by her voice. He speaks to Gertrude and admits his connection to Jenny, and identifies the unfortunate foreign woman, J.C., who gave birth to Jenny then died, as Juliana Conti. Archie tells Gertrude he has come into money and is now in a position to guide Jenny.

'She will take her rightful place on the world stage,' he says; a stage denied to him by his surgeon father.

Gertrude's hand is forced. She tells Jenny the truth of her birth. Jenny is distraught.

'I don't care if it's the truth or not. Can't you see what you're doing with your truth, Granny? You're taking everything away from me. You're taking you away from me, and you're all I've ever had.'

Can Jenny come to terms with what she learns that night, or is she destined to make one more bad decision?

PART ONE

PART ONE

AND AWAY

At six thirty on the evening of Saturday, 13 January 1946, Gertrude Foote's old cart, loaded with cartons, cases, kids and the miscellaneous, drove into the station yard. It was seen and commented on by many. Norman's railway house had to be readied for the new stationmaster. Margaret Hooper and several more decided that Gertrude's late trip into town had something to do with the clearing out of that house.

Maisy Macdonald knew what was going on. Twice today she'd spoken to Jenny. She left the dinner dishes in the sink and walked across the road to help with the unloading. The cart's contents piled down the far end of the platform, the temporary stationmaster in his ticket office, Jenny in there with him, Ray King not in earshot, Maisy took the opportunity to ask a question that had been niggling at her all day.

'Does she know what she's doing, Mrs Foote?'

'She doesn't know if she's coming or going, love.'

Gertrude had spent the day attempting to talk Jenny out of leaving with Ray King.

'What brought it on?'

'Too much,' Gertrude said. 'Too much, piled on top of too much more.'

'I've been wondering if she's heard the talk that's been going around?'

'About Amber?'

'Jim.'

But Jenny was coming, and so was the train. It was rarely on time. Tonight it was ten minutes early. They heard its elongated hoot, warning traffic — or dogs and kids — to clear the line up at Charlie White's crossing.

Two of Jenny's trio ran down the platform to watch its approach. The third of them, the oldest, Margot, ran to Gertrude.

'Not going on the train,' she said.

'It will be a big adventure, darlin',' Gertrude told her.

Adventure? God alone knew where those kids would end up tonight. Ray had a house, so he said, but what sort of a house? Gertrude had known his parents, had known the way they'd lived too.

'I offered to take Margot until they get settled in,' Maisy said.

'Jenny's intent on cutting her ties with Woody Creek.'

'Did someone mention Jim to her at the funeral, I wonder?'

'Why Jim?' Gertrude asked, but the train and the ensuing bustle killed further conversation.

'Time to go, Margot,' Jenny said. 'Say goodbye now.'

'I'm not going, I thaid.'

'We're all going. Let go of Granny.'

Margot wrapped herself more tightly around Gertrude's long, trousered leg. There wasn't much of the little girl, but what little there was was undiluted determination. Jenny turned away to lift Jimmy and Georgie on board, seemingly prepared to allow Margot to remain — or was it psychological warfare? Margot bawled as her siblings disappeared. Gertrude untangled and carried her to the train where she handed her into Ray's arms. No final kisses, no final words — it was too sudden.

Doors closing, the engine hissing, puffing dark smoke into the evening air. There was a smell about train smoke, a smell like no other, and a sadness about it tonight. Those kids had been Gertrude's life for too long. Her searching eyes sighted Georgie's hair at an open window — like molten copper, that hair. Gertrude walked down the platform blowing kisses. Two small heads out that window now, blowing their kisses back, happy little faces, eager for what was to come next. As was the train tonight. Its many wheels jerked forward and Gertrude stepped back — stepped back into Maisy.

'They're saying that Jim has been in one of those Jap prison camps, that he's in a Melbourne hospital. Has Vern said anything to you, Mrs Foote?'

'It's rubbish,' Gertrude replied.

'I'm not sure that it is.'

'Of course it is.'

Little family being drawn away by those wheels, Jenny waving, Ray standing at her side.

'The Hoopers have been down in Melbourne. I didn't know they were back until I saw Vern and Margaret at the funeral. The talk around town is that they were down there with Jim, Mrs Foote.'

No comment from Gertrude, or not until she could no longer see Georgie's hair. 'Rubbish.'

'I would have thought so too if I hadn't heard it from Sylvia, Bert Croft's wife,' Maisy said. 'She's not the type to come out with a thing like that if it had no fact to it — and at a Red Cross meeting in front of a dozen or more. Vern hasn't said anything at all to you?'

'He hasn't, and he doesn't need to hear that sort of gossip either,' Gertrude said.

'Margaret is always at those Red Cross meetings. Someone asked why she wasn't this time, and Sylvia Croft said she'd no doubt be down at the hospital in Melbourne —'

'Vern's always down there seeing some doctor or other.'

'That's what I thought, then she said that young Gloria Bull — you'd remember she went into nursing? — well, Sylvia said she's nursing at one of those rehabilitation hospitals for the returned soldiers. Her mother and Sylvia Croft were as thick as thieves when the Bulls owned the hotel. Mrs Bull told Sylvia in her last letter that Gloria was nursing Jim Hooper — that they'd flown him down from some hospital up north. She said the Japs had made a terrible mess of him. I don't think there's any mistake, Mrs Foote.'

'Vern would have told me,' Gertrude said.

'Would he though — I mean, knowing you'd tell Jenny? The last thing he'd want would be to see those two involved again, Mrs Foote.'

Gertrude couldn't deny that. She walked away from it.

Her horse, a middle-aged black gelding waiting between the shafts, lifted his head as she approached, flicked his tail at a late fly. She patted his neck for his patience, then untied the reins from the wheel — the cart's only brake, and effective enough for a horse who required no brake.

'Will you come over and have a cuppa with me?' Maisy said. 'Sylvia's got the phone on. I could give her a call for you.'

'I'll be losing the light soon, love,' Gertrude said.

The spokes of the big wheel her ladder, she climbed up to the cart's plank seat, more easily than a seventy-year-old woman should.

'I'll give her a call anyway and see what I can find out,' Maisy said.

'There'll be no truth in it,' Gertrude said. 'Young Gloria will be confusing the Hoopers with someone else.'

She flicked the reins and the old horse wheeled around and clip-clopped out through the dust of the railway yard.

Vern Hooper sat on his eastern veranda enjoying the evening air and looking to the future. And maybe he had one now. The time was ripe to go after custody of Jimmy. Given what had gone on in Woody Creek this past week, no judge would refuse a caring grandfather's claim. The papers were ready. Vern had instructed his solicitor to give that girl a week to get over the loss of her father then to get those papers in the post.

He heard Gertrude's cart coming, raised a hand as it went by, then stood to gain a better view. Margaret had seen the cart on its way into town with three kids on board. They weren't riding it home.

He limped down to the northern corner of the veranda, knowing those kids were in the cart, that he wasn't seeing them. Not there to see. She was riding alone.

'She's taken him, Father,' Margaret said, coming at a run through the rear door. 'She's taken him on the train.'

He turned to her, his long jaw sagging. 'Her father's not cold in his grave.' And he'd taken pity on the hot pants little bitch?

Cart and horse gone now, disappearing into the gloom of dusk, Vern left staring at an empty road. And his grandson on that train, gone to Christ only knew where with a bike-riding, leather-booted lout he'd been planning to use as part of his arsenal in court.

'You were advised to strike while the iron was hot. We pay a fortune for the solicitor and you chose to ignore his advice.'

Lorna, his firstborn, came from the front of the house, marched by him and around the corner. When agitated, Lorna wore out the veranda's floorboards with her marching. A know-all bugger of a woman, that one. She should have been born the male, Vern thought. No Jap would have taken her alive — nor wanted to.

She was right though. He had no one to blame but himself. The day they'd heard Jim was being moved down south, they should have got those papers underway, or got it fixed so she couldn't take that boy out of town. Too much on his mind at the time. First things first, he'd said. We get Jim well, get him home, then we get his boy. That's what he'd said.

His house, built around the turn of the century, was a classic for its period, a country classic. Tall tin roof, painted red, white woodwork, doors opening onto wide verandas, fancy veranda posts painted white; a substantial house, shaded by substantial trees, surrounded by a hedge of roses, past their best blooming but still putting on a fine show.

Lorna, black-clad, a tall ungainly woman, completed her circuit of the verandas and continued her lecture as she approached her father and sister for the second time. 'The time to make our move was when the murder was on the front pages of every newspaper.'

Plain as mud, taller than most males, tongue as bitter as gall, she was useless as a woman. Couldn't iron a shirt, couldn't make a decent cup of tea, never defiled her hands with a recipe book, but damn near ran Vern's sawmill — from a distance. Had he allowed it, she would have been down there browbeating his mill hands as she browbeat her sister, as she'd been attempting to browbeat him since his stroke. He was a match for her yet. He kept her away from the mill.

'We've had a setback,' Vern called after her. 'It's not the end of it. Not by a long shot.'

He didn't understand her obsession with Jimmy. She'd shown no interest in that boy until '42.

'Nero fiddles while Rome burns,' she snorted, again rounding the corner, this time colliding with her weeping sister. 'Control yourself, Margaret!'

The fat and skinny of them. The short and tall of them. The weeping and the snorting of them, and Vern dependent on both since his stroke.

'God will bring him back to us,' Margaret sniffled. 'The first day I held that beautiful little boy in my arms, I knew I was meant to raise him.'

'A bitch always returns to her kennel,' Lorna said and she marched on.

*

Forest darkening, black horse clip-clopping soft through the dust, old cart creaking, seat swaying, gravel crunching beneath iron-shod wheels.

How many times have I travelled this road? Gertrude thought. Countless.

The forest had a different smell to it by night, a different sound. Trees sighing, settling for the night, dust cooling, the whisper of an owl's wings, the chorus of frogs, the plaintive cry of night birds.

She lifted her face to the evening air, breathing it deep, and for an instant she was young again. I've lived alone before, she thought. I'll have room to spread myself. I'll miss those kids.

He loves her. You only have to look at his eyes when she's in the room to know he loves her — and to look at her eyes to know that she doesn't love him.

Jim alive? What if it's not gossip?

Vern would have told me. He couldn't keep something like that from me.

Gloria Bull had gone into nursing, as had her sister. Gertrude knew that to be fact. She also knew Sylvia Croft as a quiet little woman, not one to gossip.

If it's true, Gertrude thought. If it's true, Vern has known for years Jim was a prisoner. Tom Vevers' second boy died in a prison camp. They were told by some department that he was in that camp, were told when he died there.

It can't be true. I know that man like I know myself.

People become who they live with.

She'd never got on with Vern's daughters, had spent years keeping her distance from them. Vern'd lived with his grandfather for the first twenty-three years of his life, and a harder old sod had never walked this earth.

He wouldn't do that to me.

He'd do it to Jenny fast enough.

That fool of a girl, running off to God only knew where with three little kids and a man she barely knew.

Ray had a job and a house to take them to — so he'd said. He'd told Gertrude he was going to marry her. Maybe he would. And maybe she'd come home pregnant again — and God save me from that, Gertrude thought.

He'd been married before — so he said. A man accustomed to having a wife was more likely to take on a second. Look at Vern. He'd done it three times. It could work out for the best. It could work out for the best for those kids. What chance did they have in this town? Memories were too long in Woody Creek. And putting distance between those girls and Archie Foote was to the good. If that man wanted something enough, he'd pursue it until he got it.

'The bastardry of men,' she said aloud, unsure if her words were for Archie or Vern.

She'd seen Vern at Norman's funeral, or sighted him out front of the church. Too involved with Jenny, she'd had no chance to speak to him. She'd met Margaret's eyes — and they'd looked like frightened fish seeking a rock to hide behind. That girl's face was an open book. It could have been true.

Gertrude's horse, familiar with the forest road and the track leading off from the road to the boundary gate, made the turn without need of guidance, which was as well. Gertrude's mind wasn't on the job tonight.

I've got to think it's for the best. I've got to hope it's all for the best. Hope. It's all there is sometimes, she thought as she climbed down from the cart and swung the gate wide. Her horse walked himself through and kept on walking while she closed it. He knew her habits. She knew his.

The sky was clear tonight; a few stars already peeking out. She glanced up, seeking the brightest star.

'Watch over those kids,' she said. 'Guide her in the right direction.'

DISCONNECTION

Norman Morrison was murdered on or around Saturday, 6 January 1946, his battered body found in his bed three days later. For almost thirty years he had been Woody Creek's stationmaster. Three weeks after his death, the Railway Department sent up a permanent replacement. Five kids now ran wild in Norman's yard, a pup peed in his parlour, while two cats ran up and down the curtains.

Norman was not a man to be sorely missed. He had been at his best in impersonal situations, a pen and paper in his hands. The Parents and Citizens Association missed his efficiency at their first meeting in February. The Church of England Ball Committee would miss his organisational skills, but not until their first meeting in April.

Jenny didn't miss him, as in miss seeing him. In recent years, she'd seen little of her father. The gaping gash of no Norman had been inside her since she was fourteen; his death was a new bruise around the gash, that's all. It was the knowledge that she had no right to mourn him, that he wasn't her real father, that created the aching hollow of no Norman.

She should have been able to get over it. Things could have

been a whole heap worse than they were. The weather was good. Melbourne's summer days were as hot as Woody Creek's, but the nights weren't. Melbourne offered beautiful nights. And the house Ray had brought them to in the dead of night: it was a house worthy of the name. Red brick on the outside, plaster on the inside, high ceilings. Even on the hottest days, its rooms remained cool. Granny's house became an oven on such days.

Everything was good, so why couldn't she feel good?

Because she couldn't deal with knowing what she knew. Not at night, she couldn't. During daylight hours, her senses bombarded by new places, new people, with three kids dependent on her for everything, she could almost feel like their mother. It was the nights, when the kids were in bed, when their eyes were closed and she had to look out at the dark of Melbourne through her own eyes — that's when she knew there was nothing out there she wanted to see.

Thought that if she'd run fast enough, far enough, she wouldn't have to deal with what she was, who she was — who she wasn't. But how could anyone deal with it?

It was no use denying it either. She knew it was true because it answered every question she'd ever asked herself or Granny.

It was the reason Amber never could stand the sight of her. It was the reason old Noah had given her the pearl-in-a-cage earrings and pendant. It was the reason why Granny's wedding photograph had disappeared from her wall — she'd seen Jenny's similarity to the youthful Itchy-foot. The pieces fitted into place like a giant jigsaw puzzle. Everything. Every single thing. The twins' tormenting chant fitted: *Old J.C., she went off to have a pee, squatted down behind a tree, dropped her pants and found Jenny, old J.C. now stinks up the cemetery* . . . It was all true. J.C. of that little grey tombstone, who, as a child, Jenny had given flowers to, had died giving birth to her. Archie Foote, absconding husband of Granny, father of Amber, was also Jenny's sire — which made her a murderess's half-sister, which was worse than being a murderess's daughter.

Her brain crawled with it. Day and night it crawled with it. And how could anyone let go of something that was eating their head from within?

For twenty-two years she may not have liked who she was but Jenny had known who she was. Jennifer Carolyn, daughter of Norman Morrison, the stationmaster. She'd had a sister, Cecelia Louise, who she may not have been able to stand, but Sissy had always been her sister. Now she wasn't.

And Granny, the only person in the world who, no matter what Jenny had done, no matter what she'd said, had loved her. Now she'd found she wasn't even distantly related to Gertrude. She wasn't related to anyone — except Amber and Archie Foote. It was her disconnection Jenny couldn't deal with, from Norman, from Granny. It was the hollow left inside from the ripping out of that connection that she couldn't fill. Always, forever, when she'd had no one else in the world to cling to, she'd known Granny was there.

Nothing there now. And it was like drowning, it was like drowning in emptiness, from the inside out, and trying to save yourself by gripping onto a spider's web. Every time she thought she had a grip, the web melted in her hands.

Just pretending to be alive now, that's all; just doing, not being. Every day. And knowing she'd been supposed to die with Juliana, that the grey tombstone should have read: *J.C. AND INFANT LEFT THIS LIFE 31.12.23.*

Should have kept your mouth shut then Nancy Bryant wouldn't have found you, she thought. It would have finished before it started.

Before what started?

Nothing.

Jenny, an unnamed life form, exists in a brick house, in a long street, with three nameless kids, and each day, while another inch of her disappears, she pretends to be something.

Ray had introduced her to the Parkers, who shared the house, as a schoolfriend's widow, now his wife. He'd bought her a wedding ring. She hadn't put it on. Hadn't needed to put it on. She still wore Jim's ring, *Jen and Jim, 1942* engraved on its inner circle.

'Good morning, Mrs King,' the Parkers said.

She wasn't Mrs King, wasn't Jim's widow, wasn't Norman's daughter or Granny's granddaughter. She wasn't anything — and wasn't a mother either. Her kids slept on Sissy's old mattress on the floor, and she slept with them — or didn't sleep.

Ray had a good bed, a big wardrobe, beautiful dressing table. She'd done an Amber, had polished them for him. He hadn't noticed the polish. He wanted her in his bed. And she didn't want to be in it. If she knew one thing, she now knew that. 'Can we go back to Melbourne with you, Ray? I have to get out of here. I don't expect you to marry me,' she'd said.

Marrying him would get rid of the Morrison name. She'd be legally someone. Maybe this was her chance to start again.

You can't rip out half of a book's pages then, in the middle of a paragraph, become involved in a half-told story. She'd be turning pages, that's all.

She had to go.

Go where?

Nowhere.

There were three little kids in that back bedroom, asleep on their mattress, and wherever she went she'd have to take them and their mattress with her. What did they call those things the old sailing boats had dragged behind them to slow them down in a wind storm? Whatever. She had three and a mattress behind her, and she was sinking fast.

Should have left them with Granny. Should have dumped them — like she'd dumped Cara Jeanette in Sydney.

Stop.

Couldn't stand to think about that one. Wanted to vomit every time she thought about that little girl growing up in Myrtle's house, thinking she was someone she wasn't. Poor little unnamed life form, born of an unnamed life form, looking out at the world through Amberley's leadlight window — and nothing, no one, outside that window for her to run to. Blank space. Emptiness.

'Archie Foote spent his life running away,' Gertrude had said that last day. 'You learn nothing while you're running, darlin'. Look at the nomads of this world — they've had the same tens of thousands of years as civilised man to learn in, but they were too busy scratching for their next meal to learn how to plant a crop. Stay here with me. Give yourself time to come to terms with who you are.'

How could she have stayed? How could she have walked into town to buy a newspaper and seen AMBER MORRISON splashed all over the front pages? It was bad enough down here where she was no one.

AMBER MORRISON UNFIT TO STAND TRIAL.

AMBER MORRISON TRANSFERRED TO ASYLUM FOR THE CRIMI-NALLY INSANE.

Amber Morrison, mentally deranged murderess, and her conscienceless father were the only two people on this earth Jenny could claim as blood relatives, and at night she knew she was as mad, as bad, as both of them.

Look what she'd done to her life. Look at those little kids she'd given as much thought to making as she gave to making pancakes. Instead of sitting out here feeling sorry for herself, she should have been standing on some street corner selling herself. At least she'd have money in her handbag, at least she could buy those kids a bed.

Ray didn't want them. He hadn't offered to buy them a bed.

Amber had sold herself for money. That was in the newspapers too, how years ago she'd been jailed for stabbing one of her clients.

Norman must have known. And he'd taken her back into his house to mother two kids. What the hell had he been thinking of?

Question: How does a woman lie beneath multiple men for money?

Question: How does a woman stab her sleeping husband with the same knife she'd used to carve a thousand slices of meat? How does she smash his dear old face with the cast-iron frying pan he'd used a hundred times to fry eggs for breakfast, to fry cheese sandwiches for supper?

Question: How do you wipe that from your mind?

Question: How do you wipe away your last image of the man you've thought of as Daddy for twenty-two years?

It couldn't be done. Every time she closed her eyes she saw him lying on that table, covered up and cold. Every time she closed her eyes she could feel his cold dead hand in her own.

Kissed his hand goodbye because they wouldn't let her kiss his face — like they hadn't let Mrs Abbot see Nelly's face.

Stop!

Question: How do I stop?

Impossible.

The psychiatrist who had examined Amber in jail had spoken to the newspapers with great authority on the minds of menopausal woman, how they could disassociate a violent act from their conscious state. He'd spoken about Amber Morrison's constant pregnancies, her four dead babies. The following day, the newspapers printed two columns about her missing womb and ovaries.

Jenny could have told them Amber's violent act had nothing to do with ovaries or dead babies; that she'd been pregnant the first time she'd tried her hand at murder. She might have been successful that day if Mr Foster hadn't ruined her fun.

If I'd died when I was three, Norman might still be alive, Barbie Dobson and Nelly Abbot might still be alive, two newborn babies at the hospital might still be alive . . .

One murder was enough for the police, though not the newspapers. Yesterday they'd found an unsolved knife murder in Melbourne during the last year Amber had been selling herself on the streets — the victim, a younger prostitute.

God help Granny. How was she surviving those newspapers? No more 'Granny'. How was Gertrude surviving those newspapers? Her excuse for Amber had always been Archie Foote's bad seed. A very fine thing to blame — until you learn that you carry that same bad seed, until you know you've already passed it on to four innocent little kids.

They didn't have a hope! And she couldn't give them any hope.

Maybe she had, inadvertently, given Cara Jeanette a pinch of hope. Maybe church-going Myrtle and magical Amberley would eradicate that bad seed, poison it with love.

Ray's name would eradicate the Morrison name. Her kids would live in a nice house with a bathroom. And a refrigerator, an almost new refrigerator. Georgina King sounded regal.

They needed to be in school, or two of them did. Couldn't bring herself to enrol them as Morrisons; last school attended, Woody Creek. Not while Amber and that town were in the headlines.

Does a sire's bad seed, when added to a dam's lack of morals, allow the resulting life form to think about marrying a man she doesn't love, a man who can't read as well as a six year old, just to give her kids a chance at life?

He was a good man, shy, strange. He said he loved her. He told her she was beautiful. He told her he'd take care of her kids.

He wanted to have sex with her, that's why. Men had been wanting to have sex with her since she was fourteen — and had taken what they'd wanted too.

Not him. Not once had he tried to force himself on her.

Mrs Jennifer King. It sounded like someone, not her, but maybe a character in that mutilated book.

Couldn't do it — not after being with Jim, not after being Mrs Hooper.

She'd done it with Laurie, just closed her eyes and recited 'Daffodils'. He'd usually been done with her before she'd reached the third verse.

Until death do us part. That was the trouble: the forever of marriage. Didn't want that forever.

And he'd get her pregnant.

Plenty of tall buildings in Melbourne —

Everyone gets married. Not many actually die of marriage.

Norman had.

He survived twenty-odd years of it.

Question: Who else but Ray was likely to marry a woman with three illegitimate kids?

Question: What else was she planning to do with the next twenty years?

Nothing. Nothing ahead but empty space; nothing but ruin behind her — and she was never, never, never going back to face that ruin.

Ray was a Catholic. Until death do us part meant what it said if you were Catholic.

Question: Does forever have any meaning to an unnamed life form drowning in a stagnant pool?

Question: If an unnamed life form is attempting to escape the mud slide behind it, does it stop to read signposts to see if it's swimming the right way?

On Friday, 9 February, Jennifer Carolyn Morrison married Raymond Henry King at the Melbourne Registry Office. He'd wanted to buy her a white dress. He'd wanted to be married in church by a priest. He'd settled for what he could get. He'd wanted a wedding photograph to hang like a trophy on the wall. She was no trophy, but she went with him to the photographer and forced a smile for the camera.

Didn't share his bed, not that night, not until the following Tuesday.

February was gone before he picked up the photographs, one 10 x 12, coloured, framed, and two of postcard size. It was a good photograph of him. He was a nice-looking man. Her mouth may have been smiling. Her eyes weren't.

In mid-March she posted one of the smaller photographs to Gertrude. Her accompanying letter was brief. There was nothing she wanted to write. Wouldn't have bothered buying the envelope, the stamp, had she thought to bring Margot's birth certificate with her — if she had one. Jenny had never seen it. The other kids' certificates she'd found in her snakeskin handbag.

Dear Granny,

You'll probably be pleased to hear that he married me. I'm enclosing one of our wedding photographs as proof. We're all well. The girls are in school, which is very handy to Ray's house. It's a big old brick house. The kids have got a huge backyard to play in. I've met a few of the neighbours.

For obvious reasons, I'll ask you not to give my address to Vern and Maisy. If anyone asks where I am, tell them I'm in Sydney, singing with the band.

I don't know if you ever received Margot's birth certificate, but if you've got it somewhere, could you send it down, please.
Love, Jenny

THE HIGHWAYMAN

*R*ay's house wasn't his house. For a time Jenny had believed he rented the west side to the Parkers, who she'd done her best to dodge during her first weeks in Armadale. Since February, the Parkers had been making it very clear who owned the house. Like Myrtle at Amberley, they marked their territory with signs.

East-side residents' bathroom access: Monday, Wednesday, Friday and Sunday evening between 6 and 8 p.m. G&F Parker.

The bathroom was on the west side of the house, the Parkers' side, approached via a long central passage, also Parker territory, as was the front door.

Please use side door entrance. G&F Parker.

Jenny had done the washing whenever she'd raised the incentive to do it during the early weeks. The washhouse was in the backyard, on Ray's side, very conveniently placed to what might have been a back door for the east-side residents had anyone possessed the key to a heavy padlock locking the sleep-out door.

East-side access to laundry: all day Wednesday and Sunday.
G&F Parker.

Motorbike not to be garaged in laundry. G&F Parker.

Jenny and her kids obeyed all instructions. Ray had continued to park his bike in the washhouse until Georgie asked at the dinner table what *garaged* meant.

'People put their cars in garages. Cars and motorbikes are *garaged* in garages,' Jenny said.

Ray had left his meal to move his bike. That was the night Jenny learned how little he could read.

By necessity, the lav was available at all hours, seven days a week, but in March the Parkers found room for a sign behind its door.

Newspaper, cigarette butts and foreign items must not be
flushed. G&F Parker.

You can't evade housemates when you share facilities. You run into them in their passage on your way to and from the bathroom. Meet at the front gate, the clothes line. Women with kids find a way to get along. Jenny knew that Geoff Parker was a returned soldier who had served in Australia and overseas through most of the war years; that Lois, their daughter, had been born nine months to the day after their wedding in 1940. Geoff had returned intact, other than his right index finger. It was a nicotine-stained stub. Thousands of men had come home from the war unscathed. The Macdonald twins had. Not that they'd come home. They were with a peace-keeping force in Japan, and God help Japan.

Ray hadn't been in the army. Jenny didn't know why. He knew a lot about motors, held down a supervisor's job at a factory, managed the money.

There was an article in one of Harry Hall's books about tests carried out in America on a group of soldiers. It claimed that the average soldier possessed the intelligence and will power of a youth of thirteen or fourteen. *Such men, with training and drilling, and under supervision, learn to do automatically, as any child will* . . . which, at the time, had explained to Jenny why the Macdonald twins had landed on their feet in the army. It didn't explain why Ray hadn't been given a gun. He was big, strong, healthy, never missed a day at work. Maybe they hadn't made army boots in his size. His shoes looked like boats.

Big-boned like his father, Granny had said that first day when Ray had drunk tea with them in Woody Creek. Jenny had dim memories of Ray's wood-chopping champion father: huge head, neck thick enough to hold it up, broad as a tree. Ray wasn't as broad in the shoulder and chest yet, but he was heading that way.

She'd been seven years old when they'd buried Big Henry King. Ray had gone missing a week later. She'd known him at school, as a seven-year-old girl knows an eleven-year-old boy. Now, she slept with the man. 'Daffodils' didn't work with him. By April, she was reciting 'The Highwayman'. It had seventeen verses — and she knew the man she slept with no better than she'd known the giant schoolboy.

It might have been easier to get to know him had the Parkers not been a wall away. People lived where they could in Melbourne, where finding a room to rent was like winning the lottery, and finding a house was impossible. Thousands of men had been away fighting. They were home now and all looking for somewhere to live.

Ray had three rooms. The kids' bedroom was small, but no smaller than Granny's lean-to. The kitchen, a converted morning room, had a wall of windows and a glass door. Ray's bedroom was a big, beautiful old room. The position of the house was perfect — school just around the top corner, tram in High Street, train station not much further away.

She'd make a go of it. In India, marriages were arranged by the parents, so Granny had said, the bride and groom not meeting until their wedding day. Given the population of India, those marriages seemed to work well enough — not that Jenny would be adding to the population.

On a Wednesday in early April, a beautiful sunny Wednesday, her washing flapping in the breeze, Jimmy vrooming his trike around the yard, the postman blew his whistle at the front gate. There is a little of the psychic in most of us. Jenny knew he'd blown his whistle for her. She pegged Ray's working trousers and followed Jimmy out to the letterbox, where he removed a fat envelope addressed to Mrs Jennifer King in Gertrude's unmistakable large print.

She'd got full value from that stamp. Margot's birth certificate, two photographs and a four-page letter had been crammed into the envelope; four pages, filled margin to margin. Not a sad letter, just a long chat with Granny, but Jenny's eyes blurred as she devoured each word about the goats, the horse, the horse's lost shoe, the cost of shoeing a horse. She fed on news of Harry and Elsie, news of their kids. Norman's name was there: the estate was paying to have his name added beneath his mother's on her tombstone; what Jenny had planned to do before the funeral, before everything.

She read the pages to Jimmy, or parts of the pages, and when they picked up the girls at three thirty, she read them again at Ray's table. Hearing Granny's words wasn't enough for Georgie. She wanted to hold those pages, to breathe in the scent of Granny. She wanted to know who the bride in the photograph was, and why Jenny didn't have a bride's dress in her photo, and why Granny had sent those photos.

Full of questions, little Georgie, always full of questions. Jenny picked up the head-and-shoulders study of a dark-headed woman wearing an old-fashioned hat, J.C.'s brooch pinned to it. Archie Foote had left the photo on the kitchen table the night of Norman's funeral. The second photograph had been in an old trunk for years. Jenny had seen it as a twelve year old. It was of a bride, standing with a bald-headed man who must have been her father. Without doubt, the bride was a youthful version of the woman in the hat. She looked . . . maybe she looked a little like . . .

'Get your daddy's photo for me, Jimmy.'

It lived on the windowsill in the kid's bedroom, a framed photograph of her, Jim and ten-month-old Jimmy, taken in Sydney. He returned with it, and she studied the two photographs side by side. There was a similarity in the spacing of the eyes, the brow, the eyebrows and definitely the chin.

'Her hand is exactly like your hand in that photo, Jenny,' Georgie said.

Did photographers have an instruction manual on how to pose hands? Exactly the same pose, same ring displayed. Perhaps the same fingers . . .

That's when it became real, or when Juliana Conti became real. She was there, as a bride, as a woman, on Ray's kitchen table.

That's when Jenny No One realised that who she was was here, at and on this table. Those three little kids, who'd had no more say in their birth than she had, who were helpless with her, who had not much in common other than her; and those photographs. The pages of Granny's letter too, every line on them about a world Jenny knew as well as she knew her own hand. And Margot's birth certificate. *Mother's name: Jennifer Carolyn Morrison. Age 15 years. Father's name: Bernard / Cecil Macdonald. Age 18 years.* It was all there, the story of her life. And the photograph of Jim and eighteen-year-old, starry-eyed kid Jenny. And Granny's envelope, MRS JENNIFER KING in large black print, spelling out very clearly who Jenny had contracted to be. It was all there, the scattered pages of her life story. Time to accept it. Time to start gluing that book together.

'She was my real mother,' she said. 'Her name was Juliana Conti. She was your grandmother.'

'Another one,' Jimmy said.

'What's the man's name, Jenny?'

'I don't know. He was probably her father, my grandfather and your great-grandfather.'

'Are they all dead like Grandpa Norman?' Georgie asked.

'A long, long time ago, love.'

'Why does everyone get dead for?' Jimmy asked.

Melbourne's ratbag weather saved her the search for a reply. Rain had a bad habit of blowing in, seemingly from nowhere. Too many houses to hide the sky's intent? Too close to the ocean? Or perhaps the house was at fault — too solid and well established to bother about what went on outside.

She'd learn to read Melbourne's skies, and, until she did, the veranda roof would give fair warning. She'd learn to read Ray too.

MILK IN BOTTLES

A haphazard month, April: sun and rain, summer and winter, hot enough for a hat, then cold enough for a cardigan. If Woody Creek was receiving its share of the rain, mushrooms would be bobbing up their button heads in grassy paddocks. No grassy paddocks down here, or maybe there were, though not where Jenny could see them. Shops and houses replaced paddocks in Melbourne; whole streets full of shops, all manner of shops, entire blocks of houses, and in every direction more blocks of houses then more shops.

Ration coupons were a problem, tea coupons Jenny's main problem. In Woody Creek a pot of tea could remain on the hob all morning, remain hot. No hob down here. Up there if she and Granny had run out of tea coupons, Elsie and Harry always had plenty. They had kids old enough to receive their fair share. Jenny's kids weren't considered old enough to drink tea. They did in Melbourne, where milk came in bottles instead of goats, where they ran out of milk daily unless Jenny rationed it. At home they'd lived on milk, on eggs and custards. In Melbourne they ate what Ray brought home.

They ate his butter too. They'd rarely seen butter in Woody

Creek. He liked to spread it thick on his morning toast. What kids saw, they wanted. Meat had formed a minor part of their diet at home. Ray lived on it. He did the shopping on Saturday mornings, and every Saturday came home loaded down with meat. And he didn't need coupons to buy it. He had no coupons, he said, when Jenny asked him for his tea coupons.

'Everyone gets coupons, Ray.'

Not him.

He came home from work the next night with a brown paper bag of tea; not the same quality as Bushells, but tea was tea. He knew how things worked in the city. She didn't. In Sydney, Norma and Lila, girls from the factory, had known how that city worked. They'd known where to go to buy tea on the black market. They'd sold their clothing coupons to dress shops. Ray must have bought his meat on the black market — and his petrol. He had three jerry cans of it in the corner of his bedroom.

Anyone with a driver's licence received a petrol ration. Plenty of men had licences and no cars to drive. Where there is a will to make money, man will find a way. Jenny needed money but as yet had found no way to make it. Twice now she'd been into her bank account. Hated seeing that hard-worked for total going down.

Petrol rationing was a problem to Geoff Parker. In April, he had a gas-converter contraption fitted onto the rear of his Dodge. The second time he took it out, the car had to be towed home from Lilydale. Flora wasn't happy. Jenny was — because of Ray. He had no friends. That car got the two men talking.

'They're like kids with a new toy,' Flora said.

'Ray likes motors,' Jenny said.

He came in greasy when there was no more light to play in, washed his hands at the sink, sharing his black grease with sink, tap and floor. They ate late that night, the kids fed and in bed, Ray itching to go to his. He was happy, which meant 'The Highwayman'.

Then, at half past eight, Geoff Parker knocked on the passage door.

'Thought Ray might like to have a look at this,' he said when Jenny opened the door.

He had the little yellow book the gas-converter company supplied with each system fitted. The men sat at the table, smoking and leafing through the book. Jenny kept her distance until Flora came to the open door wanting to know what was keeping Geoff. Jenny asked her in for a cup of tea.

Ten o'clock, the cups long empty and the Parkers taken root at the table, Geoff dominating the conversation. An ex-army corporal, he had the voice for it.

'The gas is drawn in here; it goes through the security filter, then it's drawn along the gas line and into the mixer valve.'

His stump of finger followed the diagram in the book, Jenny's eyes followed the finger stump. That furnace contraption burnt charcoal. Bags of the stuff were now stored in the washhouse where Ray used to park his bike. Apparently some form of gas could be made by the burning charcoal, which worked more or less like petrol.

'I'm never riding in it again,' Flora said. 'I said it was dangerous all along.'

'A table fork is dangerous in the hands of a fool,' Geoff said. 'It's written in black and white for any fool to read. *Precautionary measures must be borne in mind at all times.* Follow the instructions and it's no more dangerous than petrol.'

Jenny took her precautionary measures at all times, and didn't trust them yet. Ray had been married before; she'd thought he'd know what he had to do. He hadn't. She'd gone to a pharmacy and bought him two packets of rubber sheaths, nearly died of embarrassment asking for them, and all for nothing. He'd gone red in the face and ridden off on his bike when she'd suggested he use them. He hadn't come home that night. When he did, he refused to talk about using them so she'd refused to sleep with him. There were things a woman could use. She'd visited two doctors before finding one who would tell her. The first doctor had recommended abstinence.

'The petrol ration they dole out is useless,' Geoff said. He was a salesman. He went to work in a collar and tie. 'They give you enough to do sixty, seventy miles a month, and what's the good of that to me?'

'You could have used it when you had your wife and daughter in the car,' Flora said.

'It will be no different to driving on petrol once I get the hang of it. All it is is charcoal fumes and water.'

'Water?' Jenny asked.

'Water turned to steam,' Geoff said. 'It gets drawn into the charcoal-heated zone where it hits the carbon gas, which goes along this pipe —'

'And we're supposed to drive around in a car with a burning furnace and a tank of boiling water behind us?' Flora said.

'Precautionary measures must be borne in mind at all times. I bear them in mind.' His voice was rising.

As was Flora's. 'That chap in Brunswick no doubt bore them in mind too.'

There'd been an item in the newspaper a week or ten days ago about a father of five who had burnt his shed down and burnt himself with one of those contraptions. Jenny had read it out to Ray and hadn't known what she'd been reading about. Now she knew. Flora's mother lived in Brunswick and knew the family.

Jenny eyed the overflowing ashtray as Geoff lit another cigarette. Wished he'd offer his packet. He didn't, nor did Ray. Married men smoked. Their wives emptied the ashtrays. Married men talked motors. Their wives' minds wandered. Ray smoked too much. Geoff was never seen without a cigarette in his hand, held between his stump and second finger.

She stood, replaced the full tray with an empty, washed her hands at the sink, got grease on her hand from the tap. Washed it off with a soapy rag, washed the tap with the soapy rag, then strained to turn the tap tighter. It dripped. Having a sink and water on tap was a miracle. She could stand the drips, which was just as well because she couldn't stop them. Having access to unlimited water, having a bathroom for two hours four nights a week, with a proper bath and a gas bath heater, was a miracle. Most of Melbourne was.

'He parks a hot car in a shed,' Geoff said. 'And he's got a drum full of black-market petrol in there, the bastard —'

'Geoff!'

'Well, he is.'

Jenny slept in a room with three jerry cans of black-market petrol, and Ray smoked in bed. No precautionary measures for him.

She wondered if Geoff took his precautionary measures in the bedroom. Flora wasn't pregnant.

He parked his car in the open, out front, where a lawn might have grown if someone had watered it. No one did. Ray raked up the leaves that fell to it. Plenty of land for things to grow, but nothing growing, only weeds. Miss Flowers, from across the road, had a running war against weeds. She had a beautiful garden. With a name like that, she was more or less obligated to have a beautiful garden.

Jenny looked at Ray's hand, a ham of a hand, maybe born to swing an axe. He worked at a textile factory, kept the machines going. It wasn't a confident hand. It held his cigarette back to front, the burning end protected by his palm, his knuckles lifted to his mouth. She remembered those big hands from school, the way they'd gripped a pencil — always back to front. Should have remembered he couldn't read. It wasn't the sort of thing a little kid remembered. Images stick in a kid's mind. Giant boy with lost lamb's eyes. Miss Rose, pretty auburn-haired pixie. And the smells of the school room, the chalk smell, the smell of old books. And Sissy, on stage that night, stripped to her white bloomers. Ray, his tall top hat lopsided, his eyes afraid as he'd offered Sissy her tattered green onion tunic.

Sleeping in his bed brought back memories of sleeping with

Sissy: the heat of another body, the smell of human sweat. She dreamt of Sissy some nights and was pleased to wake up and find Ray beside her — sometimes. Most of the time she woke up homesick for her sagging solitary bed in Granny's lean-to.

His nose had been broken since school. She'd asked him how it happened. Fight, he'd said and that was all he'd tell her.

'She's got a system of filters to remove any impurities before the gas gets to the motor,' Geoff said. 'That's where most of the trouble starts. There . . .' Again that stump of finger tapped the page. '*Filters must be cleaned regularly.*'

Flora stifled a yawn. 'Why don't you say *he's* got a system of filters that need cleaning regularly, Geoff?'

'Cars demand a lot of attention,' he said and winked at Jenny.

He was a married man, a neighbour, a good Catholic; he was in her kitchen, and Jenny didn't like that wink. Trust of mankind hadn't been written into her master plan — and she had reason not to trust him. During her early weeks here, when she'd slept on the floor with her kids, she'd heard the creak of floorboards, the scrape of wood on wood in the locked sleep-out, a built-in section of the eastern veranda. The kids' bedroom door opened into it, though it hadn't opened back then.

She'd asked Ray if he had a key. He'd said the door had always been locked.

Around a month ago, when she'd heard the noise again, she'd told Flora and asked her if she had the key to the padlock on the sleep-out door.

'It'll be cats,' Flora said. 'I'll ask Dad if he's seen the key.'

No more was said about it, but that sleep-out was on the east side, on Ray's side. It was his, and her inability to get into it annoyed Jenny. There were gaps in the tattered flywire. A cat could have climbed in through the hole, a kid could have climbed through it.

Then, two weeks ago, near midnight, she'd been smoking a stolen cigarette on the veranda when she'd heard definite footsteps in there. Swagman? Murderer? Her kids sleeping a door away!

She'd done her own creeping and damn near bumped into Geoff when she'd rounded the back corner. He'd been doing something to that padlock.

'I . . . found a key,' he said. 'Thought it might fit.'

Dark in the backyard. The Parkers had a light on their section of back veranda. They turned it on when they went out to the lav. It hadn't been turned on that night. He hadn't hung around to talk either. Maybe he'd found a key. If he had, he hadn't given it to her. Maybe he'd been what she'd heard in that room. She'd made up her mind to get the door open.

Locksmiths cost money. She'd already been into her bank account twice. Norman's toolbox had travelled down with her. As a kid, she'd watched him cut through a metal bolt with his hacksaw. She'd found his hacksaw and two spare blades wrapped in oilpaper. On Wednesday, Geoff at work, Flora visiting her mother, it took less than an hour to hack through the end of a slide bolt held into its slot by that heavy padlock.

Like a step back in time, entering that room: there must have been ten years of dust in there, and bird droppings, and a cat's leavings, feathers too — and areas of no dust. Something triangular had been moved recently. She'd found shoe prints, drag marks — and the key to the kids' bedroom door, in the lock. It took some turning, but a few squirts from Norman's oil can and it turned.

She'd found an old camp stretcher, dusty but still strong, old picture frames, a disintegrating cabinet that may have been expensive a hundred years ago. She'd found what might prove to be a treasure hidden beneath a dusty calico shroud: an old treadle sewing machine. Singer sewing machines never die, Granny used to say. Hoped she was right. It needed a needle, needed a good clean and oil, but if she could get it sewing, it would be coming out to live in the kitchen. Six times a week and twice on Sundays she found reason to miss Granny's sewing machine. And she badly needed curtains. All she had were sheets tacked up at the bedroom windows.

She glanced at the kitchen's wall of windows, seeing the group at the table reflected there. Dark out there tonight, but by day those windows would offer perfect light for sewing. There had never been enough light in Granny's kitchen.

She'd been so lucky. For all she'd known or cared the night they'd left Woody Creek, Ray could have taken her to a tent on the banks of the Yarra. And he'd brought her to this. No more wood to fetch in from the wood heap. Blue flames at the flick of a match. A flushing lavatory the kids had spent too much time flushing during the first days; asking too many questions about where everything went to, and what happened to it when it got there.

Certain subjects were taboo around Ray. She was learning. Her kids would learn. Given time, he'd relax. She wasn't looking for a fairytale marriage, just a good life, with a stepfather for her kids, enrolled at school as Margot and Georgina King.

'It's written on the back of the front cover for any fool to see,' Geoff Parker said. '*Carbon gas must be allowed to dissipate before vehicle is garaged.*'

Go home, Jenny thought and glanced at her watch — Billy-Bob's watch. Almost ten thirty.

Ray didn't like her wearing that watch. She'd put it away for a week or two, but with the girls at school, she needed the right time on her wrist and that watch never lost a minute. It brought back bad memories, but life had a way of overwriting the old with the new, and Cara Jeanette could have belonged to any one of five Yankee sailors. And even if she had kept her, every time she'd looked at her she would have seen Yankee in her face — as she saw Macdonald in Margot's face. She had to forget Sydney, forget Amberley and that baby.

'And what does the fool do?' Geoff said. Too loud. He'd have the kids awake in a minute. 'He parks a hot car in his shed and closes the door —'

'Keep your voice down,' Flora said. 'And he's still in the hospital, and he's got five little kids and his wife is due to have another one.'

Jenny had been following that story in the papers. The *Sun* had printed a photograph of his kids, little blonds, the oldest of them Georgie's age.

'Fools have been killing themselves off for thousands of years. That's how we swung down from the trees,' Geoff said.

'Survival of the fittest,' Jenny said.

'Too bloody right — and the way it ought to be. And the bloody government is paying them now to breed.'

'They're investing in an army for their next war,' Jenny said.

'Yeah, and they'll be doing what their bloody fathers did in the last one, breeding more morons while the rest of us are over there keeping the bloody world safe for them to breed in.'

Ray might talk cars, listen to talk of cars, all night, but the conversation having swung away to an area where he didn't want to go, he rose and walked to the window.

'You only need to look at the animals to know how man got to where he is today,' Geoff went on. 'The strongest ape breeds with his pick of the females, and the race grows stronger. The farmer knows it. He doesn't breed his cows to some mixed-breed mongrel bull. Man is no different. If you want a strong race, you breed the strong and sterilise the weak.'

'Heil Hitler,' Flora said.

'That man did a lot of good until he went power crazy.'

'There's no rhyme nor reason to any of it,' Jenny said. 'We're all numbers in God's big game of chance: the university professor and the night man. If our number is drawn out of the hat, we get whatever he feels like handing out as the prize.'

Ray had opened the glass door.

Flora's God didn't wear a hat, or play games of chance. 'It's late,' she said. 'I think Ray wants to go to bed.'

With Flora and Ray on their feet, Geoff rose reluctantly. 'The conversation was just getting interesting,' he said, and again he winked at Jenny.

A neighbourly wink? Or was he an ape, out for what he could steal from his neighbour's tree — or from his sleep-out?

She didn't rise to see the visitors out. The door was open. They closed it behind them, locked it. Ray went outside. She sat on at the table, looking down at her clasped hands, at the two bands of gold, one on each ring finger. Difficult to tell which one was which when her fingers were linked. Shouldn't have been wearing Jim's. She'd taken it from her wedding finger the morning they'd gone into the registry office, had meant to put it away with her earrings and pendant, but the engraving on its inner circle had looked so new.

Jen and Jim, 1942.

Why should one man be chosen to come home from the war with a couple of lost knuckles, and another be blown to bits too small to find — if God wasn't up there, running his daily lottery?

EMPTY-HANDED

Norman's estate — his possessions and seven hundred and fifty pounds — was to be divided equally between his daughters. He'd named Gertrude and Maisy executors in his will, which was as well. Gertrude knew where Jenny might be found, and Maisy, who had a married daughter living in Melbourne, kept in touch with Sissy.

There were legal papers to sign, and in June, Maisy was coming down to Melbourne to spend a few days with her daughter and to get Sissy's signature on her share of the papers. Gertrude suggested Jenny meet them in the city, rather than entrust important documents to the post.

A month ago, Jenny would have told her to post them. By June she wanted to see someone from home, even Sissy.

She'd started off on the wrong foot in Melbourne, with Ray and with Margot. There was too much Macdonald in that kid. The twins had been running amok since they'd learnt to run. Margot was doing the same, and something had to be done about her. Finding the incentive to do that something was Jenny's problem. Easier to give in; and, for the sake of a quiet life, the other two kids were learning to do the same.

Something had to be done about Ray's eating habits. Every Saturday morning he rode off on his bike and came home loaded down with dead cow. He expected to eat meat for breakfast. If she didn't have a bit of leftover stew to put on his toast, he wanted sausages; if they were out of sausages, he expected her to fry him a piece of steak — and facing a raw slab of steak before breakfast wasn't her idea of a good way to start the day. And some of the steak he brought home looked as if it had been slaughtered on the road.

She'd never had a lot to do with meat, had spent too little time cooking it to work out one cut from the other. She'd never looked a liver in the eye before Armadale. Their first disagreement was over a liver, be it sheep's, cow's or dead dog's, she didn't know. She'd tried to slice it and damn near vomited. She'd asked him to slice it. He hadn't got around to it. Three days wrapped in newspaper and the thing started turning green. She'd dug a hole beside the fence and buried it deep, still in its newspaper.

'I don't know how to handle innards, Ray. Don't buy any more.'

'It's ch-cheap,' he'd said.

'Mince and sausages are cheap. I can handle them.'

Sausages were for breakfast, as was mince on toast. He wanted slabs of meat at night, and potatoes.

He bought potatoes cheap, wheat bags full of them, and if she didn't serve him a Mount Everest of mashed potato, he thought his throat had been cut. He didn't eat greens. Never bought greens. Didn't own a pot to cook them in. He owned a good frying pan and a large and battered saucepan for his potatoes. He owned three plates, enamel, two stained enamel mugs, three sharp knives, one fork and two dessertspoons. If she'd come to him empty-handed, she would have been in strife. And if not for Gertrude and Elsie, she would have come to him empty-handed. They'd packed Amber's pots, her kitchen crockery, her cutlery. They'd packed Gertrude's old tin trunk with sheets, towels and blankets from Norman's house. Sissy's mattress had been tossed onto the pile as an after-thought, and Amber's preserving pan, still full of her pantry items.

They'd packed a cardboard carton with jam, chutney, tomato sauce, onions, eggs.

She'd packed Norman's toolbox, only because it had been left overnight in the yard, and while he'd been alive that toolbox had never spent a night out of doors. She hadn't been thinking straight that day, hadn't wanted to be weighed down with trunks and cartons, had just wanted to get away. She'd packed her bankbook, the account transferred to a Melbourne branch back in '44, before she'd left Sydney. She'd had visions of emptying that account, taking a train to . . . to somewhere, Queensland, anywhere. Her first withdrawal paid for a bed for the kids, a battered chest of drawers, a secondhand electric iron.

She didn't know how much Ray earned each week. From day one, she'd cooked what he brought home, grateful for what he brought home — or had been during those first months. Maybe she'd been too grateful. She'd never been a wife, didn't know how to be a wife. Flora was her only example of a suburban wife and mother, and she spent half her life yelling at Geoff, who spent half his life snarling orders back.

So much Jenny didn't know, like how often she was obligated to sleep with Ray. Someone in Woody Creek had once said it was a wife's duty to welcome her husband's attention. Someone had once said that the honeymoon only lasted for twelve months. Maybe they'd meant the sex. Most brides were pregnant within the first twelve months, which might have put an end to sex.

A long time ago, with Laurie, she'd learnt that you could let a man take your body without taking your mind. Lovemaking was a thing of the mind, not of the bits below it. It was an inconvenience in an otherwise good life. She took more than the recommended precautionary measures: rubber cap and gel, and a douche when he was done. With access to the bathroom restricted, she associated sex with the lavatory, where she prepared herself for his onslaught then washed him off, but she wasn't pregnant, and as long as she wasn't, she could stand whatever it took to stay that way.

She couldn't stand his livers. They looked and felt like monstrous lumps of congealed blood. They shivered when she picked up a knife, and her own liver shivered in sympathy. And tripe too. He'd brought that home twice. It resembled something between grey fungus and a cancerous growth.

'B-b-boil it w-with milk,' he'd instructed.

'You won't look at fish. I feel the same about cow's innards.'

She'd bought fish in celebration the day the government had started handing her a few bob a month in child endowment. She'd bought macaroni, pumpkin, cabbages, apples. Geoff Parker may not have appreciated the government paying women to populate; Jenny did. They may have paid her sooner had she felt like advertising to governmental departments that she'd had three illegitimate kids. She hadn't. Mrs Jennifer King filled in those forms. Mrs Jennifer King queued up for her monthly handout.

Jennifer Morrison Hooper's bank account supplied her kitchen dresser. The only cupboard in Ray's kitchen was the one beneath the sink, and by May the cartons containing Amber's pots and plates had started disintegrating. She'd seen the dresser in a cluttered little secondhand shop in High Street, the day she'd gone shopping for the kids' bed and drawers. Every week thereafter she'd visited it, smoothed its timbers with her hand. It had three deep drawers, three cupboards, wide shelves and a slide-out marble workbench. Then one morning she went in and the secondhand man had brought the price down by five bob, so she and Jimmy caught the tram into the city and went to the bank.

Money hadn't seemed necessary in Woody Creek. Down here she couldn't live without the stuff, and if she didn't find a way to make some soon, her bank account would run dry.

The treadle sewing machine now lived in the kitchen. The Parkers, frequent visitors to that kitchen, named it 'the old girl's' machine. They'd claimed the old picture frames and a small table; had shown no interest in the camp stretcher or a crumbling cabinet, as heavy as lead and threatening to collapse when Jenny had dragged it away from the wall. They hadn't offered to get rid of it or to help clean out that room.

They'd known that small table was in the sleep-out. Flora had asked for it. And how had she known it was in there unless they'd had the key to the padlock?

They coveted Ray's refrigerator, named it 'the old girl's' fridge. By May, Jenny knew 'the old girl' had been Flora's Aunt Phoebe, that she'd left the house to Flora's father, that Geoff was buying it from her father. She had not yet learnt how Flora's aunt's fridge had ended up on Ray's side of the house, though apparently Ray had been living there when Phoebe was alive.

'How come you lived here, Ray?'

'W-worked for her,' he said, and that was all he said. He wasn't forthcoming with personal information.

Jenny was on speaking terms with Carol from over the eastern fence, an older woman with two near grown sons who had known Ray for years. She was on garden-visiting terms with Miss Flowers, the first neighbour to knock on her door, a wee humpbacked woman of Granny's age who lived with her brother in the house directly opposite. Six weeks after Jenny had moved in, she'd come to the glass door with a posy of violets — and ended up sitting for an hour. She wasn't the type of visitor you needed in a shared house. Partially deaf, Miss Flowers over-compensated for her own lack of hearing by raising her voice. Five minutes after she'd sat down, Jenny had wanted to gag her.

She'd popped over with a bunch of beetroot the day Jenny moved the sewing machine into the kitchen.

'She used to turn out some weird and wonderful things on that when she was younger. How come the niece didn't get it like she got everything else?'

Living is learning. On her first visit, Jenny learned to say what had to be said once, to say it clearly and close to the old lady's ear. 'It was in the sleep-out.'

'None of them ever came near that poor woman while she was dying,' the old dame said.

'Have you lived in the street very long, Miss Flowers?'

'Since Howie was widowed, thirty year ago.'

Miss Flowers was Jenny's first customer. She'd made her a coverall gardening apron in exchange for the bunches of flowers and garden produce, and the old lady asked if she could make her a frock that fitted to wear to her great-nephew's wedding in June. Jenny, who had taken inordinate care in making the frock fit the old lady's shape, refused to accept payment, but Miss Flowers, as independent as Granny and more determined, hid a ten-shilling note in the tea canister, where it remained until the next pot was brewed. Ten shillings was riches. It paid for a six-pound bag of oatmeal, half a dozen eggs, golden syrup . . .

Five days later, Miss Flowers introduced a second customer, a Mrs Andrews, who was not a lot older than Jenny. She said she'd gone back to nursing and had lost a lot of weight. Everything she owned hung on her like a sack. Jenny remodelled three skirts, a pair of slacks, two frocks, and didn't charge her enough according to Miss Flowers.

'Her husband, Bill, runs a bank, and with her working five nights a week they've got money coming out of their ears, dear.'

Geoff Parker was her third customer — not quite customer. She cut three inches from the legs of his new suit trousers and turned up new cuffs. Flora was appreciative but didn't offer payment. Instead, she brought in a second pair of trousers and later a length of material — and stayed on to watch the making of a new dress for Lois. She was going to a party.

'You do it so easy,' Flora said. 'Thanks very much.'

Jenny was growing more confident with her scissors — but losing confidence in handling Margot, threatening her one minute, giving in the next.

She shouldn't have told the girls that she and Jimmy were having lunch with Maisy on Friday. Maisy was Margot's grandmother, not Jimmy's.

'I want to go, not him,' she whined.

'Friday is a school day, Margot.'

'I hate thchool.'

'If you'd behave yourself there you wouldn't hate it as much.'

Margot bawled. Jenny, having one of her non-give-in days, walked away, so Margot bawled louder.

The other kids cried on occasion and got it over and done with. Not Margot. She pursued Jenny from room to room, red-faced, fists and jaw clenched, and that inimitable wail Jimmy had labelled 'Margot's *ahzeeing*'. A good description. The *ah* was the inhalation, the *zee* created by air exhaled between clenched teeth. The girl couldn't make an 's' to save her life, but she could keep up that *ahzeeing* for an hour. It wore you down.

'If you can read three pages of your reader by next Friday, you can come with me,' Jenny said.

'And me too,' Georgie said.

'You don't want to miss school just to catch a tram into the city and home again.'

'She's your pet,' Georgie accused.

'No one is my pet.'

'Is so. I have to have yellow jumpers because she wants yellow jumpers.'

How do you explain yourself to a kid when you can't explain yourself to yourself? Maybe it takes a kid to point out that what you're doing is wrong.

Jenny escaped to the veranda, closing the glass door on wail and accusation — and wishing she had a cigarette. Didn't. Stood, fingers massaging her scalp beneath too long hair, while looking through the glass at two little girls dressed as twins. What suited one didn't suit the other — and never had. Georgie was long and skinny, Margot short and thick. But it never had been about what suited them. Knitting those two identical yellow jumpers, stitching those two brown skirts, was insurance — insurance against leaning towards Georgie, which had always been too easy to do. She'd vowed when those girls were babies never to give them cause for envy.

Childhood envy leaves scars. She still felt the scar of a young Jenny singing on stage in faded pink, the armholes rotted by Sissy sweat, looking at Sissy preening in flounced floral. And she had to stop allowing Woody Creek to dictate how she lived the rest of her life. She was an adult, a married woman, a mother. She had to stop that *ahzeeing* brat of a kid dictating how those other two kids lived their lives. And she had to alter Ray's eating habits — or she'd be a widow before she had time to learn how to be a wife. Miss Flowers said that her sister-in-law had lived on red meat and died of a stroke at thirty-three.

Margot had that door open. Her volume increased, and not a tear in her eyes.

'One more *ahzee* out of you, Margot, and I'll lock you in the sleep-out.'

'The thnib's on the inthide.'

'Then I'll put one on the outside and you can spend your life out there *ahzeeing*.'

'You didn't buy two thnibth, and I want to thee my grandmother and Jimmy, not thee her.'

CALICO SHEETS

*F*riday should never have happened. She'd left Margot wailing in the schoolyard and continued to the tram stop, stirred up by Margot, or by the thought of lunching with Sissy. She wanted to see Maisy. Didn't want to see Sissy. And of course Sissy didn't turn up. It would have been better if she had. Maisy might have kept her mouth shut.

The solicitor's papers had been signed and placed away. Gertrude had sent down two dozen eggs and a bag of walnuts, which turned the conversation to her.

'Did your gran tell you about her and Vern?'

'What about them?'

'I thought she might have written something about it to you.'

'They're getting married?'

'No. It's nothing like that.' Maisy filled her mouth, chewed, swallowed. 'Sissy doesn't live far away from you. She looks after the house for that parson uncle of your father's.'

'Uncle Charles.'

'That's him.'

'God help his stomach. What were you going to tell me about Granny and Vern?'

'Forget I said anything, love.'

'You can't do that, Maisy.'

'No. And you probably should have been told anyway — if just for Jimmy's sake.'

'Vern's threatening to go after him again?'

Maisy shook her head. 'No. They had a blazing row, that's all. Nelly Dobson told me while I was cutting her hair. She still does some cleaning for Vern, and was there the day your gran turned up at the house. She said there was fireworks.'

'About what?'

'I hoped she'd told you, love.' Maisy filled her mouth and Jenny waited, knife and fork in hand. 'I never want you to think that I've known something that you ought to have been told, that I've kept it from you. You're like one of my own kids. It's about Jim, love. They brought him home.'

'What?'

'They've taken him back to the hospital now.'

'What are you talking about, Maisy?'

'Rumours have been circulating about him being alive for months. We didn't know if there was any truth in them or not until they brought him home the weekend before last.'

Jenny placed her knife and fork down as her eyes searched Maisy's. 'He's dead.'

'He's not, love. He was in one of those Jap prison camps. Gloria Bull nursed him when they first brought him back.'

'He's dead, Maisy.'

'Nelly Dobson saw him. Young Mick Boyle helped him get in and out of his wheelchair. He says he's skin and bone.'

Maisy filled her mouth. Jenny sat, silent now, watching her chew, knowing Maisy had lost her marbles. And knowing she hadn't. Knowing it was true. Jim had never felt dead to Jenny, just . . . missing.

That nasal voice continued, Maisy's fork was loaded while blood rushed, whoosh, whoosh, whoosh, drowning Jenny's floundering heart, muffling Maisy's words.

'Your gran swears that the Red Cross got lists of the prisoners being held in those camps, that Vern and his daughters would have known all along that he was alive . . .'

Jimmy scooping ice-cream from a boat-shaped dish, ice-cream swimming in raspberry topping, triangular cone standing like the sail of a boat. Sail me away. Sail me away from this place. Watched him turn his boat, eating from the edges. Watched him bite a piece from the sail, magnified by a tear. Caught it with her finger. Caught another.

'That's what their argument was about, love. It started in the house, Nelly said, but Vern wouldn't let your gran get the last word. He followed her out to her horse. Cathy McConnell was walking by. She heard them.'

Jenny held up a hand, Norman's sign for enough. Maisy didn't read hand signs.

'You know Cathy McConnell. It's all over town.'

'Bastard.'

'I shouldn't have told you. Not here, like this.'

'Bastard.'

The woman at the next table turned to censure the bad language and saw a pretty girl, clad in green and black, her eyes leaking waterfalls. She tut-tutted and turned back to her meat pie and chips.

'Bastard.' There was nothing else to say.

'As far as I'm concerned, he always was.' Maisy loaded her fork. 'Young Billy Roberts was in one of those camps for months. Jessica's Joss saw him when they brought him back to Australia. The things he told Joss, I wouldn't repeat.' Maisy chewed. 'He's lost half of one leg — Jim.'

'Stop it, Maisy.'

'I know how you must feel.'

Know how she must feel? She couldn't feel the chair beneath her, couldn't feel the table she leaned on. Everything she'd been building for months was dropping away — and she'd barely started building it, and she didn't want what she was building anyway. Know how she must feel? She felt as if she was sinking in quicksand, no floor beneath her feet, no floor to the world, and Maisy's every word like an sledgehammer pounding her head deeper into hell.

'They say he had that disease a lot of the boys got up there. It's affected his eyes.'

Enough, Jenny's hand and her heart howled. Take his legs, take his arms, but not his eyes. Then her head was down on folded arms, at a table in the middle of a crowded cafeteria. Nothing else she could do. Nothing.

Jimmy stopped eating around his dish of ice-cream to reach out a hand and pat her head. Knew his gentle touch as she'd known his father's. Couldn't lift her head, tell him it was all right when it was all wrong.

He knew who had made her cry. 'You go away,' he said to Maisy.

'I'm sorry, love. I'm sorry I told you.'

That lifted her head. 'Granny should have told me!'

Maisy's hand on her shoulder. 'She's having a hard time coming to terms with it herself. I spoke to her before they brought him home and she swore that Vern wouldn't keep something like that from her. It's been an awful shock to your gran. She probably can't bring herself to put it on paper.'

Jenny wiped her eyes on paper, blew her nose on the paper serviette, and lied to Jimmy. 'It's all right, darlin'. Eat your ice-cream.' Walked blindly to the ladies' room, washed her face while ladies stared, blew her nose on toilet paper, held wet wads of toilet paper to her eyes. Nothing she could do about her heart.

Alive, it was pounding. He's alive.

And look what you've done.

The ice-cream dish was scraped clean when she returned. She took Jimmy's hand, said a fast goodbye and left.

And forgot her string bag, Granny's eggs and walnuts in it. Jimmy reminded her. She didn't want to go back, but eggs were eggs and her kids saw too few of them. They went back. She kissed Maisy's cheek.

'Thanks for telling me. Write to me, Maisy.'

'I haven't got your address, love.'

'Granny has.'

They caught a tram to somewhere, didn't know where, didn't care. Too early to go home and Jenny didn't want to go there. They rode a tram to the terminus and back again, and barely a word she could find to say. They caught a second tram to Armadale and arrived too early at the school gate, waited too long for the bell to ring.

And Georgie came out with a message. The teacher wanted to speak to her mother.

Her mother? She wasn't a mother. She was a half-witted fool.

'I can't, darlin'.'

'She said, Jenny.'

Too full of tears. Too full of Jim. Overflowing with tears she couldn't release.

He was alive.

Please God, she'd prayed in Sydney. Please God, don't let him die.

He was alive.

She allowed Georgie to lead her to a classroom where a middle-aged woman waited, a busy woman who didn't waste words.

'I want to separate your girls, Mrs King.'

'They like being together,' Jenny said.

'Margot is not handling the work and is making no attempt to handle it. To put it bluntly, Mrs King, her belligerent attitude is having an effect on Georgina's social interaction with the other children.'

Jenny looked at those kids waiting outside the door where they'd been told to wait, Georgie in charge. She was six years old and would have passed for eight. Margot was eleven months her senior and might have passed for a spoilt-brat five year old. Hard enough getting her to school most mornings. If she couldn't cling to Georgie, she wouldn't go.

Jenny sighed in a deep breath, attempting to get beneath the ache of half-witted fool Jenny and down to Mrs-till-death-do-us-part-King.

'Moving from her old school has been . . . very difficult for Margot.'

'As, no doubt, it has been for Georgina,' the woman said.

'She likes learning.'

'And is being held back by her sister — who will learn nothing while Georgina is doing the work for her.'

And of course she wouldn't — and hadn't. She clung like a limpet to Georgie. She hobbled her.

'Do whatever you think best,' Jenny said.

Georgie would be moving. Margot would remain with this woman. Maybe.

Home then, or back to that house that wasn't a home, Jimmy talking about Granny's eggs, about Maisy, Margot *ahzee-ing* because Maisy was her grandmother, not Jimmy's, and she wanted her grandmother, not Jenny, and why couldn't she see her grandmother?

'Shut up your *ahzeeing*, Margot,' Georgie said.

'Thee'th my grandma, not hith.'

Take her out to Box Hill and dump her with her grandma then run like hell, Jenny thought.

Can't. Four chops swimming in blood, going green around the edges. Have to cook them.

Bury them, then run.

Too much bank-account money invested in my dresser.

She sighed and lit the oven, then, eyes near closed, slid slimy chops onto the baking tray. Eight filthy potatoes, half of them attempting to take root in the wheat bag and the other half rotten inside. It would have cost him less to buy decent potatoes she could use. She peeled an onion, allowed her eyes to leak a tear or two. Ray liked onion gravy. Onions were vegetables.

Served him three chops. Shared one between three kids, doused their potatoes and cabbage with gravy. Didn't serve herself a meal. Her stomach wouldn't take it.

Didn't tell him that Jim was alive. Couldn't say his name or she'd bawl. And he wouldn't want to know. He was jealous of Geoff Parker, jealous of Flora's wood man, probably jealous of the garbage man . . .

Far better if she hadn't known Jim was alive. She'd married Ray to give her kids a name, to get rid of the Morrison name. She had to concentrate on that.

And how could she?

Jen and Jim, 1942. That's all she could think of.

And bloody Friday night and no work tomorrow, and he never missed a Friday night, and she hated the whole animal thing of his bed.

And dark in the dark old inn yard, a stable wicket creaked, where Tim the ostler listened . . . There were seventeen verses in 'The Highwayman'. 'Daffodils' had five. And she couldn't concentrate on either poem. Wanted Jim. Wanted the flight of butterflies — not a bear grunting over his fresh kill.

Ran from his bed. Ran to the lavatory, her coat over her arm. Her place. Her only place. And the washhouse. It wasn't a Wednesday or a Sunday but she washed there, washed him off her there, then felt out two cigarettes she'd wrapped in newspaper and hidden on a shelf beside the troughs. Felt for five minutes for the box of matches kept down there to light the copper. And found them, and lit a cigarette. Oh, glorious cigarette. Stood in the doorway sucking in smoke and not feeling the cold, warming herself with tears, howling in peace while staring up at Melbourne's dark sky. No stars. The stars lived on light poles in Melbourne. They went out when someone turned off the switch.

A bad Friday, it led into a worse weekend. And thank God for Monday. Ray left for work, and at eight thirty she walked the kids to school. Before she reached the house again, Margot came *ahzee-ing* up behind her.

'I'm not going to thcool if I can't thit with Georgie.'

Give up. Just give everything up. What did it matter anyway? Nothing mattered. She was empty again, an aching hollow again. Just get the tram out to Amber's asylum and ask if they've got a spare bed, ask them for a lobotomy. Why bother trying to survive when the fight wasn't worth the effort?

She had to live at least through today. She'd promised to take up the hem of a ballgown for some nursing friend of Mrs Andrews from over the road.

She got it done. Could have done a better job. She didn't charge enough anyway. Shops charged three times as much. She picked Georgie up from school. Happy little girl, she'd had a good day and was full of her new teacher, her new classroom, Gwyneth, the girl she sat beside.

Fried steak for Ray's dinner, and her mind not on steak, she fried stewing steak. It was as tough as old boots. And how was she supposed to know one slimy piece of dead cow from another? Forked it from the plates and tossed it into a saucepan with her last onion. He ate his stew late, with more mashed potatoes, ate the lot. The kids were in bed. And he wanted her in his bed, and she couldn't stand it.

And didn't.

'I've had a rotten day, Ray. Margot wouldn't go to school.'

She wouldn't go to school on Tuesday, not unless she could sit with Georgie. Georgie didn't want to be late. She ran off alone while Margot stood in the kitchen *ahzeeing*.

Jenny stood watching, listening, wondering if she couldn't say an 's' or wouldn't try. A 'z' was only an 's' with voice added. She glanced at Jimmy who stood in the bedroom doorway, fingers jammed into his ears.

Margot's noise lasted until lunchtime. They ate an early lunch that Tuesday. Like Maisy, Margot enjoyed her food.

Couldn't bribe her to go to school on Wednesday. Georgie walked home alone and found Jenny digging a grave for another liver and hitting roots.

'Will meat work like chook and horse dung works for making garden things grow, Jenny?'

'It might,' Jenny said.

'If that's rhubarb, it might make it grow and we can have rhubarb pies like at home.'

Was it rhubarb? Maybe. She got down to her knees, carefully brushing away dirt, pulling long weeds, little Georgie down beside her. And it was rhubarb. Though they found no sign of leaves, they'd exposed several crowns.

'It is,' Jenny said, and couldn't help herself, kissed that pretty little face. Loved her face, loved her mind. Just loved her. Married Ray to give that beautiful little girl a father and a chance to live a good life, and she had to stop mooning over Jim — which never could have been anyway. Vern would have stopped him from marrying her. Just a stupid kid's dream, that's all.

She dug more carefully then, and when the hole was deemed deep enough, they had a grand funeral for the liver, and maybe for a few childhood dreams.

'Ashes to ashes, dust to dust, if he buys another liver, I think I'll bust,' Jenny said over the grave.

Jimmy liked silly rhymes. 'Another one,' he demanded.

'We like macaroni and a rhubarb pie, so I'm sorry, Mrs Cow's liver, if we don't cry.'

'Now say it all again, Jenny.'

Wednesday became a better day, or it did until Jimmy recited her rhyme at the dinner table, until Georgie appreciated it anew and got the giggles. Ray didn't appreciate it, or the waste.

'What w-was wrong w-with the liver?' he asked.

'It was going green. I told you, I don't know how to cook cows' innards.'

'L-lamb's. You ssss-lice it and f-f-fry it.'

'I can't slice it, Ray. It quivers under my knife. There are things I can't do. Please don't buy any more.'

'I g-g-get what he's g-got.'

He didn't appreciate Margot's *ahzeeing* at bedtime. She wasn't going to bed and she wasn't going to school, not never.

'W-what's g-got into her?'

'She wants to sit with Georgie. The teacher split them up.'

'Tell her to p-p-put them b-back where they were.'

'She's holding Georgie back.'

'Sh-she can s-stand a b-bit of hhh-holding back.'

'No one can stand holding back.'

'That teacher ith thtupid ithn't thee, Daddy Ray?'

Embarrassed by the name, he stood to walk out, then he reached out a hand and patted Margot's head, just a brief pat, as he may have patted an unknown cat, wary, at arm's length. It was his first physical contact with either of the girls, and maybe a good sign.

Margot got herself dressed for school on Thursday morning. Ray had said to put her and Georgie back together. It was his house. He was the boss. She learned that morning that teachers were the bosses at school. She came home at midday.

On Friday, Jenny gave up the fight, and the fight with herself. She left her two kids playing with Lois in the backyard and went to the post office to call hospitals. She was married and wasn't planning to jeopardise her marriage, but she had to see Jim. She had to explain to him why she'd married. She had to tell him too that his father had let her believe he was dead.

She didn't find him that Friday but was given two phone numbers to try, though not today. She had enough coins left in her purse to buy a tin of powdered milk. Kids needed milk. Ray didn't use it and rarely bought it.

Arrived home to World War Three. Lois and Jimmy played well together. Margot was a pincher, a puncher, a pusher.

'You're going to school. Get your school shoes on, Margot.'

'I'm thitting with Georgie.'

'Georgie can read and you can't, so you can't sit with her.'

'Not going then.'

She looked too much like her fathers. Maisy should have been raising her. Jenny had never had any interest in raising her. Hadn't touched her until she was fourteen or fifteen months old. Hadn't wanted to touch her then. Didn't like her hands, her face, her hair.

I had her — had her forced on me . . .

Should have signed her away at birth.

Would have — if not for Maisy and Elsie. So let them raise her. I can't.

'Do you want to go home?'

Margot didn't understand.

'Do you want to go back to Granny and Elsie?'

Margot wasn't sure about that.

'You have to go to school. You could go to school up there with Elsie's kids.'

'And Georgie.'

'Georgie goes to school down here.'

'I want to thit with her, I thaid.'

A circular argument, going nowhere, as did all arguments with Margot. Walk away. Or fight.

An exercise book taken from her dresser drawer, a page ripped out, a pencil found. 'Kids have to go to school. If you won't go, you'll have to go to school at home. Sit down and write your name at the top of that page.'

'You're not a thchoolteacher.'

'Sit down and write your name.'

'You're thtupid.'

The page swiped to the floor, Margot left the kitchen. There was relief in watching that stocky little back disappear into the bedroom. Easier to let her go, but Jenny grasped her skirt and drew her back to the kitchen, to the table, picked her up and sat her on a chair and held her there.

'I want to play!'

'You don't play. You pinch. You're going to sit there until you write your name.'

The page flew, as did the pencil.

'Now you'll write it two times.'

Margot didn't write. She hammered the sharp end of the pencil into the table. The lead broke, she smiled and escaped.

She was the twins, tormenting Miss Rose in that classroom. She was Sissy, fighting in Norman's kitchen. She was Jenny's nemesis — but she'd taken her mind off Jim and rehabilitation hospitals.

'It's three times now.'

At four times, she locked the kids' bedroom door, locked the glass door and placed both keys on top of the dresser — as had Norman. She remained calm, as had Norman, just kept sharpening the pencil, flattening the paper.

The pencil flew at her head. Even at full *zee*, that kid's aim was good — like her fathers'.

'Every time you throw it I add one more. Keep that in mind, Margot.'

The count reached seven, the paper crumpled, ripped, flattened, the pencil sharpened for the fourth time, Margot's *ahzeeing* reaching a crescendo, and Jenny stole a cigarette, opened Ray's new packet to steal it. He'd know. And who cared? The army had supplied soldiers with cigarettes, and if that's what it took, then that's what it took. Margot had been dictating the terms of their relationship for too long.

'Eight.'

'I'm telling Daddy Ray you pinched hith thigarettes.'

'I'm telling Granny that you can't write to her because you can't even write your name.'

'I can tho.'

'Then do it! Eight times.'

Jimmy wrote to Granny, and drew her pictures. He'd been born with a pencil in his hand. Georgie wrote letters. She'd read anything: newspapers, books she shouldn't have been able to lift.

Two of a kind, Georgie and Jimmy, little sponges demanding water and soaking up every drip of information fed to them. Tell Margot the same thing twenty times and it slid off like water on glass.

'What comes after nine, Margot?'

'Ten of courth.'

'Very good. When the count gets to ten, I start increasing by five. Can you count by fives?'

'I hate you.'

'You'll hate me more when you have to write your name fifty times. If I were you, I'd start now.'

She didn't write but the page didn't fly. Jenny offered the sharpened pencil stub. Margot didn't take it. She slid from the chair and beneath the table. Jenny hauled her out by a leg. Wondered if Ray's mother had tried to sit him down with a pencil and paper; if she'd had a pencil to sit him down with.

The Palmer kids had written with sticks in the dust. Plenty of dust in Woody Creek. Plenty of sticks. The desire had to be in a kid before he'd pick up a stick and write his name in the dust.

She'd written her name, had written 'Cara Jeanette Paris', the childhood pseudonym used when she'd written to Mary Jolly. She'd written Mary's name, and rubbed it quickly away — Mary, her magical penfriend. What had Ray done through his childhood? What had he been doing between the age of twelve and twenty-six? Where had he been doing it? Who had he been married to? How had she died? Why hadn't she had kids?

He didn't want kids. He tolerated Jenny's, but was a happier man when they weren't around.

How many men would have married an unwed mother with three kids?

Jim would have — if Vern hadn't got to him.

He would have got to him.

'He's too strong for me,' Jim had said once. 'You don't know him, Jen.'

She knew that lying old bugger — knew this bugger of a kid too. She'd grown up with her.

'Are you ready to go to school yet?'

'I will, I thaid, if I thit with Georgie.'

'You'd better pick up that pencil then and start writing. Georgie can write.'

'After I play with Jimmy and Loith, I will.'

'You're not playing with Jimmy and Lois today. You pinched Lois.'

'Thee wouldn't get off the trike.'

'Your full name, nine times, please.'

Margot snatched the pencil and, for a split second, Jenny thought she'd won. It flew at her. She caught it.

'Now it's ten times. What comes after ten?'

'Eleven, thtupid.'

'Not when you count by fives. Fifteen comes after ten. Five, ten, fifteen, twenty, twenty-five, thirty, thirty-five, forty, forty-five, fifty.'

'You're fifty timeth a thtupid idiot and I hate you.'

'How many more pages will you need?' Jenny asked, reaching for the open exercise book.

'You thtop that.'

'You start writing then.'

Margot could count by fives when the kids played hidey. Ripping out a second page forced the issue. She wrote her name, once. It took an hour more for her to write it ten times, but she did, and considered throwing the pencil when she was done, but, with her arm raised, changed her mind.

Such battles aren't won in a morning, or in a weekend; some such battles will never be won. The school term ended in June. Jenny walked Georgie two streets away to play at Gwyneth's. Margot fought all the way home. She wanted to play too.

'You don't play. You pinch.'

There is a time for all things, and, if nothing more, Jenny had learnt that much. She'd been seventeen when Jimmy had been conceived; eighteen the week she'd spent with Jim in Sydney, just a kid. She was an adult now, an accidental mother, but a mother no less. She was a teacher with one focus — and her school didn't recognise holidays.

The clock on the dresser became Margot's only relief. When its little hand got to the ten and its big hand was on six, she had a biscuit and a drink of milk. When both hands reached twelve, she had a sandwich. When the little hand was on three and the big hand on six was the best time of the day. It meant Margot's torment was over.

She learned to tell the time; she learned to read, or memorise her first reader, and write her name well. She didn't surrender, or not unconditionally, but never had a child dressed so eagerly for school when the holidays were over, and never was there a mother so eager to walk her child to school and to come home to the peace of an empty kitchen and her sewing machine.

Jenny had a growing business. Rarely did a week pass without someone knocking on her door. She made seventeen and six one week and fifteen shillings the next. There was money in her purse, and money made by her hands felt so good.

She had a refrigerator. Only the rich had refrigerators in Woody Creek. She had a large wedge of cheese in the refrigerator, cabbage, carrots. She had a nice-looking husband who never missed a day at work, half a dozen roots of rhubarb six foot from her door, and, like Margot, that rhubarb was responding to her care.

And, because of Margot, because of her 'Daddy Ray', she'd got Ray playing Switch with her and the kids — and got a pencil into his hand.

Margot was never happier than when she had playing cards in her hand. She didn't like scoring: her addition was slow and painful, her figures atrocious. Ray was short on patience. He took the pencil from her hand one night and totalled the scores. Still held that pencil as he had in the schoolroom, in his left hand, between his index and tall finger, his thumb guiding its point. And how anyone could learn to write with a grip like that, Jenny didn't know. He could write figures though, good figures, and his addition was fast and sure.

She could teach him to read. She could teach him to write more than his name. He was a good man, just . . . just lost.

Dear Granny,

Margot wants to show you how well she can write. I hope all goes well in your world. As some time has now passed, no doubt you and Vern have got over your little tiff, and he has told you of Jim's whereabouts. I can assure you, and him, that I have no desire nor intention to crawl into Jim's hospital bed, but as Jimmy will need to be told that his father has arisen from the dead, it might be easier to explain if he can see the living proof of him during the explanation.

[Mrs] J.C. King

Georgie's letter was not so brief. Like Gertrude, she didn't believe in wasting paper. Margot copied five lines of Jenny's words; Jimmy drew a picture of Granny's house, eight goats, umpteen chooks, a mountain of eggs and Granny on horseback. He signed it too. With his full name.

A lengthy reply came by return mail.

Dear Jennifer,

I haven't seen Vern in months and if I never see him again it will be too soon. He did an unforgivable thing to you and to me and I don't plan to 'get over our little tiff'.

I don't know where Jim is being treated. All I know is what I've heard from Maisy. She says he had beri-beri, which is caused by a lack of decent food and can lead to all sorts of problems if it's not attended to early. A British doctor at the camp amputated his lower leg when gangrene set in. From what I know of gangrene, Jim is lucky to be alive. That's not the first time I've said that. Since his birth, that boy has been surviving against all odds.

Maisy probably told you that Gloria Bull nursed him when they first brought him back. Her mother told Mrs Croft, she told Maisy and a few more. You know what this town is like for spreading rumours. I didn't believe it when I first heard about it, and you know me well enough to know that I don't pass on rumours, not to you or to anyone else.

I know what it must have been like for you hearing it from Maisy over lunch. That woman needs her tongue putting in a vice. I intended writing, but I knew how you'd feel reading about it in a letter, so I kept putting it off. I thought I might go down with her, but things keep coming up. I'm sorry now that I didn't go.

Archie has been up here looking for you. I told him you were singing at a club in Sydney. He's living in his father's house in Hawthorn. I don't know how that came about, his father wrote him off years ago. He seems to be in the money too. He's driving a little sports car, yellow, so no one would miss seeing him. That man always was an exhibitionist. I don't know how far Hawthorn is from Armadale. I hope it's a long way, but if you see that car, run. He might look the part of a harmless old grandfather, but I wouldn't trust him within a mile of those little girls.

Tell the kids I loved getting their letters. Tell Margot I was very proud of her beautiful writing, tell Georgie that reading her letter was like reading a book about all of my beautiful grandchildren, and tell Jimmy I'm sending him six dozen eggs so he can have two for breakfast.

I don't know how well they'll travel. We've marked the carton fragile and Harry is going to drop it off at the station for me tomorrow. All things being well, by the time you get my

*letter, the eggs and things should be at Spencer Street. I dare
say I could send it to the Armadale station, but this town is
full of bloodhounds, always sniffing around after information.
Margaret Hooper has been doing her own sniffing around. She
asked Maisy only this week where you're living, and like the
fool that woman can be, she told her she'd had lunch with you
and Jimmy.*

*That's about all I can find to say today. Give the kids a big
kiss and a hug from their granny and tell them I miss their
noise.*

Love you all, Gertrude

The carton was waiting at the station, labelled MRS J.C. KING. And it
was as heavy as lead. Jenny propped it on a bench seat and counted
her coins before asking a taxi driver how much he'd charge to take
her to Armadale. She couldn't carry that carton to the tram stop,
then home from her tram stop.

Jimmy enjoyed the taxi ride. He'd had an ongoing love affair
with cars since Myrtle had bought him his first wooden car in Sydney. Jenny resented emptying her purse into the driver's hand, but
Granny's food parcel made up for it. Six dozen eggs, well packed
in newspaper, cushioned by carrots, big fat Granny carrots, fat
onions, lemons, oranges, a huge cabbage cut in half to fit, and
the eternal silverbeet filling in every gap. For once in its life, Ray's
fridge was full up with Jenny's type of food.

Dear Granny,
*I was in a filthy mood last time I wrote. I'm over it now. Sorry.
The kids thought it was Christmas time when we opened the
carton. They're starved for your greens and eggs. Not one was
broken and only three were cracked. We turned them into a
bread pudding.*

*Georgie is writing to ask you if you could send us down a
few seeds so we can make our own Granny Garden. Any sort of*

seeds will do. We've got a ton of dirt down here doing nothing bar growing weeds, which it seems to do well . . .

The seeds arrived a week later, multiple twists of paper containing enough seeds to start a market garden. She'd sent tomato seeds, onion, lettuce, squash, bean, silverbeet, pea, carrot, and on each twist of paper, she'd printed instructions on when and how to plant them. The kids hammered nail holes through the bottoms of rusting tins to make pots for the tomato seeds. Georgie read the instructions. *Set pots in sheltered spot safe from frost. Keep moist. Plant out to garden when frosts are over.*

Happy days those, waiting for winter to end, a six-by-four-foot plot of land already planted with Granny's onion and carrot seeds, the kids running out each morning to see if a seed had popped up its head — Margot always first out the door.

Jenny was better. The weather was better. There was warmth to be found on the veranda in the mornings, the rhubarb was grow-ing curly baby leaves. Then, in early August, Granny's onion seeds popped their heads out to feel the sun, and, not to be outdone, up came the carrots, and the tomatoes.

They had a thousand seeds unplanted, and on a false spring day in mid-August, Ray ridden off to buy his dead cow, Jenny clad herself in her Woody Creek shorts and shirt and worked with her kids, turning over more earth. They had a strip of earth, seven foot in width and thirty foot in length, bordered by a paling fence and a bricked path, and every one of Granny's seeds would be in that strip of earth before this weekend was over.

They worked all morning, Jenny and her kids, she tossing weeds over her shoulder, the kids carrying them to her compost bin — a large and rusting garbage can she'd found behind the lavatory, its bottom near rusted away. Norman's chisel and hammer had made short work of what was left of it. By noon, it was overflowing with weeds. Georgie climbed in to stomp them down, and it fell over, and they laughed in the sun, while time went on holiday.

He returned to weeds and earth strewn where he parked his bike and saw the mess, not the laughter or the industry. His eyes didn't like the mess.

'W-what d-do you think you're d-doing?'

'Making a garden. I'll sweep it up when we're done,' Jenny said.

'Ins-s-side.'

'In a minute. I'll finish planting this one.'

'Y-you w-want him l-looking at your l-l-legs.'

Jimmy was the only 'him' around. Seeing her legs didn't worry him. Passers-by might look over the fence, and who cared.

He meant Geoff Parker.

She glanced towards the backyard. 'He never comes around this side of the house, Ray.'

He took her arm. Big hands, strong. She dropped her shovel, kicked her soil-covered shoes off and allowed him to lead her inside. Didn't stay inside to sort out his dead cow; pulled a skirt over her shorts and went out to finish off what she'd started, visualising a long row of raised-up garden beds growing everything under the sun, loving the earth that gave back so willingly, loving the sunshine on her limbs, and wondering if he'd bought another liver. The rhubarb would appreciate it.

At eight thirty, he nodded towards the bedroom.

'In a minute,' she said. Stole a cigarette and smoked it on the veranda, delaying the inevitable.

Hated the bed part of marriage. Hated it even more now she knew Jim was alive. It was like . . . like she was cheating on him. Or cheating herself.

Big moon up there tonight, and cold enough for a frost. Not many frosts in Armadale. At home, morning after morning the grass was white with frost. Much was different down here. The kids had covered their tomato seedlings. Jenny stood with the rusting jam tins, looking out at moonlit humps of earth. You could imagine anything on such a night, almost see fairies dancing between the spindly onions.

Imagine the expression on Jim's face when he saw how big Jimmy had grown; those big china teeth flashing white, his smile growing so wide it would almost cut his face in half.

Shouldn't think about him.

Why not? He had a right to see Jimmy, and Jimmy had a right to know his father was alive.

She drew on the cigarette and allowed her mind to wander back to the cellar at Monk's old house, to where Jimmy had been conceived. She hadn't known anything until that night. She'd thought human sex was no different to a pack of dogs taking turns on a yelping female dog in the street. Loving someone changed animal sex into something else.

Had to stop thinking about that too. She was married. Her kids had a stepfather.

And she, and they, had more connection to those tomato seedlings than they had to Ray.

For richer, for poorer, for better for worse . . .

Jim was the husband of her mind and always had been. His ring meant more to her than Ray's. And he'd never been dead, not to her soul. Loved him, and he was out there somewhere tonight, looking at that same moon, maybe thinking about her.

Had they told him how Jimmy had grown?

They would have told him she'd married Ray King — which might alter his attitude to her but not to Jimmy. He'd loved him.

Should have put my age up and married him in Sydney.

Which would have achieved nothing. Vern knew how old she was. He would have had the marriage annulled.

And whether she was married or not, Jim would be interested to know what she'd learnt of Juliana Conti. In Sydney, he'd tried to tell her she hadn't been born a Morrison.

'Juliana Conti,' she whispered. It sounded like a pseudonym. She'd been real though. She'd lived. She'd died. She'd been buried.

If Granny had saved J.C.'s life that night, she would have taken me back to where she came from. I would never have known Jim, would never have had Jimmy and Georgie.

Who was Juliana Conti? Had she planted a garden? Did I get my love of the earth from her or catch it from Granny? Most of who I am came from Granny. Most of what I know I learned from her.

My singing came from Itchy-foot. Archibald Gerald Foote; old Noah of the long white beard and black coat; Doctor Gerald Archibald, abortionist — now driving a little yellow sports car — and older than Granny.

How had a thirty-odd-year-old woman become involved with a sixty-year-old man? In the photograph of Juliana wearing the hat, she looked about thirty — had looked about sixteen as a bride. She'd been married at some time. Widowed maybe. Have I got a batch of half-sisters and brothers somewhere? Where had she left her kids while she was chasing Archie Foote up to Monk's. Had he been worth chasing at sixty?

I'd chase Jim up there if he was blind and on crutches. I wouldn't chase Ray down to the end of the veranda.

Enough!

I'll stop — after I see Jim, I'll stop. I have to explain why I married Ray — and tell him his father is a lying old bastard and his sisters are lying bitches.

They might have believed for a month, two, maybe even for six months, that he was dead, she thought, but they would have known he wasn't before I brought Jimmy home from Sydney, yet all three of them had sat around Granny's table and lied when I asked if they'd heard any news of Jim.

'Bastards.'

They'd heard by then.

'Do the right thing by Jim's boy,' Vern had said. 'Do the right thing by Jim's name.'

'Old bastard.'

He'd been trying to get Jimmy since he was a baby. 'I'll have him raised by decent folk,' he'd said when Jimmy was five months old.

Marrying Ray had put a stop to that, and that's what she had to think about. And the house, and the garden.

A cold garden now. She was freezing. It would be an orange-picking night at Granny's. How many times had she and Joey run down to the orchard on frosty moonlit nights to pick oranges then sit close to the stove, peeling, eating, cold oranges?

'Don't waste that peel,' Granny used to say. Nothing was wasted up there. She'd used dried orange peel as a fire starter.

That's what I have to do. Plant an orange tree. Plant an apricot tree. Plenty of room.

A week ago, she'd looked at plum trees in a shop in High Street. They cost money.

Wished . . . wished she was rich and could buy what she wanted to buy. Wished she could get a job singing somewhere at night. She'd made good money in Sydney with her voice. Never any advertisements for singers in the newspapers. Plenty for nurses, shop assistants, house cleaners. She could get a job cleaning while the kids were at school, or she could next year when Jimmy started school.

Or plant seeds. Fruit trees grew from seed — didn't always grow true to the parent tree though. It all depended on the whim of a bee, Granny used to say. A blossom opened, it was pollinated, fruit formed and each one that ripened had its own unique seed.

My seed pollinated by Jim produced Jimmy, and look at him. He's not me, and he's not Jim, but the best of both of us. And look what I made from Laurie's seed — perfection. Margot? I had nothing to do with the making of her. I didn't know they were making her, didn't know I was having her until she was two-thirds done, so nothing of me went into her.

Cara Jeanette? God alone knew which one of those drunken mongrels made her. Was she big-boned like Hank the Yank; thick from the ears down, dark like him? Or blond like Billy-Bob? Hadn't recognised the other ones. Five of them. No room for me in Cara Jeanette — except for her hands. My hands fought that night. For a time they fought.

A shiver travelled down her spine. Just the cold. And she had to go in before she froze solid.

Didn't want to go to his bed.

The way he was about sex, she couldn't work out why he and his first wife hadn't had kids. Maybe she'd used something. Or had she died in childbirth? Not many did these days, and less down here where the hospitals were close and there were plenty of doctors. He wasn't good with kids, didn't mind her taking precautions. Wouldn't take any of his own.

She was managing.

She looked up at Melbourne's stars, not as bright as Woody Creek's, not as many, but up there, shining. She'd sat on Myrtle's front fence with Jim, searching the sky for the brightest star, sat holding hands, and hand-holding had been almost too sweet to bear.

Craved the touch of his hand, craved his beautiful mouth, craved that throbbing expectation.

And craved another cigarette. Crept inside and stole another, listened to Ray's breathing. Maybe he was asleep.

Had to get her own packet, hide it in the washhouse.

NIGHT SHIFT

*M*onday morning, Jimmy sat on the post office steps with a book and an ice-cream, while Jenny placed a call to Maisy.

'It's me, Maisy. Granny said that you still cut Margaret Hooper's hair.'

'You rang me up to talk about Margaret Hooper's hair?'

'No, and I've got no more coins to extend. Next time you see her, can you find some way to ask her where they've got Jim?'

'He's still in Melbourne. They're down there now. Nelly Dobson told me Vern has got sugar diabetes, and Lorna has gone to England for six months.'

'Is there any England left?'

'She's got an uncle over there — her mother's brother, I think he is. He's in for a shock when he sees her, though her mother didn't look much better . . .'

Once Maisy got started it was hard to cut her off. The telephone company cut her off, Jenny's precious coins wasted on three minutes of Lorna Hooper's uncle and Vern Hooper's diabetes, Margaret's bloke and Nelly Dobson's new washing machine.

Miss Flowers was out in her garden, planting pansies. Jenny

leaned a while against her fence to chat, and left half an hour later with roots of mint, thyme and a clump of parsley.

The garden was looking like a garden when Ray went on night shift. It meant more money, he said, didn't say how much more money. He was a machinery supervisor and would have been paid more than the basic wage. For some reason, he didn't pay rent to the Parkers. He hadn't told her; Flora had. He paid a half-share of electricity, gas and water rates, spent a fortune on his bike and meat, had stopped buying butter. He could have been struggling with money, but it was a waste of time asking, or asking why he paid no rent. Ray didn't talk, and he'd been talking less than usual lately.

Her fault. She'd been . . . been less available to him. Couldn't get Jim off her mind. Sat up late reading library books until Ray started snoring.

She cooked early on the Monday night he commenced his month of night shift. He ate and rode away. She got the kids bathed and into bed, then managed to squeeze in a bath and shampoo before eight. Time to read that night, the gas oven burning on low, the oven door open. It was her only form of heating and no doubt a waste of gas, but the bills weren't high. She finished her book at ten and slid into the luxury of a wide empty bed where she slept like the proverbial log, undisturbed until she heard his bike putter by the window. Out of that bed like a scalded cat; out to the kitchen, placing sausages into the frying pan before he opened the door. He ate, then, unwashed, crawled into bed.

'Shush,' she warned when she woke the kids. 'Ray's asleep.'

'Shush,' while they were eating, and when they crept down the veranda on their way out. 'Shush,' until they were out the gate and free. Ray slept a good eight or ten hours at night. Jenny, expecting him to sleep all day, continued from the school to the tram stop. She and Jimmy were going exploring.

They found St Kilda beach that day and shared a banana there, paddled in the waves. They caught a tram back to the city where they shared a milkshake. With hours still to fill, they went to the pictures. Their tram got them back to Armadale in perfect time to pick up the girls.

He wasn't sleeping. He was watching for them on the veranda, six butts at his feet.

'W-what have you b-b-been doing all d-d-day?'

'We went out so we wouldn't disturb you.'

'Where?'

'To the pictures,' Jimmy said. 'And the beach. And we paddled. And it's all salty. Trams go everywhere, Ray.'

He'd had the best day of his life. As had Jenny. Now she was home.

She found a slab of cow, tossed six potatoes into the sink, ran water on them to soften the dirt, then went to the bedroom to take off her city frock. She heard him tell the kids to go outside and play. Didn't know why — or not until he came into the bedroom.

Froze, half-clad, knowing what was on his mind.

'I'm halfway through getting dinner.' And she wasn't prepared for sex. 'I can't, Ray. I'm not ready for that.'

Ready or not, he was on her. Dinner could wait.

'Let me at least go down to the lav —'

'W-won't m-matter once.'

'It will! Just give me a minute —'

Didn't recite 'The Highwayman'. She prayed. Please God. Please God. Please God, just this once let it not matter. Please God. Please God.

Kids no longer quiet. Jimmy vrooming his trike up the bricked path, one of them running along the veranda.

Please God. Please God.

She knew it mattered when she filled a basin at the sink, the potatoes still waiting there. Knew it mattered while she washed him out of her in the bedroom; knew her seeds spent their lives standing in line, gasping for sperm. Knew by the calendar that it mattered.

Please God. Please God. Please God.

Peeled his filthy potatoes. Fried his slab of bloody cow. Got rid of him to work, then bathed, washed her hair again, and hurried back up the passage to her door, praying she wouldn't run into one of the Parkers.

'How long is Ray on night shift?' Geoff asked.

How long have you been standing in the passage? How much of what happens in that bedroom do you hear?

'A month,' she said, and hurried back to the east side.

She'd know this time next week. Not a thing she could do except wait out that week, count down the days on the calendar, and, for the remainder of his month on bloody night shift, be ready for him.

Eight days she lived through, eight of the longest days of her life, before she knew she'd been given a reprieve. A jubilant day that one, even before Granny's letter arrived, with a page from Maisy. She'd found out the name of Jim's hospital from Vern's farm manager's wife.

Bless you, Maisy Macdonald, and bless your gossiping ways. And thank you, God, for this lovely day.

She waited until Friday, until Ray was sleeping, then she dressed silently, carefully, in the green linen Jim had bought for her in Sydney. Wanted to wear it for him. Wanted him to see it and smile. She dressed Jimmy in his Sunday best, polished his worn shoes. He needed new shoes. She had her endowment money in her purse, with over a pound of sewing money. She'd get him a new pair today.

'Where are we going?' he whispered, happy to be going anywhere.

'To see someone who is sick in a hospital, someone you'll be very surprised to see.'

Let Jim tell him how he'd come back from the dead.

They rode the tram into the city and another one out. They found the hospital. She was shaking when she entered, shaking more as she followed a nurse to a sunroom, her eyes, her knees, threatening to let her down.

Found him sitting like an old man in a cane chair with wheels, staring at a window. She didn't approach him, not for a moment, just stood looking her fill. It was Jim, but so thin and grown older.

He didn't turn to the sound of her high heels on the polished wooden floor and, with a yard between them, she stilled her feet.

'What's so interesting out there?' she said.

He didn't turn to her voice.

'Jim?'

Like a wax model, no movement, no sound.

'It's Jenny,' she said. 'It's Jenny and Jimmy.'

Was he deaf? Could beri-beri affect the hearing? She closed the space between them and reached for his hand resting on the arm of the chair. It hadn't changed. It felt the same, felt warm.

'Jim. It's Jenny.'

For an instant she thought he'd heard her, thought he was going to reply. His lips parted, but they closed and he withdrew his hand to his knee and grimaced. And his teeth were wrong. No more porcelain teacups. They'd fitted him with teeth too small for his face. Clad him in a tartan dressing gown and striped pyjamas, one pyjama leg pinned up. One sharp knee bone trying to poke through the fabric; the other one . . . the other one just . . . just ending. One slipper on the floor.

He'd always been slim. Never like this, or not as a man. Skin stretched over a chiselled jawbone, stretched tighter over sharp cheekbones. So pale, yellow pale. And his dark hair greying at the temples. He was Ray's age. He was Sissy's age, twenty-seven. Men of twenty-seven didn't go grey. Wanted to howl for that grey, to touch it. Didn't.

Jimmy stood well back, his hands behind his back, being the best boy he knew how to be, but watching her with wide, worried eyes. She wasn't going to howl. She took that long-fingered hand again, and this time forced his fingers to the ring he'd given her in Sydney.

'Remember *Jen and Jim, 1942*?' she said. 'Remember having it engraved in Sydney, Jim? I'm still wearing it.'

There was no response to her words or to the ring. He didn't like being touched. Again the hand was withdrawn.

She squatted beside his chair, if only to relieve her trembling legs. Her face on a level with his own, she took his chin and turned his face, forcing him to see her. Perhaps he did, though there was nothing in his eyes. They didn't look like his eyes. They frightened her.

'It's Jenny. You know me.'

Empty eyes looking through her. She released his chin and he turned those empty eyes back to stare at the window, and she stood and stepped away, knowing the Japs had killed him, if not on that day in '43, then soon after. Only his hands had come home. And she had to get out of this place before she started blubbing like a fool.

She reached for Jimmy's warm little hand, knowing now that she had the best of Jim, the last of him, at her side. Walked him too fast from the veranda, walked him too far down that passage, and when she turned into a corridor, she came on a nurses station she hadn't seen on the way in. Lost.

Two men and a white-clad nurse, discussing papers.

'Excuse me,' she said. 'I'm trying to find my way out.'

'Go back to the first corridor on the right,' the nurse said.

'Jennifer?'

The smaller of the two men had spoken. She should have recognised the back of his head, his hair. Had she been thinking straight, she would have. She wasn't thinking straight. Recognising him washed the image of Jim from her mind. She spun around on her high heel and near dragged Jimmy back the way they'd come.

'Jennifer. Do you have a moment?'

She didn't, not for him. He pursued her down the corridor, and to the right, and out into a too bright sun. It burned her eyes. Squinted against it, she walked near blind out to the street, walked fast, believing she'd left him behind. She hadn't.

'Jennifer!'

'That man's calling you, Jenny.'

'Walk, darlin'. I don't want to talk to him.'

Archie Foote pursued her down to the tram stop, and, no tram in sight, Jenny kept walking.

'One word only,' he said.

She had no words for him.

Jimmy knew where they had to wait to catch the trams he loved to ride in. He pulled back on her hand, and she turned to face the man who had fathered her.

'You have no cause to fear me, my dear,' he said.

'I don't fear you, and I don't want to talk to you either.'

'I have only your best interests at heart. One minute of your time is all I ask.'

He was a doctor. He looked like a doctor. He spoke like a doctor, but she knew what he was. Granny knew what he was.

And what was he doing at a hospital full of returned soldiers? He was older than Granny.

Tram coming over the hill, moving too slow. She released Jimmy's hand, turned her back to Archie Foote and placed distance between them.

He spoke to Jimmy. Jimmy liked talking. He asked who they'd seen at the hospital and Jimmy told him of a man who had only one slipper on because his leg got cut off, a man who couldn't see him and Jenny, and his name was Jim, and his daddy's name was Jim too and he'd got dead in the war.

'Hooper's son,' Archie said.

One day Jimmy might learn the name of the man with one leg. Not from her, or not today. She turned to face Archie Foote, her hand raised. Stop. He read hand signals. He said no more.

Tram trundling in. She took Jimmy's hand and they boarded. Archie followed them onto the tram and found a seat across the aisle from Jimmy.

'You're having a day off from school,' he said.

'When I'm five, I can go to school. Only Georgie and Margot go now. What's your name?'

'Archibald — and I'm not even bald.'

Jimmy liked a joke. He laughed, and told him it was a funny name, like in a book. 'Why do you know Jenny's name for?'

'I knew your mummy when she was a little girl, not a lot taller than you.'

'Did you live in Woody Creek too?'

'That's enough, Jimmy.' Jenny swapped seats with him, sat him beside the window.

'You're down for the weekend?' Archie said.

She had to ignore him, that's all. He'd give up. He'd got her mind off Jim's eyes. That's what she had to think. Not a tear in her now. Her concentration on the road ahead. Not much further. She was learning Melbourne's landmarks, its streets. They were the first off the tram at Swanston Street and he still on their heels.

'What do you want from me?'

'Only to speak. I saw Tru quite recently.'

'I've made it clear that I don't want to speak to you.'

'She wasn't pleased to speak to me either. I'm an old man, Jennifer, and quite harmless.'

Armadale tram coming but she couldn't board it and go home. He'd follow her out there. Couldn't let him know where she lived. She let it go, and caught the next one, to God only knew where. He boarded behind her. They rode in silence to a suburb she'd never visited, to a street of shops where she queued to get off. He queued behind her, and she felt his breath on her neck, or maybe only the hairs on her neck standing tall at his proximity.

A threesome then, Jimmy walking between his mother and grandfather, Jimmy discussing artificial legs with the doctor.

'Will you make that man a leg he can tie on?'

'My word we will,' the grandfather said.

Madness.

'Jenny said a man in Sydney had a leg made out of wood and his knee squeaked when he walked.'

'Perhaps he should carry an oil can.'

'And he could just pull his pants up when he was walking and drip, drip, drip, and no more squeaks,' Jimmy said.

'I once knew a man with a tin leg. He could play "Happy Birthday" on it with a teaspoon.'

Just a laughing little boy and his smiling grandpa, chatting as they walked a busy street. That's what passers-by would think.

Don't be taken in by him, Granny had written. *He can put on a fine act.*

A very fine act. Jimmy was taken in. Anyone might be. No hat on his head. His mop of white curls, as her own curls, wouldn't have a happy relationship with hats. A dark grey suit, white shirt, blue tie — to match his eyes. So clean.

He'd been a too clean swaggie, his beard always Persil white. He'd looked harmless back then — and they'd locked him up for corrupting a minor — a Duffy minor.

'Ray is my stepfather and Georgie's and Margot's,' Jimmy said. Little blabbermouth. He'd never been shy. Jenny wished him shy today.

'That's enough, Jimmy. I've told you not to speak to strangers.'

He looked at her, at Archie Foote, unsure how a stranger might have known Jenny's name, but he said no more. Walked beside her and looked in windows, her obedient boy.

She'd seen today so differently, had imagined his little face when he'd learnt that his daddy from the photograph was alive. Better for him to believe his daddy lived only in that photograph, that he had big smiling teeth and eyes that laughed. Better than the reality. Nothing works out the way you expect it to work out.

Not this either. And how could a man of his age still be a doctor? And why in God's name did he have to work at that hospital?

Fate.

Maybe I'm meant to speak to him, ask him about Juliana . . .

They passed a café. 'A cup of tea would go down well?' he said. 'I thought I'd made what I want very clear.'

'Your view of me has been coloured by one half of an unfortunate marriage, I fear, Jennifer. There are two sides to each story, and expectations on either side.'

She knew all about unfortunate marriages and, for the first time, looked him in the eye; just a brief glance — but enough to know that he and Granny would have had about as much in common as she and Ray, enough to know that she'd inherited the blue of his eyes; long enough to doubt that he'd corrupted a Duffy minor. She'd been at school with three Duffy girls. They'd spent half of their time dropping their pants behind the boys' lavs — when they'd been wearing pants to drop.

He'd never tried to corrupt her. He'd never touched her. He'd never said much more to her than good afternoon, Jennifer, or good morning, Jennifer — told her once that she had the voice of an angel. Had given her that pearl-in-a-cage pendant, the first beautiful thing she'd ever owned. Posted the matching earrings to her two years later. She'd once given him a sausage wrapped in bread, dripping tomato sauce.

Don't be taken in by him.

She wasn't taken in. She was seeing him, that's all, her view coloured by an unfortunate marriage, by too early pregnancies and true brutality. She knew he was harmless, or harmless to her.

Still had to get rid of him.

Tram coming, probably going into the city. Billy-Bob's watch told her she'd be pushing time to get home before the girls got out of school. Had to get away from him.

She opened her handbag and found a stub of pencil, a small notebook. He thought she was living in Sydney, thought she was down for the weekend. The likelihood of running into him again was remote — as long as she stayed away from that hospital. She'd stay away, and not only because of him. Wrote Lila Jones's old address, a girl she'd worked with at the Sydney factory, then, just for good measure, wrote Wilfred Whiteford's telephone number, the only Sydney number she could recall. Ripped the page from the book and offered it. Didn't tell him to keep in touch.

He glanced at it, folded it. 'Tru mentioned that you were singing at a club in Sydney.' She nodded, willing Jimmy to be silent as Archie placed the paper into his wallet. 'We have that in common, my dear.'

'I thought you were a doctor.'

'I am, as ever, a man of many parts. I do a few numbers at a cosy little jazz club. If you find yourself in town on a Friday evening . . .' He had removed a printed card from his wallet. 'It would give me great pleasure to introduce your beautiful voice to our fair city.'

'It's unlikely.' She took his card, took his offered hand. And was shaken by the contact. He was her father, her blood, and her hand knew it. She snatched it free. Watched him offer his hand to Jimmy, who knew all about shaking hands.

Got away, wiped her hand on her thigh and hurried Jimmy across the road at traffic lights. Perhaps Archie followed them. She didn't turn to see. Jimmy turned.

'Was he your friend before, Jenny?'

'He was Granny's friend, darlin'.'

Granny's nemesis.

Met by accident. Fathered by him, by accident. Life was just one big accident.

It would give me great pleasure to introduce your beautiful voice to our fair city.

What if . . . what if meeting him wasn't an accident? What if she'd been . . . guided? What if she was meant to . . . to use him to get a job singing?

She didn't catch the tram. It hid her while she entered a large drapery store, where she drew Jimmy to a halt behind a chaotic table piled high with stained calico. Stood watching the entrance. No sign of him.

A large sign over that table: *Fire Sale*. The table was piled with smoke and water-stained calico sheets. And that price couldn't be right. She freed one sheet from the pile and studied it, freed another.

'They stink,' Jimmy said.

'Stink washes out.'

She bought half a dozen smelly sheets for next to nothing, and two bottles of blue dye. No new shoes for Jimmy, not this week.

BLUE CURTAINS

*I*t took three days. One day of soaking, scrubbing, boiling, then dyeing; one day to cut and stitch hems and headings; another to damp those dyed sheets down and iron them. Norman's brace and bit made the holes for large cup hooks. A hardware store in High Street supplied the dowelling for curtain rods. She and the girls carried the lengths home, cut to size by a flirty man at the shop. They hung the first curtain in the kids' bedroom, and it looked beautiful. They hung three over the kitchen windows and glass door, and had two left to hang in Ray's bedroom when he woke up.

He didn't comment on the transformation. The curtain over the glass door got in his way when he wanted to get out.

'I'll loop them back in the daytime,' she said.

'It's d-d-day now.'

'I wanted you to see how good they look.'

He wanted to get out. She looped them back with ribbons made from the off-cuts, and her kitchen looked like something out of a magazine, and his bedroom more so, after he'd ridden off to work. Wished . . . wished Granny would come down and see what she'd done. Wished she could invite Maisy and Maureen out for afternoon tea the next time Maisy was in town. Wished she could write to Granny and tell her about meeting Archie Foote. Couldn't.

Wished she'd had the guts to have a cup of tea with him and ask him about Juliana Conti. Wished she had a job singing at a jazz club. She'd made good money with her voice in Sydney.

Hadn't opened her mouth since Norman's funeral.

He'd been her father, her only father.

Archie Foote would ring that Sydney number and get some government war department, no doubt closed down. He'd know she'd lied to him.

So weird, seeing her own eyes looking back at her. Shaking his hand had been weird. He had young hands. Not her hands. She'd always known she had his hair. Wondered who cut his. Her own needed cutting and hairdressers didn't understand it. They sheared her. Granny knew how to cut it. Gained her practice on his hair? She'd lived with him for eight years. He'd drugged her and aborted her first baby. She knew him better than anyone. I have to trust her judgement, Jenny thought.

Should burn his card. She'd thought about burning it when she'd lit the copper to dye those sheets. It was in her bankbook in her handbag. Should burn it now, get him out of her head.

Better to have him in her head than the image of Jim. Jim no longer Jim.

Had to keep busy, that's all. Making the curtains had got both of them out of her head. Idle hands are the devil's tool, Granny used to say. Never put off until tomorrow what you can do today.

She washed her floors, bare boards but oiled. She polished them, as Amber had polished her boards, with a mixture of turpentine and beeswax; polished Ray's bedroom suite, then took sandpaper to the old chest of drawers she'd bought for the kids' room. Wore her fingerprints away before she was satisfied with it, then polished it with Amber's trade secret, and that old wood lapped up the polish and glowed.

Flora admired her rooms, admired the chest of drawers, asked if Jenny had found it in the sleep-out.

'I've got the receipt, Flora.'

Geoff came to stand at the door and do his own admiring — of the curtains, and his neighbour's industry.

'Why don't you make curtains?' he asked Flora.

'Buy me an electric sewing machine and I might be able to,' she said, and where did she get the nerve to speak to him like that?

'Get a job and buy your own,' he said.

'You've got money to waste on gas converters.'

He slammed the door. Flora returned to her side to slam a few of her own.

They'd been arguing on their side of the house since Jenny moved in. They argued on her side now, and in the backyard — and still went out to dances on Saturday nights, still went to the pictures while she babysat Lois. She didn't argue with Ray and he never took her out. She hadn't been for a ride on his bike since she'd married him, hadn't been to a dance. Went to the pictures with Jimmy.

'How did you cook your meals before you had this kitchen, Ray?'

'U-u-used theirs.'

'How come the old girl's fridge is on your side?'

'W-w-will,' he said.

It was the first Jenny had heard about a will. She knew Ray had worked for Flora's aunty but until that moment had been unaware he'd been named in her will.

Flora wanted curtains for her parlour exactly like Jenny's. They made them together. Flora bought the smoke-damaged sheets, Jenny mixed the dye bath. Flora rinsed them, pegged them on the clothes line. Jenny stitched, Flora ironed, Geoff hung them. They didn't offer to pay. Jenny didn't ask for payment.

Making those curtains started a habit, not a bad habit. With tea still rationed, the women began sharing their pots at lunchtime, in Flora's side of the house until Ray's month of night shift ended, then in Jenny's. The passage door spent most of its days open thereafter, or during the day it was open. The bathroom became more accessible. They weren't friends — Flora was very churchy, her life dictated to by the Pope — but they were housemates, and as long as they stayed away from religion, they found enough to talk about.

Flora watched a square of grey fabric become a pair of shorts for Jimmy. She was there one afternoon when a friend of Mrs Andrews, the bank manager's wife, came to pick up a lilac frock. Flora knew her. She saw money change hands.

'You get your money's worth out of that old machine,' she said when the woman left.

'I spent a month pulling it apart and cleaning it. It owes me.'

She was there the day Jenny found Laurie's framed mug shot tucked deep beneath Amber's embroidered tablecloths, beautiful things, rarely used. Not so beautiful that battered frame, nor the newspaper cutting it kept safe, which, a month ago, had disappeared from the kids' windowsill. Georgie must have hidden it in the drawer. Had she taken it out of its frame and read the tale of the water-pistol bandit, the details of Laurie's sentence — three years' hard labour for car theft and robbery? That kid was too old for her years, and far too smart. She had the intelligence to know that robbery and car theft were not things to be proud of.

'Where did you get that?' Flora said.

'He looked like a young Clark Gable,' Jenny said, sliding the photograph deeper beneath the cloths. 'He was my favourite movie star when I was a kid.'

'I meant the tablecloth.'

'Oh. My . . . my stepmother worked it,' Jenny said.

Stepmother — half-sister. Wondered if she was embroidering sackcloth in the asylum. The only time she'd sat still was when she'd had a piece of embroidery in her hands.

She removed the cloth with the pink and maroon roses, shook and spread it over the table.

'It looks like one of Aunty Phoebe's,' Flora said.

There was a grab-all lurking in Flora.

'There was nothing here when I moved in. Every sheet we've got, every tablecloth, I brought from home.'

'I didn't mean that it was hers! Most of her stuff was worn out anyway. I meant it's like the stuff she had here when I was young. We used to visit her a bit when she was married to her third husband. She'd put on fancy tea parties for us, spread one of her fancy cloths, and were we for it if we spilt anything on it.'

'How long have you known Ray?'

Squeezing information out of him was like trying to squeeze milk out of Granny's billy goat. Why not get what information she could where she could?

'Only since the funeral. We knew about him before,' Flora said. 'After she divorced her third, we stopped coming around. Dad used to get on well with him. I was about twelve or thirteen at the time.'

Flora was three years older than Ray. When she'd been twelve or thirteen, Ray would have been going to school in Woody Creek.

'I've often wanted to ask you why Ray doesn't pay rent,' Jenny said.

'It was in the will,' Flora said, and Jenny baited her hook with a white lie.

'He told me once that your aunty was like a mother to him.'

It sounded logical, but it raised Flora's eyebrows and silenced her for a time.

'She didn't like kids. She was on stage until she was too old to have them, so Mum says. I dare say they would have interfered with her lifestyle. I want more kids but I can't get pregnant again. I got pregnant fast enough with Lois.'

'I do it too easily,' Jenny said.

'You're not, are you?'

'No, thank God.' She turned her back. Mentions of God, in that context, equalled blasphemy.

'I thought Ray was Catholic.'

'He is. I'm not.'

'Oh, it's like that, is it.'

'Three is enough to handle at the moment.'

'Mum says that Phoebe's first wanted kids. He was twice her age. Seven years of her killed him, and less than twelve months later she married some dago bloke. He cleared out when she was in her late forties and she married a normal Australian bloke — the only one of them who was normal, according to Mum.'

The heavy knocker on the front door reverberated down the passage. That door was in Flora territory. She rose to answer it, Jenny listening while pouring a mug and a cup of tea. Flora didn't like drinking out of mugs. Cups didn't hold enough for Jenny, and she'd gone past the stage of putting on a show for her neighbour.

A woman's voice. 'The girls are wondering if you might make up a sixth tonight.' She sounded like Maisy, or one of her daughters.

'I can't stand the woman,' Flora said.

'She won't be there. That's why we need a sixth. Be a sport and sit in for her.'

'Geoff doesn't like me going out without him.'

'It's not out! It's around the flaming corner.'

Whoever she was, she hadn't been invited in, but she was in and staring openly into Jenny's half of the house.

'Look what they grow in the bush these days,' she said.

Flora introduced them as Jenny, Ray's wife, and Wilma Fogarty from down at the corner. 'We go to the same church,' she said.

'I smell floor polish. It's banned at my place,' Wilma said. 'You can't squeeze another cuppa out of the pot, can you?'

'How do you take it?'

'The same way I take my men, love: strong, white and sweet.'

She looked older than Flora, her frock was a washed-out floral, and within minutes, Jenny knew why. She had seven kids, the oldest fourteen, the youngest three.

'You've got three, so they tell me,' Wilma said. 'You don't look old enough. Where did he find you anyway?'

'Do you know Willama?' Jenny said. She never mentioned Woody Creek. Amber had put that town on the map.

'I've been as far as Frankston. Joe took me down there on my honeymoon and I've been pregnant since,' Wilma said, and she sat down at Ray's table and changed Jenny's life.

Wilma and Flora had worked together at Foy & Gibson during the depression. She lived around the bottom corner with Joe, who worked at a brewery and at weekends kept them in business, Wilma said. She was a talking machine, a city version of Maisy, not as weighty yet, but, like Maisy, could jump from one subject to the next with no breath between. She jumped from telling Flora how young Micky, the little bugger, had had enough of school, and how Joe was trying to get him an apprenticeship at that big garage in Toorak Road. She jumped from the big garage to Veronica, mad Bill's absconding wife, then, mid-sentence: 'I don't suppose you play, Jen?'

'Play what?'

'Cards. A bunch of us get together on Friday nights, and Veronica will end up with her throat cut if she sticks her nose anywhere near this street. We'll be one short tonight.'

'I do,' Jenny said, more willingly than she'd said it on her wedding day and with more conviction.

'Five Hundred?'

'Anything.'

'Tonight?'

'Once the kids are in bed.'

'You little bottler,' Wilma said. 'You probably heard how Veronica walked out on her old man last week?'

Jenny heard what Flora told her, what the kids told her, and occasionally what the twelve o'clock news told her. She'd never heard of mad Bill or his wife.

'They're in that cream weatherboard two doors up from Miss Flowers and her brother,' Flora said.

'You can't miss her. Tall, dark, good-looking — her, not him,' Wilma said. 'He looks like a mad-eyed German. Do you smoke?'

Wilma took a packet of cigarettes from the pocket of her house dress, flipped one into her mouth and tossed the packet to the tablecloth, spilling tobacco on Amber's embroidery. Amber would have murdered Norman for less — and had.

'I do,' Jenny said, helping herself to one.

She reached for Ray's ashtray and placed it, too, on Amber's tablecloth while Wilma continued her convoluted tale of Veronica, and Jenny realised she was talking about Mrs Andrews, the bank manager's wife, her second customer.

'Flora was saying a while back that your first hubby got killed in the war. I lost my youngest brother three weeks before it ended. I wish they'd dropped that bomb sooner. He was the pick of the lot. I've got six. One girl among six brothers — if you can imagine that.'

Time took wing that day. Jenny forgot to pick the girls up from school. She was on a high when Ray came home, until she told him Wilma Fogarty had invited her down for a game of cards.

He knew Wilma Fogarty. 'You d-don't w-want to m-m-mix with her,' he said.

'I miss playing cards.'

'Sh-sh-she's a b-b-b—'

His stutter was worse when he argued. The kids sat watching his mouth, Jimmy's mouth working for him.

'She talks too much, but she's very friendly.'

'Her h-h-husband's a s-s-soak.'

'He won't be there, and I haven't had a game of Five Hundred since I left home.'

'W-we'll p-play with the k-kids tonight.'

'It's an adults' game.' Shouldn't have said that. Shouldn't have. He could only play Switch. 'I won't stay late.'

But he was gone, out to play with his bike, to sweep his path, rake up leaves. She followed him out to the veranda.

'Come down at ten and walk me home, Ray.' Hold my hand, she thought, kiss me in the moonlight, make me feel something for you.

'W-w-walk yourself home,' he said.

She put on a clean frock, tied her hair back, got two of the kids into bed by seven thirty. Margot refused to go.

'I want you in bed before I leave, Margot. It's late enough.'

'I'm not thleepy yet, I thaid.'

'And I'm not in the mood for your argument,' Jenny said. 'Go to bed.'

'J-just because y-y-you want to g-go out, you're s-sending them to b-bed.'

'Just because you're not pleased that I'm going out doesn't mean that you have to take her part against me. Go to bed, Margot.'

'I want uth to play cardth with Daddy Ray.'

Gave up, or gave in. Got the cards out and a sheet of paper, a pencil. Watched Ray write the kids' initials laboriously, the J for Jimmy reversed. Didn't correct him. Georgie didn't correct him. She liked playing cards.

At eight, Jenny retrieved her cigarettes from the washhouse, from behind her packet of Persil, lit one and walked down to the corner where women's laughter drew her to an open front door.

'Get in here. You're late,' Wilma yelled in reply to her knock.

Jenny entered and followed the voices to a battered kitchen, where five women were already seated around a wreck of a kitchen table.

'Patsy, Moira, Doreen, Carol, and the lanky little bugger at my cake tin is Micky, my eldest. And I told you to get out of that cake tin and get to bed, Micky. Now!'

Jenny knew Carol from over her side fence. She nodded to the rest then took her rickety chair. Five minutes later, she was immersed in the battle of the cards.

Ray didn't come at ten to walk her home. At ten thirty she heard a bike. Hoped it was him. Hoped he'd come to take her riding through the night streets. It went by.

'I should go,' she said.

The women didn't want to break up their card game. She stayed until eleven thirty then walked home with Carol.

He was asleep when she crept in. She didn't wake him. He was a reliable worker. He kept enough food on the table. He wasn't a heavy drinker. He was young, strong. Doreen's husband had a bad heart. He couldn't work. Doreen and her two eldest daughters were the breadwinners in their house. Jenny went to sleep counting her blessings — and hoping that Veronica, the missing player, remained missing.

Still missing the following Friday evening. Carol knocked on Jenny's glass door and they walked together to Wilma's house, all three kids in bed, Ray in no mood to play Switch, and not happy that Jenny was going out again. Friday nights were his sex nights, one of his sex nights. And Veronica was a slut. Any woman who walked out on her husband was a slut, and he didn't want his wife associating with women that slut associated with, he said, though over a period of time and not in those words, or so many words.

Veronica's husband had broken her nose, blackened her eyes, and more than once, according to the card players. They discussed men around Wilma's kitchen table, discussed childbirth and washing machines, the church and contraception, kids and apricot trees. Wilma's apricot tree scraped against her spouting.

'I've asked Joe a dozen times to cut it back. He's too bloody lazy to get off his arse at weekends,' Wilma said.

'Does it have apricots on it?' Jenny asked.

'His arse? No,' Wilma said straight-faced.

There is little more raucous than the unrestricted laughter of women, and it was so good. Jenny laughed until her stomach hurt, and when the laughter died, she asked if the tree bore any apricots.

'Yeah. I keep hoping the bugger of a thing will grow bananas, but it never does.'

More laughter, the game won or lost, cigarettes lit, the scores totalled, while Jenny told the players how she and her grandmother used to make pots of apricot jam every year between Christmas and New Year's Day.

'My mother used to make her own jam,' Doreen said.

'Six spades,' Wilma said. 'It's usually loaded. Pick what you like. The birds eat what the kids don't.'

'I've been thinking about taking the kids home for Christmas,' Jenny said.

They played late that night. It was well after midnight when Jenny slid into bed. She couldn't sleep, couldn't toss around until she got comfortable either. She'd wake him. She lay on her back, her mind doing the tossing and turning.

She hadn't spoken to Ray about going home for Christmas. Had been thinking about it for a while, and hoarding sugar in jam jars. It was still rationed. A lot of sugar was needed for jam-making. The war had been over for a year. Australia grew thousands of acres of sugar cane and, like most, she'd believed rationing would end when the war ended.

Joey, Elsie's son, was engaged to the daughter of a cane farmer. He was flying down for Christmas. And Jenny wanted to see him, speak to him. As kids, they'd spent hours together, sitting by the creek, tossing in fishing lines and talking about flying away to strange places. Jenny's dream had been to fly to Paris, become a famous singer and marry Clark Gable. Joey had planned to fly to the sands of Egypt and dig up tombs filled with gold. And look where they'd ended up. He grew sugar cane and she spent her days leaning over an old sewing machine.

She still had dreams about singing in Paris. She'd had an incredible dream two nights ago. She'd been on Woody Creek's stage, but knew it was in Paris. She'd been wearing pink. She never wore pink, hated it about as much as she hated yellow. And he'd been in it — Itchy-foot. As a kid she'd named him Itchy-foot. Blame Granny for that: she'd told someone once she'd been married to a quack with itchy feet.

He could probably get her a job. He'd know all about Melbourne's night-life. She knew nothing. Clubs and bands didn't advertise for singers. Singers had to be in the right place at the right time, like in Sydney.

Occasionally when the Parkers were out, she sang.

She knew she could do it. She'd learned a lot from Wilfred Whiteford, had learnt to read music in Sydney. Ought to do it, instead of ruining her eyesight unpicking seams, stitching invisible hems. Make some real money. Pay back to the bank what she'd withdrawn.

Joey would tell her to do it. Maybe that's why she wanted to go home for Christmas. Needed someone to give her leave to do what she wanted to do. Her fishing mate, Joey, almost brother, supreme yabby catcher.

They'd never fitted into their families. Elsie had been a twelve- or thirteen-year-old kid when she'd had Joey. Granny had raised him — and Elsie from the age of twelve.

'Get out of this place,' Joey had told her when he'd come home for a couple of days after the war. 'Do what you have to to get out, Jen. There's nothing here for either of us.'

They'd got out. Jenny hoped his escape had been more successful than her own. Wondered if the cane farmer was rich, if he knew about Elsie, or if Joey was playing the grandson of a Spanish pirate. Hoped he was. He'd looked like a Spaniard when he'd had his moustache. Hoped he got married and lived happily ever after.

Her mind too busy for sleep, it didn't draw the shutters until dawn was near, until the early birds started chirping and cooing, until she woke with him on top of her.

'No!' Tried to push Ray off. She wasn't going through that again. 'Get off me, Ray.'

He was too big. Fridays were his sex nights and he'd missed out. He loved her.

A wife can't charge her husband with rape. A wife was like a cow, bought at the saleyards; once it's safe in the farmer's paddock, he can do what he likes to it.

'I l-love you,' he said when he was done.

She pushed him from her, snatched her coat and struggled to find the sleeves. 'That's not love. That's dogs-in-the-street sex,' she said. 'How dare you.'

Nowhere to wash him off her, only the sleep-out, and ragged blinds in there. She took her basin of water, her soap, her towel, out there, locked the kids' door and did what she could, emptied the water down the lavatory, then went to the washhouse for her cigarettes.

Walked her garden, cigarette in hand, packet and matches in her pocket. Lit a second cigarette from the first. Was he trying to get her pregnant? Didn't want her playing cards on Friday nights?

I'll do more than play bloody cards. I'm going home for Christmas, and going as soon as school breaks up too.

She sewed a frock for Flora to wear to Geoff's brother's wedding, and looked after Lois all day on the day of the wedding.

By Sunday she knew her luck had run out, knew she wasn't going anywhere.

PUNISHMENT

*O*ctober: plump little onions in the garden; baby carrots giving up their space early so their siblings might grow big and long; silverbeet leaves large enough to pick, and the snails feasting on them; slugs eating the lettuce.

She was six days overdue and wanted to get run over by a truck, wanted to go into the city and jump off a tall building.

You can't jump off tall buildings when you've got three kids. You can't stay inside a house when its walls are crushing your soul either. She took Jimmy into the city where they ate dishes of ice-cream for lunch at the Coles cafeteria. She couldn't stand her head, or the thoughts in her head, so she took him to a movie, uninterested in what was playing, just needing that flashing screen to turn off her brain.

She'd made a bad choice: Fred and Ginger were dancing. Loved dancing. Hadn't known the dancing would end with the wedding ring. So she'd married him for the wrong reasons, but did that mean she had to swell up like a toad every other year? She'd told him she wasn't having any more kids. How many times had she told him? Countless times.

Eyes leaking in a movie theatre when everyone else was laughing. Jimmy was laughing.

It would be different this time. She was a married woman. The kids were old enough to be interested in a new baby.

It would be worse different. It would be born in the middle of winter, and probably weigh twelve pounds, and its skull would be made of solid bone, and they'd have to cut it out of her, not drag it out like Jimmy had been dragged out.

And trying to wash napkins only on Wednesdays and Sundays. She couldn't do it. She'd be washing napkins in the kitchen sink — between sorting out his bloody meat. And how the hell did anyone get napkins dry in July in Melbourne?

No more exploring on the trams with Jimmy. No more chasing waves at the beach. No more movies. No more dreaming of singing. No time for sewing either. She'd be dependent on his roadkill.

Jimmy would be at school next year, which would put an end to their exploring anyway. Babies grew on you. Cara Jeanette had grown on her — though by the time she had, she'd no longer been hers, which was probably why she'd allowed her to grow on her.

Nine months married. February to October. She'd done everything she could to be careful. He'd done everything he could but be careful. And he'd keep on doing it. She'd probably have one every eighteen months until she went through menopause. Her fingers did the sums while Ginger danced in a gown Jenny wanted to wear at Archie's jazz club. Her sums told her she could produce twelve or thirteen more before she was forty-five — and some women didn't go through menopause until they were fifty; add three more to the total.

And knowing Ray, he wouldn't waste money on buying milk for it, not when he'd already bought the cow — or the bloody goat — for its udders. Her kids rarely saw fresh milk. At times they were lucky to see powdered milk. Breastfeeding was Elsie's only means of contraception. For self-preservation.

I'll end up feeding little Ray Kings until I'm tucking my breasts into my belt, she thought.

Which might stop Geoff Parker winking at her, which might

make Ray a happier man. He was green-eyed jealous — jealous of the secondhand man who always greeted her with a smile, who must have been sixty-five. Even he wouldn't smile at her when she had a pumpkin belly and udders hanging down to her navel.

Look on the bright side, she thought. Ray won't want to have sex with me when I'm blown up like a toad.

As if he'll care what I look like. Does any man care what his wife looks like? They do when they marry them, then their eyesight changes. A farmer has to admire a heifer at the sale yards or he wouldn't buy it. Thereafter, it's only as good as the calves he can get out of it.

That damn movie went on and on. Why did good movies end too soon and bad movies last forever? It seemed hours since they'd walked into the theatre. Not enough light to see the hands on Billy-Bob's watch, which she'd told Ray she'd found on a Sydney beach, which she *had* found on a Sydney beach, which he may have believed — and probably didn't.

And why should he trust her? She still wore her ex-fiancé's ring. It had been a tight fit on her right ring finger when she put it on there. Now she couldn't get it off — and didn't want to anyway.

When she was struggling to feed ten or twelve, she'd learn to love cooking his livers. There was something to be glad about. She'd accept his tripe as if it were a bouquet of fungus flowers.

He was getting on better with Margot. He'd probably like having his own kid.

How was he going to feed thirteen of his own kids when he couldn't afford to feed her three? She bought the milk, most of the bread, all of the fruit and vegetables.

I didn't want Georgie and Jimmy. I love them. I'll probably love it.

How can you love dozens of them? Each one snaps off a bit more of you. A woman must reach the stage where so many bits have been snapped off, there's not enough left to love anyone.

'We'll have to go, Jimmy,' she whispered. 'It's late.'

'It's not the end yet,' he whispered back.

That kid would watch anything that moved on the screen. She sat, unable to concentrate on the story — if the fool of a movie had a story to concentrate on. It ended, and while the rest of the crowd squeezed the last moments out of the credits, Jenny and Jimmy got out of the theatre.

Dazzled by the afternoon light, they made their way with the afternoon crowd towards the tram stop, Jenny knowing she'd be late picking up the girls. She felt nauseous too, and it was too early to be suffering from morning sickness, and it wasn't morning. Knowing that she was pregnant was more than enough to make a cow nauseous.

And why did it have to happen in October? She hated October. Every October she saw that little girl growing up in Sydney, saw her blonde, saw her dark, saw hands that were miniatures of her own. She would have turned two on the third of October. She tried to forget her. At times she almost did, then she'd see a little girl of around the same age and Cara Jeanette was back in her head. Once you had them, once you gave them life, they became a part of you. And she didn't want any more parts of her running around.

And what if Robert Norris hadn't returned from the war? What if Myrtle had been run over by a truck? What if that little girl was being raised in an orphanage — or by some mad, murdering bitch of a woman?

Since learning the truth of her own birth, she'd felt worse about what she'd done to that baby. People needed to be connected to someone. For months after she'd found out who she was, who she wasn't, she'd felt disconnected from life. Was connected to her kids. Even Margot, a bit. She loved cards, played like a little tooth-grinding demon.

People milling, blocking her way. She'd never seen such a crowd in Melbourne. It was impossible to get around them or to push her way through.

'Why is everyone here, Jenny?' Jimmy asked.

'Something is on, or someone important is in town.'

The girls would be walking themselves home from school today. They'd done it before, though not to a locked house. Flora would be there. And it was no use worrying about something she couldn't change. Her arm around Jimmy's shoulder, they walked with the crowd to the tram stop, where the crowd milled and not a tram in sight.

She couldn't change being pregnant either so it was no use worrying about that. She'd tell Ray tonight. He might be pleased. He ought to be. He'd done it. In the movies when wives told their husbands that they were expecting, husbands were jubilant.

'What a thing to go and do at this time of day,' a woman said.

The faces in the crowd weren't showing anticipation. It was frustration.

'What's going on?' Jenny asked.

'The tram drivers have gone out on strike.'

'Are there any trains?' she asked someone, anyone.

'Plenty of trains, love,' an old bloke said. 'None of the buggers are going anywhere.'

'What are we supposed to do?'

'Try shanks's pony,' someone said.

'We'll have to walk, love,' Jenny said to Jimmy.

It couldn't be much more than five miles to Armadale. She could do it. Jimmy was a good walker, or had been in Woody Creek. She took his hand and they joined the herd walking towards St Kilda Road.

For a time it was almost fun: strangers had something to say to other strangers, the strike melding the crowd into a group with a common grudge. There were fast walkers and slow walkers and many paths that led to home; there were taxi drivers who charged more than the recommended fee, and those prepared to pay the fee. Not Jenny. She crossed the bridge with a smaller crowd, Jimmy happy to talk about the big river — he hadn't known Melbourne had a big river. They walked by gardens, where women sat down on the lawns to remove high heels from their burning feet. Jenny's shoes were old, flat-heeled, worn comfortable, so comfortable their soles were near worn through. Jimmy's shoes were close to new, but he was happy enough to walk in them, until they passed the shrine and he realised how far they hadn't yet walked.

'It's too far, Jenny.'

'Walking makes you strong.'

He was very, very strong. He showed how strong he was until they crossed over Toorak Road. Perhaps he recognised that corner.

'How far more, Jenny?'

'Not too far. Do you want a piggyback?'

He rode for a hundred yards, but he was a big boy and heavy, and she felt heavy enough without him on her back. She set him down, held his hand and they walked on towards Commercial Road. There may have been shorter routes home; Jenny knew only one way. She followed the tramlines, be it the shortest or longest route.

'My shoes are hurting.'

'Mine too.'

They'd need resoling after today. And she was going to pay for a haircut next endowment day. Give her hair any length at all and it frizzed. She'd tied it back this morning. Somewhere between Jimmy climbing onto her back and sliding him off, she'd lost her ribbon. Her hair hung free for the late-afternoon sun to spin into gold, for the light breeze to twirl into springs of gold.

Midway between Commercial Road and High Street, Jimmy again riding on her back, a chap driving a horse and dray came alongside.

'Not going down High Street, are you, love?' he called.

'Yes, please.'

He'd already collected twenty-odd passengers. They made room for two more. It was a bumpy, slow old ride and Jenny blessed each bump. It was a happy, laughing ride; a singing ride too, like the hay ride she'd gone on once with Maisy's daughters.

They rode the dray to their corner, where many hands helped them down, and they stood on the corner smiling, waving their fellow travellers on their way, Jenny knowing she'd been closer to herself on that dray than she'd been since Norman died.

She lived a fake life with Ray, and with Flora. Rarely said what she was thinking, censored her words before she opened her mouth. She wasn't her true self with the card players either, just determined to fit in. That's what happened when you spent time being Jenny No One.

In Woody Creek last summer, she'd lived in shorts. Ray didn't approve of her shorts. She'd packed them away. He said he liked her hair long. She'd let it grow. She was losing more of who she was every day she spent in his house. He'd planted that baby in her, needing to steal what was left. Maybe he loved her. Maybe he just wanted to possess her. She didn't want to go home to him. Wanted to chase that dray and the happy travellers, ride it until it shook his baby loose.

Wanted a cigarette too. She had two in an envelope in the bottom of her bag. She found them, straightened and lit one, found peppermints, gave one to Jimmy and popped one into her mouth. Peppermints disguised the smell of smoke. Ray didn't approve of women smoking.

They walked on then, Jimmy sucking, Jenny blowing smoke, until she saw Ray waiting at the gate with the girls. She drew one last gasp from the cigarette, then dropped it, ground its ember beneath her shoe — and felt the heat of it. She'd worn a hole in that sole.

'The trams and trains have gone out on strike,' she greeted him. 'We've got blisters on our blisters.'

'Wh-where have you b-b-been?'

'To a movie.'

'You let your kids c-c-come home to a l-locked house.'

'I wouldn't have bothered locking it if you hadn't told me I had to lock it, and we would have been home in plenty of time if the tram drivers had been working, and Flora is here anyway, and she owes me for more than two hours of babysitting, and we're exhausted. We walked most of the way from the city.'

'You're always r-r-running in th-there.'

'I'm not always running in there. I haven't been in there for three weeks.'

'A man gave us a ride on his dray, Ray,' Jimmy said. 'He had a giant horse that did number twos.'

'Who?'

'A carrier playing taxi driver to us and two dozen more.'

'And we sung green bottles hanging on the wall and every time someone got off we had to sing less bottles,' Jimmy said.

Jenny slid her shoes off, poked her finger though the hole in its sole and wiggled it. Georgie giggled. Margot smiled. Ray didn't.

'You've b-been to s-s-see him again?'

Little blabbermouth Jimmy had told him about the man who had one leg and only one slipper when they went to the hospital. Wished he hadn't told him.

'We saw that new Ginger Rogers and Fred Astaire movie, and it wasn't worth seeing. And I told you, he didn't know who we were, and that we're not going back.'

Couldn't go back had she wanted to. Couldn't take the chance she'd run into Archie Foote. She might like to dream about him getting her a singing job. Dreams were free.

'H-how do I know w-w-what you g-get up to?'

'Because I tell you what I get up to, Ray, and you either trust me or you don't. And if you don't, that's your problem, not mine.'

She'd never spoken to him like that before. She'd never been pregnant to him before, and he'd had no right to get her pregnant. Walked away from him. Walked down to the lav. Thought about lighting the other cigarette, but Jimmy wanted to do wee. She gave up her space and went inside.

She'd been planning to tell Ray tonight — so he could run out and buy her a pound of tripe. And to hell with him. Anyway, after today, she may not be pregnant.

Fried chops, fried bread for the kids in the leftover fat — one of the fringe benefits of his meat: she never ran out of dripping. Saved every drip of it, clarified it and used it in biscuits, in pastry.

There were not many fringe benefits. He'd taught Margot how to write backward Js. And why should she practise her reading when her stepfather wouldn't attempt to read his own newspaper? Or bathe, when he didn't bathe often enough? The smell of his sweat was nauseating tonight.

Sighed and served the meal, unable to see a lot of good whichever way she turned. A half-house, a refrigerator, water on tap . . .

Too tired, that's all. Her legs, her feet, throbbed with weariness — or pregnancy. Jimmy was as tired. Elbow on the table, his head supported by a hand, he was too weary to eat. She got him into bed, and at seven thirty got the girls in with him. Five minutes later she was in bed.

And he came in wanting sex.

'Go away,' she said and turned her back.

'W-what's w-wrong with you?'

'I walked home from the city, half the way with Jimmy on my back.'

And your baby in my belly. And I've made a gigantic mistake. And today I know it. And I don't know if I feel like this because I'm pregnant, or if having your baby inside me is allowing me to see more clearly.

'I l-love you.'

'You want to have sex with me, Ray. Say what you mean.'

Hands all over her, one trying to get between her legs, and she rolled from the bed.

'And why the hell you'd want to sleep with me when you don't trust me, I don't know.'

'W-what d-did I d-do?'

'Who knows what you get up to,' she said.

'W-w-w-what?'

'That's what you said to me. And if you think I don't know what you meant by it, then you're wrong.'

'I w-was j-joking.'

'Saying something like that to someone like me is no joke. I've got three illegitimate kids, and you know how I got them. You either trust me or you don't, and if you don't, say it and stop hinting around it.'

She went out to the kitchen, made a cup of tea and lit one of his cigarettes, sat at the table and smoked it, and too bad if he liked women smoking or not.

Her condition was unchanged come morning, and October and the strike became worse. Other unions were now supporting the train and tram drivers. It was on the midday news when she and Flora shared their lunchtime teapot.

It was in the newspapers Ray brought home from the factory; well-thumbed newspapers and not always current. Every household needed newspaper. It polished windows and shoes, wrapped rubbish. In Woody Creek, they'd used it in the lav. Not down here. Jenny and Flora shared the cost of toilet rolls; almost shared — five backsides on the east side, three on the west.

She read the papers to Ray while the evening meal cooked, a habit she'd started during her first months in Armadale when she'd clung to hopes of teaching him to read. It had stopped his reading. She was expected now to keep him abreast of the daily news.

'*Factory workers are meeting today to discuss support for the strikers* — I hope your factory doesn't get caught up in the mess. A lot of unions are supporting them, Ray. *Rail and tramway men look set for a long strike. The Railway Commission refused to negotiate with them while they hold the state to ransom . . .*'

The strikers wanted more money, shorter hours, wanted the pegging of wages to be lifted. The papers were full of stories — bus drivers being bullied by tram and railway men, people who couldn't get to work.

'*Waterside workers said today that they won't work unless transport is provided for all.* The newsreader on the wireless said there was about three thousand waterside workers and they want transport for all of them. There's supposed to be thirty-odd ships waiting at the docks to be unloaded.'

That was the way she read the paper to him, bits and pieces interspersed with her own comments, half-pages condensed into a few lines between the turning of his steak, the mashing of his potatoes. Never read aloud about city murders, city accidents, not in the kitchen.

Days passed, too many days, and no hope left of a false alarm, a period gone wrong. He came with his paper on a Friday and she still hadn't told him she was pregnant, and he hadn't bought any bread. Her kids went through a ton of bread and without it she'd need to fill them with something. He never forgot to buy his cigarettes. She watched him light a smoke as she lifted the flour tin down and made a point of moving his newspaper from the table, replacing it with a tin of golden syrup and Amber's large saucepan. He sat down still expecting his newspaper read to him.

'I'm making syrup dumplings,' she said. The kids loved syrup dumplings with custard. Not enough milk to make custard; no eggs anyway. She was up to her elbows in flour, when he found headlines about gas rationing.

'It's the waterside workers' fault,' Jenny said. 'It was on Flora's wireless at lunchtime. It's to do with coal stocks and boats that haven't been unloaded.'

'Wh-wh-arfies striking?'

'Not yet, but if they can't get to work, they can't unload the ships, we run out of coal, then no more gas,' Jenny said, cutting the dough into many pieces, her kids crowding her, watching the process. It didn't take long to make dumplings, but, once begun, there was no stopping until they were in the pot and the lid on.

'What's coal g-got to d-do with anything?'

'They must use it to make the gas — like Geoff's coal-burning contraption. Read that bit below the picture for me, Georgie. It might say something about it.'

Georgie started reading and Ray stood and left the kitchen. Margot left off watching the making of dumplings and followed Ray out to the veranda.

Shouldn't have asked Georgie to read it. He ignored that little girl's existence and tonight Jenny knew why. She could read. He couldn't. She threatened him. Margot didn't. She lisped. He stuttered. They were forming an alliance.

I shouldn't have put Georgie in that situation, Jenny thought, watching the expression on that little kid's face. She stood at the far side of the table, staring after Ray and Margot, knowing she'd done something wrong, but keeping her place on the page with a finger.

'Finish reading it, Georgie. I'm covered in flour.'

'Use of gas will be pro-hib-ited except for two meal pe-ri-ods.'

She read words she shouldn't know the meaning of, and maybe didn't, though she did a good job at pronouncing them. Perfection, that kid — perfection with a beautiful heart and a gentle soul. She'd thought her father to be famous, like a movie star. Hadn't said a word when she'd found out what he'd been famous for. Hadn't thrown his photograph in the rubbish bin, just hidden him away in a safe place, and Jenny loved her for that, loved her soft little heart.

The dumplings boiling, the lid on, Georgie reading about Ben Chifley flying down from Canberra, Jenny staring through the glass door, her hand at her waist, wondering if she'd produce another Margot. There was no working out that kid. Georgie, she could read like an open book, and Jimmy. He was Jim. He was her.

Only a blind man might pick her kids as siblings. Georgie's hair was molten copper, thick and grown long since Granny hadn't been able to get at it with her scissors. Not straight, the barest suggestion of a curl. Margot's hair was snow-white and fine. Jenny kept it short with her dressmaking scissors. Nothing else to be done with it. Jimmy's hair was darkening each year. Jim's had been dark. His eyes were blue-grey, more blue than grey when she dressed him in blue. Georgie had Laurie's eyes, a pure green in some lights. Margot had the Macdonalds' pale purple eyes.

If I have a boy and he looks like Ray, it will be all right. A boy will balance the family.

What if it's a girl and she looks like his sister's girls?

Sooner or later I'll have one who does.

It won't happen again. I'll have a hysterectomy before I come home from hospital.

The syrup dumplings stopped her thinking. They boiled over and brought her mind back to the moment. She lifted the saucepan, adjusted the flame, smelled burning sugar and hoped the dumplings hadn't caught. Couldn't lift the lid to find out or they'd turn into hard dough balls.

She served him four sausages and a pile of potatoes. Sausages were breakfast food, but too bad. Couldn't face bloody meat tonight. She served the kids a sausage each and a pile of cabbage, cooked as Amber had cooked it, in the frying pan, fried in a little grease. Jenny hadn't learnt much from her except how to cook cabbage, make pastry, make custard — when she had milk and eggs to make it.

He'd eaten dumplings a few times, with custard. She served him a bowl full. He sat waiting for custard.

'No milk,' she said, delighted to say it.

He pushed his bowl back and left the table, went outside to sweep his path, rake up leaves, play with his bike.

How long had he been married to his first wife? How come there'd been nothing of her in his half of the house? He'd been determined to have a wedding photograph when Jenny married him. Where was his first wedding photograph? Had she left him, like Veronica had left her bank manager husband, and, unlike Veronica, taken everything with her? It was possible. He'd had nothing when Jenny arrived. He hadn't owned a change of sheets.

People can't divorce someone that fast.

What if they weren't divorced? What if he's a bigamist?

Then I wouldn't be married to him. I'd be Jenny Morrison and I'd take those kids home.

Pregnant?

She looked at her wedding ring and shook her head. Never, never would she go back there pregnant.

'Wait until you know him better,' Granny had said. 'People are what they've been raised too,' she'd said on that last day.

I'm having his baby, and I don't have a clue who he is. I mightn't have known what Laurie was, but I knew who he was.

She washed the dishes. The kids dried them. Rain sent Ray inside. Margot crawled around him, wanting to play cards. He didn't want to play cards. Jenny sent the kids to the bedroom to get their pyjamas on. At seven thirty she told them to go to bed.

'I want to play cardth with you, Daddy Ray.'

Like her aunties, flirting around boys in Woody Creek. It worked too. He lifted her up to his lap. Which was probably a good thing. Why didn't it feel good? Maybe she saw his own sitting on his lap, thirteen of his own.

She turned away and led the other two into their room, tucked them in, kissed them — while there were only two to kiss — then escaped outside via the sleep-out door, loathing herself for wanting to kiss those two faces and not wanting to kiss the third of them — and knowing she'd feel the same about his baby.

Snails on the path, dozens of them, encouraged out by the rain. She picked off three giants partying on a lettuce, found more crawling up her silverbeet. She'd dug that earth, she'd planted those seeds, and had no intention of sharing the fruits of her labour with snails. Crushed them beneath her shoe, and enjoyed crushing them, and remembered the dream she'd had in Sydney of crushing miniature twins with parachutes. While there was light to see by, she searched for more snails to crush. Scooped mashed snails up with her trowel and added them to her mulch bin — let them do something useful for once in their useless lives.

Maybe the snails caused the argument. Maybe it was the rain and the thought of trying to get napkins dry in Melbourne. Maybe it was the milk, or Margot, still sitting on Ray's lap.

'Bed, Margot.'

'I want a drink of milk firtht.'

'I've got half a bottle and it's for breakfast,' Jenny said.

'I want a drink of milk, Daddy Ray.'

'Put her down, Ray.'

He put her down and went to the fridge, took out the half-full bottle and poured most of it into a glass.

That's what started the argument. Milk and milking cows, and Margot's smirking face, and her father's stubby little hand reaching for the glass.

Jenny's reach was longer. She snatched it.

'G-give it to her.'

'It's for porridge in the morning and there's not even enough for that.'

'G-give it to her.'

'Buy enough and I will. Get to bed, Margot. Now!'

'I want milk.'

'Get into your bloody bed when I tell you to!'

She snatched the milk bottle and poured milk carelessly into it. Bottle in the refrigerator, its door slammed and her back was against it.

'It'th Daddy Ray'th houth, not your houth, and it'th hith milk too.'

'Talk back to me again and I'll slap you, Margot.'

'She n-n-needs it more than them.'

'What one of my kids gets, the others get. Now get out of my sight, you brat of a girl, or by God you'll wish you had.'

'You're t-turning a bit of m-milk into a w-war.'

'Stop taking her part against me, Ray. She's going to bed, and if she's not in it by the time I count to three, I promise she'll feel the wooden spoon on her bum.'

'You thwored two timeth now.'

'*Swore*, not swored. There is no such word as swored. I *swore*. Now get to bloody bed or your bum will suffer.'

She sounded like Wilma, felt like Norman protecting his little milk from Sissy, but she'd started the war, and if she backed down tonight she may as well throw herself under a tram.

She reached for that kid's arm to drag her to bed. Margot dodged behind Ray; he put his arm around her and that brat stuck her tongue out.

'You j-just w-want your own w-w-way.'

'Jenny wantth her own way. Jenny wantth her own way.' Margot chanting — as her fathers had chanted. 'Jenny wantth her own way. Jenny wantth her own way.'

And that fool started chanting with her.

'You pair of two-year-old idiots!'

Margot, top-heavy, short-legged, not well coordinated, pushed roughly from him, fell to her backside as the sugar bowl spun from the table, scattering precious sugar. His full ashtray followed it, spilling ash and butts to the sugar. Couldn't even sweep it up for jam-making. A chair flew at the passage door, but Margot went to bed, and without her milk.

Two kids sitting up in bed. The third between them, blankets over her head. That little bugger had started this. Now she was hiding from it.

Chairs flying in the kitchen, the table rocking. Its leg was bruised before he was done. Hoped his foot was bruised. They bruised the kids' bedroom door. He kicked it open. She kicked it shut.

'What's wrong, Jenny?' Georgie knew she'd started it with her reading.

'Margot wanted to drink all of the milk so there'd be none for breakfast,' Jenny said.

Let her take responsibility for her actions. A decent dose of childhood guilt might save that brat a whole heap of adult pain.

Ray went to his room. Jenny picked up chairs, swept up sugar-coated ash and butts, wiped sugar from his spilled cigarettes. She was sliding cigarettes into his packet when she heard a gentle knocking on the glass door. Wilma Fogarty was out there. Jenny hoped she hadn't been standing out there five minutes ago.

'Doreen's daughter just came over to tell us her father's been rushed to the hospital with his heart. Doreen has gone in with him. Could you . . .?'

The world might end but that Friday-night card game would go on. That's what women did. That's how they survived their swollen bellies and bad-tempered men who bought cigarettes instead of milk and bread.

'By God, I could,' Jenny said. 'I'll be down in five minutes.'

She didn't tell Ray she was going. She told the kids and Flora, left the passage door open. By the smile on Geoff's face, they'd heard the flying furniture. Too bad. She heard enough from their side.

VERONICA

Veronica was there; tall, dark, lean as a greyhound but more attractive, a wide mouth eager to laugh at the world, and dark deep-set eyes that never laughed. Jenny had noticed her eyes when she'd knocked on the glass door with a bundle of alterations. She'd been heavier twelve months ago. Too thin now, and tall, as tall as Granny, hair like Sissy's, nice hair. Jenny knew her as Mrs Andrews, the bank manager's wife. That night she met Vroni, the card player, who was divorcing her husband.

No one spoke openly about divorce in Woody Creek. No one did it. Granny could have. Norman should have.

Veronica spoke of other subjects considered taboo in most company.

'My new chap has got a wife and grown-up sons,' she said.

She would have been tarred and feathered for coming out with something like that in Woody Creek.

'We could have been playing cards in jail tonight — separate cells. Ian had one of his specials booked in on Wednesday, a society dame — who, I might add, didn't look a lot like she looks in the society pages. Of course I was looking at her from the wrong angle.'

The women laughed. Jenny hadn't got the point of the joke, but laughed with them.

'Vroni's chap specialises on what's below a woman's belt,' Wilma explained. 'He does abortions on the side.'

Wilma was a joke a minute. Jenny laughed again, but alone.

'It was no laughing matter on Wednesday,' Veronica said. 'We were just getting down to the business and someone started banging on the front door. I looked out the window and there's a cop at the door. You've never seen such a flurry in your life. We tossed the dame off the table, and while I pushed her into the lav and pitched her fancy fur at her, Ian went down to face him. It turned out to be nothing. The dame had parked her car around the corner, halfway across the driveway of some nob who wanted to get his limo out to take his wife to the ballet. He called the cops to move the car, and they were going door to door looking for the owner. The dame went down, moved it and fifteen minutes later she was back, demanding we do the deed — which we did.'

Jenny's heart started racing, her mind outpacing it. She played her cards, or followed suit. The hand was lost or won, the tricks totalled before she found breath enough, found nerve enough, to ask.

'How much does he charge, Vroni?'

'It depends on the case, the patient's level of desperation, how much they can afford, how busy he is. With Cup week coming up, there's been a rush.'

'Women can bleed to death from it, can't they?'

'You've been listening to the populate or perish brigade. More perish while populating than do while having abortions. There's nothing to it if you catch it early.'

'How early?' Jenny asked, the cards forgotten as five sets of eyes turned to her. She couldn't hold that many eyes. She looked at the table.

'It's your deal, love,' Carol said.

Cards scooped to her side with shaking hands, shuffled, a few spilled, collected then shuffled again. She dealt them, her heart beating like a tractor motor, shaking her bones with its beat while the conversation turned to 'bloody awful hands' to 'hands like hoofs'. They liked to moan about terrible hands.

Head down, Jenny sorted her cards into a fan, her hands shaking, shaking the fan, blinding her momentarily to the incredible hand she'd dealt herself. She had the joker, the right bower, and five hearts, three of them big hearts. Then she found the ace of clubs hiding behind the queen of diamonds. She was holding eight unbeatable tricks in her hand. Was it a sign that for once in her life she was meant to win?

She didn't want Ray's baby, and it wasn't a baby anyway. It was an overdue period. She had money in the bank. She'd spend the whole lot of it . . .

She'd killed the women's laughter. Some explanation was necessary.

'I've been pregnant for most of my life. The last thing I need right now is another baby.'

'And so say all of us. My tongue is hanging out for menopause. Six clubs,' Wilma said.

'What is said at this table goes no further than this table,' Veronica started.

'I spoke out of turn. I'm sorry.' Feeling the blood rush to her face, Jenny kept her chin down, positioning her cards according to value while the bidding continued.

'Six diamonds.'

'Seven spades,' Veronica said, then added, 'How far gone are you, kiddo?'

'Hardly at all. Two weeks.'

'Does Ray want it?'

'He doesn't know about it.' Jenny's heart upped its pace. It was going to burst out through her rib cage. Hope. Was there hope? 'He can't afford to feed the ones I've got.'

'I thought she'd left him money,' Veronica said.

Wilma held up a finger. The card players made a point of not speaking about Ray. They knew him, or Carol and Wilma knew him. They'd lived in the area for years. Veronica had lived opposite for a few years.

'Did you know his first wife?' Jenny asked.

'In passing,' Veronica said. 'Passing fast. About the other — I've been known to help out a few of my friends.'

'You need to have a good think about it, Jenny. It's not something you decide to do over a game of cards,' Carol said.

'Eight hearts,' Jenny said. 'And I've thought about it.'

'You don't need to go eight. Seven will do,' Wilma said.

'I'll go eight. If . . . if he could do it, how soon . . . could he?'

'Have a think about it for a week, and if you're sure, I'll do it here next Friday — if it's all right with Wilma.'

It wasn't all right with Jenny. She shook her head. 'I've got money in the bank. I can pay for your . . . the doctor.'

'She's a nursing sister, Jen. She's done it for me. I lived to tell the tale,' Wilma said.

'I thought it was an operation?'

'Not if you catch it in the early stages,' Veronica said.

'How much will it cost?' Jenny asked.

'I don't charge crazy card players who go eight hearts when they don't need to. I can't go nine.' Veronica lit a cigarette and counted her cards. 'You need to get yourself fixed up with a Dutch cap. They're pretty safe.'

'I did.'

'Say no more,' Veronica said. 'Nine spades.'

'You're both crazy,' Carol said.

'Nine hearts,' Jenny said.

'You kitty-happy little bugger! I can't get ten!' Veronica said. 'Get them.'

Jenny scooped in the three-card kitty and added the ace of diamonds to her hand. Had she known it was in kitty she would have gone alone. She led the joker, followed it with the right bower, then, one by one, tossed her hearts down, watching the fall of the cards for the king of diamonds. Once he'd been played, she knew she had the lot. She took two tricks with her aces, then led the queen of diamonds, the best diamond in the pack. She got the lot, and her partners applauded her play.

'Who are you?' Veronica said.

'I've never had enough time between babies to find out.'

'You're an interesting study, kiddo. You've got a forty-year-old seamstress's hands, the looks of a Botticelli angel and you play cards like a mafia boss.'

'One of my grandfathers looked a bit like Al Capone.'

The laughter was back, and Jenny loved that woman, loved every one of the card players, and stayed too late with them. They played until Joe Fogarty came home, came home drunk and happy and wanting supper, like Norman had wanted supper when he'd come home from his poker nights at the Macdonalds'.

'That's Jenny, Ray's wife,' Wilma introduced.

'Bloody hell,' he said. 'You're a bit of an improvement on his last one, love.'

'Shut up, Joe,' Wilma said.

The following Friday evening, Veronica did what had to be done, in Wilma's bedroom. It was embarrassing, but no more so than having a baby. Jenny kept her eyes closed.

'Is it gone?'

'It will take an hour or two to come away, kiddo.'

'What happens?'

'It won't be much worse than a bad period.'

And it wasn't. By ten thirty it was over. She took a Bex for the cramps and the game continued, Jenny only an onlooker tonight. The women had their original teams of players. She poured the cups of tea, emptied the ashtray, scored the game and watched the players.

They were all older than her, though they didn't know how much older. Old enough to have a seven year old, she'd replied when Wilma asked her age.

Doreen admitted to forty, Wilma was thirty-three. Carol was almost forty-five, and Patsy over fifty. A mixed batch of neighbourhood wives and mothers, apart from Veronica, who looked to be in her late twenties but had been at school with Wilma. Well groomed, well dressed. Her doctor chap looked old. He'd dropped her off at eight, and Jenny saw him again when she walked out to the car with Veronica. He was balding, had to be fifty. What was she doing with him?

'Take it easy tomorrow, kiddo. Stay off your feet.'

'Thank you isn't enough, Vroni.'

'You're welcome,' she said.

He held the car door open for her. She got in and he closed it. A gentleman. Jim had opened car doors.

Jenny walked home with Carol, and the air seemed lighter, her feet felt lighter, and her head. Free. Free. And she was going home for Christmas.

'How did Ray's first wife die, Carol?'

'She had a growth in her female parts.'

'Is that why she didn't have kids?'

'Talk to Ray about it, love,' Carol said. 'Goodnight then. And stay off your feet tomorrow.'

Jenny crept into the house and undressed in the dark. As she slid into bed, he rolled over and reached for her.

'I'm unavailable,' she said.

He understood what that meant and rolled to his side of the bed. Never touched her, never kissed her, when she was menstruating — one of the fringe benefits.

She lay on her back, feeling a far greater separation than the few inches between them, a floating separation from self.

Maybe it was the wrong thing to do, but was it any worse than climbing up onto the shed's roof and jumping, willing Jimmy out of her? It didn't feel wrong. Her body was her own again. She felt . . . intoxicated by freedom, wanted to sing, dance in the moonlight. There was no sleep in her. Every nerve ending was rejoicing.

'Were you living here before you got married the first time, Ray?'

On occasion, she could get replies out of him in the dark. Not tonight.

'W-what have they b-been f-filling your h-head with d-down there?'

They emptied my womb, she thought. They freed my head.

'They aren't gossips. We just play cards, talk about cards. Did you live here with her?'

No reply to that.

If she had lived here, then what had happened to her linen, her kitchen things? A woman needed more than a frying pan and a dented saucepan. Had he got rid of everything? If she'd died of a growth in the female parts, he'd probably found it disgusting. Women only had female parts for his use.

He had a strange head, or strange ideas in his head. He had a switch in it too. One flick of the knob and lights out. He was asleep.

Jim used to talk to her all night, talk all morning, talk of everything under the sun and beyond the sun. She'd slept close to him that week they'd shared a bed in Sydney, had gone to sleep with his arm around her, her arm over him, and woken against him. Never anyone like Jim.

She'd waited for him in Sydney; had kept herself and Jimmy for two years with her voice and what she made at a sewing factory. She'd put money in the bank.

Had to stop thinking about . . . about Sydney. She was a married woman and she had to make her marriage work. And she had to be more careful; be like the scouts — always prepared — and learn to dodge again. And find a way to make more money.

Hands like a forty-year-old seamstress, Vroni had said. Sewing was hard on hands, as was gardening. Singing wasn't. She knew she could sing. Knew Archie Foote would get her a job singing. He was like Eve dangling an apple before Adam's eyes.

Ray would loathe it if she started going out at night, singing at a club, dozens of blokes around to stare at her.

So what? Would he cast her out of Eden?

Jim would have encouraged her to sing. He had, that night in Sydney. And when she'd written to him and told him Wilfred Whiteford offered her a job singing with his band, he'd been happy for her.

Granny hadn't. *You get yourself home, my girl.*

Joey would tell her to do it. *Do what you have to do, Jen,* he'd said at the station.

Who are you? Veronica had asked.

A singer, and a bloody fool who made a complete muck-up of her life — or who had added to the muck-up the twins made of it. Couldn't blame anyone other than herself for her last muck-up. Thought she'd been running away from the mess and she'd landed headfirst in a messier mess. Mess followed her around, growing bigger every time she turned around. Sooner or later, she had to go back and start cleaning it up.

She rolled to her side, knowing there was no way to back out of this. For richer or poorer, better or worse, in sickness and in health, till death do us part. There was nothing in the marriage vows that said she had to produce a baby every other year.

Yawned, and settled the pillow beneath her head. She wasn't pregnant. She could put up with anything as long as she wasn't pregnant.

So, backbone to backbone, we'll face the world of sleep
in a bed crowded with secrets each must keep.
I'll don my mask, allow you to wear your own,
and bless your roof and think my thoughts alone.

HENRY BLOODY KING'S SON

*T*hrough the years, Vern Hooper and Gertrude had argued more or less regularly. During their long lifetimes they'd had a few blazing rows. She'd never made the first move to heal the rift. He was the one who crawled back. He missed her, missed emptying his mind to her. In all but name she'd been his wife, on and off, for forty years. A man misses his wife, and the older Vern grew, the sooner he started missing Gertrude.

He found an excuse to crawl, or to limp, back in November.

She looked out the door to identify her caller, then walked out to her chicken-wire gate and told him to stay in his car, that he wasn't welcome on her property.

He told her he was at death's door, that she wouldn't have to put up with him being on her property for much bloody longer, and to stop being so bloody antagonistic.

'We're too bloody old to hold grudges,' he said.

'Speak for yourself,' she said and went inside.

At seventy-six, Vern moved like a man of ninety-six, and today he didn't look a lot less. His once steel-grey hair had turned to silver — as had the handle of his walking stick. It was a fine stick, purchased for his last birthday by his daughters. His old stick had become a familiar friend, the new was still a visitor, but he leaned on it heavily as he made his way to her gate, and through her gate.

He had money for one daughter to waste on overseas trips, for the other one to waste on a fancy walking stick, fancy furniture that wasn't fit to sit on; he had money to burn — and what use was it to a man if it couldn't buy him his health, his son's health, or buy his grandson out of purgatory? It made him sick to the soul to think of Hooper blood being raised by Henry bloody King's stuttering, bike-riding lout of a son.

Everything made him sick to the soul these days. The thought of Henry and Leticia Langdon floating back to Australia with Lorna made him sick in his gut. They'd turned up in the thirties for months, had driven him out of house and home. The only bloody thing he had in common with them was food. And his city quack, a scrawny, mean-eyed bastard of a man, had taken that away. Food had been one of Vern's lifelong pleasures. If he wanted to live long enough to get his grandson, he had to stay clear of anything with sugar in it. Take sugar out of a man's life and what's left that's worth eating?

He'd lost a lot of his girth since they'd let him out of the hospital, and, as it decreased, so did the grease between his joints. His back ached, his knees, his ankles, ached. He was one elongated bloody ache, and with too much height in his bones, there was too much bone to ache. Pain wore a man down. He didn't stand as tall as of old, didn't bother ducking his head as he went through the doorway.

'I've got nothing to say to you, Vern, other than you're a lying bastard of a man.'

'Then don't say it,' he said.

A determined race, the Hoopers, and neither age nor ache could erode that determination. Half-cousins, Vern and Gertrude, born six weeks apart, but try telling anyone Gertrude was seventy-six. Most would laugh in your face. She mounted her horse every Friday morning — or every Friday morning when Vern was in residence — and rode by his corner on her way into town, not because of her need to buy, but to rub in his face the fact that she was still capable of sitting a horse. Always cantered by his house, willing him to be sitting on his veranda watching her go by. Never looked to see if he was sitting there.

Her hair was white at the roots. She and Elsie went looking for those white roots with a toothbrush dipped in dye and painted that give-away stripe a dark chestnut brown. There were things folk needed to know and a lot more they didn't, and her age was one of the latter.

She had all of her teeth, barring two molars she could do well enough without. Every night of her life she brushed them with a finger dipped in salt. She had great belief in salt. Four times in her life she'd cured serious infections with salt and water, and one of those times it was Vern she'd cured. She'd saved his hand and maybe his arm twenty years ago. She hadn't saved his teeth. He'd never been a man to willingly take a woman's advice.

He sat with some effort at her table. She hadn't invited him to sit, but for fifty years he'd required no invitation to sit in her kitchen. She could have walked out. She could have loaded Lenny's pea rifle before he'd got out of the car. It had been leaning against her dresser this past month. She hadn't. Habits of a lifetime won't die easily. She made a pot of tea, took her tin of biscuits from the cupboard and watched him bite into one, wondering how a man with a mouth full of dentures could chew a biscuit. He could and reached for another.

'You're not supposed to be eating too many of them.'

'Why put them on the table and tempt a man if you know he shouldn't be eating them?'

'I can eat them — and how would I know anything I didn't hear third-hand, you lying bastard of a man?'

He reached for a third biscuit, maybe to change the subject. She snatched the tin.

'Don't want me to die yet, Trude?'

'How could you do that to me of all people? I trusted you.'

'I'm not down here to go into that.'

'Then don't come down here. How could you look me in the eye and lie to me for three years?'

'The same way you lied to me. You knew he was on with her when I had my stroke. The Japs as good as killed him anyway. I can't get through to him and neither can anyone else. He sits on his arse, staring at nothing, saying nothing, doing nothing . . .'

'Shell shock?'

'Bloody bastard Jap shock, having his brains belted out with a gun barrel shock, starved —' He stopped for a breath, then changed his mind about breathing, and lit a cigarette. 'And if you'd kept that hot pants bitch of a girl away from him, he never would have been over there.'

She filled the kettle, offering him her back and wondering why she offered him that much. Blood, that's why, and because they were the last Hoopers standing, or the last with the old man's blood running through their veins. And because they'd been more than half-cousins for too damn long. She'd never married him, never lived with him — no doubt would have been dead by now had she married him. He'd gone through three wives.

Only two men in Gertrude's life, and in the past two days she'd entertained both of them — though the other sod hadn't got as far as her kitchen. When she'd heard Vern's motor, she'd thought it was Archie come back for another attempt. Two obsessive old men, both in pursuit of Jenny. Vern wanted his grandson; Archie wanted to put Jenny on the world stage. So he said — not that she'd ever believe a word that sod of a man said, or not after the first twelve months of living with him.

He'd said yesterday that he'd run into Jenny at a city hospital, that she'd given him her Sydney address. Gertrude believed that.

She hadn't armed Amber against her father, but it seemed that she might have been more successful with Jenny, who'd had the good sense to give him a fake address.

'Your bastard of a husband is staying up at the hotel,' Vern said.

That's the trouble with knowing someone for too long. They learn to read your mind.

'I had him down here yesterday,' she said.

'He's using his own name at the pub. Doctor Archibald bloody Foote.'

'That's not news either.'

Not news but an embarrassment. Foote wasn't much of a name to wear, but she'd worn it since turning nineteen. Should have taken her maiden name fifty years ago. She hadn't, for Amber's sake — and that girl would have been better off if she'd never heard the Foote name, never met her sod of a father.

He'd always dressed like a toff, spoken like a toff. Too good-looking for his own good, saintly. He had the appearance of one of Jesus' retired disciples now, a sprightly retired disciple. And he had to be eighty. He was four years Gertrude's senior — and he drove a sporty little yellow car, drove it with the hood down so no one could miss seeing him behind the wheel. An exhibitionist, Archie Foote, never happier than when he had centre stage.

She'd greeted him with a rifle salute yesterday — and Lenny's little rifle didn't aim true. She'd gone closer to his car than she'd intended. He hadn't hung around to argue. Got back in behind the wheel faster than an eighty-year-old man should have been able to.

She smiled, wondering at Vern's reaction had she given him a two-shot salute. He would have kept coming. She hadn't. And maybe that said it all. And maybe she'd missed seeing him sitting on that chair, missed talking to someone who remembered what she remembered, those she remembered. Too many of their age group had moved on to the graveyard.

'I still swear he fathered that girl,' Vern said.

'There's no doubt.'

'So you're admitting it now?'

'You're losing your onions. I told you, he admitted it the night of Norman's funeral when he came down here.'

'I'm talking about Margaret, not that hot pants little bitch.'

'Give it up. Margaret's a better daughter to you than your hawk-faced, globe-trotting lamp pole. When is she due home?'

'Too bloody soon, and she's bringing them back with her. I was stuck with them for two months the last time, and I was a healthy man and could take off somewhere.'

'Where have you got Jim?'

'At a private place that promised the world and is doing bugger all. We were down there the weekend before last.'

'There's talk going around that he's lost his sight.'

'Sight? He's lost his leg. They've got a fake one on him. He could get around on crutches, but won't.'

'Bring him home.'

'Margaret's got a bloke, and enough on her plate. And we've had him home twice. We took him out to see Monk's place. Before he joined up, he conned me into spending a fortune on that bloody house and we couldn't get him out of the car to look at it. He doesn't want to be home, or any-bloody-where else. Where has she got his boy living?'

'Sydney,' Gertrude said.

'She's doing very well for herself up there too.'

'She is.'

'Yeah. She can afford to take a flight down from Sydney to take that boy hospital visiting. Like bloody hell, she can. She's got Jimmy living somewhere in Melbourne.'

'Joey's flying down for Christmas.'

'Stop changing the subject. Where has she got him?'

'You brought up flying. He's getting married in April to a nurse he met when he was in the army hospital up north.'

'Is he bringing her down?'

'He's coming alone this time.'

'And every time. I'll bet you a pound to a penny she doesn't know he's a darkie.'

'He's got a whiter heart than you, you lying sod.'

'Speaking of liars. We've contacted that Sydney boarding house and the landlady hasn't set eyes on your granddaughter since '44. You're a bare-faced liar, Trude.'

'And the longer I know you, the better I get at doing it.'

He'd spent a lot of money in looking for his grandson. For months now he'd been paying a retired police detective to search Sydney for him. The chap had found the boarding house; he'd been to Sydney schools searching for Morrison or King kids — found plenty, though not the right ones.

'Maisy Macdonald met her in Melbourne for lunch. Did she fly down that day too?'

'Go and clutter up Maisy's kitchen. She'll be happy to gossip with you all day. I've got better things to do.'

'We bought a train set for Jimmy's birthday. I need her address.'

'I'll post it up to him for you.'

'You've known me for seventy bloody years and you don't trust me to send my own grandson a birthday present?'

'Because I've known you for seventy years. She's married. She's happy. They're living in a nice house. The kids are happy. Leave them alone.'

'If she'd left Jim alone, he would have been taking care of me now, not the other bloody way around.'

'And you wouldn't have had a grandson to buy train sets for — and with luck, you could see him at Christmas time. She said in her last letter that she's thinking about coming home when school breaks up. And you hound her while she's up here Vern, and, by God, I will greet you with my rifle.'

*

Archie Foote hadn't appreciated Gertrude's bullets. They'd kicked up dust two foot from his front tyre. His '39 Auburn roadster had been suffering from shell shock since, and while old lovers sparred in Gertrude's kitchen, Archie stood in the sun out front of a tin-shed garage watching his pride and joy subjected to the garage man's greasy hands and his screwdriver poking around in its bowels.

The car had done very few miles before the war; had spent most of the war years up on blocks, according to its previous owner. This morning, it had woken up with the hiccups. Some blockage perhaps, diseased petrol more than likely. He'd blamed country fuel when presenting his case. There were sufficient cars in Melbourne to guarantee the product was fresh. The Auburn's fuel tank had been topped up last night in anticipation of making an early start and arriving home in time to freshen up for an evening engagement. Now this.

'A blockage of the arteries?' he asked.

'Doesn't look like it,' the garage man said.

Three days in Woody Creek was a week too long. He'd come in quest of information on the whereabouts of Jennifer, and had learnt nothing, other than her older sister was living with her father's relatives in Richmond and that Jennifer sang with a band in Sydney. She'd given him a phone number, an address. He'd placed a call to that number, and, on the off chance he'd managed to transpose the last digits, had placed the call again. Apparently she'd moved on. He'd written to the address. Not a word.

Gertrude, his only conduit to Jennifer, was a blocked conduit. She'd pulled a rifle on him forty years ago and her bullets had set the dust dancing at his feet. He'd raised the dust himself yesterday in his haste to get his vehicle out of rifle range.

The garage man removed a spark plug. Archie could just about recognise a spark plug. He drew nearer, his manicured hands clasped behind his back while the mechanic walked into the tin shed wiping large greasy paws on what looked to be a pair of his wife's bloomers. He returned with a dialled implement, which

Archie watched him attach to the sick motor. A minute or two later he had a diagnosis.

'Your compressions are down to buggery,' he said.

Archie had learnt the art of driving a vehicle back when the horse had first made way for the combustion motor. He'd known nothing of a car's internals back then and knew less today.

'Some clarification perhaps?'

'Valves,' the garage man said. 'I'll need to take your head off to make sure, but I'll hazard a guess that you've got a couple of burnt-out valves.'

'Operable?'

The greasy chap wiped the dialled implement on his wife's bloomers, slowly, carefully, his eye not on the task, but sizing up his customer's ability to pay. He saw a dapper little man in a pin-striped suit, dark hat, white shirt, maroon tie.

He knew who he was. A stranger didn't remain a stranger in Woody Creek, not if he hung around for more than a day. An hour after booking in at the hotel, he'd been connected to Gertrude Foote, and through her named as the local murderess's father. A few hours more and they'd connected him to the Monk family: big property owners and the town's toffs until the bank sold them up during the early days of the Great Depression. Old man Monk's son had wed Archie Foote's aunt, which made Dr Archibald Foote MD a first cousin to Max Monk. After he'd been three days as a guest at the hotel, there wasn't a lot Woody Creek folk didn't know about Gertrude Foote's husband. Nelly Dobson, the hotel laundress, could tell you he wore black silk underdrawers.

No one had yet connected him to Albert Forester, the bearded old coot who had hung around town during the depression years. Horrie Bull, the previous publican, may have made the connection, but a year or two ago he'd sold the hotel to Fred Bowen and bought a pub in Carlton. Denham, the previous copper, would have recognised him. The Denham family had moved on to

Bendigo. Betty Duffy gave Archie the evil eye, but she'd lost most of her marbles and even her family took no notice of anything old Bet raved on about.

'It won't be cheap,' the garage man said.

'Time is the priority, sir, not cash,' Archie said.

More specifically, how much more time he now must spend as a guest of the local publican, the one place in Woody Creek where a stranger might find a bed. There were two establishments where he might buy a meal, both of them greasy.

'I'll need to strip her down.'

'How long?'

'A day. Two if I run into problems. You never know what you'll find until you get inside these old girls.'

Archie had a response on his lips but held it in. This was Woody Creek, not the city. He glanced past the mechanic and into his shed. Barely room for a car between the piles of junk and tin cans.

'I believe I'll allow her to limp home.'

'She might get as far as the ten-mile post,' the mechanic said. 'I charge for towing.'

'No doubt you do — and provide car-washing services too?' he added as a mangy and somewhat greasy fox terrier lifted his leg against a back wheel.

He was not the first dog in town to lay claim to it, and no doubt would not be the last. The town was full of peeing dogs. Archie didn't like dogs, abhorred cats, had a bird phobia.

'I've got Joe Flanagan's brakes coming in after lunch. If nothing urgent comes up, I'll get on to yours this evening.'

The keys were changing hands when something more urgent came up. A girl of twelve or thirteen rode into the yard. The terrier left off his peeing to bite at her wheel.

'Mum says can you come quick, please. Trevor just fell off the roof and he's out cold.'

'I'll be there in five minutes,' the garage man said and started stripping off his overalls.

Archie laughed, amused, as always, by this town. 'Does the town doctor moonlight as mechanic — or the reverse?'

'Taxi driver,' the garage man said, again utilising his wife's bloomers. 'Always someone wanting to go somewhere.'

'In my long experience I've found that most children bounce.'

'He's one of Tom Vevers'. He lost his oldest boy in the creek, and lost his second in the war. Young Trevor is his last — or his last boy.' He eyed his customer. 'Go around and take a look if you like. Save me a trip, and you'll get your car faster.'

Archie was watching the girl and the bike disappear up the road, the dog near hanging off her back wheel. His credentials were current. Doctors came under the heading of essential services, and those employed in the essential services gained an extra portion of the rationed petrol. He was well beyond the age of wanting to poke around at unclean bodies, but always eager to obtain more than his fair share of whatever was going. In retirement, he'd gone into the study of shell-shocked minds. An American chap by the name of Freeman had been having some success with them. More recently, Archie had volunteered his services one day a month at an asylum for the criminally insane, where he documented many similarities between the shell-shocked boys and his vacant-eyed firstborn, locked behind those walls.

'They're over the lines and through the park. The third house on your left. They'll know who you are. If they don't, tell them I sent you.'

He found Tom Vevers' house, found the thirteen-year-old youth, no longer out cold though maybe suffering a mild concussion. He suggested they keep him under observation for thirty minutes; and, an hour later, ate a nice lunch with the woman and her daughters.

Mrs Vevers turned the conversation to Gertrude, to Amber, who she'd gone to school with. She spoke of the Morrisons' lost babies, and how losing a child was something parents never got over.

Archie turned the conversation to his granddaughters, and,

over a second cup of tea and a slice of fruit cake, edged it around to Jennifer.

'They say she's singing with that band again in Sydney,' Mrs Vevers said. 'We heard her on the wireless years ago. She was very good, doctor, then she went right off the rails.'

Archie nodded, his expression, one of disappointment, not a perfect match for his thoughts — and where was the fun in walking that straight and narrow rail?

I KNOW YOU

*B*etween the hours of ten and three thirty on the third Wednesday of each month, Archie Foote could be found at an asylum for the criminally insane. His interest in the dysfunctional mind was genuine. Throughout her lifetime, his sister had suffered from a recurrent mania, which had, more or less regularly, seen her carried away to a private sanatorium, where, removed from the stresses of a family hell-bent on educating the ineducable, she had regained her senses and been returned home until the next episode. He'd seen little of his sister during her adult years, too little to make a study of her mania. Not so his firstborn, a permanent inmate of the asylum. Each month he spent time with her, documenting her responses, watching her actions as a child may look on a caged creature at the zoo, with consuming interest but little concern for the animal's welfare.

She'd been a pretty enough thing in her youth, as had his sister, Victoria. The Foote females bloomed early and faded fast. Like his sister, this one had evolved into a skin-and-bone hag.

It was the first time he'd seen her on her feet. On his previous visit she'd been a screaming, spitting shrew. She was walking in circles today, her narrow shoulders hunched, head down, her right finger and thumb pinching the bruised skin on the rear of her left hand. Self-mutilation? Counting her steps? Perhaps a pinch for each circle completed. Was she capable of counting?

'How many circles have you completed?' he asked.

No response, he added to the already copious notes compiled on his firstborn.

New drugs were being developed, which, in some cases, made the handling of the insane easier on their keepers. This one had murdered her husband, which, in the state's eyes, made her a fair enough guinea pig.

Check recent medication, he wrote. Something had got her on her feet and seemingly tamed.

He stood for ten minutes observing her circles and that pinch, and he smiled, recalling his own time spent in a similar cage.

Twice in his life he'd been incarcerated: for the best part of two years in Egypt; and over fourteen months in Pentridge. The human mind is a magnificent creation. Take away the printed word, take away paper and pencil, take away light, and the strong mind will find a way to fill a day.

The males of the Foote line were a strong race, which may have accounted for the mania that ran through the female line. He'd given life to two. His first seed had grown twisted in Woody Creek's dust. The other had taken root in the same dust and bloomed. This circling hag, having been planted in the strong-willed daughter of a hovel-dwelling dirt scratcher, would, in all probability, have wed a dirt scratcher and lived out her days in penny-pinching poverty with her umpteen dirt-scratching offspring. His second seed, planted in the wife of an Italian banker, should have been raised in a Catholic orphanage. Some manipulative hand had seen to the meeting of his two daughters. The older had raised the younger.

Four years of mopping up the blood and guts of war and Archie had washed his hands of religion, and, like many, had spent the early twenties partying. Even so, the perfect symmetry of life was, at times, almost sufficient to convince him there was a greater being than man; a grand old clown balancing on a cloud while pulling the strings and, with raucous amusement, watching the dance below. He'd manoeuvred Archie into a corner in '23.

Stony, motherless broke, reduced to penning a begging letter to his father when his current meal ticket had started pining for London, a city Archie had never been fond of. He may have gone with her had his father not replied. He'd give him no more money, but a position might be found for him in the family business. Dear old Dad or dear old Lily? One as bad as the other, he'd taken a wander down to the shipping company's office where he'd learnt that a cruise ship's surgeon had slipped on deck and broken his leg. Two days later, Lily deserted, Archie had been pandering to the rich on a luxury world cruise. The puppet master had got him exactly where he'd wanted him.

They were two days out of San Francisco when she came to his surgery, a dark, sad-eyed woman, edging towards thirty-five and more beautiful for her maturity. She'd had little English. He'd mixed her a headache potion and she'd gone on her way. That night he was called to her cabin with a repeat of the potion. He'd sat on her bed and spoken to her in her own tongue. As a youth he'd excelled in schoolboy Latin. His interest in the study of languages had taken him to many shores.

She'd been desperate for companionship. She'd told him that her husband had two sons, that she had five grandchildren. She'd told him that her husband lost much money in the gambling room. Archie knew the fat old coot who spent his evenings playing cards for high stakes. He'd watched him later that night, his own fingers itching for cards. Had his pockets been up to it, he may have taken Conti's money instead of his wife. Alas for empty pockets.

The signora's debilitating headaches had continued. The banker and his much younger beauty had been on that boat for months.

'You are missing your children?' Archie had asked.

'No baby, I am flower only for my husband to wear in the buttonhole.'

'But such a beautiful flower,' he'd said.

He diagnosed her headaches as sexual neglect. His cure was simple enough. He should have known better, but he'd never been one for self-control. A pleasurable game, the initiation of a thirty-five-year-old woman to the joys of the bed. Each night he'd carried a sleeping potion to Juliana's cabin, and on several of those nights he'd locked the door behind him.

They were docking in Sydney on a pretty morning in late April, Archie on deck taking in the view, when Conti's wife approached him, told him she had been touched by the hand of God. Likened to the angel Gabriel in his youth, to Jesus on occasions, God's representative on earth had considered jumping overboard and swimming for his life when she told him she was with child. He'd quelled the desire and patted her hand.

'Your husband will be delighted, my dear.'

'He does not bruise the display flower.'

More quietly, Archie had offered to fix her problem, between Sydney and Melbourne. She'd run from his suggestion.

The shipping company paid him well for his dance of attendance on the rich. Impregnating the wife of one of their richer passengers was not in his contract. He'd gone to her that night, calmed her with lies. A woman desperate for love is easy to calm with lies of undying love. They rocked his narrow bed in Sydney Harbour, and after he explained that he was a penniless doctor who owned no house and had no savings. Though nothing would please him more than they should raise their love child together, he was not in a position to do so. He too was wed to another. He told her she must make love with her husband, and soon.

'He is no good down there for the woman. Ten year he is no good down there.'

Archie's contract with the shipping company being open-ended, he'd decided to end it in Melbourne and go home to dear old Dad, join the family practice for a month or two. The mean old bugger had his fingers into many rich medical pies. He was first down that gangplank in Melbourne, off and running home to dear old Dad for the reconciliation of the century.

Three weeks later, the ship well on its way towards Africa, Archie spending his days in consultation rooms, private lying-in hospital, sanatorium, generally keeping his nose clean, or clean enough when it needed to be clean. If he'd given one thought to the beautiful Juliana, it was given with a smile. Like the cuckoo chick, his offspring would be raised in a nest feathered by a lesser bird.

The ship may well have been on its way to Africa, but the fat banker and his wife weren't on it. Archie was at the lying-in hospital when they found him; and where else might a doctor be found than at a hospital, and where else would a rich man take his pregnant wife but to a doctor at a private lying-in hospital? Archie had wished he'd taken a job as a night man. Conti's English was little better than his wife's. Archie, ready to deny all accusations, to blame early menopause, the hand of God, if he must, listened to his ramblings intently and was relieved to learn that the grateful Juliana had accused an unknown sailor for her predicament.

Bald, tubby, olefinic, Conti was not a big man, not in stature, although a giant in name and bank account. His beautiful Juliana was an old man's final trophy to display in fine garments, to hang with jewels. He would not display his trophy with a belly swollen by the leavings of a rutting 'animal'. And thus, the 'rutting animal' became further embroiled. Conti agreed to pay for his wife's lodgings at a respectable house, to place money enough at her disposal to pay for her confinement, and to leave a donation to be given, with the infant, into the hands of the holy sisters when it was over.

'Then you buy ticket home for my beautiful Juliana. Yes?'

'Indeed. Indeed, I will, sir.'

'I give . . . my treasure; you protect. Yes.'

'She will be well protected,' Archie had said.

Conti took the first available berth home, leaving his wife in the protection of the good Doctor Foote, who was not good, who had never been good, who, for most of his life, had lived off women, and who had been finding his father's house stifling, his sister unforgiving, unrelenting, uncompromising, and mad into the bargain. He moved Juliana from her respectable lodgings into a room at a city hotel, a fine room, large enough for two, where Mr Albert Forester and his wife enjoyed a few interesting months before she started growing out of her clothes.

Some see beauty in the pregnant belly. It repulsed Archie, but, no longer gainfully employed, he had to live somewhere. He remained the thoughtful lover until Juliana's money ran out. She had jewellery; they sold a few pieces. There'd been a ready market for good jewellery in Melbourne. One chap had made a damn fine offer for her brooch, her mother's brooch. She'd dug her heels in over the brooch, refused to part with it. Most women, when they dig their heels, in are hard to budge. Juliana was immovable. Archie's desire to cut loose and run had grown daily.

One morning he'd done it, had taken off with only the shirt on his back, caught the train to Three Pines Siding. His cousin gave him a clean shirt and a bed. To this day, he didn't know how a woman with limited English had managed to track him down. Had she found something in his luggage? Had she returned to the hospital where the elderly Foote brothers laboured? Had she found the house in Hawthorn? His sister would have told the devil where to find him.

He'd been with his cousin for a week when a woman was found dead outside of Woody Creek. He'd left Juliana in a hotel room, had assumed that's where she'd be still. He hadn't put two and two together, not then. A week later, with fifty quid of his cousin's money in his pocket, he'd returned to the Melbourne hotel to fight her for his luggage. She wasn't there.

The infant near ripe for the picking, he'd visualised her sitting up in a hospital bed, and had asked at the hotel reception desk if Doctor Foote had perhaps been called to his wife's room. The reception clerk called the hotel manager, who told Archie that his wife hadn't been sighted in eight days, hadn't paid the bill, and if it wasn't paid by today, they'd be out on their ears without their luggage.

His cousin's fifty quid paid the bill. He'd sold Juliana's prized fur coat and a garnet necklace to recoup his losses, then waited; and searched for her brooch while he waited. He'd sold a tiara, no doubt worn to some royal gathering. He'd sold a fancy ballgown and three pairs of Italian shoes before he'd seen that newspaper.

DO YOU KNOW THIS WOMAN?
Foreign woman dies in childbirth beside a railway track . . . four miles from Woody Creek . . .

The photograph hadn't done her justice, but he'd recognised her features. For a time he'd considered claiming the body — or claiming the brooch, which must have been on the body. But that would have meant claiming the female infant, who, according to the newspaper had survived — and there had been no mention of any jewellery found.

Fate being ever kind to Archie Foote, he'd picked up a job on a cargo boat leaving for Egypt. No luxurious cabin that time, but he'd never been to Egypt. He'd seen the Pyramids. He'd ridden on a camel's back, picked dates fresh from the palms, and more. Some of his better stories came from Egypt. He'd enjoyed every day of his time there — until the bastards locked him up.

He'd got out, with a shattered upper arm. It still ached today. Two of the four he'd got out with had been felled by a hail of bullets. Archie had crawled into a hovel to bind his wound, and there, hanging behind its door, was one of the black face-covering sacks worn by some of the old Muslim women. He'd lived in it for two months; had gone openly about the job of surviving, and not a soul dared lift his veil. Few would have recognised what came out from beneath that rag. He hadn't recognised himself, and it had been safer at the time not to be himself.

Albert Forester had sold the Contis' jewels. A bearded form of old Albert made his way to Paris, not a good place to be at that time. He'd hoofed it down to Spain, which had been worse, but he'd got a boat there heading for Melbourne, had worked his passage home in the ship's kitchen.

Like the rest of the world, Melbourne was in the grip of the depression. His father was dead. His sister was installed in the house with a maid. They were heavy sleepers. He'd been breaking in and out of that house since infancy. He'd helped himself to what he could, and for months lived where he could; had queued with the starving thousands for his tin cup of soup and a slice of bread, promising himself that one day he'd write his life story — when he found the time. He'd look on his 'blue period', his poverty-stricken period, as research.

He'd been taking the sun in Bourke Street, reading a discarded newspaper, the day he sighted his fighting bitch of a wife walking with Vern Hooper. He'd followed them to their hotel, assuming they were wed. Watched them for days; safe to watch from behind his beard, his newspaper. Few of the prosperous gave a second glance to derelicts. He'd followed them to the station when they'd checked out of the hotel, and that night made another visit to his father's house. Poor, bearded old Albert bought a ticket to Woody Creek, chuckling in anticipation of his fighting bitch of a wife's face when he told her he'd have her up on charges of bigamy.

She hadn't wed. She'd been where he'd last sighted her, in her hovel. He'd walked out to his cousin's house and found it empty. Vern Hooper moved him on, and that big bastard hadn't recognised him. Archie had chuckled about that.

He'd moved on, into town, and holed up in a hut near the bridge. Raked up the pub's backyard for a meal. Stacked crates in the grocer's yard for a pound of flour, a packet of tea. Raided Gertrude's henhouse, pinched her figs, and anything else that was handy. It was all a grand game until the day he sighted Jennifer out front of the grocer's. Does blood recognise blood? If he'd given

Juliana's offspring ten seconds of thought in the years since its birth, he'd seen it raised by the nuns in an orphanage, as Conti had wanted it raised — without the donation.

A golden child that one, gold of hair and complexion, long in the shank, fine-boned — something of his sister in her build, but more of the boy he'd been in her face.

He knew himself as a man of obsessions. He'd become obsessed with her before he'd heard her voice at that Christmas concert. The applause had roused in him the pride of the creator. Hung around too long. His firstborn had approached him in the park.

'I know who you are,' she'd said.

He'd denied it. He'd denied it again when she'd bailed him up down at the bridge. Walked away from her and the town that night, vowing he wouldn't go back.

He'd gone back.

'I know you.'

Past and present mingling. Archie lifted his head; eyes, concentrated too long on a page of notes, didn't immediately refocus.

The circling hag had stopped her circling, had stopped pinching her hand. She stood staring at him. He took a reflex step back and closed his book with a snap.

'As well you may,' he said. 'We have spoken before, Amber.'

'Lying bastard,' she snarled.

Turned on his heel and, ten minutes later, left the facility, consciously slowing his retreat when his every nerve ending told him to run. Perhaps it was time to discontinue his voluntary work.

GIFTS FROM HOME

20 November '46
Dear Jenny,
Just a quick note. Maureen Macdonald and her husband came up for the weekend. They offered to take a few things back for you. I don't know how far Box Hill is from where you are, but Ray should be able to strap the carton onto his bike. Maisy is here with me now. She's writing him directions on how to get out to Maureen's.

Archie has been up here for a week. He told me he ran into you at a hospital a while back and that you gave him an address in Sydney. I think he's left.

Vern has been down. He said he wanted to send Jimmy a present for his birthday. It's in the carton. He knows you're not living at Myrtle's boarding house. From what I can gather, he's got some investigator chap trying to find you and Jimmy.

He said Jim's been fitted with glasses, and an artificial leg, but according to Vern, it's not his leg or eyes that are troubling him. He says it's his mind. They've moved him to some private place out of the city.

I have to finish this off. Maisy is going to post it for me on her way home.
Kisses to all, Granny

27 November
Dear Granny,
Jimmy and the girls love Vern's train set. You can thank him from my kids and spit in his eye for me. I've seen similar sets in Myer's and they cost a fortune.

Thanks for your food parcel. The kids sat on the veranda cracking walnuts with Norman's hammer and eating as many as they put into the basin. They brought in enough to make a batch of your oatmeal biscuits.

I haven't told them yet about Christmas just in case we can't make it. Have you got any more details on how Joey is getting down . . .

27 November
Dear Mum, Dad, Dawn, etc, etc . . .
Jenny turned up to get Mrs Foote's carton and you could have knocked me over with a feather when I saw her at the door. She was pushing a pram. I thought she must have had another one we didn't know about, but she said she'd borrowed it from a neighbour to push the carton home in. I was expecting Ray to come for it, or to come with her. I've been dying to see what he grew into. She looked well but wouldn't come in for a cup of tea. She had to get home to Jimmy, who she'd left with her neighbour, she said. I asked where she was living. She said it wasn't that far away, and that's all.

Got to go. I'll phone you on Sunday night.
Love, Maureen. X

Dear Jenny,
How did you get out to Box Hill? Harry says that Armadale is

*miles across country. I spent a weekend out there years ago and
it seemed miles from Hawthorn . . .*

Dear Granny,
*Trains and trams go everywhere down here. Do you know yet
what day Joey will arrive in Melbourne? Tell him if he's looking
for a bed, I've got a camp stretcher he's welcome to use, and that
we'll travel up there with him on the train. It will only be me
and the kids. Ray said he'd ride up when his factory closes . . .*

Said he might. Nothing was positive, but everything was possible
by mid-December, so she told the kids they might be going home
for Christmas.

Kids are renowned for taking a *might* and turning it into a
when.

'If we go, how many more days, Jenny?'

'Sh-she's your m-mother,' Ray said.

He didn't like Georgie. She'd corrected Margot's back to front
'J' for 'Jimmy'. She'd picked up the rules of Canasta in one sitting. Ray had trouble holding eleven cards in his hand. Margot
could hold eleven. She'd learnt the rules almost as fast as Georgie.
There was not a thing wrong with that kid's mind. Pure, unadul-
terated wilfulness was her problem and determination to get her
own way.

There was something wrong with Ray's mind. A week before
school ended, a week before Joey was to fly down, Jenny paid for a
haircut — paid twice for it. He accused her of having it cut for her
old boyfriend, and when she told him not to be so crazy jealous,
that Joey was her little brother, the furniture suffered and the walls.
A chair leg went through the plaster.

Her haircut was only the beginning. She made up the camp
stretcher, tacked a sheet over the disintegrating flywire in the sleep-
out, making that room as nice, as cat-proof, as she could. Ray

didn't like nice. He pitched the camp stretcher at the disintegrating flywire and made a larger hole for the cats.

Then, two days before school broke up, a letter came from Granny. Joey wouldn't be flying into Melbourne. He'd found out that he could get a small plane in Sydney that would take him to Albury. Billy Roberts drove a truck to and from Albury. He and Joey had been in the same army unit. Billy would pick him up in Albury and deliver him back there on Boxing Day.

And without the leverage of Joey, Ray changed his mind about riding up.

'You used to ride your bike up every weekend before we got married,' Jenny said.

'I'll g-go with you on the train when I f-f-finish work.'

She didn't want to wait. The kids didn't want to wait. They'd been counting down the days. But it would look better going back as a family. She'd have less time up there, more competition for Joey's time, but she agreed to wait.

That final night: her red case packed and waiting beside the glass door, two string bags bulging beside it, weighty with newspaper-wrapped, sugar-filled jars, hoarded for months for jam-making. The kids had gone early to bed, too early, wanting tomorrow to come fast.

And he said it. 'I haven't g-got money to go w-w-wasting on h-holidays.'

Stunned silent for a second, for ten seconds. 'I told you I'd pay for the kids and my fares. It won't cost us anything while we're up there, Ray.'

'H-happy to p-pay your w-w-way when you're g-going home to s-see your old b-boyfriend — with your n-n-new haircut.'

'I spent half of my life yabbying with him, fishing with him, setting rabbit traps with him! He's not my boyfriend.'

'H-h-hooper,' he said.

'Jesus Christ, Ray! He's in a sanatorium down here! He's crippled! I'm married to you. I sleep with you. And you had no intention of ever going, did you? It's got nothing to do with money.'

'D-d-didn't g-get your h-h-hair cut for m-m-me, did you?'

'I got it cut for me, for God's sake. It was driving me mad! For me! And I'm not disappointing those kids, or Granny. We're going in the morning.'

Excited kids don't sleep well. They have big ears that hear more than they're supposed to hear. Kids creep from beds to stand in doorways like three silent little mice. Their eyes ask questions.

'G-get b-b-back to bed,' he roared.

Jenny ushered them back to bed, then continued on, through the sleep-out door and down to the washhouse, where she snatched up her cigarettes, lit one and stood blowing smoke at the encroaching night. And one wasn't enough. She lit a second from the first, sucking in smoke until she was calm enough to speak to him.

'I want to take you up there, Ray. I want people to see my good-looking husband. I want to go to the New Year's dance with you.'

'Y-you couldn't w-w-wait to g-g-get out of the place.'

'And I'll be eternally grateful to you for getting me out of that town. But I miss Granny, and the kids miss her.' She hated the wheedling tone of her voice, her attempt to reason with one who was not reasonable. 'It's just for a few days.'

Her handbag hung over the bedroom doorknob. She fetched it and brought it to the table, opened it, counted pound notes, money she'd withdrawn from her bank account to pay for fares, money saved from her endowment and her sewing.

'W-w-where d-did you get it?'

'Where do you think I got it?'

'Wh-ooo knows w-w-what you g-get up to?'

'Right. I'm at it every day,' she said. 'I've got my own corner in Fitzroy. Threepence a ride and a discount for twins.'

She had excellent reflexes. His backhand missed her ear.

She stood on the opposite side of the table and swept up her notes, stuffed them into her handbag, then took her bankbook from a worn side pocket, Archie Foote's card still in it. Stuffed the card back into her bag — not that he'd be able to read it. He could understand figures.

'That's where I got it,' she said, pointing to a fifteen-pound withdrawal. 'I earned it in Sydney with my voice. People used to pay me to sing, Ray. People used to treat me as a person, not a live-in prostitute-cum-cook-cum-laundry woman.'

Angry, fiery-eyed angry, and vocal tonight. He couldn't fight her with words. Maybe he knew he was in the wrong. He walked away from her bankbook, went to his bedroom and slammed the door.

She stood leafing through the book, looking at the pitiful little figures. The first page was all withdrawals, then the pay-ins commenced: *7/6*; *5/0*; *15/0*. Pages of money squirrelled away, the sums growing in size as she progressed through the book. Then the last page, after those Yankee bastards had raped her, when the storing of money had been her only security: *3/0/0*; *2/10/0*; *2/7/6*. Followed by Melbourne withdrawals. Going down, down, down. And what for? For the pleasure of living with him?

She opened his bedroom door. 'I drew that money out so I could take the kids home, and I'm not disappointing them. You come or don't come, but we'll be on the train in the morning.'

'D-d-don't bother coming b-back if you g-go.'

'You made the mistake of marrying me, Ray. We'll come back.'

'You w-w-won't get in,' he said, and he kicked the door and damn near took the tip of her finger off.

She walked outside, sucking the pain from her finger, stood on the veranda sucking and staring at her garden beds, the bankbook still in her hand, handbag over her shoulder, breathing fast and fighting back tears.

Tomato plants grown tall, plenty of fruit on them, though not pinking up yet. Onions aplenty, carrots standing in rows, lettuces sunburnt, full of slugs and snails, but they washed off. The rhubarb had gone mad. She'd made rhubarb pies, they'd eaten rhubarb with macaroni puddings, with their Weet-Bix for breakfast — all thanks to his bloody livers.

She'd created that garden, she and her kids. They'd brought a little of Granny, a little of home, to this place that wasn't home, that would never be a home. The kids had dug holes all along the fence line and planted his withered potatoes, grown now into a long row of dark healthy greenery. Below the earth they were making babies. She'd tunnelled beneath one of the plants just to prove it to the kids.

Am I prepared to leave my garden? Can I leave my dresser, my electric iron, his fridge? I'd leave him a damn sight easer. I'd leave him tonight without a backwards glance.

The pain gone from her finger, she placed her bankbook into her bag and considered returning to Woody Creek as a failure, married for less than twelve months. And after what she'd written to Granny, she couldn't.

He turned the kitchen light off. He was going to bed.

Walk up to the phone box and call a taxi. Get the kids up and take them to a hotel. One way or the other, she was going home tomorrow. She walked out to the gate and stood leaning on it, knowing she couldn't disappoint those kids.

And knowing too that she couldn't stand being the subject of Woody Creek gossip again, couldn't stand having half of Woody Creek whispering behind their hands every time she walked into town, couldn't stand to walk by the raping-eyed blokes who congregated on the hotel corner, who had probably placed their bets on how soon she'd come running back pregnant.

Worse than that: Vern Hooper would be on the phone to his solicitor five minutes after he learned she was home. Jimmy had a father now, a returned soldier, heroic survivor of a Japanese prison camp. Every newspaper in Australia had published photographs of the walking skeletons they'd brought out of those places, every newsreel in the theatres had shown those men and the conditions they'd survived in. That hard old swine would use Jim's war record in court, and how many judges would deny a serviceman's claim on a son he hadn't seen in five years? None — not if she took that son back to live in two rooms and a lean-to.

She left the yard to walk, uncaring of where she walked, turning when she felt like turning, as she had the day she'd heard Jim was missing in action. She'd lost herself that day. Wanted to lose herself tonight, but, unlike Sydney's roads, Melbourne's went to where you expected them to go. She kept finding herself.

Ray was jealous of Joey, jealous of Jim, jealous of Georgie, probably jealous of Granny . . .

If he didn't care about me he wouldn't be jealous.

Jealous or possessive?

Wanting to possess someone isn't loving them. It's owning them. Telling her not to come back wasn't loving her. It was proving to himself that he owned her.

And he didn't. And she was going.

And what if he'd meant what he'd said?

Georgie loved her school and was doing so well there. Jimmy was eager to go to school next year, and over-ready to be there. She had a growing business with her sewing. She had her garden, her card-playing friends, Miss Flowers over the road, Carol next door. She saw all of the new movies. Delete Ray from the equation, delete fear of pregnancy, and she had a good life down here, a better life than she'd ever expected to have.

Not the life she'd wanted.

A damn sight better than the one she'd have if she went home.

Tyrants are created by those who give in to unreasonable demands.

She had to give in. She had no choice.

She took a road leading back to High Street and to a telephone box, where she looked at her watch. Not nine thirty yet. Maisy wouldn't be in bed.

If I haven't got the right coins, I'll call a taxi and to hell with the consequences.

Of course she had the right coins.

Maisy must have been sitting next to the telephone waiting for it to ring. Jenny said what she had to say. She lied about Ray's factory, said it had been involved in the strike, that he was still catching up with the bills and could Maisy please let Granny know that they wouldn't be coming up. Maisy filled the three minutes. She'd had a card from Sissy. Patricia was having another baby. Rachel's oldest had been rushed to hospital with . . . then the money dropped and Jenny was alone, holding on to a dead phone line.

Wanted Maisy's voice back, wanted to hear news of anyone, wanted the normalcy of . . . of home.

Not enough coins to call her back. Plenty of pennies.

Empty streets out there. Didn't want to leave that phone box for emptiness.

She had a number she could reach with pennies. Had it in her handbag.

Couldn't.

He wouldn't be home — so it wouldn't matter if she tried his number.

And what if he was home?

Was he any worse than Ray?

Tonight no one was worse than Ray.

Ringing. Ringing somewhere. Where?

Five. Six. Seven rings. He wasn't at home. Then the pennies dropped.

'Good evening.' A bored voice, maybe a sleepy voice. 'Good evening.' Repeated. An educated voice, distant, but in that phone box with her.

Hang up.

'Are you there?'

She was there. 'Merry Christmas,' she said.

'Jennifer?' How could he possibly recognise her voice? 'Where are you?'

'I flew down,' she said. 'Just for the night.'

'My Christmas was looking very bleak. What a delightful surprise.'

He spoke of his recent trip to Woody Creek. She told him she was on her way there, on the morning train. She told him she was staying at a hotel in the city. Just a fairytale, spun in a phone box, on a street corner, just fiction travelling down a line. It didn't matter. He replied, and not in monosyllables.

He asked if she'd seen Jim Hooper recently, then told her he'd lost track of him, that the family had moved him to a clinic specialising in the care of shell-shocked servicemen. She didn't want to talk about Jim. Didn't want to think about Jim. She wanted to ask him about Juliana Conti, but couldn't raise the nerve, so she wove more stories about the club she sang at in Sydney — had, once upon a time.

'Granny always told me I got my voice from you. She said once you could charm the natives from the jungles with your voice.'

'Dear Tru,' he said, then he asked after her fine friendly son. She told him he'd be going to school next year. He knew about the girls. She didn't want him to know about the girls or ask after them. She spoke about Wilfred Whiteford and his band, no doubt disbanded by now, but so very fine to speak about as if it were today. He spoke of the jazz club, of his concert group.

'If I could get work down here, I'd consider moving closer to home,' she said.

'I have many contacts in the industry, Jennifer.' Was it an offer? Did she dare? She was searching for a reply when he continued. 'There are no limits as to how far your voice, your appearance, may take you.'

Who amongst us doesn't want to hear such praise?

No praise in Ray's house. No singing there — nothing to sing about there. And she had to go there. Her watch face told her over half an hour had passed since she'd placed her call to Maisy. That's what happened when you spoke to someone who replied. Time disappeared.

'I'll have to go,' she said. 'The train leaves early.'

'Having broken the ice, do keep in touch, Jennifer.'

Goodbyes then, a promise to keep in touch. Promises don't count when you're spinning fairytales in a telephone box.

'Oh, before you go, dear, should you find yourself back in town on the fourth, my concert group is putting on a performance at the Hawthorn Town Hall. I would be truly delighted to introduce your voice to our southern city.'

'I don't know where I'll be on the fourth,' she said.

'Don't lose my number.'

She had no intention of losing it, not now.

Life is a current. Get caught up in it and it can sweep you into dangerous waters, take you to where you don't want to go. Fight it though and you'll surely drown. Far better to float with it, hope that sooner or later it will wash you close enough into shore for you to get your feet on solid ground.

Jenny floated through Christmas, and it was like all of those Christmases with Amber, those silent Christmases of no laughter, no Granny, no love. It was a Christmas of children's eyes watching her, watching him, of staying out of his way, and waiting for what came next.

Jenny didn't know what came next. Her mind halfway between pretend-land and hell, she cooked a form of Christmas dinner: roasted chops and potatoes, pumpkin, carrots and onions; picked a bunch of silverbeet and made white sauce to pour over it. He liked gravy. She didn't make gravy. He liked his potatoes and pumpkin mashed. He got what she cooked that Christmas Day.

She made a treacle pudding and poked a threepence into each serving. Hoped he choked on his. He didn't, but he swallowed it. The kids found their threepences.

Slept on the camp stretcher she'd prepared for Joey — or didn't sleep. Spent the night . . . floating . . . replaying the telephone conversation, replaying it word for word. Near dawn, the old Christmas tunes began playing in her mind, and she sang along with them, soundlessly, and thought of Granny, of Joey, of Christmases past and those ahead. A confusion, her mind on

Christmas night, thoughts crisscrossing like the city train lines near Flinders Street, a confusion of tracks, leading out, leading in. She travelled to Sydney, then diverted to Norman's funeral, stood again in the telephone box, hid behind a tree spying on old Noah the swaggie.

Itchy-foot. Always Itchy-foot. Always knew he could sing. Could old people still sing or did their throats become wrinkly?

She could hear him on the fourth — if she had the guts. Did she have that much guts left? She'd had guts once. Gone to Melbourne at fifteen, to Sydney at eighteen.

Was that concert a doorway?

What would be on the other side?

Don't be taken in by him, darlin'.

More confusion on the far side, more trouble. She had to stay on the safe side — which wasn't safe anyway.

A sleepless night, a bad Boxing Day, a day of dodging the blackmailer, and on Boxing night, sleeping again, or not sleeping, on the camp stretcher, letting him know that he may have been able to blackmail her into not going home but he didn't own her.

Between Christmas and New Year, he tried to prove he owned her. She'd spent the day making jam from Wilma's apricots, made eight jars of it, and went to bed early. He came into the sleep-out in the middle of the night and tried to take her on the camp bed, then the floor, her kids only a door away. She knew the layout of that room better than he did — climbed over the old cabinet and dived through the cats' hole in the flywire. Rusting flywire scratches those without fur, but she showed him who she belonged to. Climbed over Carol's fence and hid in her garden, in her nightgown.

Shades of yesteryear. How many times had she scaled Mr Foster's fence when Amber had been the one chasing her?

Ray paid her back with a liver. She fertilised her rhubarb with it while it was still fresh, while 1947 was still shaking off its newness. He fought fire with fire. He stopped buying bread. She had money in her handbag. She bought her own bread, her own milk, cheese, fruit, loaded his fridge with her type of food and left no room for his.

Then Granny sent her a ten-pound note in the post, which wasn't at all like Granny. She'd wrapped it well in three pages — one page from Joey, which Jenny couldn't read for tears, couldn't read aloud to the kids. It wasn't fair. Nothing was fair in this bloody world.

'Get your shoes on,' she said.

Worn-out shoes, but they got them on.

'Get your hats on.'

'You don't wear a hat.'

'I don't burn. Do as you're told, Margot.'

They rode the tram into the city where Jenny paid back to the bank the fifteen pounds she'd withdrawn from her account, knowing she'd be desperate for it one day, maybe one day soon.

Later, loaded down with three pairs of new school shoes, after lunch at Coles cafeteria, she gave the kids five shillings each of Granny's money and let them spend it in Coles. You could buy a lot for five bob in Coles. Watched them choosing how to spend their coins. Jimmy spent his on a wind-up monkey who played a drum when you wound his key. Georgie wanted a floral dress. Only one on the rack, one with leaves as green as her eyes, flowers the colour of her hair. Margot wanted one the same, but couldn't have it. Didn't want the yellow dress, or the one with blue flowers. Georgie got her dress. Margot bought a big bag of butterscotch, a packet of cards with Mickey Mouse on them, and two pretty pins to keep the hair out of her eyes.

As much as she, those kids had wanted to ride the train home to Granny. They knew who to blame for their lost Christmas. Even Margot knew who to blame.

She blamed Georgie for not buying the dress with the blue flowers. Coles had two of them.

'We're not twins,' Georgie said.

She'd turn seven in March. Margot would turn eight in April.

Jimmy had turned five in December. And look at them sitting there, little city slickers, holding on to their parcels, going home to a nice house in a nice street.

I did the right thing, Jenny thought. I've given them a chance at life. Now I have to give myself a chance. I'm going to Itchy-foot's concert.

She rang him from the post office, the kids sitting on the steps, licking ice-cream.

'I'll be here on the fourth. I'd like to sing at your concert,' she said.

'And you shall, my dear. And you shall.'

She told Ray she was going to a concert, that he could take her to it on his bike if he felt like it. He didn't feel like it. He took off alone on his bike. Flora had already agreed to look after the kids. At seven, Jenny left them with her, Georgie in charge of Jenny's old book of fairytales, her precious book from Sydney, only brought out on special occasions and treasured by all three of her kids.

She wore her blue linen, Norman's blue necklet at her throat, its matching drop earrings swinging from her lobes. She caught two trams to the Hawthorn town hall and to the strangest, out-of-this-world night of her life.

She heard Archie Foote's voice, heard the age in it, heard him reach for the high notes and listened in awe to the pure rich tones of his lower register. He sang 'Autumn Leaves' and, to her, it would ever be his song. Since Christmas, anything could make her cry. She fought back tears that night, unsure if it was his voice, his age, or the words of the song that moved her — or maybe something deeper. He'd given her life. Him. He'd given her his voice. He was her sire, if not her father.

He claimed their connection, in part, when he introduced her. 'My beautiful granddaughter, Jennifer Morrison,' he said.

She didn't embarrass herself on that city stage. She sang 'The

White Cliffs of Dover'. And, when the night was near over, they sang 'We'll Meet Again', father and daughter standing side by side. Their voices accepted their connection. They blended.

He wanted to drive her back to her city hotel. She got away from him, though not before he gave her the address of his jazz club.

'I'm there every Friday night,' he said. 'If you find yourself back in town . . .'

It wouldn't happen again. It couldn't. She didn't want . . . didn't want to know him better. He was too . . . too easy to trust.

Jimmy was enrolled at school as James Morrison King. She got rid of the Hooper name. Hoped Jimmy would forget it but doubted he would. He had the memory of an elephant. Her days were long without him. She picked home-grown tomatoes, pulled home-grown onions, bought a pound of cooking apples and made eight jars of chutney to add to her pots of jam, stored now in the old cabinet in the sleep-out. Jenny wrote to Granny about her chutney, her jams. In February Miss Flowers' tree had supplied plums. She didn't mention Ray. Made no mention of singing with Archie Foote. She wrote about a wedding dress.

Doreen, a friend of Wilma's, asked me to make a wedding dress and two bridesmaids' dresses for her daughter's wedding. I almost had a stroke when I saw the material they'd bought. I looked at it for two days, too scared to cut into it, then I went out and bought a roll of calico and made the entire frock out of that, just tacked it together. Once it fitted, I unpicked it and used the calico pieces as the pattern. It looked so good, I couldn't believe I'd made it. Even the inside looked good. I didn't have a clue how much to charge them so I rang up a dressmaker and asked what she'd charge to make me a wedding dress and bridesmaids' dresses. I almost fell over in the phone box. I ended up charging eight pounds for the lot and even Wilma said I was mad. If you happen to be talking to Miss Blunt could you ask her what she charges these days?

Flora had watched the making of the bridal gowns with great interest. She'd played model for the smaller of the two bridesmaids' frocks and wanted one the same. It took a day to make it, and maybe Jenny shouldn't have made it look so easy. Flora didn't offer to pay. She wore it to a ball; Jenny envious when she watched her neighbour leave, leaving her at home with the kids, Lois asleep on the camp stretcher.

Jenny had moved back into Ray's bed. She'd asked him to take her to a jazz club on Friday night.

THE BREEDING OF MONEY

She went alone and couldn't find the club that first night. She walked by the entrance three times, was ready to turn around and go home, when she realised the club was down a set of old stairs, in a cellar. Jim had always wanted to hear what her voice sounded like in Monk's cellar . . .

A crowded, smoky place; eyes turned to her as she entered, clad again in blue, her frock too tame for that place, out of place there, as was she.

Itchy-foot had been watching for her. She'd phoned him to let him know she'd . . . flown down again. He introduced her to Monique, clad in slinky and low-cut black, and to her husband, Ralph, as slinky in his black dress suit. Not the same atmosphere or clientele as the club in Sydney. Archie sang; Monique sang; her husband, Ralph, played the piano; and the bug-eyed club owner considered himself a dirty-mouthed comedian.

Jenny sat at a small table in a smoky corner, partially screened by a dusty palm in a pot. Archie had supplied her with a jug of water; she shouted the palm a glass. It was late when Archie introduced her to the protruding-eyed manager.

She hadn't expected to be asked to sing, but she sang 'Blue

Moon', Ralph on the piano, adding bits never written into the music of that song, but she wasn't booed off stage, which wasn't a stage anyway, just a corner crowded by a piano.

'Like a breath of fresh air,' the bug-eyed coot said — and invited her back — or maybe offered her a job.

After eleven, when she left to catch the tram home, the party in the cellar was still warming up. She was going back — whether to donate her time or not, she didn't care. She'd got a foot inside that door and it wasn't closing on her.

That week she ripped the guipure lace from the neck of the black frock she'd worn to Norman's funeral and hadn't worn since; the once-red frock Laurie had bought for a fifteen-year-old Jenny in Melbourne. She'd dyed it black in Sydney, when she'd had nothing to wear to the Sydney club, had added the lace to give it a respectable neckline. She didn't need that same respectability at Itchy-foot's jazz club.

The frock was a heavy silk. It fitted at the hip, flared at the knee and looked fashionable enough for after five. She bought a gold silk rose to pin on its shoulder, wore her pearl-in-a-cage necklace and earrings, then covered the frock's low neckline with a button-up cardigan until she got to the club.

Itchy-foot noticed the pearl-in-a-cage pendant at her throat — or her frock's neckline. He reached to touch an earring, smiled, but didn't comment.

A few world-weary eyes concentrated on her neckline while she sang, but who cared. The bug-eyed coot discussed money that night. She rode the tram home with cash in her handbag.

Ray wasn't happy. Nothing she did could make him happy. She read his newspapers to him, cooked his meat, slept with him — or spent time in his bed. She did most of her sleeping in the sleep-out, in the narrow camp bed.

Sewed for herself that week, made a black wool gabardine suit and a black and white print blouse. With her next week's wages, she bought a pair of ultra high-heeled black shoes and two pairs of fine stockings with black seams, paid for a haircut and dictated every snip.

Put money in the bank the next week and read of trade unions to Ray. Everyone was chasing money. The trade unions wanted more of it for fewer hours, which was madness. Before the war, anyone who could get a job had been happy to work as many hours as it took to keep it. Two years ago, most of the unionists were overseas shooting people and being shot at. Now there was no war and there was enough work, so they waged war on people who were fighting just to keep their heads afloat.

A child of the depression, Jenny worked when she could. She had a big sewing job in March, making curtains for Carol's sister's brand new house. No more card games on Friday nights, but Wilma was more than a card-playing friend now. She popped in every Wednesday while Flora visited her mother. Carol popped in too. She'd elected herself Jenny's agent — sent a heap of sewing work her way.

There is something very strange about money. Get a little of it into one place and it breeds more.

In April, Norman's estate was finally wound up. Granny wrote the figure on paper: *Three hundred and forty-seven pounds*. It was a fortune. It was enough to . . . to . . .

She couldn't stand Ray's touch. Couldn't stand living with him, watching him eat. Loathed the sound of his bike put-putting in through the gate. Didn't have to live with him, not with a job and three hundred and forty-seven pounds, but where else was she going to get rooms and someone to look after the kids on Friday nights? They liked their school, were doing well there. Even Margot was coping.

Already caught up in a whirlpool, for two days Norman's money stirred it.

Dear Granny,
See if you can invest Dad's money for me. The banks were offering good interest for three-year investments . . .

The papers came in the post, the figure typewritten and not so real. Maturity date: 19 April 1950. Jenny placed the envelope and its contents safe in her cake tin, with the birth certificates, her marriage certificate, then put the lid on it — until April of 1950. That would be her running date. By then Georgie would be ten, Jimmy eight, Margot eleven. They'd be old enough, she'd be rich enough. All she had to do was keep on singing, keep on sewing, until 1950.

She bought herself a black sweater to wear with her suit skirt. It showed her shape. Her ultra high heels showed the shape of her legs. She spent more time looking after her hair, powdering and painting her face.

'You're m-meeting someone in there.'

'I take the tram in. I sing. He pays me. At eleven I ride the tram home. Ride in at eleven and pick me up, Ray.'

'G-get yourself home.'

'Then stop accusing me. Do I accuse you when you stay out all night?'

Like hell, she accused him. She blessed him.

'You're d-d-dressed up l-like a t-tart —'

'I can't please you when I dress up. I can't please you when I don't dress up. I can't please you, so I've stopped trying.'

'You're m-m-my wife.'

'And I've got three kids who need to eat, and you don't feed them so I do.'

Apart from his roadkill and rotten potatoes, she paid for what she served on his table. And she had her own potatoes too, big fat home-grown potatoes she boiled in their jackets and ate with butter and salt and pepper. She bought milk each day after school, large loaves of bread. Washed his clothes, swept up butts from his bedroom floor, cooked his meat, changed his sheets, did her wifely duty with gritted teeth, and did what she'd been born to do on Fridays; the one thing she could do effortlessly, the one thing she enjoyed doing.

Could have picked up a dozen blokes at the club if she'd wanted to. Leo, the bug-eyed owner, told her he knew a chap in the recording business, and asked if she'd be interested in meeting with him. Of course she was interested, and she'd shown her interest — in the recording chap. Just another come-on. She knew how to deal with come-ons.

'My husband picks me up, Leo,' she'd lied.

And he could have. In Woody Creek, she'd loved riding on the back of his bike, and he knew it. He could have taken her riding through the night streets of Melbourne and she may have gone more willingly to his bed. That wasn't the way Ray's head worked. You don't court wives.

And it didn't matter any more. She had a big neon sign flashing before her eyes: 19 April 1950. She'd rent her own house, or put a deposit on a brand new house, like Carol's sister. A lot of people were paying off new houses.

In June, she lost track of the date and forgot to pick up her child endowment, her lifeline of not long ago. That's what happens when you're caught up in a whirlpool.

In June, Flora told her she wouldn't be able to keep an eye on the kids next Friday night — or any more Friday nights.

'You said they're no trouble.'

'They're not. It's Ray. He told us he doesn't want me to do it. We have to live with him, Jenny.'

Why did they have to live with him? They were the ones paying off the house. Why didn't they tell him to go? She wanted to ask why, wanted to tell Flora to tell him to go, to tell her she'd pay rent for those rooms. She got as far as, 'Why?'

'Men like to be the breadwinners,' Flora said.

Geoff didn't. He wanted Flora to get a job. Lois went to school, to the Catholic school.

'Don't worry about it, Flora,' Jenny said.

Janice, Wilma's thirteen-year-old daughter, was happy to earn five bob babysitting. The following Friday, Jenny left her playing cards with the kids and returned to find her in bed with them. She woke her and walked her home.

Wilma popped in on the Monday to tell her Janice wouldn't be back.

'He came in drunk and told her to get. Bring your kids around to my place next Friday.'

They enjoyed their night at Wilma's house, were full of it on Saturday.

'It's like at Elsie's down there, Jenny, when everyone used to laugh and play cards,' Georgie said.

Not much laughter in this place.

One memory will raise another. Jimmy spoke of Myrtle's leadlight window when Jenny served up bowls of macaroni cheese casserole.

'Did we live a long time before in a house with a magic window, Jenny?'

'How was it magic?'

'Like colours, like in that church we see when we go into the city.' He spooned in macaroni. 'It made rainbows on the wall.'

Only one window had painted rainbows. And how could he possibly remember Amberley? He'd been a month away from three when they'd left Sydney.

'Do you remember Myrtie?'

He shook his head. Maybe he remembered Myrtle's macaroni cheese casserole. He cleaned his plate, scraped up the last of the sauce.

'Can you remember the lady who used to make this same dinner for you?'

'Did she have a baby that cried very loud?'

She had a baby, a tiny bald mite with Jenny's hands. Hoped he'd forgotten Myrtle and that baby. Jenny questioned him no further.

In July, she bought a roll of flywire and on Saturday morning, while Ray was out raking up his roadkill, she and the kids ripped the old flywire from the sleep-out and began tacking up the new. Geoff heard the hammering. He came around to help.

'A cat sleeps in there,' she explained. Didn't tell him the fool of a thing had landed on her camp stretcher and frightened ten years' growth out of her. She'd thought it was Ray.

The following week, she bought a roll of canvas, green canvas, and forced the old sewing machine to stitch new blinds. Geoff took the old blinds down and tacked the new canvas to their rollers. They worked all afternoon together, Ray watching from a distance. The sleep-out a cosier bedroom now, with new blinds to keep the wind out.

In July, she moved the last of her jams and chutney into the fridge and dragged the dilapidated old cabinet away from its wall to form a partial barrier to her camp stretcher, leaving a small passageway between the kids' bedroom door and the back door. Well used that back door. That week, she took to the cabinet with Norman's tools, repaired its drawers, used Norman's screws to fix the backboards on firmly. Elbow grease and sandpaper removed the years of abuse; Amber's furniture polish made the old unit glow.

She moved out of Ray's room for good that day. He knew why. She'd told him she'd been raped by drunks before; called him a raping bastard. Wished she hadn't invested Norman's money. Bought an old wardrobe from the secondhand man; no drawer space in it, but she had three drawers in that old cabinet.

'You're m-m-married to me.'

'You spell wife with a "W". Prostitute starts with a "P". Take a trip to Fitzroy, Ray.'

A school of life, that jazz club, a fast-talking place. She was a fast learner. She bamboozled him with words.

He pitched chairs, ripped her frocks from their hangers, stamped on them. She washed them, ironed them, hung them again. A big man, Ray, grown more solid on her cooking. She had to go.

But not yet, not until after September. She was going to make a pile of money in September, all thanks to Itchy-foot.

He had a persona to suit every occasion. At the hospital, she'd seen the doctor; at the concert, he'd played the kindly grandfather;

at the club, she glimpsed the man Gertrude may have known. A big talker, always another story to tell. He'd lived history. He'd been on a boat little more than five hundred miles away when the *Titanic* went down. He'd spoken to survivors. He'd seen the carnage of the first war, had operated in field hospitals. Such a little man, so much smaller now than he'd seemed in his long black Noah coat. Maybe her high heels made him smaller. Been everywhere. Done everything.

And I've done nothing.

I will. After the school holidays.

She'd asked him about Juliana.

'A victim of circumstance,' he'd said. 'A beautiful and tenacious woman.'

She'd wanted more, had pushed him for more.

'I'm not one to look back, Jennifer. The present is far too interesting to go puddling in the past.'

Wished she could tell Granny about him. Wished she could tell her she was singing, putting money in the bank. Wished she could tell her to come down in September.

She was playing Snow White in a pantomime. Itchy-foot was playing Grumpy, and he was so good at it. They were doing five performances at the Hawthorn town hall: Wednesday, Thursday and Friday afternoons and two shows on Saturday. She'd be out all day Saturday.

Ray would get drunk and pitch the furniture. And Granny would murder her if she knew she was allowing those kids to live like that.

Wanted to play Snow White. Wanted fairytales. Wanted . . .

Had to keep her eye on the main prize, that's what she had to do — and write fairytales to Granny.

Seated on Granny's tin trunk at night, she scribbled pages of the truth in an exercise book. Couldn't see what she wrote, so just wrote it, then hid the truth deep in Granny's trunk, between the clean linen.

I planted a penny and tended it well
It grew into a green bank-note lettuce.
But marauding snails feast well in the night
And how far will nibbled notes get us?

I planted a sixpence. It thrust flowers from the earth
Each one a small handbag, gold filled.
But a black frost came down, now the flowers lie dead,
Not a coin have those small handbags spilled.

I planted a shilling. It grew into a tree
And silver and gold were its leaves.
But a woodchopper came and he stripped the trunk bare,
My hope in the pockets of thieves.

SHEEP'S-HEAD STEW

*A*ugust. Cold. Wet. Windy. The kids had colds and Jenny's world was black. He came home at noon on Saturday and dumped down a pile of newspaper-wrapped roadkill. He'd scraped up the lot this time. She unwrapped the largest parcel, expecting something she might roast for Sunday, and was confronted by a skinned sheep's head. Covered her mouth and ran to the glass door.

'Get it off that table, Ray.'

'What's w-w-w-rong w-with you n-now?'

'Get that thing off the table or I'm going to vomit.'

'M-make a s-stew out of it.'

Margot poked a finger into one of its eye sockets and Jenny was out the door. The wind caught it and flung it back hard. She waited for the smash of glass; when it didn't come, she ran for the lavatory and lost her breakfast.

'He's stopping you from singing the only way he knows how,' Wilma said.

He'd stopped everything. She no longer wanted to sing. Had to. Couldn't let everyone down and needed the money. Sick in the stomach, sick at heart, and Fridays kept coming around, rehearsals kept coming around.

He boiled his sheep's head while she and the kids were down at Wilma's, and when she returned the stink of it was in the kitchen and he was sucking at its eye sockets. She ran for the lavatory and vomited again, lost a cup of tea and the biscuit she'd thought she was keeping down. She could keep cigarettes down. Smoked too many. Sat on Granny's trunk, wrote the truth and chain-smoked.

Never this sick with any of those kids. Not sick at all with Margot. Hadn't known she'd been having her, that's why.

Veronica was away for six weeks, cruising the tropics with her sister, the trip booked and paid for by her doctor chap. The newspapers and police were running a witch-hunt on abortionists. Veronica's chap had taken his wife to England.

The card players knew she needed Veronica, who wouldn't be back until late September. They needed Jenny. With Veronica missing, they didn't have a sixth for Five Hundred. Friday night was club night. Jenny couldn't make up the six.

Had to keep going. That was all she could do: keep doing what she'd been doing, hide it from him until September.

She became devious in late August and slept with him again. You can't get pregnant when you're already pregnant. It made him happy until Friday, until she dressed for the club, painted her face, until Mrs Firth, her babysitter, arrived, a tough old bird in her sixties. Maybe Ray had respect for her age. He stayed out of her way, took off on his bike when he saw her at the door.

Wrapped in her overcoat, scarf around her head, the wind attempting to blow her back the way she'd come, Jenny boarded a crowded tram on that last Friday in August. There must have been something good on in the city.

Archie Foote bought her a coffee. Tonight she couldn't stand the smell of it. She ordered a glass of wine. Sipped it, with a cigarette, while Archie spoke about nothing in particular and she nodded. Ralph and Monique were late. No audience other than she, he found a persona between doctor and grandfather. Her tolerance levels low, she lit a second cigarette. He was a man of vices,

Granny had said. Smoking wasn't one of them. She found out why that night.

'The smoking habit is harmful to a singer's throat,' he said.

She had bigger problems than her throat. She nodded, politely. Didn't put her smoke out.

They arrived, Monique windblown. Her hair was long. She went to the ladies' room to do something about it. Archie transformed; interesting watching it happen, the altered vocabulary. He was old and he wanted to be as young as Ralph. Jenny was young and she wanted to be fifty and menopausal.

She sang. Ralph played the accompaniment. He was probably a musical genius. He probably knew it.

His wife was back, and probably as fake as Archie. There was a Monica Fulton in Woody Creek. Had Monique been baptised Monique or just plain Monica?

The whole world seemed fake tonight and Jenny didn't belong in it. Like with Laurie, when nothing had been real. Pregnancy did something to her brain.

Her old snakeskin handbag looked real, worn real. Why was it still with her? She'd looked at other bags, never liked them enough to waste money on them. Why? It was a part of her past, that's why.

She emptied her wine glass and looked out at the tables between the leaves of the sick palm tree, sick for need of the sun. Sun and soil and room to grow wasn't much to ask for, was it? She couldn't have any either. Never had.

Not a full crowd in tonight. Some nights the place was packed, the ceiling blue with smoke. Too cold to leave warm houses, warm wives in warm beds?

She sang two ratbag songs, and tonight she wanted to sing the old, sad songs. Wondered if Ralph would notice if she broke into 'Blue Moon', if he'd follow her as the organist had at Norman's funeral when she'd started singing the Twenty-Third Psalm. Or maybe she'd sing 'The Last Rose of Summer' for Jim, let him hear how it sounded in a cellar.

No Jim here to hear. Wished he was here. He wouldn't have got her pregnant to stop her singing. Closed her eyes and saw him as he'd been that night in Sydney, so proud of her; maybe the only person in the world who had ever been proud of her. She saw the Sydney crowd, yelling out for their favourite songs, clapping, whistling. Just a well-mannered patter of applause from this lot. Maybe they wanted the old songs but were too, too modern to admit it.

Archie ordered a second glass of wine for her, which seemed happy enough to share her stomach with whatever was in there. She lit another cigarette. Ralph playing, Archie discussing a singing teacher he knew, his eyes on Jenny. He'd offered to pay for a few months' training with a singing teacher. She needed money, not lessons.

'I had eight years of lessons,' Monique said.

I had five years of pregnancy, Jenny told her wine glass. 'It shows,' she told Monique, and wondered if her years of pregnancies showed.

'Then I did two years at the Conservatorium.'

I did two years in Sydney free of pregnancy — between Jimmy and Cara Jeanette, Jenny explained to her wine glass.

She liked what that wine was doing, liked how it felt in her stomach, so she sipped more, drew on her cigarette and wished she was at Wilma's playing cards. The card players weren't fake. They were who they were. Wilma had been five months pregnant with Micky when Joe Fogarty married her and she didn't mind who knew it. She was a Catholic, and she'd had one of Veronica's abortions. Now she wouldn't let Joe come near her unless he used a rubber.

'I've warned him that if he gets me up the duff, I'll get rid of it again,' she'd said.

Up the duff. A bun in the oven. In Woody Creek, women had 'fallen in', or were 'in the family way'. Same women; different words for different worlds. None of them got pregnant. Cows got in calf, goats got in kid, dogs got in pup . . .

Women didn't drink wine in Woody Creek. Jenny ordered another and reached into her bag for a cigarette. Monique eyed her bag, eyebrows raised — at its age, or its worn shoulder strap? The strap, replaced in Sydney, had never matched; now, worn ragged, it was a better match for the bag. So what? It looked how she felt: a little worn on the outside, tattered on the inside, soiled by too much handling.

Like Granny's house too, that handbag. She could put her hand on anything. To prove it, she put her hand on a lipstick, on her endowment book . . . what the hell was that? She withdrew a new packet of sewing machine needles bought months ago. Thought she'd left them on the shop's counter. She needed machine needles. Hoped tomorrow she'd remember they were in there. Found her smokes, and a choice of two boxes of matches.

Monique didn't smoke. She had respect for her trained vocal cords. Her husband smoked. He didn't need vocal cords, only his fingers. Jenny had no respect for her fingers or vocal cords or her head tonight. She drank half of her wine in a gulp.

That's what she'd do. Spent the next three weeks drunk. Laurie had given her wine. It numbed the brain. She'd get drunk and sleep with Ray, keep him happy for three more weeks.

Laurie had always been happy. He'd been happy when she'd unwrapped that handbag. He'd been happy when she'd noticed he'd filled it with stolen money.

Hadn't known much at fifteen. Hadn't known they made handbags out of snake's skin either. It must have had a tough hide. You needed a tough hide to be a dirt slider in this world — though it hadn't done the snake a lot of good, had it. The hunters had still got it, skinned it, hung its skin out to dry.

Her hand, still searching, withdrew a crumpled shopping list. *Vinegar, Baking powder, Cornflour.* Which just went to show how often she cleaned out that bag. She'd bought baking powder months ago, months and months ago.

The men were discussing America. Itchy-foot had lived there for a time. Itchy-foot had lived everywhere.

'I spent some time at an asylum,' he said.

Inmate? Jenny thought, and peered again between the palm fronds, allowing her mind to wander far away.

What a ridiculous life I've led. What the hell is Jenny Morrison doing in this place?

Who is Jenny Morrison?

And what the hell are they talking about?

'He went in behind the eyes,' Archie said. 'The skull is quite thin at that point.'

Did any of his convoluted stories have a point?

'The eyeball was pushed to the side, a few taps of the hammer and it was over in minutes. I was lucky enough to watch a few of his operations.'

She frowned and met his eyes, her eyes, though her own would look numb tonight. She felt numb, and numb was good.

'The asylums were full of shell-shocked boys and there was little anyone was doing for them. He offered a solution.'

'What was his success rate?' Ralph asked.

'A third showed improvement. There were deaths, of course.'

'As one would expect,' Jenny said, very carefully. She put her hand on a stub of pencil. Wrote *Lobotomy* beside *Vinegar, Baking powder, Cornflour.* She needed one of those badly. *I am lost,* she wrote.

A half-page, ripped from an exercise book, crumpled, soiled by months in the bottom of a handbag, forces a pencil stub to be brief.

Lost in the chill depths of his eyes,
Captivated by his eloquence,
I listen.

Monologue
of self-appreciation,
Monotonous hum

of words
unheard.
I nod.

My gaze, it hovers somewhere
north of eye but south of brow.
Unmoving now,
I nod, politely.

Attentive puppet, his voice controls my strings
while my own thoughts compete
in chaos of race-meet
around the circuit of my mind
where streams of lost and wandering dreams
ride dodgem cars that grind and grate,
while I nod, and nod,
and I self-negate.

And he fills the still receptacle he sees,
as empty shells long left behind he's filled
throughout his years.

Vibration in his throat,
old cat in silken coat,
soft fur,
gentle purr,
a hidden claw?

His face in profile, darkening
against the lesser dark
of open door.

Hovering now, a floating thing.
The room, retreating.

Table where . . .
. . . where the chair.
As I regulate my breathing to that deep, that droning hum,
and I grow numb,
become,
not yet begun.

Regression to the place before the being,
retreat into a greedy sack,
unwilling to expel
and to set free
the me
I yet may be.

Refused exit,
I watch myself decay,
while the walls of a womb shed wasted cells
and cleansed again, its tissues wait
to yet create . . .

'Jennifer?' His hand was on her arm.

She was here to sing, though not quite here. She crumpled the paper, stuffed it into her handbag, dropped the pencil in and stood, or didn't quite stand, or not on her initial attempt.

'Are you quite well?'

'You're the doctor,' she said.

She sang two more songs then left while Itchy-foot was up there singing; left without her money.

Always next week, and the week after that, and the week after that. The calendar was full of weeks, and she was drunk.

THEN THE SKY FELL IN

*S*eptember near gone. The kids back at school today. Spring-time — or the blossom trees thought it was spring. This morning, the path Jenny walked was strewn with wet petal confetti, and before she reached Veronica's street a fine rain was falling again. Cold rain, blown in from the South Pole. The map, hurriedly drawn with pen and ink on the rear of an envelope addressed to Mrs Fogarty, was wet, its ink bleeding.

Veronica had been home for two weeks. Wilma had put Jenny's case to her over a hand of cards, then told her about the pantomime, showed her a flyer, a photograph of the cast on it, and Jenny's stage name: *Jennifer Morrison.*

Jenny's kids had been given free seats at every matinee. Wilma and her troop sat with them at two sessions. Carol and her husband drove Miss Flowers to the Saturday night performance, the hall crowded that night. Like one of Miss Rose's school concerts.

She could have had it done before the pantomime. Maybe she should have. Scared something might go wrong, that she'd be denied her days of magic, denied her line in the newspaper: *Jennifer Morrison's voice carried an otherwise unspectacular performance . . .*

Wondered if Granny would see it, if someone up there would

see it. Barely a line, near the rear of the paper. Probably not. Probably a hundred Jennifer Morrisons in Melbourne, and she was Jennifer King now.

She found Veronica's house, one in a row of small narrow houses; found Veronica standing on the veranda watching for her. No time to waste this morning. She had to be at work by ten thirty.

'How far along are you, kiddo?' she asked, taking Jenny's coat, scarf, both damp.

'I missed in late July.'

'You can't keep doing this, you know.'

'I know. I'm going to leave but I need enough money behind me when I do.'

Narrow staircase; Jenny followed her saviour up to what must have been her doctor chap's surgery. Was it murder like the newspapers said; like Granny said? At what stage did it become murder? It was no longer an overdue period. She felt bloated with it this time, her breasts felt sore with it. She was vomiting her heart out morning, noon and night with it, had lost a ton of weight.

Getting rid of this one had nothing to do with babies. This time it was all about Ray. He'd put on such a shy, pleasant face in Woody Creek when he'd been the visitor. He'd worn that face for a month or two after she'd married him. You can't wear a visitor's face when you live with a person, sleep with a person. She didn't like the man behind the mask.

He hadn't got what he'd thought he was getting either. He'd wanted her, not someone he had to share with three kids. Should have married a girl fresh from the schoolroom, who had no life apart from him, who might willingly spend her life feeling her way around whoever was inside him. She wasn't that girl. She'd had a life, and, with luck, might yet carve out the life she'd dreamt of living as a kid.

Couldn't have done it without him. Would have still been in Woody Creek, old dames looking down their noses at her, the Hoopers still threatening to take Jimmy. Down here, there was hope. But not with him. He hated Georgie. She'd always kept her distance from him — a better judge of character than her mother. Jimmy used to follow him around at weekends; he'd loved the motorbike. Not any more. He and Georgie disappeared when they heard the bike coming.

'What do you weigh, kiddo?'

'Everything is loose on me except my bras. I haven't stopped running since August.'

He probably knew she was pregnant. He hadn't asked. That was too personal for him.

And it was done, and she felt worse for it, but she'd feel better soon. Vroni phoned for a taxi. She made a cup of tea while they were waiting, had a smoke, then wrote her phone number on Jenny's palm.

'Closed fist, kiddo. Memorise it, then wash it off. If you need me, call.' Taxi tooting out front, coats on. 'Don't panic if the bleeding is heavier than last time. You were further gone with this one.'

'I won't.'

'I'll get the driver to drop me off at work, then he can take you home.'

'Bless you, Vroni.'

'You're welcome, kiddo. Keep your feet up tomorrow.'

Vroni paid her share of the taxi fare and then some. Jenny told the driver to drop her in the city, out the front of Coles. She went to the cafeteria, chose a table close to the ladies' room. It had happened fast the last time. She expected the same this time; wanted it to happen before she went home.

Always people about in the city. Wind and rain didn't keep them indoors. It hadn't kept her indoors. At any given time, enough Melbourne people had to be somewhere. She watched them come and go that day, mothers with daughters, sisters with sisters. She sat alone, sipping black tea and picking at a toasted cheese sandwich. Always loved toasted cheese sandwiches. Sometimes they tasted like Norman's fried sandwiches. Not today.

She sat for two hours and nothing happened. Absolutely nothing. She sat until people started staring, so she walked over to Myer's and sat in their cafeteria until Billy-Bob's watch told her it was close to three. Had to go home. Not home. She had to collect her kids from school. And it would probably happen on the tram.

It didn't. It didn't happen when she walked to the school, when she stood with Gwyneth's mother discussing the awful wind. She repeated identical words to Billy's mother. Just a normal day.

She wasn't feeling normal. The pains were starting. She leaned against the school fence, willing those kids out and the bleeding to stay in.

Jimmy too slow in coming today. Jimmy's best friend was Billy, and they had a lot to say to each other.

'Would you like to bring Jimmy around to play on Saturday?' Billy's mother said.

'He'd love that.'

Had to get away. And stop halfway up their street, grit her teeth, ride the pain and pray it didn't come away. It didn't.

Peeled pumpkin between agonising pains, peeled potatoes, fried sausages for the kids and steak for him and watched the clock. Eight hours since it had been done. She took two Bex tablets when she heard his bike. Served the meal, didn't serve herself. Went down to the lav.

Just pains. Just agony. She sat until Geoff came out to knock on the door. Had to vacate her seat and go inside.

Told the kids to get ready for bed at seven. Margot wasn't sleepy.

Couldn't fight her tonight. She lit a cigarette and went outside.

The tablets had done nothing to dull the pain. It was worse than having a baby. Fear that something had gone wrong multiplied each cramp. She walked the bricked path, walked out to the gate, wanting to call Veronica, just to talk to her, to have her say it was normal. She needed to know it was normal.

Walked and smoked and thought of Granny. She'd encouraged her to walk when Georgie was coming. Walked back inside. Two kids in bed. Margot playing Patience at the table, Ray flipping the pages of a newspaper. Waiting for her to read it to him? Not tonight.

Swept up Margot's cards and slid them into their packet. Margot went to bed *ahzeeing*. He went to the bathroom, and she boiled water to wash the dishes. She was standing at the sink when it started happening. She made it as far as the glass door, then it was like a rush of life leaving her and she was on her knees, her face pressed to cold glass.

He came with his towel from the bathroom and saw her crouched there, saw the blood, and called Flora to deal with it.

'Jenny's haemorrhaging,' Flora yelled. 'Get the car out, Geoff.'

Don't panic if there's heavy bleeding, Veronica had warned. *Don't go running to a hospital if there's heavy bleeding.*

Margot standing in the doorway, grinding her teeth at the bloodbath.

'Get her into bed! I'm all right. Get me a towel, Ray, and go away,' said Jenny.

He tossed her the towel he'd used in the bathroom and went away.

'I'm all right, Flora.'

'You're not all right. You're haemorrhaging,' Flora said. 'Bring a blanket, Ray.'

She tried to get up, to argue. Couldn't get her feet beneath her. Submerged by pain or fear or pills, and where did heavy bleeding stop and haemorrhaging begin? She didn't want to go to the hospital. Didn't want to bleed to death either. Granny said she'd almost bled to death when Archie had aborted her baby.

Fear of dying overrode fear of the hospital. She stopped arguing. They wrapped her in a blanket; Ray carried her out to Geoff's car. He drove them to the closest hospital, the Alfred, where a nursing sister diagnosed a miscarriage.

'Is it your first, Mr King?'

Maybe Ray didn't understand miscarriage. Geoff understood. 'She's got three,' he said.

They hurried her away. They strung her up by her legs like a cow in a butcher's shop. They peered into her, prodded her, lights blazing, sisters bustling. Then the breathing in of chloroform and that dragging away from consciousness.

I'm sorry, Granny.

Is it your first, Mr King?

I'm sorry, Granny.

Is it your first, Mr King?

Woke up in a bed, woke up vomiting in a world of punishing white light, and she wanted the dark back. Hands handling her like a butcher handles a dead cow's carcass.

Is it your first, Mr King?

Slept again, dreamed mad dreams of pantomimes and the factory, of Lila and Norma, dwarves, standing around a giant inspection table, packing the pressed bodies of babies into cardboard cartons. Came to her senses in a panic, and rose up from her pillows, knowing where she was, or where she wasn't. Remembered the hospital, remembered Ray and Geoff Parker, remembered Veronica. Didn't know the time. They'd taken Billy-Bob's watch. Didn't know if she'd been in that bed for a day, a week, or a month, or who was feeding her kids.

A nurse told her the time. She found her watch in the tin locker drawer. It was dead. The nurse resuscitated it, strapped it on, and Jenny knew it was ten o'clock. Morning or night, she didn't know.

'My kids?'

'Fast asleep, Mrs King.'

Night-time.

She slept deeply, for an hour or a day. They woke her to drink tea, to eat a hospital biscuit, and later they woke her with a sandwich.

Her watch needed winding.

Then he came, her shoes and clothing stuffed into a string bag. For an instant she was relieved to see him, until she saw his eyes, until she saw the bulging policeman at his side.

They knew.

THE FALLOUT

Jenny slid lower in her hospital bed. She couldn't look at Ray, couldn't look at the policeman who leaned over her demanding the abortionist's name. She turned to a young doctor, her eyes pleading with him to pull the bedcovers over her head and pronounce her dead.

'We need his name, Mrs King,' the policeman said. 'What was his name?'

How did they know? Did they know?

Ray's eyes knew. They hated her.

'You were lucky. Other women have not been so lucky,' the policeman said.

Wanted him to put her in jail. Wanted to be anywhere away from Ray's eyes.

'We need an address and his name, Mrs King.'

Wished she'd never heard of Mrs King. Wish she'd never heard of Raymond King, never heard of Armadale — and they could stick red-hot needles beneath her fingernails and she wouldn't give them her saviour's name.

'The abortionist's name, Mrs King.'

He was like a stuck record. She had to turn it off, but if she said anything then she was admitting that she'd had an abortion.

They knew. Policemen wouldn't waste their time on every woman who'd had a miscarriage. Somehow they knew.

'Myrtle,' she said.

Didn't know why she'd said that. It came out, that's all. Myrtle had taken Cara Jeanette. It was an abortion without being an abortion. Had to . . . had to think before she answered. Couldn't think.

'We need more than her Christian name.'

'Norris. It was Norris.'

May as well be hung for a sheep as a lamb, Granny used to say. Sydney was a long way away.

And he wanted her address.

'I don't know.'

'Where did the procedure take place, Mrs King?'

'Nowhere. At the house.'

'Where is the house?'

'I telephoned her. She came to . . . to Armadale. She did it in the bedroom.'

The first time, Veronica had done it in Wilma's bedroom. It had been over and done with in less than three hours, no repercussions.

'The phone number.'

'I can't remember it.'

She could remember Veronica's. She could still see those numbers written on her hand. Had tried to wash them off with spit and her handkerchief. Handkerchief in her handbag.

'It's in my bag.'

Safe to say that. Her handbag was at home. Sewing money in it, singing money from last Friday in it, her bankbook. She had to get home, get it, get the kids, get what was in her cake tin and go.

Where were the kids? Had the police taken them away? Women who had abortions were unfit mothers.

'Where are my kids?' Scared for them. Scared of Ray's eyes. Scared of the policeman. 'Who's got my kids?'

'Who gave you the phone number, Mrs King?'

If she invented someone, they'd want to know where she lived. This wasn't a game she was playing with Archie Foote, fairytale lies of singing in Sydney, of sharing a house with her friend. If she lied to a policeman, it was true lies, and they multiplied into worse lies. And they'd probably put her kids in a home, and she'd get five years' jail, and her kids wouldn't know her by the time she got out, and they wouldn't want to know her, and Vern would get Jimmy. She turned her face to the pillow and bawled for the hopelessness of life, and because Granny wouldn't want to know her either, and . . . and because she'd end up on the streets like Amber, or in a madhouse like her.

'Who gave you the phone number?'

'Please go away!'

'We need names, Mrs King.'

'A woman in Coles cafeteria gave it to me.'

Always a crowd in there. She'd shared tables in there. She'd discussed her kids with strangers. It could have been true.

'Her name?'

'I didn't ask her name!'

He wanted a description and, defeated, she gave him what he wanted. She described Margaret Hooper, which was easier than making up a description she'd probably forget — and Margaret deserved it anyway. She'd lied about Jim being dead. They'd all lied about him being dead.

'Frizzy platinum-blonde hair, short, plump, glassy blue eyes.'

He asked for a description of Myrtle Norris, the abortionist, and it seemed rational to describe Lorna.

Nothing was rational. The look on Ray's face wasn't rational. He was rigid, frigid, his innocent lamb's eyes burning like the devil's.

'You'll have every other bastard's kids but mine, you she-dog slut,' he said.

And not a stutter, not the hint of a stutter. This wasn't Ray. Ray stuttered. None of this was real. She was dreaming it. Wanted to wake up.

And he wanted her to wake up. He flung the string bag of clothing at her head. Her shoes were in it. They hurt.

Got rid of the policeman though. He and an orderly marched Ray from the ward while she cowered in the bed, finally knowing the man who hid behind the stutter, and knowing exactly what he thought of her.

Is it your first, Mr King?

It hadn't been his first. She'd got rid of his first too. Hadn't thought about it . . . them as babies, just blood. Maybe the last one was threads of baby.

How had they known? Had she screamed it while fighting her way free of the chloroform? Had Veronica left something inside her?

Hadn't thought about what might happen if something went wrong; hadn't thought about much other than getting it out of her. It was out, and she wanted to die, wanted the doctor to put her to sleep with an overdose of chloroform before the policeman came back.

'Where are my kids?'

The doctor didn't know. And the policeman didn't come back. She found out why when a nursing sister came to help her dress. She was being discharged.

'Am I going to jail?'

'You're the victim, Mrs King. They're not after the victims.'

They weren't sending her home? Not with him. He'd murder her.

'Do you know who's got my kids?'

The nurse didn't know.

And Ray hadn't waited. Maybe they'd put him in jail. She stood at the hospital entrance looking towards Armadale. She had to go back there, get her money, and find out who had her kids. Probably with Flora. She'd hate her too. She wanted more kids and couldn't get pregnant. Everyone wanted what they couldn't have.

Jenny wanted sixpence for the tram. She had a ton of money at home, plenty in the bank, and not sixpence in her pocket for a tram fare. Didn't have a pocket. Didn't have the strength to walk to the tram stop even if she'd had sixpence.

Sat on the hospital step catching tears with her fingers, until a middle-aged bloke sat beside her and offered his well-ironed handkerchief and his packet of cigarettes.

'Lost someone have you, love?'

Shook her head.

'It can't be as bad as all that,' he said.

It was worse than all that. She'd finished everything this time. Everything.

She smoked his cigarette and a taxi arrived. The bloke was waiting for it. He got in, then, his head out the window, called to her, 'Which way is home, love?'

'Armadale.'

He gave her a lift to her corner, patted her shoulder when she slid out. 'Take care of yourself,' he said.

Gone then, never to be seen again. Wondered if he had a wife; if he loved his wife, or if he looked at her with hatred in his eyes.

She'd walked that block and a half to Ray's house a hundred times. It had been as nothing. She walked it slowly that Wednesday, stopping to rest, to study shrubs not worthy of study, but she got there.

His motorbike was parked against the veranda. She walked around to the back door. It was open. And her kids ran to her, all three of them, and she held them to her, feeling a rush of love for and from those massed little bodies. Held them to her until he came dancing into the sleep-out like Granny's mad rooster.

The kids ran out the door. With no strength to run, Jenny backed away, backed away to Granny's old tin trunk, where she sat, watching the mad rooster's dance.

'It w-wasn't mine,' he said. 'You've been m-making m-m-money on your b-back, you sh-she-dog slut.'

She could absorb punishment, had learnt the art early. She sat watching the dance, waiting for it to end.

He wasn't a man of many words. He ran dry. The kids came back when they heard the bike roar into life. Quiet kids, clustering around her, knowing something was wrong but afraid to ask.

'It's all right,' she said. 'We'll go.'

'Where?' Jimmy asked.

God knows.

'When?' Georgie asked.

'I'll think about where tomorrow.'

She made a cup of tea. Georgie was frying pancakes when Flora opened the passage door. She didn't come in.

'I had the police here today,' she said.

'I'm sorry.'

'No woman came here that day. You went out with the kids and you didn't come back until school came out.'

Jenny didn't deny the accusation. 'I'm sorry,' she said.

Didn't eat a pancake. Had no strength to wash the dishes. She left them on the sink and crawled into the kids' bed, needing its comfort that night, needing the comfort of her kids. A crowded bed, but she slept, surrounded by warm little bodies.

And woke to him leaning over the bed, and the smell of drink, the smell of his sweat.

'Please don't start on me again,' she said.

'S-start on you, you she-dog s-slut? The whole b-bloody town s-started on you.'

'Get out of my kids' room with your dirty mouth.'

'You g-got rid of it because it w-w-w-wasn't mine, you slut.'

Jimmy awake and clinging to her, Georgie out of the bed.

'We're leaving in the morning. Now get out. You're scaring my kids.'

He slammed the door, slammed his own; she slid from the bed and, on bare feet, crept out to the kitchen. She'd leave before he woke.

Then what?

Get a hotel room until she felt strong enough, felt capable of making the right decision. Had to make the right decision this time. Had made too many that were wrong.

Had to get her handbag. It was in his room. Should have got it instead of sleeping. She looked for his cigarettes in the dark. There was always a packet around somewhere. Not tonight. She had cigarettes in her handbag. Sat watching his door, giving him time to fall asleep. It felt like midnight or later. The city grew silent in the early hours, its hum of life stilled.

Hungry, and no milk in the fridge, no bread in the tin. A few sultanas in a jar. She ate them, made a cup of tea and drank it black.

Granny used to say she had the recoil of a rubber band. She was recoiling. She had a plan. Get her bag, get the kids up before daylight and get out, and who cared to where. Ride trams all day if they felt like it. Ride a tram to the end of some line and get a hotel room there. Her case was in the sleep-out. Her clothes were out there. She'd take what she and the kids could carry.

Stood and crept to his door, listening to the in and out of his snore, the choking inhalation, the moaning exhalation. He was dead to the world. Slowly she opened his door, just a little, just enough for her reaching hand to locate the bag's strap. She unlooped it, withdrew it and closed the door silently. Back through the kids' room then, through to the sleep-out, where she turned on the light and opened her handbag.

No cigarettes. She'd had half a packet left. No red purse. It had last Friday's jazz club money in it. She felt the pocket where her bankbook lived, found her endowment book but no bankbook. It had to be there. She emptied her bag onto the camp bed, shook it. Lipstick, pencil, notepad, junk and fluff, old shopping list, but not a threepenny bit.

He didn't want her to leave in the morning. He wanted to keep her here to punish her.

That book and purse had to be somewhere. They'd be in his room. She wasn't going in there, not tonight.

In the bags on his bike maybe?

She crept outside and up to the front of the house, and in the dark searched the leather saddlebags, the little tool bag. No bankbook. No purse.

They'd be in his bedroom. She'd have to wait until he went to work. He didn't like missing work. Wait, and hope he didn't take them with him.

She slept the last of the night on the camp stretcher. The kids woke her at eight. She hadn't heard Ray leave, but he was gone and the kids wanted to go to school. Jenny was home, life was back to normal, or it would be once they were back at school.

No bread to cut school lunches. She spread Weet-Bix with jam; they liked that. She walked them out to the gate, watched them to the corner, was still leaning on the gate when Flora returned from walking Lois to the Catholic school. She barely acknowledged Jenny's 'Good morning'.

Here we go again.

No time this morning to worry about Flora; she had to find her bankbook and purse.

She emptied Ray's drawers, his wardrobe, went through the pockets of his grey suit, his trousers, his jacket. She stood on a chair to look on top of the wardrobe, she looked beneath it, pulled his mattress from the bed, moved his dressing table. No bankbook, no red purse.

Knew they wouldn't be in the kitchen, but she searched it, and felt like Amber, who had periodically turned rooms upside down and shaken them. She progressed to the kids' room, then the sleepout. Every drawer in the house was emptied, every cupboard. She emptied the rubbish tin, poked with a stick through ash in the incinerator, raked out the copper's firebox, searched her garden, wondering if he'd buried them, or burnt then buried them.

She was on her knees, peering beneath the veranda, when the kids came home. They got down on their knees to search with her. They found a tennis ball, found Jimmy's wind-up monkey, wondered who had hidden it there. Its works had gone rusty. It wouldn't play the drums.

Dinner that night was boiled macaroni served with vegetables, cheese and a mixture of tomato sauce and chutney. Ray didn't come home. And something in the fridge stank. Chops there since Saturday morning were turning green; steak was threatening to do the same. She tossed the chops out and made a stew from the steak.

A WONDERFUL LIFE

*S*unday, washing day. Ray hadn't been home since the night he'd taken her purse — shouting himself a hotel room with her earnings? She didn't know where he'd gone, didn't care, just as long as he stayed there. She was hanging a multitude of little socks on the clothes line when Flora walked by.

'Still cool enough,' Jenny said.

Flora looked the other way and didn't reply. It hurt; it hurt enough to drop both sock and peg to the dirt.

She was hanging Ray's work trousers when Lois came out to show Jimmy her picture from church. Flora came at a run to drag her away from pollution. That hurt more. What she'd done was now affecting Jimmy and he didn't understand.

Pancakes for lunch. No complaint from the kids. They loved pancakes, spoke of eating pancakes with lemons and sugar like they'd had at Granny's house. No lemons down here, and little sugar. The canister was empty, sugar bowl almost empty. There was enough stew for the evening meal, or there was until he came in for a change of clothes and found their stew. He heated it up and looked for bread to toast.

'No bread,' Jenny reported.

He ignored her and ate the stew from the saucepan.

'Give me my bankbook and we'll leave. It will be faster than starving us out, Ray.'

'G-get your s-s-singing p-p-pimp to feed your k-kids,' he said and pitched the saucepan at the sink. One of Amber's saucepans. He dented its lip.

Two kids skedaddled. Margot was playing Patience. She had the reading skills of a five year old, but those stubby little hands handled playing cards like a thirty-year-old woman.

'T-tell your m-mother she's a she-she-dog slut,' he said.

Too many S's in the sentence for Margot. She left her game on the table and followed the other kids. He changed his shirt and rode away — stayed away.

Monday, the kids took pancake sandwiches in their lunch bags. Jenny saw them off then came inside and dressed for the city, hoping she'd strike a decent tram conductor. She had to get to the bank and report her lost book. She was locking the glass door when a couple of police officers came around the corner of the veranda, a male and a female. She had to unlock the door, had to take them inside. Had to stick to her hospital lie.

The female did the talking. She told Jenny that Mrs Parker had stated that she'd seen her leave the house before nine and not seen her return until after three thirty on the day of the abortion.

'I don't know if she was out or in,' Jenny said. 'I don't know if she's in today.'

Not a sound issued from the west side. The wireless had been playing while she'd dressed. Not playing now. Not a footstep, the rattle of a dish. Flora would have seen the police coming. She was probably standing with her ear to the passage door — only ever unlocked between six and eight on bathroom nights now. They'd gone the full circle, from enemy to almost friend, back to enemy.

Jenny's reply had silenced her visitors. Mrs Parker was at home; minutes ago, she'd directed them to the eastern door. They listened for fifteen seconds, then asked if they might sit, asked her to sit.

She sat, and the female of the duo asked what implements the abortionist had used.

'I don't know.'

That was the truth. She'd closed her eyes, just wanting done whatever had to be done. The first time, at Wilma's, she'd been watching for Veronica to arrive, had seen her slide from her chap's car out the front of Wilma's house, and shuddered at the small brown case she carried, afraid of what may have been inside it.

'She brought a case about the size of a school case. I didn't see what she had inside it.' The truth was easier. 'A man dropped her off and picked her up.'

'Can you describe the driver, his vehicle?'

Veronica's chap drove a maroon car, low-slung, classy, but why not keep it all in the one family? Vern Hooper had driven a dark green Ford before the war. She described the old Ford but stilled her imagination before describing the driver.

The male policeman was eyeing her. He was one of the dominant bulls of the human race. Ray was one of them gone wrong. Vern Hooper was the king of the bulls. They had a way of looking at women, of seeing them as service centres, easy on the eyes, vital for breeding stock, but not quite human. Vern had gone through three wives. According to Granny, Lorna's mother had been dead when they'd cut her baby out. Jim had been cut from his mother a month early and she'd never got over it. It was a woman's lot to die pushing out the next generation. Plenty more where they'd come from.

She could have died with Jimmy's head stuck halfway out. Little Lenny Hall had ridden in to get someone with the car to take her to the hospital. He'd had Vern Hooper's door slammed in his face. Maisy had got her down to the hospital. Doctor Frazer had given her chloroform and dragged Jimmy out.

She'd told Ray about Jimmy's birth. She'd told him before she married him, and he'd listened to her, told her he wanted her, not kids. How many times had she told him she was never having another baby? Four? Five? Six times, the last after she'd gone to the chemist's shop and bought him two packets of rubbers, knowing that day that he was too embarrassed to go in there and stutter his needs. He'd never opened them. Had never discussed why he wouldn't open them. A nod towards the bedroom was as close as Ray had come to discussing sex.

The female policewoman was discussing sex across the kitchen table — or speaking about a fourteen-year-old girl who had died as a result of sex, though it wasn't the sex that had killed her; it was the abortionist.

No ring on the female cop's finger. Was she a cop because she cared about fourteen-year-old girls, or was she making her single-handed attack on the dominant bulls' paddock?

Hoped she was.

Jenny picked up the framed photograph of her and Jim and ten-month-old Jimmy. Jim had been big enough to be a bull. Born with the wrong mindset. Gentle Jim. Loved his face, his eyes, his big hands. Loved his mind. She glanced towards the kids' bedroom and considered rising and returning the photo to the window-sill. Jimmy had brought his daddy out this morning so he could watch them eating their funny breakfast — one and a half Weet-Bix spread with jam. She'd eaten the leftover half, the last of the Weet-Bix.

In photographs, people stayed forever young, forever happy. Jim's eyes still smiled at her, he still flashed his big teeth. Fat little Jimmy showing his front teeth, not so big as his daddy's. She looked like a kid in that photo — had been a kid. Eighteen when she'd gone up to Sydney, a kid with a kid and two more at home. Strange studying her own eyes, seeing things in them and not knowing what she was seeing; eighteen-year-old Jenny calling the twenty-three year old a bloody fool —

'Mrs King?'

Bull cop's eyes appreciating her; female eyeing her, waiting for a reply. Jenny hadn't heard the question so she asked her own.

'Was she raped? The fourteen-year-old girl who died?'

Shouldn't have said 'raped', should have asked if she'd been taken advantage of. Bet a bull male had used that term first — after he'd taken full advantage. They weren't in her kitchen to discuss the how, the why, the when, but the where. They didn't care if that fourteen-year-old kid had been held down on a tombstone and split in half by two bulls who had taken full advantage.

She turned the photograph face down and stood. 'If hospitals were allowed to do abortions, she wouldn't have died, would she? It should be written into the law that fourteen-year-old kids are not allowed to have babies.'

Wrong reply, but it got them back to the script. The female gave her a spiel about the sanctity of a life newly formed; how abortionists and those who seek their criminal services are not only violating the laws of the country but committing a sin against heaven. She didn't read it from a pamphlet, but the depth of feeling she put into her spiel suggested she'd learnt it by rote from the abortion witch-hunt manual.

'God has got no more interest in pregnant women than he's got in pregnant cows.'

It came out uncensored, out of the mouth of another fourteen-year-old kid, still cowering somewhere inside Jenny, or maybe not cowering today.

And why should she cower? That kid had done nothing wrong. She'd come third in a radio talent quest, had won a five-pound note; she'd sat for a scholarship that would have got her out of Woody Creek, and she'd got it too. She could have been . . .

The five-pound note! That's what eighteen-year-old Jenny's eyes had been trying to tell her! She was sitting on a five-pound note.

Jenny snatched the photograph and stood. How had she forgotten that? There was something very definitely wrong with her head. She'd never spent that talent-quest money. It had come from the time before her dreams had been ripped out of her. She couldn't spend it. Years ago, before she'd come home from Sydney, she'd hidden it behind that photograph, when Jim, like her old life, had been dead. And he wasn't dead; and that singing kid inside her wasn't dead either.

Her visitors weren't done with her yet. They asked her to sit down. They wanted her to describe Myrtle Norris the abortionist.

She didn't sit, but stood, the photograph held to her breast, and with great pleasure described Lorna Hooper. 'At least six foot, with ears to match her height. She wears her dark hair in a bun. Narrow hawk-beak nose, fingernails like a hawk's talons, lisle stockings, lace-up shoes, old maid's black dress . . .'

What if Lorna Hooper was walking down a city street and the police recognised her by that description? What if they marched her off to prison in handcuffs?

Jenny turned quickly to the dresser to hide the twitch of her lips, and, to prove she had a better reason, opened her three cupboard doors. Not a lot in them apart from Amber's pots and basins, her spices and empty canisters.

'I'm not twenty-four yet,' she said. 'I've got three school-age kids and nothing in the house to feed them when they come home.'

She reached for the tea canister, removed its lid and placed it upside down on the table; offered the sugar canister, also upside down and lidless. They weren't interested in Amber's empty canisters, so she opened the refrigerator.

The female asked her again to sit, and when she didn't, they stood, maybe to arrest her. Jenny offered her dripping bowl.

'If I can't feed three kids, tell me how I'm expected to feed four, six, eight? I'm young enough to have twelve more.'

Neither one wanted the dripping bowl. She returned it to the fridge and closed the door.

'I've still got an inch of flour in my tin. My kids took pancake sandwiches for lunch today.'

'There are charities, Mrs King —'

'I don't sing alms for the poor on street corners.'

The male wanted the abortionist's phone number. Her hand-bag was on the table. She opened it, upended it. Lipstick rolled to the floor. She picked it up.

'When I told my husband I was taking my kids home, he took my money and bankbook so I couldn't. The abortionist's phone number was in my bankbook.'

Or Archie Foote's phone number was. Should have phoned him.

Look, no pennies.

She had a five pound-note though. She was getting out of this place as soon as the kids came home from school, taking what she could carry.

They wanted to know where her husband was employed. She told them, and when they were done with searching her handbag, they left, and she locked the door, closed the curtains, and with the help of a knife removed the back from the photograph. The envelope was there, and the note.

Just holding it, just smelling it, brought back memory of that night. She could feel the weight of the frock she'd worn, so little of it, but heavy, silky, against her skin. Fourteen-year-old Jennifer Morrison, the golden girl with the golden voice. That's how the master of ceremonies had introduced her. She'd felt golden that night, standing up there clad in Juliana Conti's gold crepe frock, in Juliana's shoes. Hadn't known who the dress had belonged to then — or maybe some primitive section of her brain had. She'd felt so tall, so powerful. And that bank note meant more to her than what it would buy. It was like holding hope in her hand — and she wasn't going to give that hope into a stranger's hands to soil.

Had to. It meant she could get the kids away from here tonight. She slid it into the patched pocket of her handbag, slid her child endowment book in beside it. Then spun around on her chair to stare at the calendar. She hadn't bothered to collect her child endowment for months, not since June. Had no time; had no need to queue up with those desperate for the few bob incentive to populate. It was due on Tuesday week, and four months of the governmental incentive would be no pittance.

She kissed the five-pound note, and Jim's photograph while it was free from its glass, then placed photograph and talent-quest money back, safe. She'd go into the city, report her bankbook missing, and if they wouldn't give up her money, she'd wait for endowment day. She had vegetables, dripping, chutney, two-thirds of a jar of plum jam. If she stretched that flour, they'd manage.

The photograph back on the windowsill in the kids' room, she left the house. It took two trams to get her into town. The first conductor, a thirty-year-old woman, eager to flaunt her little power, didn't care if Jenny had lost her purse or not. She'd put her off the tram. The second conductor, a battle-scarred male of sixty-odd, winked at her and allowed her to ride without a ticket.

And the bank needed identification before they could issue her with a new book.

'I know to the penny what I've got in it. There's eighty-seven pounds, four shillings and sevenpence.'

They had no argument with the figure, but still needed identification. Jennifer Morrison Hooper had no identification on her, other than Mrs Jennifer King's endowment book. She had Jimmy's birth certificate at home: James Hooper Morrison; and her own birth and wedding certificates in the cake tin on top of her dresser. Or Charlie White — he was a justice of the peace. He'd write her a letter of identification.

On the tram home, she chose a seat beside a middle-aged woman with three wailing kids; the conductor didn't try to sell her a ticket; and when she stepped down from that tram, she knew she wasn't up to repeating that trip, not today.

Pulled two carrots, an onion, picked a bunch of silverbeet. Inside, she chose two big potatoes. The kids turned Amber's mincing machine's handle while Jenny fed it with vegetables. She had no egg to bind the mixture, but plenty of flavourings. They added a spoonful of chutney, a shake of curry, two shakes of ground ginger, salt and pepper, then a heaped tablespoon of flour. A fast fry in plenty of dripping, then into the oven to roast a while.

The kids wanted more. There were no more, and not much dripping left either.

He came while the dishes were being washed. He'd bought a loaf of bread, a bottle of milk and some sort of meat. It could have been sausages, or minced steak. Jenny unwrapped the newspaper parcel. Tripe. She rewrapped it.

He cooked it, wasted half of the milk on it, the kids standing big-eyed, watching the level of milk in that lone bottle drop. Jenny snatched it before he could waste the lot. She took it and the kids out to the veranda to share the last of it from the bottle.

Maybe he tasted his tripe. Most of it was in the saucepan when he rode away. It looked like glue and smelled worse. Even Margot, who would eat anything served up on a plate, turned her nose up. They buried it.

'I wish Granny sent some eggs to us,' Jimmy said.

'Me too, darlin'.'

'Can we have two eggs each when we go there?'

'You can have eggs every day, buckets of milk every day.'

'When?'

'Soon.'

Jenny wrote to Charlie White that night and posted her letter the following morning when she walked the kids to school, hoped it didn't get lost in shop mail, hoped Charlie picked up on its urgency.

Hoped someone would come to her door wanting a hem taken up, trouser cuffs let down. No one came. A day is slow in passing when the kids are at school; when your housemate snubs you if she runs into you on the way out of the lav.

Then Wednesday, and Wilma Fogarty knocked on her door.

Before the abortion, she'd popped in for a cup of tea every Wednesday while Flora was visiting her mother.

'Veronica told me to thank you for keeping her name out of it. She said she'll come around once things die down. How did Ray take it?'

Jenny shrugged.

'Men's memories are in their trousers, love. He'll come around.'

Didn't want him to come around. Wanted him to stay wherever he'd been staying.

'I hear that Flora is giving you a hard time.'

How had she heard? Carol spying over her fence? She hadn't been in to visit.

'I can't offer you a cup of tea,' Jenny said.

'You're wiping me because I go to church with her?'

'Because I've got no tea,' Jenny said.

They had a smoke and drank water. They had two smokes. Wilma may have stayed longer had she brought more cigarettes. She left at three with a bunch of silverbeet and two carrots. At four, Janice, her daughter, came around with a bit of tea, a cup of sugar, a bottle of milk, a few cups of flour and three cigarettes.

Charlie's letter came on Friday. *To whom it may concern. I have known the bearer of this document since birth . . .*

Good old Charlie. His half-page would satisfy the bank. Too late today though to run the gauntlet of tram conductors. Monday would be soon enough.

No sign of Ray or his meat on Saturday. They heard his bike on Sunday night, and went quickly to bed and stayed there until the bike left on Monday morning. He came in at six on Monday night with a loaf of bread and a bottle of milk. No tripe. No liver.

On Tuesday, Jenny lined up with two dozen women as desperate as she for the governmental handout — all strangers, and a good few bellies advertising that they were doing what they were being paid to do, breeding up the next army. Not one face amongst them she recognised, or who recognised her; not a sneer out of one of them. Loved the anonymity of Melbourne, the thousand faces she didn't know. She loved the government that morning, loved Charlie White. By ten, his letter, plus the birth certificates and her marriage certificate, had convinced the bank manager she was who she claimed to be. They'd issue her with a new book in her married name. It would be posted to her.

'Why?'

'Bank policy.'

'I need the money today.'

'Bank policy.'

She'd already waited too long, but she had money to wait with now. She bought tea and a six-pound bag of flour, a large tin of powdered milk, four pounds of brown sugar, half a dozen eggs. She bought a pound block of lard from the butcher and half a pound of minced steak; a large loaf of bread and a few ounces of yeast from the baker. Fried the steak with vegetables and served the lot, then for sweets she mixed up a batter with just a smidgen of yeast and, when it doubled its size, deep-fried spoonfuls of it in pure white lard. During the depression, the Palmer kids had lived on dough-balls tossed in brown sugar and cinnamon. Jenny's kids pronounced them delicious.

She made bread that night and the kids sat up late, wanting to see one of Granny's loaves come out of their own oven. It smelled like Granny's bread, smelled better than it looked. They ate it for breakfast, slices of it dipped in egg and milk, then fried. For two mornings, they ate fried bread for breakfast, with the last of the plum jam.

Her new bankbook arrived in the mail the following Tuesday, alongside a letter from Granny. Jenny read it on the tram into town.

An English migrant family who had moved in with Tom Vevers had three kids down with something that looked a lot like polio to Granny. It was always around. Every few years there was an epidemic. It killed kids, and if it didn't kill them, it crippled them.

Elsie and Harry had a tribe who caught everything that was going. And she was taking her kids up there in the morning. Couldn't think about that, not right now.

Later, thirty pounds in her handbag, she went to Coles and bought a new purse, black, transferred her money into it, then took a tram down to Spencer Street station to check on the train time and the availability of seats to Woody Creek. When she'd left the house this morning, she'd planned to book and pay for the tickets, to book and pay for a hotel room for tonight — the train left early. She didn't book seats or hotel. Knew she couldn't take those kids anywhere near polio.

Her mind on other things, she was approaching the Swanston Street tram stop when she sighted the back of the abortionist she'd described to the police. Knew that head. Knew that long black skirt, the lisle stockings wrinkling around sparrow ankles, that long-legged, striding walk — like Jim's walk. Jenny stopped dead, her eyes searching the crowd for the dumpy little platinum blonde. See one of the Hooper sisters and you usually saw both. Lorna was with an elderly couple, a dumpy little dame and a lean English squire in his hunting gear.

Jenny stood in the middle of Swanston Street, forcing the crowd to walk around her, her mind dancing from Vern to polio, from polio to Ray, all three as bad as each other.

So she'd go somewhere else.

Where else?

Queensland. Joey.

What do you use for money when your bank account runs dry?

I had a plan. What did I do in my past life to deserve this? Survived my birth. Opened my mouth when I should have kept it shut.

She turned on her heel and walked back the way she'd come, walked with the crowd to the lights, crossed over with the crowd, no aim in mind, crazy thoughts in her head. Itchy-foot had a big empty house. She had plenty of pennies now. Give him a call.

Out of the frying pan into the fire; the ensuing results could be worse than dire . . .

Had to think straight. Had to think further than the immediate. Three laughing women walked by her in a hurry to get somewhere. She followed their laughter into a picture theatre, stood behind them at the ticket office. She had plenty of time, and she'd be better off the street if the Hoopers were on it. The theatre was showing *It's a Wonderful Life*; James Stewart and Donna Reed starring in it. She'd read about it. It was supposed to be good. Not in the right frame of mind to appreciate it though; just a place to hide today, a place to sit and think and kill a bit of time.

Newsreel playing: prime minister, girls in bathing costumes, boats in the harbour, a male voice attempting to make it all so highly interesting. Just light and dark flashing before her eyes to Jenny, making no contact with her conscious mind — a mind too busy refereeing contests. Ray wrestling in there with Vern Hooper. Polio stepping in. Ray versus polio and Vern Hooper. It was no contest . . .

Charlie White — he had her address! Hilda, his daughter, would have it, and she was a worse gossip than Maisy — and a nasty bitch with it. That's why Lorna Hooper was down here! They had her address. Vern would be at her door when she got home. Or he'd already kidnapped Jimmy from the schoolyard! She had to go!

Then the picture started and it was a magical show. From the opening scene, it wiped her mind clean of Vern, polio and Ray.

She found herself relating to the James Stewart character, stuck in a tin-pot little town, spending his life wanting to break away and do something grand. Something always came up to stop him. He was ready to end it all in the river when an elderly angel, still working for his wings, gave him his wish and took back his insignificant life. The story was about how one insignificant life had changed the lives of many, had changed an entire town, maybe even the world.

While the credits played, Jenny considered her own impact on the world.

Had she not survived her birth, Amber may not have gone mad. Norman may have been alive. Sissy may have married Jim. Jim may not have joined the army. Laurie may still have been dodging the police. Granny may have married Vern Hooper. Myrtle wouldn't have had her baby. Ray could have married some girl who might have been pleased to spend her life pregnant and frying livers. The world would have been a better place.

Except there'd be no Georgie and Jimmy in it. The world may not have missed Jenny Morrison, but her kids were destined to leave their mark.

Not if I take them home and they get polio. Kids of their age are more vulnerable to it than older kids. I'll have to wait.

Only one place to wait.

She left the theatre with the crowd, squinting at her watch-face as she walked from semi-dark into natural light. Over two hours had disappeared. It never failed to amaze her how a good movie could swallow time and a bad one lengthened it.

As she slung her handbag's strap over her shoulder, it caught on her wedding ring. She felt its slide too late to save it. She looked at her feet, turned. A young chap had stopped its run with his shoe. He was looking for the owner.

'Thank you,' she said.

Shouldn't have thanked him, should have walked on fast. When it was in her hand, she knew she didn't want it and never had. Didn't slide it back onto her finger. Walked on towards the tram stop, looking at her naked finger, skinny, like the rest of her. Sick before the abortion, she'd lost a ton of weight since. The skirt she wore told her so, as did her sweater.

Poor worn old finger, its fingernail ragged. She had useless fingernails, flat, weak. A long ring finger, and his brand worn into it.

Branded first by Jim's ring. She glanced at her right hand, at an identical gold band. Only she knew the difference. And in the middle of Swanston Street, she worked the smaller band of gold over the knuckle of her right ring finger. It slid eagerly onto her left — and *Jen and Jim, 1942* was back where it belonged; secure there too, sized six years ago for a girl's slim finger.

A tram trundling by, not her tram. She crossed at the lights, gripping Ray's ring, punishing her palm with it for her stupidity. God works in mysterious ways, his wonders to perform, they say. The sign was on the corner, on a barred jeweller's door: *Turn your unwanted gold into cash.*

She had unwanted gold.

The jeweller bought the ring. Jenny didn't know, nor care, if he was robbing her blind or paying a fair price for it. Just took what he offered and ran to catch her tram.

Ray had promised to look after her kids, so let him feed them — and put a roof over their heads — for a week or two more.

WEAR AND TEAR

*M*en's memories may well have been in their trousers. It was their wives and mothers who remembered who could take up those trousers, make false cuffs when lanky-legged sons grew tall. Money no longer a priority, it started trickling in again. On Friday evening, a middle-aged woman knocked on Jenny's door.

'I'm Mrs Carter from two doors up. We moved in yesterday and the lady next door said you took in sewing.'

Mrs Carter had a daughter turning twenty-one on Saturday week, and she was wondering if Jenny could possibly run her up curtains for three rooms, and if she could do the lounge-room curtains first.

'I brought my curtains from the last place, but my new windows are longer, and with the party . . .'

There was nothing to making curtains, just the measuring and a bit of straight sewing. Jenny had the lot done by the following Wednesday and Mrs Carter told her she was worth her weight in gold. She added a fifteen shillings tip to her cheque. Jenny ran a cash business. The cheque presented a problem. Not to the bank though. They accepted it.

On the Sunday morning after the party, two of the younger Carter girls came to the door with leftover cake and a plate of pastries.

No more pancake sandwiches in school lunch bags; no more time to make Granny's bread or to fry it for breakfast. Porridge with milk was back on the breakfast menu, sausages or minced steak on the dinner menu, and Jenny's new purse, bulging with money, safe in Granny's tin trunk, tucked deep between Norman's sheets, beneath his towels, while her snakeskin bag hung empty over a doorknob — a snake decoy.

Ray came and went. He noticed the full canisters. He ate their bread and leftover mince stew. At times he came in while she was pressing a garment, measuring up material. He didn't speak to her. She didn't speak to him. She washed his clothes on Wednesdays and Sundays, ironed his shirts. He wore them, then pitched them soiled to his bedroom floor, with his cigarette butts. She made a big minced steak curry one night. He found the leftovers and heated it up for his breakfast, on toast made from her bread.

She dodged Flora. Flora dodged her. Geoff no longer winked at her. Lois was rarely sighted in the backyard and Jimmy stopped looking for her. Each night, Jenny sat on the kids' bed spinning bedtime stories about a small colony of Earthlings who lived in an enclave on Mars, Earth and the rest of humanity a spaceship away — or a gate. The small group lived happily, while the Martians kept their distance.

'What happened to them then, Jenny?'

'That's for tomorrow night.'

'Give us a hint,' Georgie said.

Who knew what tomorrow might bring?

October had grown old before their enclave was invaded by the Martians. Jenny, up to her elbows in Earthling food, turned to the sound of the key in the passage door. It wasn't bathroom night. Then someone knocked.

'Come in,' she called, hoping the Martians were friendly.

They didn't come in. They stood side by side in the doorway, their small Martian behind them. She looked friendly — the adults not so friendly.

'We've come for Aunty Phoebe's sewing machine,' Flora said.

Syrup bubbled on the stove, dough waited on the table, already cut into eight. Jenny gathered the eight onto a floury palm and placed each piece carefully into the boiling syrup, placed the lid on to the saucepan, before turning to face them.

'Going into the tailoring business?' she asked.

Flora couldn't sew a straight line.

'You've had the free use of it for twelve months,' she snapped.

Jenny walked to the sink, splashing water while washing flour and dough from her hands. Old treadle sewing machines were two a penny; she could make her choice between half a dozen at the secondhand shop — and she was going home anyway, as soon as she heard from Granny.

'Take it,' she said.

'It's not for you to tell us to take what's our own,' Flora said.

'Then don't take it, Flora.'

'You're lucky we're not charging you for wear and tear on it. Your type need to learn that nothing is free in this world.'

'If you believed that, your type would have paid me for the sewing I did for you,' Jenny said, removing a folded brown-paper bag from the middle drawer of her dresser. She proceeded to empty the machine drawers into it; Geoff now on the east side, leaning on the machine, Flora watching Jenny from the doorway.

'Those scissors are Aunt Phoebe's,' Flora said.

'I bought them. Want to see my receipt?'

Norman had kept his receipts. He'd kept account books listing every penny he'd ever spent. Jenny may not have been his blood, but her bookwork was as accurate. She'd glued every receipt she was given into the rear pages of an exercise book, recorded every item she stitched in the front pages. The paper bag on the table, the machine lifted around to make its way west, Jenny took her account book from the drawer, flipped through receipts until she found the one she was looking for.

'They cost twelve and six.'

Flora had lost interest. She left the doorway.

'If you want the thing, give me a hand with it,' Geoff yelled.

The machine's frame was cast iron. It didn't lift easily. Lois came in to help, Flora rushing in behind her. She couldn't allow her daughter to set foot on the polluted side alone.

Lois was wearing a frock stitched on that sewing machine, as most of her frocks had been stitched on it. That frock, and five-year-old friends caught up in an adult war, raised anger in Jenny. Flora's parlour curtains, visible through the open door, added fuel to that anger. She may have been raised as Norman the pacifist's daughter, but she wasn't.

She opened the account book to the front page where the Parker name was repeated five times with the date — and not one payment.

'If you can hang on for five minutes, Geoff, I'll get your wife's dressmaking account ready for you.'

'You're the one who owes us, babe.'

'And you can add on the cost us of taking you to the hospital when your abortion went wrong,' Flora said.

'Oh, the jars of jam, the chutney, should cover that. The eggs, vegetables —'

'It's our land they're growing in,' Flora snapped. 'And we didn't come in here to fight in front of the kids either.'

'Of course you didn't. You came in to take away my livelihood so my kids can starve, like any good Christian would.'

'You're sitting in here rent-free, babe, the lights on until all hours, sewing on this bloody thing. Your husband hasn't paid the last light bill and the gas bill is due,' Geoff said.

Syrup dumplings threatening to boil over, Jenny grabbed the

saucepan and held it high while turning the gas low. The machine she could live without. Electricity and gas she couldn't.

'If that's all that's niggling you, I'll pay it.'

'You should be paying two-thirds of it with that fridge going all day and nothing in it,' Flora said.

'How do you know there's nothing in it, Flora?'

That got rid of her. She scuttled back to her side as Jenny walked between her kids — standing together, watching, wondering what was happening now, what would happen next. They followed her to the sleep-out where she flung the lid of Granny's battered trunk open and dug deep for her purse, took a pound note from it and returned to the kitchen, placed it on the sewing machine bench.

Geoff picked it up. 'We're struggling to make the payments every month on this bloody place.'

'Why doesn't Ray pay rent, Geoff?'

'He must have been bloody good in bed, that's all I can —'

'Geoff!' Flora hadn't gone far. She was back at the door.

'If you want the bloody thing, help me lift it,' he said.

Lois was again deep into enemy territory.

'I told you to stay away from them. Get back in here, Lois!'

Geoff left the machine, picked up Lois and carried her back to the Martians' side. The door closed, the key turned.

'What's wrong, Jenny?' Georgie asked.

'Just something grown-up.'

'He took your money.'

'It's to pay for our lights. We've got plenty of money.'

And she had to use some of it, go somewhere. This was no life for kids. Was a two-and-a-half-room hut any better? Was a two-mile walk to and from school better? Was being the illegitimate kids of the town slut better? Maybe it was. From day one, her kids had been unwanted lodgers here.

Too many reasons why she couldn't go right now. The dresser she'd paid big money for; Norman's linen; those curtains too, the blinds, the new flywire. She'd put too much into these rooms to walk away from them.

The machine was moved back to its place beside the windows with little effort. It had little metal rollers on one set of its cast-iron legs. Just a case of lifting the bench and steering it — if you knew how. She hadn't told Geoff about those wheels. Wouldn't tell him the next time they came for it either. And they would.

No sign of Ray that night. She got the kids into bed at eight, then made a cup of tea and sat at the table flipping the pages of her account book, mentally totalling Flora Parker's sewing account. She selected a clean page and wrote an itemised account — and the Parkers would get it too, the next time they came for the machine.

She sighed, knowing she'd resent someone living rent-free in a house she was struggling to pay off. Anyone would.

She'd given Flora what she could, and much more than free dressmaking services. Every time Granny sent down eggs, she'd given Flora a few — a full dozen once. She added eggs to the account, walnuts, half a cabbage. How many bunches of onions? God knows. Bunches of rhubarb too, silverbeet.

All forgotten now. Jenny had done the unthinkable.

And Granny would agree with Flora, which was one of the reasons Jenny didn't want to go home, one more secret she'd have to keep forever. Too many secrets. Granny didn't know about Cara Jeanette, didn't know she'd been seeing Itchy-foot, didn't know she'd played Snow White to his Grumpy — who had looked so much like old Noah with his white beard.

Should give him a call. She could probably remember his number. And if she couldn't, the exchange would soon find it. How many by the name of Archibald Foote lived in Hawthorn? Maybe tomorrow.

Or give Maisy a call and find out if they did have cases of polio up there. Could have. Granny hadn't written for weeks. She didn't like writing bad news.

Would she go up there if there was no polio? Should she try to work out some arrangement with Ray? Offer to pay for the gas and electricity, cook his meals, wash his clothes.

And ring Itchy-foot, claim sudden illness and see if they'd take her back at the jazz club.

OLD PHOEBE FISHER

*R*ay slept at home on Friday night. Jenny wouldn't have known he'd been there if not for the pile of clothes in the corner of his bedroom, the butts on his floor. She was sweeping them up when he came home with his roadkill. He dumped it on the table and left again.

No liver, no tripe; a pile of minced steak, which would last longer cooked than it would raw. She made a large pot of mince stew; and that night, roasted chops, cooked a pot full of potatoes, made gravy. The way to a man's heart is through his stomach, they used to say in Woody Creek. She wasn't interested in Ray's heart, only his share of the roof, and tonight was determined to work out some compromise, at least until the school year ended.

She and the kids ate at six thirty. He came in at eight, smelling like a walking brewery. She'd kept his share of the meal warm over a saucepan of water. He ate it without comment and went to bed. So much for working out a compromise.

She left the kids eating porridge on Sunday and went down to the washhouse to get the copper boiling. When she returned to the house, he was heating up a portion of mince stew and making toast. Margot was with him; the other two were in the sleep-out, playing with the train set. Jenny stripped the beds, swept up more butts, picked up his pile of washing and returned with her bundle to the tubs. Sheets and towels went directly into the copper to boil clean. His working trousers required a soaking then a scrubbing brush. She dipped half a bucket of boiling water from the copper, enough to warm the water in the trough, then stood handwashing small frocks and underwear.

It must have been well after ten when the kids came down to tell her Ray had asked them if they wanted to go to the shops and get an ice-cream.

In the early days, before she'd married him, when things had been good, he'd taken the kids up for an ice-cream one Sunday morning. They'd brought one home for her. Maybe he had appreciated his chops and mash last night, his breakfast this morning. She didn't want to give up Melbourne's unlimited water, its electricity, its anonymity, his fridge. She had to at least try.

'Can we, Jenny?' Jimmy loved ice-cream.

'Walk together and hold hands when you cross the road,' she said.

Time has a habit of disappearing when you're at the wash-tubs, while your hands rub and the mind is free to plot courses, dream a little. Sheets and towels bubbling, she poked them down, added a few more sticks to the firebox before hanging her first load out to the clothes line. She couldn't hear the kids. They hadn't brought her back an ice-cream.

A dozen socks pegged, small frocks flapping, she glanced at her wrist. Her watch was on the kitchen dresser. She hung the underwear, gave his work trousers a scrub, then left them soaking while she went up to the house to get her new packet of blue bags. Amber had always used a dash of the blue bag in the sheets' rinsing water. It kept them white. No sign of those kids, no sound of them, and it was almost twelve o'clock.

'Georgie?' She opened the glass door. 'Jimmy, where are you?'

She got what she'd come inside to get, then walked out to the veranda. The trike was on the front section.

'Jimmy?'

Down the side of the house and back to where she'd come from.

'Georgie! I'm not in the mood to play hidey.'

Hoped they were playing next door with Lois. Small hope. A curtain lifted at Flora's kitchen window but no kids came out.

What time had they left? It must have been well before eleven. His bike was in its usual place, his bedroom door was closed. She knocked then entered. He wasn't in there. She looked beneath the bed, hoping those kids were playing games with her.

'Georgie!' she called over Carol's fence. Carol's oldest son, mowing the back lawn, turned to her call. 'Have you seen my kids, David?'

'I saw them walking off with their father when I was doing the front.'

Ray wasn't their father. He wasn't anyone's father — and he was paying her back because he wasn't anyone's father.

Is it your first, Mr King?

He'd kidnapped them.

She ran out to the front gate, fear growing in her. He'd been in touch with Vern Hooper. They'd formed an alliance . . .

Stop it, you fool. Vern had no interest in the girls.

Archie Foote then. Ray had found his telephone number in her old bankbook. He'd formed an alliance with Vern and Archie Foote. Or he'd taken them down to the Yarra and drowned them like a bloke had drowned his kids six months ago . . .

Georgie could swim like a fish.

Not with Margot clinging to her neck.

Stop! There were three of them and all three could yell.

She was on the street when Veronica walked down her husband's driveway, waving both arms. She'd gone back to him!

That's what we do, Jenny thought, then shook her head. That's what women with kids might have to do. Veronica had no kids. She had a trade, could get work anywhere, work day or night. So what was she doing back there?

'Where are you off to in your apron?' Veronica said as she crossed over.

'He took my kids for an ice-cream hours ago.' Jenny reached to untie the tapes and remove her washday apron. 'I thought they were back.'

'Make me a cup of tea, kiddo. I want to tell someone my news.'

'You've gone back to him?'

'When hell freezes over. The mad bugger is in jail. I wanted to see what he'd done to my house while they've got him locked up. He's put his boot through a couple of walls — and better them than me.'

'A bank manager? In jail?'

'Unless his old man bailed him out, which I strongly doubt. They've had enough of him.'

'What's he done?'

'They caught him with his fingers in the coffers. They reckon he's embezzled thousands.'

The curtains moved at Flora's parlour window. Jenny waved a hand as she led the way inside.

'He's always liked the gee-gees,' Veronica said. Jenny held a finger to her lips. Veronica sat, then in lower tones continued. 'Every Saturday he'd head for the races with a wad in his pocket. The last of the big spenders, my Bill, which was the reason I went back to work in the first place. I hated leaving that house. I'd put so much of myself into it.'

'Was he always . . . you know?'

'He was a different bloke when he was young, before the war.'

'Was he in it?'

'For six months. He was in an accident and it ruined his back for marching. How did you get mixed up with Ray?'

'I knew him at school.'

'He looks a damn sight older than you.'

'Five years. He's twenty-eight.'

And just like that she'd given up her age. No comment though from Veronica, only an offered cigarette. Jenny lit one, lit a gas ring with the same match and put the kettle on. Or no comment for a time.

'You're twenty-three and you've got a seven-year-old daughter?'

'She's eight now.'

'How did you manage that, kiddo?'

Jenny measured tea into the pot. 'I had no say in the matter.'

'Your father?'

Hands rose to push those words back where they'd come from; then, to save a good and gentle man from accusation, she said more. 'A neighbour's twin sons raped me when I was fourteen.'

'And they let you raise the kid!'

'They tried to marry me off to one of them — for my good name's sake. I took off down here and as they say, jumped out of the frying pan into the fire. I ended up having Georgie.'

And she'd said too much. She set two mugs on the table, the sugar basin, milk.

'How has Ray been about the abortion?'

'He hasn't been around much, and when he is, he doesn't talk.'

Kettle boiled, she poured water over the tea leaves then turned to the clock. 'They've been gone too long. I should call the police, Vroni. There could have been an accident. He could have been in touch with Jimmy's grandfather. He's got the phone on, and Ray knows he's been threatening to take Jimmy for years.'

'I hate to be the one to tell you, kiddo, but the cops would side with them.'

And of course they would — as soon as she said her name. A woman who aborted a baby wasn't fit to raise a litter of rats.

'He's not going to make any phone calls.' Veronica went on. 'He came to my door when old Phoebe was dying and he couldn't get a word out. It's Sunday. He's taken them somewhere.'

'Down to the river to drown them.'

'If he'd been going to drown anyone, it would have been old Phoebe or her housekeeper. Want to hear the rest of my news?'

Veronica's chap had bought an old guesthouse in Frankston which he was planning to set up as a health farm, with fringe benefits, and Veronica would be running it. She was full of news that morning. She spoke while the clock ticked away the minutes, while Jenny stared at her wedding photograph and a cobweb dangling from it. It hadn't been dusted since the abortion. She couldn't stand to look at it long enough to dust it.

'How come Ray's first wife didn't have kids?' she said.

'You're joking?'

Jenny's eyebrows rose. 'Did you know her well?'

'No one wanted to know her well, kiddo.'

'What was she like?'

'Smoked cod,' Veronica said. 'Dried smoked cod.'

'Do you know how long they'd been married?'

'She made an honest man of him on her deathbed, according to popular belief. I don't know the ins and outs of it. Carol says he moved in here when he was a bit of a kid. She'd been in that house for twenty years.'

'What connection did she have to Flora's aunty?'

Veronica squinted around the smoke. 'That's who we're talking about.'

'Who?'

'Old Phoebe Fisher. That's who he was married to.'

'What?'

'Watt invented the steam engine, kiddo. The old dame who owned this house, Phoebe Fisher-King — or, so it said in the death column, *loved Aunty of Flora* — like hell, she was — *passed away after a long illness*. She took six months to die, and sometime before she did, married Ray, though none of us knew — until we saw the funeral notice. *Survived by her devoted husband, Raymond.*'

'I feel sick. She was . . . old.'

'Sixty-seven — according to the death column.'

'He worked for her. He told me he looked after her yard.'

'He did. He spent his life cutting limbs off the neighbours' trees then cutting them small enough for her to pitch back over the fences. At the best of times, old Phoebe was as mad as a rattlesnake. Riled up, she was a sight to behold. When Carol's lilly pilly trees were shedding their berries, you could hear her from one corner of the street to the other. The year I moved in, I watched her carry two buckets full into Carol's. One of the boys opened the door and she let him have them, then danced what she could into the floor-boards.' Veronica laughed, and lit another smoke.

'It's no laughing matter. It's sick.'

'It was no love match.'

'Stop it, Vroni.'

'Flora reckons she did it to get back at the family. Her brother got the house but Ray got free tenancy for life.'

And Jenny finally knew why Ray didn't pay rent.

'A tricky old bugger was Phoebe Fisher, supposedly a big name on stage in her youth. Even as a smoked cod, she could dance. When I was going out with Bill, we used to see her and Ray at the dance halls, long before I knew who they were. I used to think she was teaching her grandson to dance. He was well dressed, not a bad-looking boy, and she was this gruesome old hag, bewigged, make-up plastered on with a trowel, eyebrows drawn in with a black pencil, wrinkled old lips weeping scarlet lipstick. Ramón, she called him.'

Not a word could Jenny find to say. Someone had taught him to dance. Now she knew who.

'He told you he'd been married?' Veronica asked.

'The first time he came down home, he told my grandmother and me that his wife was dead.'

'Never told you who he'd been married to?'

Jenny shook her head. 'How come the Parkers are buying the house if he's got free tenancy?'

'According to Wilma, Flora's father worked out some deal with Ray. Flora had been living with her parents until Geoff got out of the army. They had to live somewhere — and her old man can't stand Geoff. Flora's family are rabid Catholics and Geoff's not — and he refused to change his faith. She had to marry him.'

'She told me Lois was born nine months to the day after the wedding.'

'Try seven. Who did you think Ray had been married to?'

'One of Phoebe's relatives. Her housekeeper . . .'

'She was older than Phoebe. You could have knocked a few of us down with feathers when he turned up here with you and three kids. Your ears must have burned for months, kiddo.' She offered her cigarettes and Jenny took one, lit it. 'We all felt sorry for the poor coot but rent-free or not, he was stark raving mad to bring you to this street.'

'I was stark raving mad to come. And I've got sheets boiling to death in the copper. I'll have to get them out.'

Veronica helped wring the sheets, helped hang them. Ray's working trousers went into the copper to boil clean.

Almost two o'clock. Those kids had been gone for at least three hours.

'I'll have to call the police, Vroni. I'm getting scared.'

'He'll bring them back,' Veronica said. 'He's weird but he's never been a danger to anyone. He looked after old Phoebe for months when she was dying and was as gentle as a woman with her. Ian is picking me up at three. If they're not back by then, I'll get him to take us to the cops. They'll take more notice of him than they will of you.'

They had another cup of tea, another cigarette, and at quarter to three Veronica took a roll of ten-pound notes from her handbag and tossed it across the table.

'It's Ian's. He asked me to give it to you.'

Jenny swept it back. 'I don't want his money!'

She was up. She'd heard the gate open. Stood listening for kids' voices. Heard someone knock on Flora's door. Waited, expecting the police to come around her side and tell her her kids had been drowned. No. Flora had visitors, loud voices in the passage.

'I could have got five years' jail, and Ian could have been dragged into it with me and lost everything. Take it, kiddo. He can afford it.'

'If I was pregnant now, I'd be pulling my hair out in a madhouse. Put it away.'

Veronica walked out to the veranda, the notes and her cigarette packet left on the table. Jenny rolled the notes, five of them, slid them in with the cigarettes and followed Veronica to the gate. No imported maroon car waiting, but her small trio approaching, holding hands. Jenny ran.

Georgie's face was sunburnt; Margot, who usually looked as if the vampires had been at her, was red raw, arms, face, scalp.

'We went to the zoo,' Jimmy said. Already tanned, he showed no sign of burning.

'We saw elephants and tigers and everything,' Georgie said.

'Where's Ray?'

'He said go home.'

'From where?'

'Just the tram,' Georgie said. She walked on ahead as Margot started *ahzeeing*. Her feet were sore, her head was sore, and no doubt the rest of her. Jenny picked her up and carried her inside. Georgie was at the sink, filling a mug with water.

'He let you cross the road by yourselves?'

'After we crossed the big road, he said go home,' Georgie said around the mug.

'Why didn't you wear your hats?'

'We were only going to get an ice-cream at first.'

'Then he said the zoo,' Jimmy said. 'And we said yes.'

She'd never taken them to the zoo, had promised to. Sunburnt or not, they'd had a good day. She found zinc cream, olive oil, mixed up a plaster of it, and the two women plastered the girls, then, warning them not to step outside the door, they returned to the gate.

'If you decide you've had enough of him, I'll need staff down at Frankston.'

'Me and my three kids, Vroni.'

'The old servants' quarters are well detached from the house. There's six rooms that could be made habitable.'

'I don't know what I'm going to do from one day to the next,' Jenny admitted.

Maroon car approaching.

'That's him.' Veronica waved to the driver, who looked older in daylight than he had by night. 'The phone will be connected down there after Christmas. We're calling the place Veronian — which is as close as I'll ever get to joining my name to another man's. The exchange will give you the number if you need me.' She kissed her cheek. 'Bless your tight little mouth,' she said, and kissed her other cheek, gave her a Granny hug.

Jenny held her for an instant. 'Bless you too,' she said and turned away, tears blurring that brick house. There'd been a lot of months between Granny hugs.

She had an option now, if she could hang on here until Christmas, until after Christmas. Had to hang on, that's all.

TEN-POUND NOTES

She was sewing when Ray came home. The kids were in bed, Margot silenced with half an aspro and a glass of milk. Jenny had a skirt to finish off before next Wednesday, and the hand-stitching on a ballgown — six yards of its hem to roll by Friday. She had a list of Miss Blunt's prices too, glued into her account book. She'd put hours of work into that ballgown — had hoped to put a few more hours into it tonight. Packed it away when he came in, slid it safe into a pillow slip, with the skirt. Sewing expensive fabric was a dangerous occupation when there were little fingers around — and Ray, on the hunt for food.

She watched him open the fridge and stand before it. Still some mince in there, a bowl of mashed potatoes. They could be heated. She'd gone past her first feeling of abhorrence about old Phoebe and was edging back towards pity. He'd left Woody Creek as an eleven- or twelve-year-old kid and somehow found his way to a safe harbour, and whether he'd shared old Phoebe's bed or not, was that any worse than what she'd done with Laurie?

He removed a plate of greaseproof-paper-covered steak, dripped blood to the floor as he took the paper off. She rose to save further disaster.

'Do you want me to fry a piece for you?'

He wanted; she read desire for steak — or her — in his eyes. He didn't reply, but turned to the bread tin. Plenty of yesterday's bread for a sandwich.

Veronica's cigarettes were on the dresser beside the bread tin. She'd placed them there before she'd started plastering the girls with zinc cream. Forgotten to give them to Vroni. Capstan cigarettes, not Ray's brand, but in his hand now, and he was looking at her, his eyes accusing her of infamy.

'Veronica was here. She forgot to take them.'

She reached for the dishcloth, stooped to wipe up the blood spill as he opened the packet.

'S-s-spent your f-f-free day on your b-b-back, you slut.'

'Veronica popped in to tell me her husband —'

The open packet flew at her head, missed, hit the wall, cigarettes and ten-pound notes spilling.

'— is in jail.'

She retrieved the scattered notes, aware she couldn't explain why Veronica had left them. Retrieved the packet, was sliding them back in when she was hit by a truck.

Flew. Hit the dresser. Plates rattled as the floor rose up to meet her.

'B-been at it for months, you sh-she-dog slut.'

Dragged up by an arm, smashed down again, landed hard on her elbow. Shock of pain overriding the shock of his attack. Paralysing pain.

'That's how you've b-b-been feeding your bastards.'

Flung at the wall, she offered no more resistance than a kitchen chair. Chairs didn't have hair. Dragged her up by her hair. Fist in her face. Stars, then lights out.

A haze of pain. A chorus of screaming. Lying face down. Trying to roll over, see the screaming.

Georgie, screaming little warrior wearing white warpaint, throwing herself on Jenny. Jimmy, wrapping his arms around the monster's leg. Margot, a foot-stamping fire imp. 'Daddy Ray. Daddy Ray.'

Perhaps that name reached his mind. He went away. Only the bike howling its pain then.

Georgie kneeling at her side, pushing a tea towel into Jenny's face. One elbow trying to get her up, the other arm too useless to push the tea towel away.

'It's getting everywhere, Jenny. It's running all on your dress.'

'He's gone now Jenny. His bike's gone now Jenny.'

Scared little kids, and she'd done this to them. She'd given them a name, and done this to them. Raised herself up onto her backside with her one good arm, got her back against the wall, took the tea towel and held it to her nose.

'I like Granny's house best,' Jimmy howled. 'Jenny, I want us to go to Granny's house.'

Head hurting. Hip, elbow hurting. Mouth, face, back hurting. Trying to get onto her feet. Too many little hands trying to help, hindered. She stayed down.

'Get Lois'th mother?' the pudgy fire imp said.

'No.' She'd get up. 'No.'

Two hands on the dresser, she got one foot beneath her, then the other. Stood leaning there, her head circling, little faces circling.

'I'm sorry,' she said. 'I'm sorry. We'll go home.'

Literal little beings, kids, they ran to the bedroom to dress for home. She limped, via the dresser, via the table, to the sink. Stood there, her nose dripping great splotches of blood to metal, her elbow doing its own dripping. Hard to see an elbow. She felt for damage, felt an inch of skin flapping in the breeze. Washed it, and pink water ran down into Melbourne's anonymous drains, disappeared into anonymity.

Blood everywhere. Nose running like a tap. Mrs Carter's daughter's ballgown in a pillow slip on the table. Wilma's sister-in-law's skirt in with it. Had to stay away from that table. The tea towel held to pinched nostrils, she limped to the door and locked it. Only glass. Glass wouldn't keep a monster out.

The kids came to her side, shoes and socks on, all ready to go to Granny's house, Jimmy holding the photograph of his daddy. She held them to her, her bunch of babies, held them hard and knew that being nameless wasn't the worst thing in the world. They gripped hold of parts of her and every part they gripped hurt; still held them though. Dripped blood to Margot's white hair. Let it soak in, please God, let it fuse me to that kid.

Later, when her nose stopped dripping, when the tea towel and her blood-stained frock were soaking in the sink, when she knew her lower lip was split, that her nose may have been broken, that she wasn't going anywhere, not tonight, she walked out to the sleep-out to check the rear door. Just a tiny snib on it, barely enough to keep a cat out.

Norman's toolbox lived beneath her camp bed, heavy enough to assist that snib. Too heavy for her tonight. She opened it and removed Norman's hammer, his tommyhawk. The kids following at her heels, wanted to go to Granny's, not for Jenny to start fixing something. Nothing to say to them, not yet. Too sore for words. Too sore to take her green linen from its hanger, but she got it down, found a clean petticoat in the drawer, took them, with hammer and tommyhawk, to the kids' bedroom and locked that door.

'Hop back into bed, darlin's.'

They weren't getting into that bed. They were going to Granny's.

This night would be etched into their memories forever. She hadn't wanted them to have bad memories.

Too late now.

'The doors are locked. Pop into bed for me. Leave your clothes on.'

'He might break the glass. I don't like glass, Jenny,' Georgie said.

'Glass makes a big noise when it breaks. We'll hear it.'

'Not if we're atheep,' the fire imp said.

'I won't go to sleep.'

Not until their shoes, their socks, Jim's photograph, had been placed into a string bag and hooked over the doorknob with the snakeskin handbag did those kids get into bed.

He didn't return.

Jenny didn't go to bed. She slept at the table, head on her arms, Norman's tommyhawk at her elbow.

The kids didn't go to school on Monday, or on Tuesday. Margot's sunburn needed more than zinc cream and olive oil. Jenny had nothing more, and couldn't leave the house to get more, so she plastered her with what she had.

He didn't come home on Tuesday night. Spending Veronica's money on accommodation, on prostitutes? He'd taken it, and the cigarettes.

'When will we go, Jenny?'

'When Margot's sunburn is better.'

She didn't mention her own face. They could see her face.

He came at six thirty on the Wednesday. She was boiling macaroni, a sheeting bandage restricting her elbow's movement. How else do you keep an elbow still enough for it to heal? He tried the door, stood a moment looking in, expecting someone to open it. No one moved in the kitchen, other than Jenny, who picked up Norman's tommyhawk.

He left the door. They heard the howl of his bike fade in the distance.

Georgie and Jimmy went to school on Thursday. They walked there alone. Margot looked less like a boiled yabby but the skin on her face had wrinkled as it dried. She was more gnome now than fire imp.

'You'll remember your hat next time, won't you?'

'He thaid we'd jutht get ithe-cream.'

'You have to learn to think for yourself, not expect other people to think for you, Margot.'

'You thaid he was our thtepfather and to do what he thaid.'

She had, back in the early days of hope. She smoothed on more zinc cream, learning that jaw-clamping little face as her hands followed its contours, learning her arms, the backs of her knees. For the first time in eight years, they had a common bond, Jenny and Margot. Jenny's left eye was swollen, near closed, and underlined by dark purple and black bruising. Both of Margot's eyes were slits in a piebald face.

On Thursday, he came at six to that locked door. The kids watched him place a load of shopping down: four bottles of milk, a large loaf of bread, butter, sugar, newspaper-wrapped meat. And Veronica's cigarettes.

He didn't wait at the door that night. They waited for the bike's howl. No howl. He was out there somewhere. They waited for fifteen minutes, listening. Couldn't hear him. Maybe he'd walked off somewhere.

'Can we get it, Jenny?'

Great respecters of food, Jenny's kids, and right outside that door there was a glut of it.

She unlocked it, picked up the cigarette packet to check its contents. Three cigarettes and the red roll of ten-pound notes. Removed them. And he must have been on the front veranda. He came around the corner while she was counting them.

'I d-d-did something s-stupid,' he said.

The kids separated. Jimmy ran for the backyard. Georgie stepped back to Jenny's side. Margot scuttled inside, a bottle of milk in each hand.

'H-h-h-he h-hung himself.'

Jenny didn't know who had hung himself and didn't care. She backed inside, walked to the table and picked up the tommy-hawk. Vegetable pancakes burning on the stove. Georgie lifted the pan.

'He g-g-got away w-w-with f-fifteen thousand.'

Knew then who had hung himself. Knew that Vroni was free.

Knew too that Ray thought it was over. He'd done something stupid. Admitting it was his apology.

She took the pan and turned the pancakes. Still edible. Placed them back over the heat.

He'd bought a pound of sausages, his second apology. She fried them and served four meals.

He served himself from the pan, cut bread and sat with them at the table. Maybe he thought it was over.

It wasn't.

When her face looked normal, when Margot's face had finished peeling, then it would be over.

She finished rolling the hem of Mrs Carter's daughter's ballgown that night while he prowled. Three times he went to his bedroom and closed the door. The third time it opened, Jenny stopped her hand's reflex move towards the tommyhawk. His lost lamb's eyes were back. He looked lost.

'I l-l —' He came to the table, shielding his eyes from the glare, or from the sight of what he'd done to her face. 'I l-l-love you.'

Couldn't raise one word in reply. Made a careful stitch, then another.

'I g-g-got n-n-no one, Jenny.'

She sighed and made three more stitches.

'I l-love you.'

Raised her eyes to his then. 'You don't love me, Ray. You married me because you thought I was the town slut and you didn't deserve anything better. I married you because I thought I didn't deserve any better. I deserve a whole heap better, and so do my kids.'

PACKING UP

On Thursday, 21 November 1947, the day Princess Elizabeth was to marry her Prince Charming, Jenny was leaving her marriage — and doing it right, using her head for once in her life.

She'd filled in forms to have her child endowment transferred to Woody Creek; had filled in more to have Jenny Morrison Hooper King's bank account transferred to the Willama branch of the National Bank. She'd found the name of a local carrier in the telephone book and made the phone call. Yesterday, she'd spoken to the secondhand dealer in High Street who'd sold her the kitchen dresser. He would buy it back, along with the kids' bed, their chest of drawers and maybe the sleep-out cabinet.

Sissy's mattress was going home. It was a good one. Granny's tin trunk was packed again with Norman's linen, blankets, Amber's tablecloths; a new label pasted over the old.

She'd mass-produced labels, eight of them, cut from heavy cardboard, her name in block print: *J.C. KING, C/O MRS FOOTE, WOODY CREEK STATION.* Holes made with the point of her scissors, she threaded lengths of twine through them and set about tying one to each item. They were numbered: Norman's toolbox was number one; three large rope-sealed cardboard cartons were two, three and four. Then the red case, the trunk, the mattress, the parcel of pillows.

On the run since Tuesday, she'd spent last night packing quietly. This morning, once the kids had gone off to school, she'd rolled their mattress and roped it. Roped the blanket-wrapped pillows.

Nothing she'd brought to this house, or paid for in this house, would remain, only her labour. No use taking down curtains. She'd considered it. No windows for them to shield at Granny's house. She'd left him bread, butter, dripping, a bowl of sugar, a little tea. He'd bought the potatoes; she'd left them. Amber's canisters, her spices, were going home, packed with Jenny's empty jam jars. Granny was always searching for jars.

Her account book lay open on the table. She checked the list made during the past three days. All items ticked. On the opposite page she'd made a list for the secondhand man. Hoped he wasn't late.

Twice she'd thought about writing a note to Ray. Twice she'd picked up her pencil and attempted to find a word or two for him. He'd been coming home every night sober, with milk and bread, butter too, and meat he knew she'd cook. Whether his offerings were further apology, or insurance against her showing her face to the street, she didn't know. She hadn't shown her face. She hadn't opened the curtains, or the glass door to Wilma last Wednesday, or to a possible customer last Friday.

Georgie had delivered the ballgown to Mrs Carter. She'd delivered the skirt for Wilma to give to her sister-in-law.

A swollen nose will shrink back to its original size in days, split lips heal quickly, bruising takes longer to fade. Still shades of his bruising beneath her right eye, a large ugly scab on her elbow, the remains of a football-sized bruise on her hip, but she was fit to be seen.

Margot was fit to be seen too. She'd been back at school since Monday.

Dear Ray, her pencil wrote.

He could work out words if they were spelt phonetically. Her pencil laboured for a time, attempting to find words spelt phonetically. Still pitied him, always would. He had no one, no friend to talk motors with, a landlord who wanted him out — if a landlord he was when he received no rent from his tenant. She'd pitied the old swaggies who had stopped for a day or two in Woody Creek, pitied the derelicts lying beside their bottles on Melbourne park benches. Didn't pity them enough to want to live with them — and feared Ray enough to not want to live with him. Feared him as she'd feared Amber. You can't live with a walking time-bomb. You can't wander around in a blindfold listening for its tick-tick-tick-tick-tick. Kids got stuck in whatever situation their parents stuck them in. She wasn't a kid, and she was getting her kids unstuck.

I'm taking the kids home, taking what I . . . would he work out *brought*?

He'd know as soon as he opened the door that they'd gone, and know why. No need for a note. She crumpled the page and stuffed it into her handbag.

Apart from Laurie's stolen money that day in Geelong, she'd never seen so much of the stuff before in one place. She had twenty left from what she'd withdrawn from her bank account, plus Veronica's five ten-pound notes, and change. And she'd have more after the secondhand man had been.

Wished he'd come. He'd promised to be here by one. Loathed relying on others. Loathed watching the hands of her watch eating away the minutes. Plenty of time though.

She lit a cigarette and watched the hand holding it shake. It would stop shaking once she was on her way — or maybe it wouldn't. Maybe she'd damaged a nerve in her elbow. Granny would want to know how she'd done it. Tripped over in the dark on the way down to the lav and banged it on the washhouse wall, Granny . . .

Jimmy would tell Granny how she'd done it. Little blabber-mouth Jimmy.

She sat smoking, flicking ash into the sink and watching the hands of her watch move to one fifteen. Stubbed out the butt, washed the ash down the sink, then set about moving her belongings outside. She'd done her packing silently, aware of Flora's footsteps a wall away. Gave up on silence now, pushed and dragged the tin trunk out to the veranda. Tin on wood is noisy. Cardboard cartons slide silently. She carried her old red case; rolled and dragged the mattress, not heavy but bulky, as was the parcel of pillows. The toolbox was as heavy as lead.

Little case waiting open on the table. It would travel with her. Her alarm clock, nightclothes for herself and the kids, clean socks, a few items of emergency clothing. They'd stay tonight at a cheap hotel in Spencer Street, already booked and paid for, as were the train tickets. Everything was done.

Looked at her watch again. After one thirty. She lit another cigarette. She'd opened a fresh packet this morning and gone through half of them already. Granny didn't approve of smoking. It ruined the lungs, Granny said. It cured the head — and what use a pair of healthy lungs if you were off your head?

Outside, then, to sit on Granny's tin trunk, to flick ash to the bricked path where he parked his bike. She could watch the street here and not be watched by Flora. Sat feet tapping, willing the secondhand man to stop out front.

Possessions, like kids, grew. When she'd left Myrtle's boarding house, all she'd owned had fitted into two cases and a string bag. Had left a lot behind in Sydney.

Today wasn't the time to start thinking about that.

She tossed the butt to the path and reached for her handbag. Its clip would no longer keep it closed. One more journey and she'd put it out to pasture. She removed Granny's letter, delivered on Tuesday morning, and already well read. That letter had chosen the day of her escape.

Dear Jenny,

It's been a madhouse up here and it doesn't look like improving soon. Harry took Elsie down to the hospital this morning. She's pregnant and been having enough trouble keeping it before she got the disease that's been going around up here. Harry is worried sick. Tom Vevers died of it. Old Mrs O'Donald and three more are in the hospital . . .

The secondhand man caught her unaware. She led him and his offsider indoors, pointing with Granny's letter to the items she wanted to sell.

He offered a third of what she'd paid him for the dresser. He offered five bob for the sleep-out cabinet she'd repaired and polished, which may not have been hers to sell, though if not for her it would have ended its life on the wood heap.

'It can stay,' she said.

He liked the old chest of drawers, obviously didn't recognise it as the battered wreck he'd sold her. He said old beds without their mattresses were two a penny. He'd said different when she'd bought it. He offered her two bob for both iron and toaster. She told him they could stay. A man with Ray's needs would move in another woman in a week. At least she'd find an iron, a toaster, curtains.

The kitchen looked bare when the men carried her dresser away. The kids' bedroom was bare. She followed her furniture out to the gate, watched her dresser loaded, almost waved goodbye to it.

Seated again on Granny's tin trunk, she opened the letter.

. . . Harry said he'd stay down there with her. You know what Elsie's like with strangers.

It's a terrible thing. I swore it was polio when I saw the first cases — sore throat, fever, pain in the limbs — but it's striking the old as well as the young and there's been no paralysis with it. There are a lot in town blaming an immigrant family for bringing it to town. We've got a couple of English families up here. Tom Vevers came out from England as a boy. One of the migrant chaps is a cousin of his. Tom had them staying with him for a time.

Archie is up here again. He says the disease is a form of the pneumonic flu we saw a lot of just after the first war. He probably knows what he's talking about. He was a good doctor when he put his mind to it, and I've never said different. It's staying power he lacks, and if the truth is being told here today, I hope he stays longer. I'm too old to be running in and out from town and so is my horse.

I started this on Thursday, now it's Saturday, and all I've got for you is bad news. Doctor Frazer told Harry that Elsie isn't pregnant, that what is going on in her womb could be a tumour. If they can get her over this flu they want to take her down to the city next Thursday. They've got someone else going down that day. Harry asked me to ask you if you could find him a corner. Try to keep the kids away from him as much as you can. He's showing no signs of it, but you never can tell with this swine of a disease. When it hits, it hits sudden, and take it from me, you don't want those little kids catching it.

The Dobsons have offered to take Teddy and Maudy in while Harry is away. Maisy has already got Brian and little Josie in with her. Lenny, Joan and Ronnie will stay down here with me. You might give Maisy a call when you get this. We should know more by then.

Love to all, Granny

Jenny had spoken to Maisy on Tuesday night. Elsie would be at the hospital by now, and Harry walking the polished corridors. She'd told Maisy to tell him she'd meet him at the hospital after the kids got out of school. He wouldn't be looking for her yet.

The carrier had said he'd be there between three and three thirty. Anonymous Melbourne where anonymous people could make arrangements with anonymous carriers, then rely on them to come when they said they'd come. In Woody Creek they came; and whether they did or not in Melbourne, she was leaving at three thirty. He had the address. He knew where her goods were to go. He'd see her pile, see her labels.

You can't pay via telephone. So . . . leave the money somewhere. Write him a note. Where do you leave the note? Should have made some arrangement to leave it in the letterbox.

Knock on Flora's door and give her the money . . .

Jenny shook her head.

He hadn't arrived by three, or quarter past three. She walked down to the corner to meet the kids, kept glancing back, unsure from which direction the carrier might come.

Margot's face looked piebald. Georgie's nose had peeled. Jimmy was as brown as a berry — and he needed a haircut.

'Rough nut,' she said, ruffling it.

They saw the pile on the veranda. They knew.

'When?' Georgie asked.

'When Daddy Ray cometh,' Margot replied.

He'd been eating with them. Margot had forgotten, or forgiven, the night of the bruising.

Maisy had known how to forgive, or to forget. How many times had Amber screamed at her to get out and not to come back? How many times had she come back for more of the same?

'Why can't we take my trike, Jenny?'

She'd forgotten it. 'Get it, darlin', and be quick.'

One final piece of cardboard cut, one final time she printed, *J.C. KING C/O MRS FOOTE, WOODY CREEK STATION*. She added a bracketed nine beneath the address, bored a hole through cardboard with the point of her scissors, threaded one final length of twine.

'What's the time, Jenny?' Georgie wanted to go.

'Quarter to four.'

Harry would be standing out front of the hospital now, looking for them, wondering if she'd forgotten to meet him, if she'd gone to the wrong hospital. The kids followed her out to the gate, and this time they saw a horse-drawn dray turn their corner. It had to be the carrier. It would be him. They stood at the kerb, willing him to stop out front of their house. And he did.

'Mrs King?'

'Yes,' she said. 'I'd given up on you.'

'Trams on every corner today, love, and the trucks are starting to think they own the road.'

He lifted a two-wheeled trolley down from the dray and she walked with him to her pile. The trunk was heavy. He handled it. Jenny carried the battered red case, eager to see it loaded.

Flora watching from behind her parlour's lace curtains, needed to be told she was visible from the street. She'd stood there when the secondhand dealer had loaded the dresser, no doubt keeping an eye out for the sewing machine. Poor old sewing machine, destined to end its life on one of the verandas, rusting away.

Poor old garden too. Who would give it water? Everything was doing so well. She had a beautiful healthy crop of rhubarb, begging to be harvested. Fat white onions. Ray might pull an onion. Flora and Geoff would pull more. Jenny didn't need them. Plenty of everything where she'd be tomorrow. She'd stay there this time, milk goats, feed chooks, grow vegies, make jam and live man-free — as Granny had lived her life man-free.

'That's it, love?'

'That's it.'

She paid the man, then her goods moved away. 'That's it,' she repeated and went inside for the last time.

Small leather case waiting open for her scissors, the last of the twine, the exercise book. She packed it, closed it, the kids at her heels like three eager puppies waiting for her to pick up their leashes and say 'walk'.

'Run down to the lav before we leave. It'll be a while before we see another one,' she said, and like three good little puppies they ran to obey.

She opened the case and ripped out the page containing the Parkers' itemised account. She'd added to it during the past week.

Flywire for sleep-out.
Canvas for blinds.
Curtains for three rooms.
Reconditioning of sewing machine.
Oil and needles.

Repairs and polishing of sleep-out cabinet, she added now, and, *Garden produce.*

About to slide it beneath the passage door, she changed her mind. Why not leave Flora a double-edged message? She placed it beneath the sewing machine's stitching foot, aware the passage door would be unlocked two minutes after she and the kids had closed the glass door.

Patted the machine's head as she may have patted a faithful dog's. Then away.

'*Old J.C., she went off to find happy, found a flushing lavatory, ended up in purgatory. Old J.C., she's better than she used to be, many long years ago,*' she sang as they walked. Kids like lavatory humour, and Jenny's troop had insufficient religious training to understand the literal meaning of purgatory. They laughed and marched, and Jimmy wanted her to sing it again.

They saw a horse and dray as they turned the corner, and ran hand in hand to catch up. It wasn't their carrier. Georgie asked how Granny's Nugget would like driving down roads with all of those trucks and cars. There would come a day soon when the horse and dray would be forced from city roads, but not yet, not while petrol was rationed, not while one-horse motors worked on hay.

Trams worked on electricity. They went fast. The tram caught up to their carrier three or four blocks on, and the kids laughed at the wheel of Jimmy's tricycle spinning at a hundred miles an hour.

'Goodbye, red racing trike,' Jimmy called to it.

'Goodbye, mattress,' Georgie called.

'Goodbye, Armadale,' Jenny said.

It was not at all like her leaving of Sydney and Myrtle, not one little bit like that. This was breaking out of prison with a bunch of happy kids. This was escaping to the paradise of Granny, to buckets of free milk and chooks that laid golden eggs.

'*Old J.C. is heading to paradise, finding it so very nice, like dough balls with lots of spice. Old J.C. can live well without fridge ice, for many long years to come.*'

Laughing on the tram with her kids, loving them and their laughter, and making even sillier rhymes so they'd laugh more.

Lanky Harry standing out front of the hospital, rolling his inimitable slim cigarette, his watery blue eyes searching for them. A lean, rusty-headed, snub-nosed boy of eighteen when he'd married Elsie, Gertrude's darker-than-average adopted daughter. Twelve-year-old Jenny had been at his wedding. He didn't look much more than a boy now. They waved to him as the tram went by, then all four ran back, all four grabbing a part of him to hug. Plenty of length to go around.

'Any news yet?' Jenny asked.

'They're not mucking about, Jen. They'll do a hysterectomy tomorrow morning the chap said. Doctor Frazer warned us what to expect. He knows his business. He got her onto some new drug to clear up her chest. They say she's well enough to stand the operation.'

Slim cigarettes burned fast. He tossed the butt and his hands wanted to roll another one. 'I was convinced the flu would take her, but it turned out to be a blessing in disguise. If she hadn't got it, I wouldn't have got her down to see Frazer. He knew right away that there was no baby inside her.' Harry was wound up, words spilled from him as they walked to the tram stop. 'She's been having trouble for months. Mum kept telling me to get her down to a doctor.'

'She's with the best of them now,' Jenny said.

'If it's cancer, it could have gone further, one of the doctors told me. He said there's no way of knowing if it is or not until they get in there and have a look.'

'Wombs are made to hold babies in. Whatever it is, it's locked in tight.'

'What's wombs, Jenny?' Georgie asked.

'Gardens inside ladies' tummies where baby seeds grow,' she said, and turned again to Harry.

'It's the same hospital Dad died in. It's like it's all happening again. I can't lose her, Jen.'

'You won't,' she said. 'Doctors have come a long way since you were thirteen.'

'There was nothing of her before she got crook. There's nothing left of her to cut into . . .'

'She's a sparrow with the heart of an eagle. She'll breeze through it.'

The tram coming, she gathered the kids in close to board. Harry had been raised in the city. He hadn't been back since his father died, but he remembered the city streets.

'Isn't it going the wrong way for Armadale?'

'Yeah,' she said.

Georgie remembered her father. 'I forgot my photo, Jenny.'

'He's packed, Georgie.'

'And mine?' Jimmy said.

'They're together in one of the cartons.'

Harry followed them onto the tram. He asked no questions, not until they'd found seats, he and Jenny side by side, the kids opposite.

'I hope I didn't cause trouble between you — asking for a bed?'

'You gave me a date to leave, Harry. I've been putting it off since last Christmas. I've booked a family room for the night. I hope you don't mind sharing.'

During one of Laurie's poorer periods, Jenny had spent a week with him at a Spencer Street hotel, almost opposite the station. It hadn't changed: not the reception desk, the tired furnishings, the creaking lift, or the musty odour of the rooms. A crowded little room, three single beds; they wouldn't be spending a lot of time in it.

For dinner they bought fish and chips at a little shop near the corner of Flinders Street, also unchanged in eight years. Nothing better in the world than fish and chips eaten out of paper, with a large bottle of fizzy lemonade to wash the salt and grease down. They picnicked on a street bench, spoke with their mouths full, the kids giggling when Harry burped.

Bliss is to be free in the city with giggling kids and someone from home to talk to. Bliss is a thousand words tossed to the wind, and a thousand words returning.

At seven they caught the tram back to the hospital. The kids weren't allowed on the wards. Told to be as quiet as three little mice, they were left in a downstairs waiting room while Jenny followed Harry to a four-bed ward.

No bliss there. Overwhelming sadness washed through her, and fear, at the sight of capable little Elsie, frail, lost in the space of a city hospital bed, her birdlike hands reaching for Harry, grasping him. And that lovers' kiss. They had seven kids at home: five of their own and two of Elsie's sister's kids. Harry must have been six foot four; Elsie might have stretched to five foot before that bed had swallowed her. Two unrelated entities, fate had stitched into one. And Jenny wasn't needed there.

She kissed Elsie's cheek, told her she'd see her at home soon, and she took her kids outside to a city night where they didn't need to be as silent as three little mice.

After nine they returned to that bed-cramped room, and too much talking, too much laughter, when they got there. Jenny turned off the light and told the kids they had to get up very early. Kids don't sleep when they're on holiday. They thought they were having a holiday. They spoke of Granny's surprise when she saw them coming tomorrow, and asked if they'd still sleep in her bedroom like they used to. And why was Elsie in the hospital? And would everyone be in the same classroom when they went back to their old school? And would Mrs McPherson remember them, and would they be Morrison at their old school or still King? Eleven o'clock before their eyes gave up the fight to stay open; when they closed them just for a second, then forgot to open them. One by one they succumbed.

Cigarettes lit, two heads out the window, and Harry raised the subject of the Hoopers — or Elsie.

'Vern's wife died of a growth,' he said.

'It wasn't in her womb. They cut that out of her when Jim was born.'

'Is he the reason you're going home?'

She drew in smoke and breathed it out. 'He's the reason I know I have to go home.'

'They had him up there again a while back. Nelly Dobson says he's still — not himself.'

'He was a starburst in the black night of my life, Harry. Some stars burn so bright they burn out,' she said. 'Keep your head out the window for a minute while I get into bed.'

She took her frock off, hung it, and made room for herself down the bottom end of Jimmy's bed. Harry kept his head out the window for ten minutes more, then the creaking of bedsprings told her he was lying down.

Room full up with breathing. No rhythm to it. Harry's breathing deep, slow. He'd had a long day, a stress-filled week. Georgie had a clicking little snore. Margot's sleep was sound. Jimmy's feet ran. What was he dreaming?

She rolled to her side, her mind too busy for sleep. Wondered what Ray had done when he'd opened the door and found the dresser missing, when he'd found the kids' room bare. Wondered if Harry was fated to lose Elsie, as he'd lost his brothers, his parents; if God was really up there ticking off names in his account book. She yawned and hoped Norman was sitting at God's desk tidying up his bookwork. Harry and Elsie were family.

Hum of the city, rattle of a lone truck, tick-tick-tick of her alarm clock, the alarm set for five thirty . . . and before the city placed its head down for the night, Jenny was asleep.

PAINTING THE CLOUDS

Jenny had paid in advance for the hotel room, paid for two nights. She could have changed her train tickets and stayed another day, but if things went well at the hospital, Harry wouldn't need her with him; and if the news was bad, three excited kids wouldn't be his preferred companions.

He walked with them to the station, stayed with them until they boarded, but his mind was already at the hospital with Elsie and he had little to say.

Then goodbye land of electricity and refrigerators and flushing lavatories.

'Goodbye, trams,' Jimmy yelled.

'Goodbye, powdered milk,' Georgie yelled.

'Goodbye, thtupid thchoolteacherth,' Margot yelled.

'Goodbye, dear old sewing machine,' Jenny added.

'Goodbye, tell-tale Loith.'

'Goodbye, zoo.'

'Goodbye, elephants.'

'Goodbye, monkeyth.'

No one said 'goodbye, Ray'.

*

Jenny had made this trip at fifteen, with the Salvation Army couple, Dorothy and Donald. She'd made the trip with three-year-old Jimmy, and surely the train moved faster this morning than it had back then.

They ate railway-station fruit cake and shared a bottle of lemonade when the train stopped for twenty minutes at a large station; they walked the platform, looking out at a strange town, then the train called them back and they took their seats. Jenny sat staring out of the window, waiting for the land flatten out, for the green paddocks to change to brown, for the white sheep to become dusty.

'How many more stations, Jenny?'

'Two little ones.'

As a three year old she'd known the name of every station, every siding, on Norman's line.

'How many more miles?' they asked when there were no more stations to count.

'About twenty.'

They wanted to get there. She wanted to get them there. The best cure for bad memories were happy times.

'Close your eyes and count up to a hundred, and I bet when you open them we'll see a herd of white-faced cows.'

They counted, and when they opened their eyes they saw two blue dogs herding those white-faced cows.

There was something about Woody Creek country, something the years were incapable of changing. She recognised a family of argumentative crows bickering on a barbed-wire fence. She recognised a stand of blue gums still sprinkling their shade to the Tylers' rusty-roofed farmhouse. And Lewis's dam with its white clay walls. And his cluster of sheep watching the train go by and still resenting its disturbing hoot.

Same old fig tree leaning over the same old convent fence. More rust in the fence, more bulges in the corrugated iron. And Blunt's shop roof, and the train's elongated warning to kids and dogs at Blunt's crossing. Unchanged, forever unchanged.

And Norman's station — no longer Norman's station, though it would ever be his and little Jenny's. A part of her was still there somewhere, still colouring newspaper pictures with her box of crayons.

The kids, eager to board the train in Melbourne, were as eager to leave it. They ran ahead down the corridor.

'Be careful stepping down!' she called after them.

They weren't careful. She should have been more careful. She almost fell on her face. He was waiting for her. He'd ridden up. Should have known he would. Why hadn't she known he would? Because Friday was a working day. He hated missing work.

Margot ran to him. The other two looked at Jenny for answers. Unable to find her own answers, she took Jimmy's hand and walked down to the goods van to watch her pile unloaded.

Red case. Bedding. Then the cartons, three of them. All there. Jimmy's trike, Granny's tin trunk.

The stationmaster approached her. He wanted her tickets; didn't know he was the interloper here, didn't know she'd lived half her life on this platform, that she knew more about what was beneath it than he'd ever know; of what was beneath his house, buried in his garden. Wondered if he'd unearthed the wooden spoon that had dug its own grave beneath the oleander tree, wondered if it was still blue. Full of memories this place, chock-a-block full.

He took her tickets. Ray hadn't moved, nor had Margot.

The ability to forgive was a good trait. It said so in the Bible. Forgive us our trespasses. Turn the other cheek.

'You'd be a relative of Mrs Foote, would you?' the stationmaster asked.

Jenny turned to him. 'Granddaughter. Is Mick Boyle still the carrier?'

Stupid question. She'd been gone for less than two years, and in fifty years' time Mick Boyle would still be Woody Creek's carrier; Mick or his son, or his grandson. That's the way it was in a town that stood still.

'If he comes by, could you ask him to deliver this lot, please?'

'My wife and myself have got good reason to be grateful to your grandfather,' the stationmaster said. 'There's a bad dose of the flu going around.'

Jenny nodded, glanced at Ray.

'Holidaying, or moving?' the man asked.

Two years in Woody Creek and he was already cataloguing new arrivals like one born to the town. He'd be standing on this station twenty years from now, married into the place by his kids.

'Can I ride my trike home, Jenny?'

'It's too far,' she said. 'Mr Boyle will bring it down.'

'When?'

'Soon. Margot! If you want an ice-cream, walk with us.'

Margot wanted an ice-cream.

They waited for the train to clear the lines, then the kids ran ahead, remembering well where to buy ice-cream. Jenny walked behind them, her heart lurching when the bike roared into life. Thought she'd left the lurch behind. Hoped Ray would be pleased to be rid of her and her kids. Hoped another woman would plug in her iron, her toaster, pick her rhubarb, slice up his livers, boil up his tripe with one of her onions.

The bike roared over Blunt's crossing, turned left into North Street and drove by them as they waited to cross the road. Hated the sound of that motor. It turned into the hotel yard and died. They crossed over to the café.

Mrs Crone standing behind her counter, unchanged, as was her Madonna, still claiming its corner, both untouchable. A good Catholic, Mrs Crone; a good businesswoman too. She still knew how to use that scoop so the ice-cream ball looked solid but wasn't.

He was standing beneath the pub veranda, lighting a cigarette. They'd have to walk by him or go the other way. She'd changed enough habits because of him. This was her town. She walked her troop by him. Didn't look at him. Didn't look at Clive Lewis either. He'd had a talent for football. He'd got out of this town and tried to make it big in Melbourne. He'd come back. Shaky, they called him now, Shaky Lewis. He didn't sleep at the pub, but he lived there.

The kids holding hands, they crossed over Three Pines Road, then, hands freed, they walked down the far side of the road, placing distance between them and Vern's hedge of roses, Jenny pointing out landmarks, hoping Jimmy wouldn't look east, wouldn't remember where Grandpa and Aunty Maggie lived. He remembered and stopped to stare.

'No dawdling,' she said and took his hand again, drawing him on towards Macdonald's mill.

They stopped to give way to a log buggy hauling bleeding logs into the yard, and they smelled again the smell of chewed-up forest while a giant saw screamed its victory over timber and sawdust flew. The mountain of sawdust had grown taller since she'd been gone.

She knew Ray was behind them. The hairs on her neck felt him there. She didn't look back, or not until McPherson's bend when she glanced over her shoulder.

She didn't fear him, not up here. She feared what he'd tell Granny. Feared that he'd been down there already, had already told her what she'd done.

Is it your first, Mr King?

Always afraid of something, of someone. She'd probably pushed her head out of her dying mother's womb afraid. And why not? She'd had a head-on crash with life.

Just get there, find out the worst and deal with it. No use imagining the worst. What you expect never happens.

'Keep up, Margot. And slow down, you pair.'

You pair with those long walking legs, her legs. Margot had the Macdonald short pins — and Maisy's desire never to walk if she could drive.

Ray's legs were long enough, solid enough to walk a hundred miles. He rarely used them to walk on, and was well behind when they crossed over the road and entered into the trees.

The smell of the bush never changed: eucalypt, honey, rotting leaves, fungus, dust. She didn't know if she liked that smell or not. It was the smell of home, that's all.

'Will Granny have some baby goats?'

'She might.'

'And baby chickens?'

'Granny'th alwayth got baby chickenth.'

Cooler walking that bush road. The day wasn't hot, but hot enough to appreciate shade.

'Don't run, Georgie!'

Almost there now, and Georgie wanted to get there. Jimmy had fallen back to Jenny's side, Margot lagged behind, Ray behind her — strung out on that road like a herd of cows at milking time.

Should have known he'd follow her. He loved her — so he said, had said, the second time he'd taken her out. Ridden his bike up here to take her to the movies, to a New Year's dance. He'd probably ridden up last night, while she'd been eating fish and chips, while she'd been standing, head out of the window, smoking with Harry.

Had Margot told him they'd spent the night at the hotel with Harry? Hadn't considered that either. There was something wrong with her head. It didn't think far enough forward, or not about certain things. Free, that's all she'd thought about last night; getting free of him, sleeping free.

The trip up on his bike used to take three or so hours he'd said once. Only eleven o'clock. He'd probably ridden up this morning and gone straight to the station.

''member that train before, Jenny?' Jimmy's hand had crept into her own.

'Everyone can,' Georgie said.

'You weren't there. I mean just me and Jenny, a long time before when we went on the train. And we got a pink ice-block, not an ice-cream.'

'You couldn't possibly remember that,' Jenny said.

'Can so. I dropped it in the dirt.'

She could remember being three; just snapshots. Had his three-year-old mind taken a snapshot of that pink and brown ice-block lying in Woody Creek's dust?

'*When I hold back a tear to make a smile appear,*' he sang. ''member that song, Jenny?'

She remembered, and she sang it with him, sang as loudly as she had when they'd come home from Sydney, knowing Granny would hear them coming, as she had the last time — wanting her to come at a run up that track . . .

Ray was a good fifty yards behind them when they poured in through the boundary gate.

He wasn't wanted here. Wasn't wanted anywhere. Never had been. His mother hadn't wanted him; his father had begotten him then forgotten him. There was little Ray recalled of Big Henry King, other than a roaring presence. And a toy motorbike he'd brought home once from a gymkhana. For a day or two it had raced across the floor.

Raymond King was seven years old before he learned about fairytales and happily ever after. He'd been given the role of Cinderella's coach horse at the school concert. Clad by the town ladies in a crepe-paper costume, told to pull a golden billycart slowly across the town hall stage, little Raymond had done it well and the town ladies and the audience had applauded him. His memory of each concert, each costume, was vivid. The following year, he'd played the woodchopper in Snow White and carried a broadaxe made from cardboard. At nine, he'd worn a clean white sheet and presented a gift to baby Jesus. He was ten when he played the role of Father Bear in Goldilocks. He'd stuttered his first lines that year. Grumpy old bears were allowed to stutter, Miss Rose said.

Eleven was his finest year. Clad in Mr Blunt's suit, a colourful waistcoat and a tall top hat, he played the ringmaster, and for three hours he'd been on that stage, cracking his whip, opening and closing the curtains, bowing and lifting his hat to the audience. Each time he'd walked on, he'd been applauded.

He had never worn the Prince Charming costume. Paul Flanagan wore it in Cinderella. Billy Abbot wore it in Snow White. In The Frog Prince, the Macdonald twins had played both frog and prince. The Prince Charmings of this world didn't stutter.

Ray's first wail may have been a tremulous plea to be someone's prince. It went unheard in Big Henry King's shack, where a bowl of burnt porridge was as close as it ever came to happily ever after. Filth and neglect should have killed him before his first birthday. Five of his eight siblings had succumbed before reaching school age.

On his first morning in the classroom, he'd fallen in love with Miss Rose, the infants mistress, in love with her name, her pretty clothes, her perfume, her gentle voice, and her fairytales. Her concerts had transported him into a magical world.

Ray was eleven when the fairytales ended. Big Henry King, woodchop champion, drunken giant, was crippled by a falling branch at work. When they carried him home from the hospital, he'd shrunk. Spent his last days sitting in an invalid chair on the veranda while his bitch of a wife sat with her crones around the kitchen stove, a coven of draggle-haired witches, their strident laughter a cackling insult to the cripple who sat in messed pants.

Big Henry had needed someone to run up to the pub for a billy of beer, and for much else that no father should ask of his eleven-year-old son. For Ray, being needed was similar to being loved.

On the last morning of Big Henry's life, he'd needed his son to bring him a basin of hot water and his razor. He'd wanted to have a shave because it was Sunday.

Ray would never forget that cut-throat razor. It had a white bone handle and a blade so sharp it could slice through Big Henry's beard like a spoon through porridge. He couldn't find a piece of soap that morning. Big Henry couldn't shave without soap. By the time he'd found a bit of soap, the razor had been on the floor, its handle painted by the dark red blood spouting like a tap from his father's throat.

To his dying day Ray would see that blood. To his dying day he'd remember running for Constable Ogden. He could see them now, Ogden, Vern Hooper and half a dozen more standing looking surprised that so much blood could have come out of one man. To his dying day Ray would hear his nasty bitch of a mother telling those men how her brainless, stuttering oaf of a son had handed his father the razor so he could cut his own bloody throat.

As a kid, Ray's eyes had shuddered when he'd fought too hard for words. He'd fought for words that day, needing to tell the constable that his father had said he'd wanted to clean himself up for Sunday. Palms pressed to his temples, Ray stood before those men striving to push those words down and out through his mouth. They wouldn't come out.

They'd taken Henry King away and left Ray alone with that nasty bitch who wouldn't stop blaming him, wouldn't stop calling him a stuttering idiot, an overgrown oaf.

He'd done something stupid. It hadn't felt as if he'd done it. He'd felt icy-cold, that's all, crackling cold, as if the words in his head had turned to ice and were burning holes through his skull. He'd heard the devil's words cursing his mother to hell. Had seen her fly the width of the room but couldn't remember hitting her. To Ray, it had felt as if those iced-up words in his head had blown like a gale from his mouth, that he'd blown her over with words.

His two brothers came home for Big Henry's funeral. They were twelve and fifteen years Ray's senior. Molly, eighteen years his senior, told them how Ray had knocked his own mother down. The brothers took him out to the wood heap to teach him what happened to stuttering, overgrown bastards who hit their widowed mothers. They'd blackened his eyes with their lesson, they'd broken his nose and left him lying on the wood heap. And later, when that nasty bitch saw what they'd done to him, she'd laughed.

God paid her back for that laughter. She went to bed one night and didn't get up the next morning. She was still asleep at midday. Ray had stood at the foot of her bed playing with one of the brass knobs on the old iron frame, spinning it with his finger until it spun off and flew like a spinning top to land on her pillow, on her hair. He'd expected her to sit up and call him names. She hadn't. She hadn't moved when he'd retrieved the knob and screwed it back where it belonged, or when he'd pulled her hair, pulled a bit out by the roots.

He'd gone to get the constable again, not running this time, but walking slowly and twisting that length of hair around his finger, like a ring.

Ray would never forget his father's funeral. It was like one of Miss Rose's fairytales. The men had made Big Henry King a heavy rough-cut red-gum coffin; eight wood cutters strained to carry it. Outside the Catholic church, two long lines of timber workers, axes over their shoulders, had sung Henry off to the grave. They hadn't honoured Ray's mother when she'd been planted in the same grave ten days later. Ray hadn't honoured her either. He hadn't gone to her funeral.

He'd ridden into town with his sister, but when they went to the church, he'd gone home.

Anything worth taking had been taken. Big Henry's work boots were still there. Ray's brothers couldn't fill them. Ray's feet had almost filled them. He'd felt taller with those boots on. They hadn't taken an old tweed sports coat. It made Ray's shoulders broader. A worn-out felt hat had covered his clipped-to-the-scalp head, had made him old enough.

He'd left the shack with a wheat bag over his shoulder; inside it, a broken pocket knife, half a bag of porridge, two rabbit traps, a rag of blanket, a dented saucepan, half a box of matches, his toy motorbike and half a tin of treacle. He'd walked down to the forest road and kept on walking, walked out past Nurse Foote's land, out past Wadi's camp, just walked; lost track of how far, for how long, where he'd walked.

Walked a lot of slow miles in Big Henry's boots, learned where to set his rabbit traps, to cut and stack a ton of wood for a corned beef sandwich. He'd slept in hollow logs, in sheds, under bridges, followed rivers and sometimes roads.

He'd followed a railway line for a few days. Rabbits liked railway lines. Ray had liked rabbits. He must have been thirteen, as tall as he'd ever be, when he'd found himself amongst a thousand houses and no more rabbits. Plenty of cats. They had more fight in them and hadn't tasted as good.

He'd knocked on a few suburban doors asking to cut wood. Most had turned him away. Hungry, so hungry his gut had stuck to his backbone. Starving, footsore, he'd leant against a fence to watch a woman trying to chop a branch as thick through as she was. She was wearing a pretty flyaway gown, green, had looked like Miss Rose — until she turned around.

'What are you staring at, boy?'

He hadn't replied. Ray had given up on talking.

'Can you use an axe?' she'd said.

He could use an axe when he was five years old.

He'd swung that axe for her that day, and when that branch was down, her front yard lost beneath it, she'd applauded him. It had been a long time since anyone had applauded Raymond King. She'd gone inside, but minutes later came out with a meat sandwich and a mug of sugared tea. He'd never forget the taste of that sandwich, that cup of tea.

He'd trimmed the branch later. She'd pitched what he trimmed over her neighbour's fence; and when there was no light left to trim, to pitch, her decrepit old housekeeper had come out with a plateload of mashed potatoes and hunks of meat swimming in gravy.

He'd eaten in the yard. They'd stood, two crazy old dames, on the veranda, choking with laughter while he shovelled in that pile of potatoes.

'Raised in a pig pen were you, boy?'

Maybe he'd nodded.

'Dumb are you?'

Maybe he'd nodded again.

They'd laughed at Big Henry's boots. He'd wired a bit of car tyre to the soles. It stopped his feet from wearing out.

Boy, they'd called him. 'I'd change my boot repairer if I were you, boy.'

They'd tossed him a pair of fancy shoes and a blanket later, and told him to be on his way by sun-up. The shoes were too small for his feet but he'd cut the toes out of them with his pocket knife.

The sun hadn't come up the next morning. A fine rain drizzling down, he'd started cutting the solid section of that limb into foot blocks, stacking them down behind her wood heap. The old dame had watched him from her veranda, sucking on cigarettes she poked into an eight-inch holder. They'd fed him breakfast: two eggs, toast with butter and three sausages. He hadn't known there was so much food left in the world.

She hadn't liked trees. Her neighbours had been too fond of them — every leaf in Armadale fell in her yard, she said. That afternoon he'd climbed a ladder and cut more limbs. They'd kept feeding him.

He must have been going on for fourteen. His birthday was in July. It could have been July the night she came out to the wash-house and told him to get inside. Freezing cold, half asleep, he'd followed her into a house the likes of which he'd never seen. It had a bathroom and a tub full of steaming water, big pink towels hanging on a rail, and a brand new bar of pink soap sitting in a china dish shaped like a swan.

'Get yourself clean, boy. You stink,' she'd said.

He hadn't known folk had rooms used for nothing but getting yourself clean in. He'd never sat in a bathtub of hot water. He'd used her pink soap that smelled like Miss Rose and he'd watched the water turn brown. She'd come in while he was sitting there and placed a bundle of clothing on a stool, then she'd washed his hair.

No one had ever washed his hair. At home, his mother's clippers had never left him any to wash.

The night of his first bath he'd told old Phoebe his name and she'd stopped calling him Boy. She'd had a different way of saying Raymond: *Ramón*, she'd said. After a time he'd got to feel like he was playing Prince Charming in one of Miss Rose's concerts. Old Phoebe had dressed him in fancy costumes, bought him soft shoes that fitted his feet like a second skin. He'd got to like playing Prince Charming, winding up her gramophone in the dead of night and dancing with her in her parlour.

He must have been sixteen when she sent for a tailor. He'd made Ray a three-piece suit. When she was happy with it, she'd clad herself in scarlet satin and scented furs, and, like the nobs, they'd travelled in a taxi cab to a dance hall.

Travelled to many more in the years thereafter. Rode in taxis to theatres, to balls, old Phoebe clinging to Prince Ramón's arm.

He'd been old enough for the army when war broke out. Couldn't get a word out the day the army doctor checked his heart and lungs. Maybe the forms the doctor filled in said *stuttering, brainless oaf.* The army hadn't wanted him.

Factories weren't so particular. He'd worked at a few through the war years, working six days a week and raked up the old girl's leaves, lopped intruding branches on Sundays. They'd fed him, clothed him.

He'd squired old Phoebe to theatres and dance halls through most of the war years, then one day she'd stopped dancing. She hadn't stopped thumbing her nose at her neighbours; thumbed it every time she'd dragged herself out to the letterbox; hadn't stopped hosing the neighbours' kids when they'd thumbed their noses back.

She'd sent for her solicitor a few months before she died. They'd all come when old Phoebe called: butcher, baker, hairdresser, doctor, tailor. She'd been someone once. Miss Fisher, they'd called her. The parson came one day, with the solicitor and his clerk. They witnessed the marriage of Phoebe May Fisher and Raymond

Henry King, then the parson witnessed the signing of Phoebe's last will and testament.

In Miss Rose's fairytales, witches were all wicked. They died badly. The old girl had died by the inch. He'd looked after her. He'd looked after her for so long he'd started wishing she'd ask him to bring her a razor. She'd never done that to him.

He'd wound that gramophone and cared for the old girl to the end, believing he and her antique housekeeper were the only souls on earth she had to care for her. Not until she died did he find out just how many had cared. They'd come out of the woodwork at her funeral: her brother and his wife, her niece, cousins, a lover or two, a couple of discarded husbands.

A smart old dame, she left her money to her housekeeper, her jewellery to her antique hairdresser, with her furs. Most of her furniture went to the Salvation Army. She left the house to her brother. Left Ray her bedroom suite, her small dining-room suite, her refrigerator — and free tenancy of that house for his lifetime. Twenty-six at the time, he might expect to live rent-free for another forty or fifty years.

Her brother wasn't happy about that. Phoebe hadn't expected him to be happy. Smart as a whip, that crazy old girl, she'd invested a thousand pounds with her solicitor in Ray's name. He'd get it on his thirtieth birthday, if it hadn't been swallowed up in court costs.

She hadn't been cold in her grave when her brother's solicitor sent the first letter. Sending a solicitor's letter to Ray was as much use as handing a small-toothed comb to a bald man; he could just about work out the headlines in a newspaper. He'd found *Phoebe May Fisher-King* in the funeral column, and filled in a few nights working out *passed away at home after a long illness*. He didn't waste five minutes on a letter couched in language designed to confuse a university professor. Pitched it out with the rubbish. Pitched the next one too.

Phoebe's brother knocked on the front door on a Saturday morning six or eight weeks after the funeral. Ray didn't invite him inside. The brother told Ray, and most of the neighbours, that the will of his crazy bitch of a sister wouldn't stand up in court. Ray locked his front door, went out through the back door and caught a tram into the city where he spent a portion of his hoarded wages on a motorbike. The following week, he spent a bit more on a leather helmet, goggles, leather jacket and riding boots.

Someone turned off the electricity, but he wasn't home often enough for lack of light to bother him. That bike introduced him to another world. Girls liked it. Turning off the gas was of no great concern either. Pubs served up what he ordered, and with a glass of beer.

They came to his door in force three weeks after the gas was turned off, Phoebe's brother and his solicitor. They suggested that given the drastic housing situation, empty rooms were sacrilege. They suggested that the house, if split into flats, could house three families. They suggested too that unless he agreed to their terms, the electricity and gas would remain disconnected until after the court case. Then they suggested that for a nominal fee to cover electricity, gas and rates, Ray might retain his bedroom in the eastern section of the house.

Ray told them he liked living alone, thanks, though not always sleeping alone.

They came again, the brother, the solicitor and Geoff Parker, and told him there was nothing in the will stating that anyone other than he had free tenancy, and if he brought a woman into the bloody house again he'd be tossed out on his ear.

Then his sister died. No one told him. No one knew where he was to tell him. He'd taken to reading the funeral columns in the rear pages of the *Sun*. They were repetitive; work out one and you could work out a lot of the next one. He learned that Molly Martin had *died after a long illness, at her home, in Woody Creek.*

Molly was his sister. He could probably thank her for his survival, or curse her for it. He didn't know why he'd got onto his bike that morning, but once he'd been on it, he'd kept on riding.

Being back in that town, seeing Big Henry's shack, had made him sweat. He'd gone to the draper's to buy a clean shirt for the funeral and chanced upon pretty little Jenny Morrison, the singing petunia from that last night of Miss Rose's concert fairytales. Couldn't believe she remembered him. Fifteen years since he'd walked away from that town. She couldn't have been much more than six or seven years old at the time.

'Ray King,' she'd said. 'I went to school with you.'

She'd gone with him to Molly's funeral, maybe only to ride on his bike, but he'd seen how his brother looked at her, how his cousins looked at her. He'd never owned anything that every other bastard in the world had wanted. He'd decided that day to have Jenny; and when next Phoebe's brother, solicitor and son-in-law turned up, Ray told them he'd think about giving up the west side of the house, the hottest side of the house, that he'd pay half of the bills, as long as he could have a wife living there with him, as long as they fixed up a bit of a kitchen for her on the east side.

They'd turned up the following evening with papers for him to sign. It had taken four months for old Phoebe to die and she hadn't done it silently. Ray told the brother's solicitor to give his papers to Phoebe's solicitor, that he'd sign them where and when Phoebe's solicitor told him to sign.

They'd worked it out between them while Ray continued his pursuit of Jenny. And he'd got her.

And now he'd gone and done something stupid and lost her.

He'd done a few stupid things. Maybe he had hit his mother like she'd said he had. He knew he'd hit Jenny. Had seen it written in those kids' eyes. He'd seen her face.

Hated himself for what he'd done to her face. He loved her beauty. If someone had asked him to describe his wife, if he'd had the words, he might have said, *She's a petunia, fighting for space to grow in a bed of onions.* He didn't have the words.

A MILLION EGGS

Gertrude didn't hear them coming. Her goats did. Six or eight of them stood at the fence, big and small. The chooks cackled their welcome, the rooster high-stepped towards them, wings spread wide to scare off rivals. The kids remembered mad roosters and dodged behind Jenny as she opened the chicken-wire gate.

'Granny?'

The door was shut. Jenny opened it.

'Granny? Are you in there?'

She must have gone to Maisy's to wait for Harry's call.

One foot inside and Jenny knew. Smell of sickness in a cold kitchen. No stove burning. No kettle singing.

And from the bedroom, a death-rattle cough, and a voice that didn't sound like Granny's. 'I told you kids to stay out of here.'

Jenny's kids stayed outside. She didn't. Nor did Ray. At the station she hadn't spoken to him. She spoke to him when he came to stand at the curtained doorway.

'We have to get the ambulance.'

257

And Granny, choking for air, trying to rise up and fight for her right to die alone, vomited on her bed, and not for the first time.

Gertrude Foote had cared for the sick for fifty years. She wasn't going to be seen by ambulance men lying in her own vomit.

'I'll get you clean, Granny.'

Hated the howl in her voice. Howling would do no good.

The bed she'd expected her kids to sleep in tonight was down the northern end of Gertrude's room, piled high with cartons of God only knew what. Jenny pitched them to the floor, pitched a pile of newspapers, a box of empty jars, not seeing what she was pitching or where she was pitching it, just working her way down to the bedcover. When she stripped it back, there were no sheets on it. Sheets behind the middle door of Granny's wardrobe. She snatched two, found pillow slips, and felt him behind her.

'I have to get her clean.'

Hated howling in front of him, hated herself for speaking to him. Would have spoken to old Wadi had he been here; would have spoken to Lorna Hooper — or to the Devil.

'I'll f-f-fix it,' he said, taking the sheets from her hands.

She filled the washbasin at the tap, found soap, a piece of towelling and old towels, and, when he left the room, she rolled the soiled blanket back and saw an old woman in a fouled bed.

Ripped the nightgown from buttoned bodice to hem, got it off the only way she could. No fight left in Gertrude. She lay like the burning dead, offering no resistance while Jenny soaped her with her hands, washed her as she might wash a baby, with water cold from the tank. Gertrude's heat would turn it to steam. Hated seeing the age of her, cried for her age, welcomed her tears for their blurring of the evidence of age.

Had to leave her to fetch clean water. He was in the kitchen. He took the basin from her hands.

'More,' she said.

He brought more.

She washed the end of Gertrude's plait, then released it and washed her hair. Perhaps soothed by the touch of cool hands, Gertrude went away, her only protest from lungs bubbling like a pot of porridge, groaning like a wind storm.

Clean gowns in the bottom drawer, where they'd ever been. Getting that gown on was like dressing the dead, but she fought old arms into the sleeves, pulled the gown down to cover her.

'Ray. Can you help me?'

He came, carried Gertrude to the clean bed, supported her while Jenny propped her high on pillows and spoke again of the ambulance.

'L-l-let her g-go in her own b-bed, J-Jenny.'

'She's dying.'

He didn't deny it. She looked at him, wanting him to deny it; looked at Gertrude, resting on clean pillows, and knew that the last thing in the world she'd want would be to die old and helpless in a hospital bed. How many times had she said she'd die with her boots on, after a good meal?

Howling hard, Jenny turned away. He reached out a hand to her, but she walked to the other bed, blindly bundled the soiled bedding, nightgown, the towels she'd used. Halfway to the shed and she changed her mind and carried her bundle down to the rubbish heap, pitched it. He came with Gertrude's mattress; nothing else to be done with that bedding.

The three kids behind him, wanted to know what they were doing.

'What's wrong with Granny?'

'She's sick,' Jenny said. 'And stay away from me. I'm covered in her germs.'

Watched the mattress tossed to the pile, not knowing what to do, what Granny would want her to do. Birds warbling, chooks clucking, bees buzzing, Gertrude's land speaking to her.

She turned towards the orchard. 'Lemons. Run down and find me a couple of lemons, Georgie.'

Granny had sworn by her flu brew: the humble aspro, brandy, honey and lemon juice. They'd been her medicines the last time there had been flu on her land. All three kids ran. Ray reached for a cigarette.

'Wash your hands,' she said. 'That mattress will be covered in germs.'

Like one of her kids, he jumped to do her bidding, and sadness, pity for him, near overwhelming her, she followed him to the tank, couldn't hold his big brown lost lamb eyes when he passed her the soap. He was Dr Jekyll and Mr Hyde and she was married to both of them. And she couldn't think about that now.

'You might light the stove for me, please, Ray.'

Wiped her hands on her hips and walked across to the shed. The worn-out mop was where she'd left it — Granny had never liked mops. A floor wasn't clean unless you got down on your knees and scrubbed it clean. Jenny liked mops and boiling water. A cold-water wash today, but plenty of phenol on the shelf beside the old wooden wash trough. It got Gertrude's room smelling clean. Later, the old brown curtain ripped down and pitched to the rubbish pile, the lean-to shutters open, kitchen window open, stove burning, Jenny reached for the packet of aspros on the top shelf of the dresser, for the brandy, always kept up there, safe from the hands of kids. Honey in the Coolgardie, safe from ant attack, and that safe not cool like it should be. It required water. She filled a bucket at the tank and poured it into the metal-lined reservoir on top of the safe.

This place needed people, that's all. Everything was here, just needing hands to make it function. You could put your hands on anything in Granny's house if you knew where to put them. Jenny knew. She found the lemon squeezer, the sharp knife to cut the lemons.

'What's the time, Jenny?' Georgie said.

'After twelve.'

The clock on the mantelpiece told a different time. It didn't wind down in a day. Fix it later.

Two aspros crushed to powder, mixed with a dash of brandy, a good spoonful of honey, the juice of a lemon, a spurt of water from the kettle, already warm, and she entered the phenol-scented bedroom to feed the brew into Gertrude, a teaspoonful at a time. A new-born will reflex-swallow. Gertrude swallowed.

The stink of burning feathers infiltrated the room before she was done. Ray had lit the stove; now he was attempting to burn Gertrude's feather mattress — or send smoke signals to the cavalry. Hoped they'd come to the rescue.

It brought the Hall kids running through Joe Flanagan's wood paddock, thinking their house was on fire.

'How long has Granny been sick?'

'She got it when Brian got it, and told us to stay away from her — that Dad didn't need to be worrying about us as well as Mum,' Joany said. Just a kid of twelve or thirteen. 'I came over this morning and she yelled at me to get out.'

Lenny was fifteen; Ronnie, the youngest, the tallest of the three was the scrawniest — another elongated Harry in the making. He had Harry's rusty hair, his blue eyes. None of them looked like Joey, were like Joey. He wouldn't have left Granny to die in her own vomit.

'How's Mum?' Lenny asked.

'The doctors will be operating now. Your father said he'd phone Maisy tonight.'

Or phone earlier if the news was bad. Enough bad news in this place. It wasn't going to be bad.

She left the kids and walked over to Ray, poking now at the mattress with Granny's rake. 'Would you have a spare cigarette?'

Too willingly, he dropped his rake and offered the packet. She got one out. He struck a match. God, let me hate him, she thought as she leaned in close to get a light. Couldn't hate him, not when he was like this. Stood with him for a minute, sucking in nicotine but smelling the stink of feathers.

'There'll be a tin of kerosene near the wash trough in the shed,' she said. 'Toss a bit on with some wood. If you can get what's underneath it burning, it might catch on.'

He knew how the city worked. She knew how this place worked, knew without thinking. And she couldn't afford to think, not right now. Just do; just do what had to be done and think later.

She sent the kids off to find eggs. They found dozens of them, precious as gold in Melbourne and here for the taking. Jimmy loved fried eggs.

'There's millions everywhere, Jenny.'

A food market, Granny's land. Milk on the hoof, vegies in the garden, meat on the wing in the chook yard.

The kids were eating fried eggs and potatoes when Mick Boyle arrived. No room for more in Gertrude's house. The lean-to took most of it; the bottom end of the kitchen absorbed the rest.

She must have known something when she'd rolled Sissy's mattress. Had to scrub Granny's bed first, then it would absorb Sissy's mattress and the pillows. She made up the sleep-out bed with Norman's sheets, his blankets. Emptied one carton into Gertrude's dresser cupboards. The rest could wait.

She was cooking scrambled eggs and potatoes at six when Elsie's kids walked by again, taking the diagonal short cut through Joe Flanagan's wood paddock to town. They'd want to be at Maisy's when Harry made his phone call.

Seven o'clock, seven thirty, and they hadn't returned. If the news was bad, Maisy wouldn't allow them to return. Jenny looked for them when she tucked her kids into the lean-to bed, all three worn out by their day. Left their window hatch wide open, fresh air blowing through, blowing the germs away, please God.

Ray left for town at eight, the same way as Elsie's and Harry's kids had gone. Hoped he'd find his way through. She watched him hold down the wires of the dividing fence and step over, watched him head into the trees. Then picking up the milk bucket she walked out to the paddock to call the goats in, as Gertrude had called them, by tapping on the bucket's base. She'd milked goats before. Hoped they'd allow her to milk them. They came, three gentle old nannies to stand in line. They didn't argue about her out-of-practice hands either, maybe relieved to give up their load.

She'd learnt a lot on this land. Hadn't learnt much in Melbourne. Loved and loathed this land. Loved its bounty, its sky, its moonlight. Same moon as Melbourne's, but bigger up here — more sky for it to grow fat in. More stars too. Different sounds. Different smells.

Still loathed the smell of goats, but by the time that orange moon had escaped the hump of dark trees, she had two-thirds of a bucket of free milk; pints of milk for porridge, for puddings. She had wood on the wood heap; an old black stove where the kettle was always boiling, the oven always ready to cook. If she belonged anywhere, it was here. If she'd learnt anything in her twenty-four years, it was how this place worked.

'It's all pre-recorded somewhere up there,' she told the moon. 'I was meant to come home today. It's all written down. I'm just following a script. If you're sitting up there waiting to scratch Granny's name out, don't do it, or I'll walk off the stage.'

Bone tired when she carried her milk back to the house, that happy train ride now light years away. She'd been picked up by a time machine, moved from 1947 twenty years back. Same table lamp burning on the same old kitchen table. Same milk strainer. Same chipped enamel jug. No Granny sitting beside her stove. Granny burning up in bed.

Another lemon squeezed, Jenny was crushing aspros when the Hall kids came home, came to stand at the door, all three talking at once.

'Mum's good, Dad said. It doesn't look like cancer, the doctors reckon. She was still asleep, Dad said.'

'That's a weight off your minds,' Jenny said.

'How's Gran?' Lenny asked as they were leaving.

'Bad.'

It took too long to spoon in the flu brew, and Gertrude choked on it and stopped breathing. Jenny hauled her away from the pillows, shook her, held her against her and thumped her on the back. That forced a breath in. She held her with trembling arms for minutes, then, more carefully, spooned in the last of the brew.

Probably the wrong thing to do. Not knowing the right thing, she did what felt right. Fetched a basin of water from the tank at ten — and the old climbing rose bush grasped at her arm, asking for news of Gertrude.

'I've got to cool her down,' she told it, or told herself. 'That's what she'd tell me to do.'

Bathed her with cool cloths, bathed her long legs, her long narrow feet, and by lamplight they looked young, too vulnerable without their boots. She washed old work-worn hands, kissed those hands and thought of kissing Norman's dead hand, and she held Gertrude's face between her hands, kissed her cheeks, her brow while she could, spoke weary nonsense to her while she could.

'I'll let your goats go dry, my old darlin'. I'll sell the young ones to the butcher. I'll eat your chooks — the ones I don't let starve. I came home so you could save me, so wake up and save me. That's your lifetime job, so wake up and get to work.'

Not a movement out of her, barely breathing, but cooler maybe. She lifted her away from the pillows and propped her higher, placed an ear to her chest where the wind storm still raged. It would be all over by morning.

Or maybe it wouldn't.

Ray was back, with his bike, and wherever Gertrude was, she heard that motor and flung her arms attempting to rise from her bed. Someone needed her.

'It's Ray. It's Ray's bike. We're here with you, darlin', and I'm never leaving you again. Wake up and talk to me.'

He came in with a bottle of lemonade, a loaf of bread, two packets of cigarettes; and maybe she was pleased he'd come back, certainly pleased to see the bread, the cigarettes. She washed her hands, her face, combed her hair, and cut bread, ate it with honey, drank tea with goat's milk, helped herself to a cigarette, and reached for Granny's matches to light it.

Always a box of matches on the mantelpiece, on the dresser side of the mantelpiece. Always and forever they'd been kept in that same place. They'd lived there long before Jenny could reach them. Reaching that mantelpiece had been a childhood measuring stick.

Twelve years old when she'd outgrown Elsie. Fourteen, and as tall as Amber, when she'd stopped growing, stopped being. Stopped. Believed for a long time that if not for the twins, if not for Margot, she would have grown as tall as Sissy, as Granny. Knew now that height had never been written into her master plan. Archie Foote measured five foot six, an inch more than Juliana Conti; their offspring had been lucky to ever reach Granny's matches on that mantelpiece.

'She's spent her life running around after the people of this town,' she said. 'Why didn't those kids tell someone she was sick?'

'Old Ph-Phoebe w-wanted to die in her own b-bed.'

He'd said her name.

'How old was she, Ray?'

'Y-y-younger than your gran. H-how old is —?'

'Seventy-odd.'

Didn't want to work out the odd bits, not tonight. Didn't want to know how many odd bits there were.

'Did you get a room at the hotel?'

He shook his head. She was relieved about that. Didn't want to be way out here with three — six — kids, not tonight.

'Toss one of those blankets on the couch,' she said. 'I'll sleep with Granny. She won't dare to die if I'm beside her.'

Joany was the first of Elsie's kids to take to her bed with the disease. Ronnie had it but refused to lie down. On Sunday morning, Margot started her *ahzeeing*.

'I'm thick.'

She was. She wouldn't eat, and when Margot wouldn't eat, she was sick. Two lots of brew to mix that morning, but Gertrude was improving. She took her midday brew from the cup, then coughed like a dog with distemper.

Six o'clock on Sunday night when Jimmy vomited. She settled him in beside Margot; knew she had the disease too, but refused to admit it. Once Ray was gone she'd deal with it, and Harry was coming home tomorrow.

Ray had brought no change of clothes and little money. He knew he had to go home. She wrapped a dozen eggs, placed them into a brown paper bag. He liked eggs. It was all she had to give, and a ten-bob note for petrol.

She walked with him out to his bike, watched him place the eggs into his saddlebag — from a distance. She expected him to mount the bike. He didn't.

'I g-g-get c-crazy jealous, Jenny.'

Didn't want this scene. She wanted a strong dose of flu brew and to get her limbs down. Had to play it out to the end, and play it the right way.

'I couldn't have managed here without you. I'm grateful, Ray.'

'I d-d-don't know w-w-w-what I'm d-d-doing when I'm drunk.'

Sometimes there was no answer to make. Sometimes there was nothing to do but look up at a sky lit like a Christmas tree, to reach for a cigarette just for something to do. She lit one. The smoke hurt her lungs. They felt raw. Her throat felt raw.

He reached for her. 'I w-w-want us to m-make up, Jenny.'

She stepped back. 'There's nothing to make up, Ray. We're parting as good friends. I'm grateful to you.'

She sounded like a cracked record. What else was there to say?

'I'll c-come b-back on F-Friday.'

'No. I came home because I want to be here. I'm not leaving Granny again.'

'I'll g-get a mill j-j-job.'

'You've got a house and a good job down there. You belong down there.'

Bats flying, feasting on unseen bugs; music floating across the paddock. She used to sit in the moonlight with Granny listening to Harry's wireless.

'We're m-m-married.'

'I'm sorry, but I'm not the wife you need.'

She drew on the cigarette and the smoke tasted bad. She tossed it down, ground it out, sighed in air. And fresh air hurt her lungs.

'I'm sorry you found out I got rid of that baby, but I'm not sorry I did it. I'd do it again. Having kids splits a woman into pieces. We leave pieces of ourselves in every one of them. There wasn't enough of me at fourteen to split, and I've done it again and again. Just go, Ray. I don't want to be your wife or anyone's wife.'

'I n-need y-you.'

'You need a girl who's got no scars, someone who wants nothing more than to go to bed with you and have your babies. You're a nice-looking man. You'll find her. And when you do, take her riding in the moonlight, talk to her. Don't close yourself off from her like you did from me.'

'I'll u-u-use those things you b-bought.'

'Oh, God.'

She had to get him gone. She had to breathe, and get this scene played out calmly, decently. Just get him gone then go to bed and sleep until she woke up. That's all she needed. For him to be gone and a long sleep. She'd be fine in the morning.

'I w-won't t-touch you if you d-don't tell me I c-can. I p-p-promise —'

'It's too late, Ray.'

'I g-g-got n-no one, Jenny.'

'I'm sorry.' The howl was back in her voice and she had to control it. 'Why didn't you tell me that in Melbourne? Why didn't you tell me you'd nursed old Phoebe for months, that she'd wanted to die in her own bed? You hid your best parts from me.'

'Y-you would h-h-h-have said what they all s-s —'

'I would have said you were a kid, like I was a kid when I got pregnant with Georgie, that we did what we had to do to survive. I would have been pleased that the big boy who'd saved me from Sissy had found a way to survive when everyone in town thought he was dead. We were two kids dealt unplayable cards, Ray. We make bad partners but good friends. We can stay friends.'

'I g-go m-mad when I g-get drunk —'

'Getting drunk makes people into who they want to be. It made Norman brave enough to fry cheese sandwiches in Amber's kitchen; made eighteen-year-old twins fearless enough to rape me. You wanted to kill me. I can't live with that.'

'I'll c-come on Friday n-night.'

'You've got grounds to divorce me. Go home and do it.'

Walked away from him. Left him standing out in the moonlight, looking like a Roman gladiator, tall, strong-featured, unarmed — and waiting to be eaten by the lions.

WAITING FOR PETROL

She slept for five hours on the cane couch. Georgie woke her. Jimmy had vomited all over the bed.

Jenny washed him on the table, changed his pyjamas, placed him into her couch bed, made up Granny's spare bed for the girls and got them settled before hauling the new mess out to the shed. Carried water from tank to shed and howled for Melbourne's water.

This too would pass. In a day or two, it would pass. Harry would be home this morning. Just get through this morning, leave the mess soaking in the trough, a shake of Persil, a dash of phenol to kill the germs.

Jimmy on the floor when she returned, his big eyes open but no longer seeing her.

Aspro. It was all she had. And while she was feeding it to him in honey, his skinny little body went into convulsions. He wet his clean pyjamas, soiled them, and was unaware of what he'd done. Held him and howled on him, and, when his little body relaxed, ran with him in her arms to Elsie's house.

'Lenny! Lenny!'

He came to the back door, pyjama-pants-clad.

'Get the garage man. Jimmy's bad. I have to get him to the hospital. Get Maisy. Get anyone with a car. Hurry.'

Carried Jimmy home, praying, pleading for Lenny to hurry, for the garage man to hurry, Archie Foote, anyone. Maybe it was too early for the garage man to be at work. What time did he open? Her watch said eight.

Holding Jimmy was wrong. He was burning. She was burning and heating him more. Had to cool him down. That's what she had to do. Wet cloths. That's what she had to do.

Got him on the floor, a towel beneath him, got water. She was on her knees, bathing his half-naked little body, when she heard the motor. Thank God. Thank God. Thank God. Wrapped his lower half in a towel, pulled a singlet over his head.

Motor running, car door slamming, the gate squealing open. She was wearing the wraparound gown she'd worn since Georgie woke her. It was crushed, wet, gaping. She pulled it straight as a long shadow fell across the floor. Expecting the garage man, or Maisy, for an instant she didn't recognise Lorna Hooper's silhouette against the light. Saw the white handkerchief held to her nose. Get anyone with a car, she'd told Lenny. Garage man not at his garage, he'd got someone. That was all that mattered.

'He took a convulsion. I have to get him to the hospital.'

'Clothe yourself,' Lorna Hooper said.

Red case open on the stripped lean-to bed. Chaos in there. She grabbed the first frock she put her hands on, the blue linen. Got her wrap off, got it on. Shoes? Where had she left the shoes she'd worn home? In the kitchen.

Lorna was halfway out to the car, Jimmy in her arms, before Jenny located her walking shoes beneath the couch. Got them on, snatched her handbag from behind the door, then, with no word to Granny or the girls, she ran, her frock unbuttoned.

She was opening the chicken-wire gate when Lorna did a reverse spin. The wheels of the big black car bucking, gears grinding, the car took off up the track, Jenny left standing, belt dangling, bodice gaping.

She'd get Jimmy to the hospital. That's all that mattered. Couldn't have the air in her car polluted by the town slut. Of course she couldn't. That didn't matter. It didn't matter if her beautiful boy rode with the devil's handmaiden as long as she got him to the hospital.

She was still standing at the gate when a second car drove onto Gertrude's property and came bumping down the track. Gone from town too long, she didn't recognise it. Someone wanting Gertrude? Nurse Foote wasn't available.

She buttoned her frock, did up her belt then recognised Lenny seated beside the garage man. She met the car in the yard, not understanding why they were here.

'Lorna Hooper took him.' Giving voice to those words made her understand, and her heart lurched. 'Who told the Hoopers?'

'Miss Hooper was waiting for petrol,' the garage man said. 'You'll be right, then?'

Vern was Jimmy's grandfather. He'd get him to the hospital. He'd demand the best attention for him. That's all that mattered. Nothing else mattered. That's what she told herself. Her stomach told her a different story. It wanted to vomit. Nothing in it to vomit out.

Garage man leaving; Lenny's bike in his car boot. Lenny ran after the car. It stopped. She watched the bike lifted out, knowing she should get in that car and follow the Hoopers to Willama. But he'd be safe in hospital. He'd be safe there until . . . until Harry came home. Quarter past eight. The train got in between ten and ten thirty. He'd be safe until then.

Car bumping up the track. Watching it go.

'Joany's pretty crook with it,' Lenny said. He sounded like Harry.

'Aspros,' Jenny, mother of three, said. If she'd learnt anything in Melbourne, it was how to be a mother. 'There's plenty of lemons on the tree. Sweeten it with honey.'

She swallowed two aspros with water, picked up Jimmy's soiled pyjamas and the towel and took them out to the shed to be tossed in with everything else. Not enough water to cover them. Wanted Melbourne's taps.

Drank black tea with a squeeze of lemon, and when the aspros reached the aches in her, when they wrapped a cushion around her nerve endings, she filled the copper, got it boiling, tossed all bar the blanket in to boil clean. Washed the blanket; heaved everything over the clothes line.

Ten thirty: Granny coughing her lungs out but wanting news of Elsie.

'It's not cancer. Harry will be home soon to tell you all about it.'

'Ray?'

'He had to go back to work.' Tell her about that later.

Looked for Harry at eleven, wanting another adult close by, needing him to convince her that Jimmy was safe in hospital. Watched for Vern Hooper's car, hoped it would come, didn't expect it. Watched and listened until eleven thirty, walked outside each time she heard a motor approaching. Trucks drove by. A tractor. No Harry.

Mixed up a double dose of flu brew for Granny and drank half of it before offering the rest.

Margot had the constitution of an ox. She wanted to get up to go to the lav. Jenny carried her out, carried her back to bed. Georgie had the disease, or the headache and sore throat of it.

'Stay in bed,' Jenny told her.

'What brought you home?' Gertrude asked.

'Homesick.'

At twelve Lenny rode off to town to find out what had happened to Harry. He came home with aspros and honey and the news that Harry had missed his train, that George Macdonald was in hospital.

One o'clock. 'I'm going into town, Granny.'

She cut through Flanagan's land. The last paddock looked too wide. But she crossed it, climbed between the last wires, and the stooping lifted her head from her shoulders. Walked up Blunt's Road, her lungs straining to feed limbs sufficient air. Legs of lead, trembling at the distance they still had to go. They carried her down to Hooper's corner.

His roses were an assault, their massed blooming wrong today, red, pink, orange, heavy giant blooms. Too much colour, too much perfume. And no car in the yard. She walked by the roses, following a bricked path between green lawns to the front door where she knocked.

The hollow empty sound of her knock put the fear of God into her heart. She hammered at that door, then forgot her legs were leaden and ran around the veranda to the back door to hammer there. Locked.

Ran then, up past the hotel and over the railway line, each breath of air hurting. A twin opened Maisy's door. Looked by him, looked for Maisy. She came, dressing-gown-clad, a small coughing boy behind her.

'Can I use your phone, Maisy? Jimmy's in hospital.'

'We took George down last night.' Maisy's nasal voice was a croak today. 'He's in a bad way.'

Didn't want to hear about George Macdonald. Didn't want to hear about Harry's missed train, or about Elsie's chloroform.

'Harry said he slept for the first time last night, slept through until seven,' Maisy said.

The phone in her hand, Jenny placed the call.

'The operation knocked her about, he said, but she was talking to him last night. The doctors seem to think she came through it well.'

Nodding, barely listening, waiting for that call to go through. 'What's taking them so long?'

'The place is chock-a-block,' a twin said.

'They say Ernie Porter's in a bad way with it,' Maisy croaked. 'He's been down there since Saturday.'

A woman's voice on the line.

'I'm enquiring after my son, James Morrison — Hooper. He was admitted this morning.'

The woman had no record of a James Morrison Hooper, no Hooper-Morrison, no Morrison-King, nor any near-six-year-old boy admitted to the hospital this morning.

'He has to be there,' Jenny said. 'His grandfather took him down early this morning. Vern Hooper.'

The woman didn't know Vern Hooper. She gave Jenny a list of local doctors and their telephone numbers. No pencil. No paper. A twin offered a pencil and pad. She touched what he'd touched. Sometimes there is no choice. Legs shaking, stomach shaking, head pounding, only fear keeping her on her feet now, fear and her need to locate Jimmy.

A twin brought a chair from the kitchen. She didn't thank him, didn't sit down. Her third phone call located Jimmy, or located where he'd been. Mr Hooper and his grandson had seen Doctor Frazer this morning.

Almost two o'clock. Where had they taken him?

'They'll be staying at the Farmers' Arms, love,' Maisy said. 'They'll want to keep him down there close to the doctors.'

'Why isn't he in the hospital?'

'They put the old man out on the veranda. It's wall-to-wall beds out there.'

Maisy gave her a Bex tablet and a glass of lemonade. 'One of the boys will drive you home, love.'

She'd crawl before she got into a car with one of them, and she wasn't going home. For years she'd feared Vern would steal Jimmy. In Sydney, when Jim had been listed as missing, she'd feared every car that pulled into the kerb out front of Amberley. She'd feared Vern when Norman had died, had feared leaving Jimmy at the school gate in Armadale.

And she'd brought him back to this town.

Constable Denham knew her. He knew the history. He'd find Jimmy.

She left Maisy's house and walked the short distance to the police station. A stranger answered her knock.

'Is Constable Denham in?'

He'd moved on to Bendigo. And her legs gave up the fight and sat her down on a weather-worn bench seat; and her mind gave up the fight to remain coherent. She said too much, spoke too fast. The constable told her to slow down, to start from the beginning, but the beginning had been too far back. Today, there was only today.

He brought her a glass of water. She didn't want water. She was breaking up — head, body, heart. He told her he knew Vern Hooper and his daughters, that they were good people. He knew Mrs Foote too, knew where, how, she lived. He drove Jenny home and told her he'd contact his Willama colleagues, get in touch with Mr Hooper, that he'd contact her when he had news of her boy, and to pop into bed and get some rest.

She poured the last of the brandy into a glass when he'd gone. Its taste was vile but she drank it and lay down on the cane couch to die. And did, until seven that night, when she rose to dose the rest of them, and herself, adding rum to her brew this time. If anyone called for her in the night, she didn't hear them.

The constable woke her at nine. He stared at the girl who had difficulty opening the door, a girl who might have been a movie star playing the role of destitute wife, and he imagined what she might look like in high heels and fur coat, stepping into a limo.

He knew now that she'd been involved with Vern Hooper's son, had been engaged to him, had a baby to him that the son spent two years in a Japanese prison camp, that she hadn't waited for him but wed a stuttering, bike-riding lout. He'd heard it all this morning on the telephone, from Miss Hooper. He'd heard that she and her father had been in touch with the city police, that her brother, the war hero, had charged Jennifer and Raymond King with the wilful neglect of his son.

The constable saw, smelled, the neglect that morning.

AN UNFIT MOTHER

*H*arry didn't miss Tuesday's train. He came home to his own houseful of sickness, came home with his other kids, four of them and two coughing.

The constable's car returned at three, Vern Hooper in the passenger seat. Jenny walked out to the gate.

'Is your husband about, Mrs King?' the constable asked.

'Where's my son?' she said.

'Mr Hooper and myself would like a word or two to your husband, if we may, Mrs King.'

She pushed the gate open. 'Jimmy is my son,' she said, bypassing the constable to approach the passenger side of the car. 'He's my son.'

'Your son, and my grandson,' Vern said.

'Where did you take him?'

'Where he'll be well looked after.'

'I want to talk to Jim.'

'All you need to hear from Jim is that he's charged you with neglect of his boy.'

Vern remained in his seat. The constable stood looking across at Harry's house, at smoke billowing up from its chimney, a swarm of kids playing outside.

'You know he was never neglected. His teacher, everyone knows . . .'

Too sick for this; back aching, neck, her limbs felt like bruising on bone, head aching, throat too raw to fight any more.

'Tell it to the judge, girlie,' Vern said.

'You can't do this, Mr Hooper. I love him.'

'If you loved that boy, you'd do the right thing by him. A fight in court will do him and no one else any good, and you can rest assured I'll take it to the highest court if I have to. An agreement between you and Jim will be the best way to handle this, best for all concerned.'

'Where is he?'

'With his father, where he should have been two years ago.'

'I want to talk to Jim.'

'He doesn't want to talk to you.'

She turned to the constable, two hands holding her head onto her shoulders. 'He wasn't ever neglected. He was sick. I sent Lenny in to get the garage man.' Tears blurring the constable, blurring Elsie's house. 'The garage man will tell you he came down to take him to the hospital. She came in and she took him.'

The constable had spent the past half-hour speaking with Vern and his daughter. They'd passed on information received from their investigator. Miss Hooper may well have walked into that shack and taken her nephew, but if a judge got to hear half of the dirt the investigator had dug up on Mr and Mrs Raymond King, he'd no doubt hand her a medal for kidnapping that boy.

'You haven't got a leg to stand on, Mrs King,' he said.

Her legs were leaving her; she gripped the police car's door-frame, the windowsill, and hung on. Harry coming across the paddock, Josie in his arms. Had to hold on, that's all. Harry knew she'd never neglected those kids. Head spinning, or the yard spinning, roar of the ocean in her head, shaking her head, forcing her eyes to see the face at the window.

'You know me, Mr Hooper. You know me.'

'I know you, girlie. I know about that filthy abortion business you got involved with down there too. And if you've got the brains you were born with, you'll want to keep that from your grandmother.'

A punch below the belt. It wrung the air from her raw lungs. And he saw what his words had done and hit her with more of the same.

'Any woman who'll do to her unborn what you did to yours is no fit mother for my grandson, or for the others you've got. I'll see them all taken away from you.'

'You would have let him die unborn.'

It was the howl of old ammunition, useless against him. He waved it aside with his hand.

'Make it as dirty as you like. It won't do you one iota of good.' He raised a finger, Jim's finger, Jimmy's finger. 'You went after my boy to ruin your sister's wedding, and there's never been a doubt in my mind of that. You got Jim so screwed up about you, he didn't know if he was coming or going.'

Then he hit her with his death blow. 'We've got our investigator chap looking into what you got up to in Sydney. He's already found the lodging house. He'll know more by the date of the hearing.'

The devil was in Granny's yard raising a heat haze. Blurred white chooks swaying, yard trembling, walnut tree shaking, pecking chooks vibrating the earth beneath her feet.

She'd used Jim's name in Sydney. Jenny Hooper had been six months pregnant when she'd left the clothing factory. They'd found Amberley. They'd find Cara Jeanette. Little three-year-old girl with Jenny's hands.

Just one more rape, Jenny Morrison. God's account book fallen open again at that old dog-eared page. Lie down in the dirt and spread your legs, Jenny Morrison. It's no use fighting any more.

She fell to her knees. Vern didn't bother opening the car door to put the boot in. He did it seated.

'Do you want your grandmother to see your name plastered all over every newspaper in Australia? That's what's going to happen if you force me and Jim to court. We'll do it. You've got my promise on that.'

Sky darkening, raining newspapers. ABORTION emblazoned on the front pages. Raining photographs of wide-eyed, smiling kid Jenny, holding fast to her talent quest envelope. WOODY CREEK SONG BIRD SWAPS BABY FOR FREE BOARD. The headlines buried her. They blacked out the day.

The constable carried her inside, and, having got her there, found a coughing old woman collapsed beside a bed, two little girls trying to lift her.

He drove Jenny to the hospital.

WITHOUT COERCION

*N*ight of the long nightmare, of Norman's train racing in her head, the roar of it, the circling of its hundred wheels. Factory in her head, piles of prison-camp bodies on the inspection table, wire trolley full of body parts she had to sew back together. Had to find the right bits, do what had to be done.

And voices. Voices too loud in her head.

'Mrs King. Mrs King.'

Not the factory. She hadn't been Mrs King at the factory. Everything was wrong. Sissy was there in her rainbow taffeta. Everything was wrong.

Beside the lake, beneath the trees . . .

'I'll put a cheque in your hand today.'

Had to sign the cheque for Sissy's dress. That's what they wanted. She'd got Norman's money. Nineteenth of April 1950. It was wrong. Couldn't sign it yet. Sissy always wanting something. Always getting what she wanted. Let her wait.

'A couple of signatures today will bury what I know.'

Words hammering against her eardrums. Wheels. Clacketty-clack, clacketty-clack, clacketty-clack. Stowed away on the ghost train to hell, old devil squatting down there, waiting for her soul.

Two devils, bargaining for her soul . . .

'Money is nothing to me, not without that boy to plan for. She's had him for six years.'

Six, sixty-six. He wasn't six. Third of December he'd be six. Cara Jeanette was the third of October. Couldn't know one without the other. Tried to lift her head to tell them he wasn't six. Magnetic pillow beneath a head of iron. Iron coffin. Hot.

Contract in the devil's hand. Why didn't it burn?

'W-w-what's it s-s-saying?'

'That he'll end up owning every penny I own, every penny his father owns too. What more can she want for her boy?'

Chuckling papers.

'I n-need g-g-glasses.'

'It's simple enough. This one says, *I, Jennifer Carolyn Morrison King, without coercion, and being aware that it is in the best interests of my son, James Hooper Morrison, do hereby relinquish* . . . This second one is to do with the legitimising of the lad's birth. He'll be his father's son, and my legal heir.'

What's in a name? A rose by any other . . .

'Your father's name is still respected in Woody Creek. They'll spit on it if I'm forced to use what my investigator chap dug up on you and old Phoebe Fisher. Her brother is prepared to stand with us in court and swear that you wormed your way into that old lady's affections. And don't doubt I'll use him if you force me to. I'll use that abortion business, drag up the business with her mother. Our team can keep this in the headlines for months if we're forced to. Or we do it clean. We do it here today.'

And all our yesterdays have lighted fools the way to a dusty death . . .

'For Jim's and the lad's sake, I'd prefer to do it clean. Your boy will be raised in a mansion to know the best that money can buy, girlie. He'll be educated at the best schools. It's his father's turn now. He's missed out on six years of watching his son grow. You do the right thing by him now.'

'T-t-take the p-pen, Jenny.'

You can't fight two. Lie down and take it. Sign away your soul and they'll go away.

White paper chuckling in her face. Gold and maroon pen dripping black insects to the sheets.

Just a fly in everyone's ointment, Jenny Morrison. That's all you ever were. Drag your feet across their chuckling paper. Then lie down and die.

There was a landlady called Myrtle,
Who lived in a shell like a turtle,
Until one fine day, she decided to play,
and Myrtle the Turtle was fertile.

SCATTERED CHILDREN

Cara Jeanette Norris, born on a kitchen floor, her swaddling cloth a striped tea towel, was, at the moment, walking with her father, Robert, looking at the pretty flowers.

A pretty child, clad in a red tartan and lace frock, shod in dainty shoes, her head a golden halo of tight-spring curls, her eyes as blue as the early December sky. Pretty as a picture, tiny Cara Norris, and full of questions.

'Is stars a bit like . . . like the sky's flowers, Daddy?'

'Stars are like suns, poppet.'

'Where did them all go . . . when . . . when it gets light time, Daddy?'

'They're still up there in the sky. Our big sun is so bright we can't see them.'

'Why?'

Environment is seventy-five per cent of the child, the experts say. Experts are often wrong. Environment may influence a child's aspirations, her vocabulary, the tone of her voice, but Cara Jeanette Norris was Jenny's child.

Robert Norris had met the girl who gave birth to his daughter. He recalled a pretty young thing, country-clad, a chubby babe on her hip. Myrtle had known her well. She spoke often of their daughter's resemblance to Jenny, and since the chap had come knocking on her door enquiring after a Jennifer Morrison who had lodged at Amberley during the war years, Myrtle had argued to sell the house and move far away.

'A house is only a house, Robert.'

But a house can be much more than a house if it is in a familiar area, in a familiar city, when well-known shops are just around the corner, the station a few blocks away. A house as large as Amberley can also provide a good income.

'You're worrying needlessly,' Robert Norris said.

'Mrs Collins has commented on Cara's hair a dozen times. She knew Jenny well.'

'She knew her as an adult, not as a child.'

'She was little more than a child when she was here.'

'Mrs Collins will move on when she retires. Her son is in Melbourne.'

Had Lorna Hooper not been abroad with her Langdon relatives at the time, she may have travelled to Sydney with her investigator and seen Cara at play. She would have recognised her hair, her eyes, as Jenny's. Vern's retired policeman investigator had sighted the infant at her mother's heels when he'd knocked on Amberley's door but had not known of nor had he been in quest of that child.

Twice he'd knocked, and once Myrtle had come on him in the laundry, speaking to Mrs Collins, a sweet-natured woman, but far too chatty.

'Who sent him here, Robert?'

Their daughter had been fathered by one of the five American sailors who, Jenny claimed, had carried her down to an unknown beach where all five had had their way with her, then left her naked there. Had she lied? Had the boy been in love with her? Had he known there was to be a child? Was he attempting to find that child?

'If that chap comes back, Robert, I'm taking her to New Zealand. You can stay behind and sell the house.'

The investigator didn't return. Vern Hooper had his grandson.

On Christmas Eve of 1947, Father Christmas found the scattered children of Jenny Morrison. He delivered a fluffy black and white puppy to Amberley, a puppy that moved its head and yapped when a key was inserted into its tummy and given a few turns. Cara named him Bowser, like the shadow puppy dog Robert created on the parlour wall.

To a substantial house in a tree-lined street in Balwyn, a north-eastern suburb of Melbourne, the bearded old chap delivered a shiny red and silver bicycle, fitted with small trainer wheels. Or Aunty Maggie pretended Santa had left it beneath the tree. Michael, Jimmy's new friend, said Santa wasn't real, that mothers and fathers bought the presents.

While the Christmas chicken roasted, Jimmy rode the bike in circles around the garden and remembered riding his old red tricycle. He thought about its wheel spinning around and around so merrily the day it travelled away from Ray's house on the cart. He knew his trike was very lonely, and sad too, because Jenny and Granny and everyone had gone to live with the angels. Aunty Maggie said so.

Angels were good though, and they could sing, and Jimmy bet that Jenny was singing 'Painting the Clouds'; and she might even really be painting the clouds because she'd told him his daddy had painted the rainbows when he was dead. He wasn't dead any more though, because after Christmas dinner was finished, everyone was getting in the car and going to see his daddy, who wasn't living with the angels, anymore, but with the nursing sisters, who were like halfway to angels, Aunty Maggie said.

It was good that people who had gone to heaven could come back sometimes. Jesus had. Jenny hadn't told him about Jesus coming back from being dead. She hadn't told him about Santa Claus not being real either. He wished he could ask her if he was real. He'd asked Aunty Maggie, but she always said just nice things, not true things. Jenny had said true things. Like Aunty Maggie said babies came from stars falling from heaven, but Jenny said they grew from seeds planted in the mother's tummy gardens.

Around and around he rode on his new bike, his mind making its own small circles. Nowhere else to ride down here but in circles. The house had a tall fence and iron gates so no one could get in and he couldn't get out, except in the car. Or sometimes he went out with Aunty Maggie and they rode on a tram exactly like the same tram he and Jenny used to ride on. The city was exactly the same, though it didn't feel like the same, unless he closed his eyes very tight and just listened.

He couldn't close his eyes on the bike or he'd run over the garden beds, then Grandpa wouldn't take the little balancing wheels off. When he did, it would be a proper grown-up bike, and one day, one day when the gate was open so Lorna could get the car out, he'd ride that bike out, ride it very, very far until he found the 'just one' railway line, that went all the way to Woody Creek and he'd ride there. Jenny and Granny and everyone might have come back from heaven.

In Gertrude's house, no one believed in Santa Claus. Margot and Georgie received new school shoes, new frocks and two giant balloons.

While Elsie and Granny were serving out Christmas dinner, Teddy Hall blew Margot's yellow balloon up until it burst. She howled and hit him with Gertrude's poker, and he punched her, and Harry took his pop gun away from him, because boys didn't hit girls, even if they deserved it.

'She told me to blow it up bigger than Georgie's,' Teddy argued. 'You didn't have to buthted it.'

Always bedlam at Gertrude's on Christmas Day.

Elsie's kitchen table carried across the paddock, any Hall kid capable of carrying a chair carrying one, the cane couch moved out to the yard to make room. They'd made enough room for thirteen. Home-grown vegetables crowding the plates alongside home-grown chicken, Granny's seasoning, Elsie's gravy.

Jenny's plate was as crowded as the rest. She pushed it away when she heard that motorbike.

He kept coming back, and coming back.

He bought Margot a doll's tea set, bought Georgie a picture book, bought Jenny a ring, two hands clasped. A friendship ring? He didn't know his wedding ring had bought flour, porridge. She placed the ring back into its box and, with nothing more to give, gave him her meal, her chair at the table, then walked away from the house.

He found her mid-afternoon, sitting on the water-dipping log at the creek.

'Th-th-this is no p-place to l-live, Jenny. C-c-come home.'

She took her shoes off and slid into the water, swam to the other side where he couldn't reach her. He couldn't swim.

For two hours he sat on the log waiting for her to swim back. She didn't, and when his cigarette packet was empty, he walked back to his bike. Left without a word to the girls, to Gertrude.

He didn't come back.

THE BRIGHTEST STAR

Vern Hooper came back. He made his final trip out along the forest road on a Saturday in January when 1948 was still brand new. He knew he'd get no welcome from Gertrude. He wasn't looking for a welcome. He wasn't too sure what he was looking for; maybe to make peace with himself. He'd done the right thing by that boy. There was no doubt in his mind about that. Maybe he wanted to convince Gertrude that he'd done the right thing by that boy.

The boundary gate was closed. He had one foot on the ground when she came out of the trees.

'Where is he?'

He hadn't expected to see her. Nelly Dobson had told him not half an hour ago that Jenny Morrison hadn't been sighted since they'd brought her home from the hospital. He got his foot back into the car and closed the door. He wasn't down here to get into a slanging match with her; wouldn't have come near this place had he known she was down here. He slapped the gearstick into reverse and the big car moved back.

'You answer me!'

He didn't.

The track was narrow and overhung by trees. His head through the open window, watching the path of his rear wheels, he didn't see her pick up a solid length of fallen timber. He heard it smash into his windscreen.

'You wild little bitch.'

'Tell me where he is!'

A bankbook he'd intended giving to Gertrude to post to her was on the passenger seat. He reached for it, spun it at her.

'Take your money and get your life sorted out or you'll lose the other two.'

Wind currents on a warm day can't be relied on. Spin a flat stone and if it's done right, it will skip on water. Spin a slim book by its corner and if it catches the right air current, it will fly. He didn't wait to see where it landed but continued backing up the track. She didn't chase her money. She chased his car, and got his driver-side door open. The track wasn't wide enough. He hit the brake.

'He's mine.'

'He was, now he's mine. Let go of that bloody door.'

'I want to talk to Jim.'

'He doesn't want to talk to you.' Or anyone else.

Vern fought her for that door. He was stronger. He got it shut, got it locked, tried to wind up the window but her hand was inside, gripping the doorframe. He stopped winding before he cut it off, then he slipped the car out of gear. His bloody knee was throbbing with the effort of holding down the clutch.

'Your boy shook his father's hand on Christmas Day, and if you could know the feeling raised in a man's guts at seeing those two Hooper hands meeting, then you mightn't begrudge it to me.'

These were the words he'd prepared for Gertrude. They cut no ice with Jenny.

'He's mine. I carried him. He's my son.'

'He's my grandson, a Hooper. The papers you signed at the hospital state that you'll make no attempt to see him. It's over. Now let go of this bloody car.'

She clung to her only contact with Jimmy, and Vern was too old for this.

'For all I know or care, you might have been the best mother in the world to him. You might have even loved his father at one time. It makes no difference to me. Can't you get that through your head? You had the misfortune of giving me my only grandson. He's the reason I've kept on living, and now he's living like he should have been living five years ago. Christ almighty! Can't you see what we've done for him? You named him Hooper. What the hell did you expect a man to do?'

'You let me think Jim was dead.'

'And thanks to you, he may as well be.'

Again the gears engaged and the car moved back. You can't back a car up a narrow track while arguing. He clipped a tree, heard the screech of his paint peeling away from metal as he hit the brake.

'Now look what you made a man go and do.'

His car would wear the scar of this day, and his overbearing bitch of a daughter already spent enough time telling him he was unfit to drive the bloody thing. He drove forward, heard a second scrape. Unfit to drive; unfit to get out of the car and look at the damage too.

'You've got time to have ten more and no doubt will. I've got no time left. I've got no legs left to walk on. All I've got is money, and your boy to leave it to when I'm gone. Now for Christ's sake, let go of my car and pick up your money. Let it buy your life into some sort of bloody order.'

Then, too fast, carelessly, he backed up the steep rise to the forest road, determined to shake her off. She stumbled, but didn't let go.

The gearstick slapped into first, he hauled on the steering wheel and turned that big car towards town.

He shouldn't have come down here. He'd been coming down here for too bloody long. Her face was close, a face he'd known through every stage of its life. Her eyes had lost none of their colour, though the light behind them had gone.

'You fool of a bloody girl. You were the brightest star this town ever grew. You could have bought and sold every bugger in town if you'd played your cards right — and look where you've ended up.'

He took off then, the motor roaring, those big wheels spraying gravel, whipping Jenny with gravel as she ran beside him.

She let go.

An eye for an eye, laddie, his grandfather whispered in his mind. And fair enough too. She'd killed the life in Jim's eyes. He'd killed the light in hers.

An eye for an eye.

It had taken him six years, but he'd done what he'd set out to do. His grandson wouldn't grow up a bastard in this town.

PART TWO

JIMMY'S GONE

A blistering, smoky month, January 1948. The forest knew Jimmy was gone. It burned for him. Then the storms came, and for days on end the thunder gods beat their drums and lightning lit the land, but not a drop of rain fell on the blackened earth. The creek was down to a trickle out near the bush mill. Teddy Hall hooked a mighty Murray cod. It was damn near as big as ten-year-old Teddy, but he landed it, and dragged it home in a wheat bag.

Then March, and the heat worse than midsummer. They blamed lightning for the fire out at Three Pines. Not much they could do about it but let it burn. They saved Monk's old house, lost a few outbuildings and most of the fences, a few head of sheep.

Then the mother and father of all storms hit Woody Creek. Hail as big as golf balls hammered the town. Gertrude's goats ran bleating from the bombardment; Georgie stood in the doorway watching them run, watching lumps of ice dance on dust.

For two days more, the sky wore black, then its days of mourning passed and that violent summer of no Jimmy gave way to the wet ash smell of autumn without Jimmy.

The girls stopped asking when he was coming home. Gertrude stopped saying, 'Jim will look after him, darlin'.'

Jenny sat. She slept, and sometimes walked while others slept, or slept while others walked.

Elsie came to the house to help with the sauce-making. Tomatoes mutilated by hail were good enough for sauce.

Maisy drove down with a bicycle for Margot, who didn't like dogs, who wouldn't cut through Joe Flanagan's wood paddocks to school with Georgie and Elsie's kids. She didn't like bikes either. For a week, Maisy supplied a private taxi service to and from school. At the end of the week, she suggested it would be easier if Margot moved into town from Monday to Friday.

Silence in Gertrude's house then. Long, long nights of Jenny's silence. It made Georgie scared; she wanted Jenny to talk to her.

'Will I read the paper to you, Jenny? Jenny, you know that man in Brunswick? Remember that man who got burned in Brunswick — well, he stole a big heap of ration coupons. Will I read it to you?'

'Read it to me, darlin',' Gertrude said. 'My old eyes aren't much good by lamplight.'

Georgie read of thieves and politicians, of cricketers and unionists, of murder and beauty queens — just the same old news, only the dates on the newspapers altered, only the names of those deemed newsworthy.

Margot had more interesting news to relay at weekends.

'Nana Maithy'th got proper lightth like in Armadale. I can't even thee to read with that lamp.'

Long weekends.

'Granny said to stop your *ahzeeing*, Margot. Jenny's asleep.'

'Why can't I thtay with Nana Maithy all the time?'

Please God, let her stay all the time with Nana Maisy. Please God, take this cup away from me. I never wanted it.

Never wanted Jimmy either. Jumped off the shed roof to shake him out of me. A Richmond doctor would have got rid of

Georgie. I would have got rid of Cara.

Is it your first, Mr King?

It wasn't his first. His first had gone the same way as his second. She'd done it. Her fault. She'd given the Hoopers the ammunition, and they'd shot it back at her, straight through her heart.

'Nana Maithy'th got a vacuum that getth all the dutht out of her houth.'

'I'm very fond of my dust,' Gertrude said.

'You get thick from dirt.'

Monday night, a quiet night, Georgie reading of Jews moving back to the land of Jesus, now the land of the Arabs.

'Was Jesus an Arab or a Jew, Jenny?'

British troops were getting out of the place, packing up to go home, or packing up to get on a boat to Australia. Georgie read about British migrants by lamplight.

'Why are they all coming out here, Granny?'

'They've got millions of people in England, darlin'. The government doesn't think we've got enough,' Gertrude said.

Australia was prepared to take in the world — as long as they were white.

'*Those of colour who found sanctuary in Australia during the war have been given notice to quit the country,*' Georgie read. 'What's *sanctuary*, Granny?'

'A safe place, darlin'.'

'Like here is a sanctuary?' Georgie said.

'A sanctuary from what, darlin'?'

Georgie glanced at Granny, thinking before she replied. 'I liked school in Armadale, and the trams and everything, when Jenny was making heaps of money.'

'From her sewing?'

'From singing mostly.'

'Singing?'

'She got lots and lots of money from that. When she was in the pantomime, me and Margot and Jimmy didn't have to pay, but hundreds of people had to buy tickets, and she came home with piles of money.'

'Is that true?'

'She was Snow White. In the last September holidays.'

'She didn't tell me she was singing down there.'

'You were sick when we came home, then she got sick.'

'Why did you come home, darlin'?'

'If we didn't, the Hoopers wouldn't be able to get Jimmy, would they?'

'He's with his daddy who loves him.'

'Is Margot going to stay with Maisy and her fathers, Granny?'

'She'll come home again when Jenny is well.'

'My father can't ever get me, can he? Even if she's not well?'

'Never, my darlin' girl.'

'I don't even want one now.'

You can hold your mind still. Sometimes. You can hold your limbs still. You can't hold time still. Old clock hands jerk forward, deducting minutes from hollow days, and when enough hollow days erode, they turn into hollow months. Enough of them, and the first autumn of no Jimmy gives way to the bitter winter of no Jimmy.

White frosts that winter, bleak foggy days, and the old black stove, too hot in summer, insufficient to take the chill away from the dark kitchen.

Gertrude and Georgie sat close to the stove at night, the oven door open, icy feet propped on the hearth tray before it. Jenny didn't sit with them. Bed was her sanctuary, bed was one more day over, bed was dreams. Sometimes they were kind.

'She's going like Amber, Mrs Foote. We need to get her to a doctor.'

'All she needs right now is peace and quiet, Maisy.'

'Margot says she won't talk to anyone.'

'She's got nothing she wants to say to anyone.'

'I remember those terrible days with Amber. The only thing that would shake her out of herself was the doctors.'

'She's not Amber.'

Never, never Amber.

Recovery started with the blood plum tree. It looked like a snow of blossom in the spring of '48. Then the peach trees joined the display, and the apricot. The climbing rose, not to be outdone, unfurled its insignificant buds and Gertrude's west wall and half of her roof bloomed pink. A bunch of roses ventured in through the bedroom's window hatch and Gertrude didn't have the heart to cut them off or lock them out — or not until the petals fell.

Jenny slept in the spare bed in Gertrude's room. She liked that hatch closed, liked the dark. Bright as day when the moon rode high.

Ghostly galleon, tossed upon cloudy seas . . .

Given time, the petals fell. Jenny closed the hatch and brought the dark back, but bruised petals stuck to bare feet. She opened the hatch to see where they'd fallen.

Someone had to sweep them up. She came to the hearth for the small shovel and brush, and those green eyes that darkened to black by lamplight watched her, followed her, and when she returned the shovel and brush.

'Princess Elizabeth has got a baby boy, Jenny.'

Baby boys and baby girls. Babies, babies, babies. That's what life was, babies and war and more babies for more wars.

Nature fought its own wars on Gertrude's land that spring. The wisteria — a mass of perfumed lilac beauty for a month, and for the rest of the year a rampant weed — was doing its best to rip the boards from Gertrude's shed. Harry took to its main trunk with the wood axe and cut it down, cut it below the earth, buried it. Within a week it sent up a hundred suckers to continue the war.

Each year the forest sent in its young to reclaim the lost territory of Gertrude's land. A clump of saplings had taken hold near the main gate; a veritable forest of saplings had claimed the eastern end of her rear boundary. The pumpkins, demanding more than their allocated patch, fought the silverbeet for space to extend their empire — and won. It was everywhere: the winners and the losers. That's what life was about. The winners and the losers.

Pumpkins dictated time passing. Each day their fruit doubled in size, feeding well on goat and fowl manure. And the tomato plants — their tiny golden star flowers fell away to expose green berries, and too soon the weight of tomatoes threatened the branches they grew on.

Old garden stakes from last year, from ten years before, still leaned where they always leaned, in the eastern corner of Gertrude's shed.

Gertrude and Georgie heard the hammer, and together they walked to the window to watch Jenny hammering stakes into the earth.

'She's very good at growing things. We grew heaps of tomatoes in Armadale, Granny. We made your chutney, and when he wouldn't buy anything, we had chutney pancakes.'

Gertrude hadn't lived for near on eighty years and not learnt to read between the lines. She asked few pointed questions but a good listener learns enough.

In December, Jenny saw the first blush of pink amid the rich green of Gertrude's tomato patch. That's how she knew the first year of no Jimmy had passed. That's how she knew he'd turned seven. She hadn't been there.

That's how she knew she hadn't been here for little Georgie. Not so little now. Big teeth growing, filling up the gaps. Worried eyes, as green as Laurie's, watchful eyes.

Mine. No one else ever for little Georgie.

'My beautiful girl.'

Little Georgie running from her words, running down to the

orchard. Jenny thought she'd left it too late, but Georgie returned to her side with a handful of apricots.

'They're nearly ripe, Jenny. I like them best when they're just nearly ripe. You do too, don't you?'

Little shadow stuck to Jenny's elbow that day, eyes full up with hope, that day. You have to feed hope. You have to. All there ever is is hope.

The heat came too fast. It ripened the apricots early; big apricots, tasting as none other.

'Armadale apricots looked like marbles, Granny. They didn't even taste like your apricots but they made good jam.'

Christmas only days away and the jam jars found, boiled clean, paraffin wax seals melted down. Elsie and her girls came over to sit five around the table, cutting fruit, pitching the stones into a bucket. Little Georgie sat with them, using that sharp knife like a woman — not so little Georgie, grown out of the faded orange and green dress she'd chosen from Coles.

'Why do yours grow so big and in Armadale they didn't, Granny?'

'It's all of my good manure,' Gertrude said.

'We used Ray's livers to grow good rhubarb down there.'

'Ray's livers?' Joany Hall asked.

'He used to buy livers and we used to bury them near the rhubarb. Jenny used to say a poem over the grave. Remember, Jenny, about Mrs Cow's liver?'

Jimmy had bought a tin monkey the day Georgie bought that dress. Wind up its key and it played the drums. Someone had hidden it beneath the veranda and its cogs had rusted.

Georgie and Gertrude had allowed Jenny to hide, but they'd wound her key daily. She found a sharp knife and joined them at the table, cutting apricots and tossing the stones into the bucket.

SO MUCH FOR DREAMS

Cars were big news in 1949. Few had been built during the war. Australia was now building her own: the Holden, 'designed in Australia for Australian conditions'. A farmer from out on the Willama road was the first in town to buy one. He parked it out front of the post office one Friday where it spent most of the afternoon, bonnet up, men clustered around it, peering into its works.

Two months later, the farmer's seventeen-year-old boy decided to see if the car would go as fast as its speedo promised. Seventeen-year-old boys are indestructible — though he'd turn eighteen before he was released from hospital.

'The buggers roll too easily,' the farmer said. 'There's something wrong with the design of those Holdens.'

Vern Hooper's car needed replacing. Lorna was hard on gearboxes and clutches. In May, he spent a few hours wandering around the Exhibition Building, his grandson holding onto his hand. *Acres of cars with free-flowing lines and jewel-like paintwork*, the newspaper advertisement had said. It hadn't mentioned the acres of car enthusiasts. Vern's legs weren't up to negotiating their way through crowds. He stood a while, getting his breath, and admiring a black Daimler with a price tag big enough to choke an elephant.

'Will we get that one, Grandpa?'

So much taller than he'd been at six, the last of the baby gone from Jimmy's face. His hair, always allowed to grow a little longer than fashion decreed by Jenny, was well trimmed now. It showed the shape of his head, showed his small neat ears, his skinny little-boy neck. He'd adapted. Life is what it is to a child.

He wasn't Jimmy any more. He'd been taken to the church and baptised with his proper name: James Morrison Hooper. Vern still called him Jimmy sometimes. Most times he called him lad. Lorna called him James. Margaret called him her darling boy.

The Menzies government got into power in December of '49. Few in Woody Creek voted for him. It was a labour town, full of labourers. They called Menzies 'Pig Iron Bob'. You can't please all of the people all of the time, though he pleased a lot of drivers when in February of 1950 he ended petrol rationing.

Road traffic increased. Car accidents increased. Road deaths increased. The police blamed worn tyres, so the price of tyres increased.

Georgie turned ten in March of 1950. Sissy turned thirty-one on the same day. In April, Margot had her eleventh birthday, and Norman's money, invested so long ago, matured. A lot of dreams had been pinned to 19 April 1950. So much for dreams. Maisy took the cheque and Jenny's unworn bankbook to Willama when she drove down to visit her daughters. She paid the money into Jenny's bank account.

In June, the rationing of butter was abolished. In July, coupons were no longer required for tea. The country was racing forward under Menzies. Work commenced on a bridge out near the Aboriginal mission, a bridge promised back in the twenties. Men and machines were ripping up the old stock-route road. The work brought the first foreigners to town: blond-headed, blue-eyed blokes, ten or twelve of them, housed in hurriedly erected huts not far enough from Gertrude's boundary gate.

Vern missed Woody Creek, missed his roses, missed Gertrude. Melbourne wasn't home and would never be home. Its winters played hell with his arthritis; his bed was as hard as the hobs of hell; the sounds outside his window weren't the right sounds. He spent half of his nights listening to them and planning a train trip to Woody Creek. He put himself to sleep at times with his planning of that trip, but woke knowing he couldn't go near Gertrude if he did make the effort to get on the train.

His grandson was his comfort. He loved that boy, wanted ten more years of life in which to watch him grow — and doubted he had ten more months.

His mind wandering his life, Vern Hooper wandered the Balwyn garden, killing colonies of aphids sucking the life from immature rosebuds. He'd planted two-dozen cuttings from his Woody Creek roses in the Balwyn garden. Half of them had taken.

In Woody Creek, that hedge would be in full bloom. No one there to snip the best of them, to bring them indoors. A lonely house, its blinds drawn, no furniture on the verandas, no movement.

Vern hadn't married off any one of his three offspring. He'd educated the female out of Lorna — if she'd been born with any female in her. Margaret, all female, might have caught herself a man had she been able to break away from Lorna. Like a wolfhound and a yappy little chihuahua, those two; and let the chihuahua put one foot out of line and the wolfhound snapped. He'd done his best when Arthur Hogan had started hanging around Margaret, but Hogan hadn't stuck. Blame Lorna for that. He'd packed her off to her Uncle Henry in England for six months when Ernie Dalton, a widower, had started showing an interest in Margaret, and Lorna had ended up bringing Henry and Leticia back to torment him for three bloody months. That got rid of Ernie Dalton.

Jim? He'd never been able to work out. That boy had too much of his mother in him. A bookish bugger, he'd never had a girlfriend until he'd got himself engaged to Sissy Morrison — not Vern's choice of daughter-in-law, but any port in a storm, he'd told himself at the time.

'Bloody fool of a boy. He never should have been in the army.' He squashed a mass of green aphids, and allowed his mind to return to the day he'd taken Jimmy out to meet his father, convinced that Jim would shake off whatever was shaking him up when he saw his son. They'd got a reaction out of him — not the expected reaction.

Jim hadn't noticed his boy was with them that day, or not for a minute or two. Jimmy had been hiding behind Margaret.

'That's your own dear daddy,' Margaret had said. 'Aren't you going to say hello to your daddy?'

If he closed his eyes, Vern could see that day now.

There was no denying little Jimmy was the dead spit of that hot pants little bitch — and he'd looked like her that day, standing there, hands clasped behind his back, wide eyes watching everything, and silent, maybe awe-struck by the magic that had brought his father back from the dead — or halfway back.

Then Jim must have sighted him. His eyes, fog shrouded since they'd brought him back to Australia, had changed. That fog had lifted — for a time it had lifted — then a rain storm set in.

Vern never could stand to watch his son blubbering. Jim might have been three years old the first time Vern had told him to be a man. He said it that day and today he wished he hadn't.

'Be a man,' he'd said. 'Shake your son's hand.'

Jim's hand had remained where it was, pleating the knee of his trouser leg, tears rolling, his eyes never leaving the face of that boy, seeing her in him, and Vern knowing what he was seeing, and knowing too that they'd made a mistake in taking Jimmy out to that place.

'Why is he crying, Aunty Maggie?'

'Because he's so pleased to see you, darling. Go over to him and kiss him better.'

Vern had never encouraged kissing between males, had never been guilty of doing it. 'Shake his hand, lad,' he'd said.

Someone had trained that boy well. His hands had come out from behind his back and he's stepped forward, and when Jim wouldn't take that little hand, Jimmy had picked up his father's trouser-pleating hand. He'd shaken it, then given Jim a quick kiss on the jaw.

Fairytale princesses are woken with a kiss. They'd stood stunned, he, Lorna and Margaret, watching Jim wake from the half-dead and grasp that boy to him, watching Jimmy take it for a while, but when he wasn't released, looking at Margaret for guidance.

She'd walked over and kissed her brother, smoothed down his hair.

'Jen?' he'd said.

'Jenny and everyone got very sick —' Jimmy started.

'Take him out to the garden, Margaret,' Lorna commanded. They made a point of not mentioning his mother's name in Jimmy's presence.

Jim's eyes had found Lorna then. They visited him every month, but by the look on his face, he'd been seeing her for the first time since he'd handed her his car keys back in '42.

She hadn't been looking at him. Had she been, she might have left those papers in her handbag. Always had more interest in papers than people. She'd wanted her brother's signature on her papers that day, and while Margaret, the weepiest woman Vern had ever had dealings with, led Jimmy from the room, Lorna removed the cap from her fountain pen.

'Is Jen with you?' Jim had asked.

Back when he'd been in that first hospital, Vern had told him what that hot pants little bitch had been up to. He'd forgotten, or hadn't heard. He'd told him again about Henry King's stuttering fool of a motorbike-riding son, while Lorna flattened her papers then offered the pen.

Jim had signed before without question. He questioned today, or swiped at the hand offering the pen.

'They are to do with me adopting the boy and legitimising his birth,' Vern had explained.

'You,' Jim said. Just that. It wasn't what he said. It was the way he said it that cut Vern to the bone. 'You!'

'You can play a role in your boy's life if you get up off your arse and get yourself out of this bloody place.'

'No,' Jim said. 'No!'

'His mother signed him over to me a while back —'

'What have you done to her?'

'Taken your son out of the purgatory you allowed him to be born into,' Lorna snapped.

And he'd got up on his feet, or on to his one foot and his peg. He'd gotten out of that chair unassisted. Damn near fell on his face while he was getting his crutch, but he got it under his arm, then stood leaning, breathing too fast, wanting to follow Margaret and his boy outside. Maybe the distance looked too great — until Lorna opened her mouth.

'I need them signed today, boy.'

He'd moved then, unassisted. They'd watched him to the door, where he'd lost his balance and come crashing down.

Vern barely had strength enough to get himself on his feet. Lorna never touched anyone if she could walk around them. A chap on the staff got him up, and suggested they leave.

'We require a minimum of sanity out of him today,' Lorna said. 'Settle him down.' She'd chosen the sanatorium for its compliant staff. She said crap and her trained rats squatted down to obey.

Jim hadn't been as compliant. He'd lifted his crutch and sighted down it like he was sighting down the barrel of a rifle.

'If this was loaded, I'd shut you up,' he'd said.

She'd got no papers signed. She'd told Vern and Margaret not to take the boy in there until she'd got them signed. She was always right, though he hated to admit it, and hadn't that day. He'd sent Margaret back in with them. She wanted that boy safe as much as he. She was back in minutes, bawling her eyes out, and still no signatures.

They had the mother's. They'd be able to get something from Jim's doctors, stating he was unfit to make decisions on his son's life.

Lorna drove home. Margaret dripping, Jimmy asking why, Vern sitting, uncertain of how he ought to be feeling. He'd seen life where there had been no life in two years — and for a minute there, had seen the light of battle in Jim's eyes. He'd felt hope, hope that the electric currents they'd been shooting into his head might bring him back from wherever his brain had gone to. He'd known too, that if he ever came back, things mightn't go the way Vern had been planning for them to go.

Not a good night that one, then the next morning, at seven-thirty, they were awakened by a call from the hospital. Jim had tried to hang himself from the shower pipes in the bathroom.

He'd had too much height to get his foot off the floor. No real damage was done, other than by the note he'd left for the staff to find. A suicide note, they'd called it.

It stated that he wanted his son to be raised by his mother, and that the money in his trust fund was to be transferred to them. He'd had his signature witnessed by a couple of inmates — patients — whatever.

It was a well-put-together letter, which more or less proved he still had a brain in his head — if a man with a brain would attempt to hang himself. Vern hadn't known what to think about that letter.

It was Lorna who had seen the value of a signed, witnessed document, in which Jim had made no mention of hanging himself. It was Lorna who suggested that the addition of a date, prior to the date on the papers signed by the Morrison tramp, may be accepted by the courts, as proof that Jim had given up all claims on his son to the Morrison tramp, months before she had signed him over to Vern.

Lorna had added in a date. She was good with a pen and ink.

They hadn't taken Jimmy back for a second visit. He believed his mother and sisters were dead and far better he continue to believe it.

Vern and Lorna hadn't been back. Margaret went out there once a month with Ian Hooper, her cousin. On two occasions, she'd come home jubilant. Jim had walked around the gardens with them. On more occasions, she'd come home weeping because they couldn't move him from his chair.

RUNNING FROM THE HOUNDS

*O*n a Sunday morning, while his neighbours drove off to church, Archie Foote cut a half-pound block of butter into careful squares, made neat holes in their centres, measured in a little arsenic, then sealed the holes. When the neighbours went to bed, he crept around his garden placing bone-china saucers loaded with small golden treats for the umpteen wandering cats who used his front lawn as a public lavatory and bordello. He had never been fond of cats, and not because they killed birds. He wasn't fond of birds either.

No doubt the greediest of family pets died in agony on Sunday night. He was called in to assist with grey and white Tom on Monday morning. It wasn't pretty. He diagnosed a bait, offered his condolences to two pretty girls, and returned home delighted that one less feline would be peeing and pooping on his lawn.

The following week, he mixed up a few similar, if smaller, treats, which he offered to a family of cawing crows. They'd taken a particular liking to his oak tree, where they spent their days bickering and splattering his new car, a cream Holden. He would have liked something a mote more sporty. Economics had dictated his choice of vehicle.

Given the life he'd led, he should not have owned a lawn for cats to yowl on, a new car for crows to poop upon, nor butter to waste. Disowned in his twenties, declared dead in his sixties, and happy enough to stay dead for a decade, Archie had, like Jesus, arisen. It had taken Jesus a bare three days to do it. Paper hadn't been invented then. It had taken Archie a damn sight longer, and a veritable mountain of paper, but he'd done it. His father's house, willed to his cousin, was Archie's, if only for his lifetime. A pity. It was worth a fortune. He'd got his father's money too, never a fortune, but enough, or it had been. It was damn near gone now.

He would have gone easier on it had he expected to live past eighty. There had been times when he hadn't expected to see thirty, but he was hanging together better than he ought to have been — apart from his eyes. Always an avid reader, a reliable keeper of journals, he'd taken his good sight as God-given. To read these days required good light, which he found on a sunny corner of his father's front porch, if the sun was shining.

He enjoyed his newspapers: they told him of a world he could no longer travel. He'd seen most of it. Had few regrets. Would have appreciated a longer relationship with Jennifer; still, their brief acquaintance had been enough to recognise Gertrude's distrust in her every nuance.

He'd brought that fighting bitch of a woman to this house as a bride, and known within days what he'd let himself in for. The house had been surrounded by an acre of garden back then; she'd spent more time with the gardener than with her in-laws. She wouldn't recognise the street today: the busy road, vehicles spewing exhaust fumes. She wouldn't recognise the kindly old gentleman who raised his hat to neighbourhood women when he took his daily constitutional around the block. She was more familiar with the old bastard who had prepared the arsenic and butter baits. Archie chuckled and flattened his copy of the *Melbourne Truth*. If he had one ambition left in life it was to sing at Tru's funeral.

August almost over, spring sunshine seeping into his sheltered corner, two buttered biscuits set on one of his mother's hand-painted plates, teacup close at hand, Archie settled down to read a witness's report on a double murder. The *Melbourne Truth* could be relied upon to give a few gory details on the front page, then force the reader to flip through seeking the tale's continuation. He licked a finger and flipped to page five, where the photograph of a tombstone caught his eye, its details too clear not to have been enhanced by an artist's hand. CLARENCE, SIMON, LEONORA APRIL REGINALD.

A sorry tale, two columns of it beneath the photograph. Archie sipped his tea, scanning down the column to the brutish husband who had kept his wife pregnant since her wedding night.

He threw me to the floor and had his way with me while my daughter screamed from behind the locked door, Amber Morrison . . .

Archie placed his cup down, seeking more information.

The reporter claimed to have spoken to a third party, one of a group of Samaritans intent on gaining Amber Morrison her freedom.

'Some chance — a fine piece of fiction.' He smiled attempting to visualise Norman Morrison throwing any woman to the floor and having his way with her, or having his way with any woman. For a few years, during his blue period, Archie had made a study of Woody Creek's stationmaster, a worm of a man if ever a man was a worm.

He turned the page and settled to read about a different breed of man, one driven to murder by his nagging wife. They'd given that poor sod life.

Maisy Macdonald sat at her table reading a copy of that same newspaper. Amber's best friend since kindergarten, she'd introduced her to Norman — and never forgiven herself for doing it.

'Poor Norman,' she muttered.

An inveterate, though never vicious, gossip, Maisy enjoyed a good talk — and at times knew she did too much of it, but when someone popped in for a cup of tea, someone had to do the talking, didn't they.

It was the following Tuesday, the lunch dishes washed and packed away, a lemon meringue pie cooling on the bench, when someone knocked on her front door. Most of her visitors yelled out at the back door. She ran a comb through her hair, removed her apron. It was a stranger, a young chap, city-dressed, his car parked out front.

'Mrs Maisy Macdonald?' he asked.

'That's what they call me.'

'I was given your name by Amber Morrison. I'd like to have a chat to you, if I may.' Then he introduced himself. He was a city newspaper man.

'What's she done — I mean, what else?'

'May I?'

He wanted to come inside. She let him in and led him down to the kitchen.

'I believe you have known Amber for some time, Mrs Macdonald?'

'All of my life. We started school the same day,' she said, and he took out a fountain pen and a pad to write in. 'I would have been her bridesmaid if I hadn't been pregnant at the time.'

He'd driven all the way up from Melbourne. Of course she made him a cup of tea. She told him she had a daughter and four grandchildren living in Melbourne, out at Box Hill. She cut two slices of her lemon meringue pie, which never cut well when it was hot, asked him if he'd like a dollop of cream with it.

He ate her pie, told her it was the best lemon meringue he'd ever tasted. She told him the trick was in only using fresh eggs; that Amber's mother supplied those eggs, that she had a little farm two miles from town.

He stayed for two hours and for those two hours Maisy talked. Before he left, she brought out her old photograph albums. There were a few shots of Amber, a few of Jenny and Sissy, and the most God-awful shot of Norman.

'He didn't look that bad in real life,' she said. 'Or not to me, he didn't. I got used to seeing him, I suppose. He wasn't a bit like they said in that newspaper. He was like . . .'

What was Norman Morrison like? Like that photograph: fat and faceless; nothing around him, a brick wall behind him, always there, but never quite . . . quite present.

The chap was more interested in Amber and her girls. He asked if he might borrow three photographs.

'Oh, I couldn't do that,' Maisy said. 'Or not that one. It's the only shot I've got of me as a girl. I was raised by my aunty who was as mean as a meat axe. She didn't waste money on photographs.'

He worked for a big newspaper. He gave her his card with his business address and a phone number, and if you can't trust newspapers, what can you trust? He wrote her a receipt for the three photographs and promised to post them back, registered mail, within the week.

She asked him what his interest was in Amber, and he told her that three specialists had pronounced her sane, that he and a few more were interested in obtaining her release.

'She was never charged with the murder of her husband, Mrs Macdonald,' he said.

'They didn't need to charge her, did they? Everyone knew she did it. She hid him in the house for two or three days and told everyone he was missing. And she stayed in there with him. Anyone who did that had to be stark raving mad. I mean . . . I helped clean the place, after they'd taken him away, and with every window in the house open, you could still . . . It was terrible.'

'You believed she was out of her mind at the time, Mrs Macdonald?'

'Of course she was — and had been on and off for half her life. She cleared out and left Norman when the girls were about three and eight. No one knew where she was for six years. Her mother paid doctors a fortune to cure her, but she never was cured — which is the only reason she wasn't charged for Norman — and for little Nelly Abbot and Barbie . . .'

He closed his book with a snap and rose, thanked her again for the splendid pie and the photographs.

'Pass on my regards to her,' Maisy said. 'Not that I mean my regards, but you know what I mean. Tell her I'm in touch with Sissy.'

'Sissy?'

'Cecelia — her daughter. Everyone called her Sissy.'

'Would you have her address handy, Mrs Macdonald?'

'No,' Maisy said, aware she'd already said too much. 'No. She moved recently.'

She didn't lie easily and, feeling the blush begin, walked ahead of him to her front door and got rid of him.

Over dinner, she told George and Dawn about her visitor. They told her she shouldn't have let him in, that she should have kept her mouth shut.

'Don't you go mentioning it to Mrs Foote,' Dawn said.

'As if I would.'

On a Thursday in late February of 1951, Archie, seated on his front porch, was attempting to encourage his eyes to read. Blindness lay in wait for him; he knew it now. He had cataracts on both eyes, so an eye specialist had told him yesterday. His left eye was damn near useless, his right was going fast the same way. He didn't need his magnifying glass to read the headlines.

PLANE CRASH EIGHT DEAD.

'A good way to go — up in the clouds, flying free, then gone,' he said.

A man needed his eyes. A man was up shit creek in a barb-wire canoe without his eyes. He'd gone into that surgery thinking he required stronger glasses and come out with blindness lying in wait for him.

FREE MEDICAL TREATMENT PROPOSED FOR PENSIONERS.

He'd be on the pension soon, a blind pensioner, tapping along with his white cane. No more books, no more newspapers, no more diaries. No more dreams.

I flew in the clouds with the eagle, at one with supreme nobility. Time's arrow stills man's flight when cataracts steal his light . . .

He flipped a page and found the report on the hanging of a prostitute and her two pimps. They'd tortured then murdered a seventy-three-year-old bookmaker. Archie used his magnifying glass to read all about that.

SCHOOLGIRL RAPED.

Again his magnifying glass was lifted. A man of his years takes his pleasure where he can. He took his time studying a photograph of two pinafore, boot-clad country girls. He hadn't seen kids dressed like that in half a century.

'I was twelve years old when my father bought me a pretty new dress and my first pair of pretty shoes, then took me for a walk down to the bridge and raped me in the dirt.'
Amber Morrison is the daughter of . . .

Cataracts or not, under double magnification Archie's name was too large. He pitched his magnifying glass and that puerile rag. The glass landed on his front lawn, where February's sun glinted on it, blinding him. A gusty north wind picked up the newspaper, separated its pages and sent them scuttling across the garden.

Rape? He had never been guilty of rape.

On his feet now, he attempted to recall the schoolgirl in pinafore and boots who he'd no more raped than he'd raped his own sister. He recalled buying her a pretty frock, recalled the rain storm and his ride home to his cousin's house. Soaked to the skin, he'd taken a severe chest cold, which had kept him to his bed for much of the following week — not always alone. His recollection of a flighty little blonde-headed nursery maid who on several occasions had joined him in his bed was significantly more vivid than his brief dalliance beneath the bridge with his daughter — not acceptable in civilised society, but not rape either.

Three times in his life he'd been accused of that heinous crime.

Sixty years ago, his sister had screamed rape. A sociable couple, their parents, always out and about, his sister crawling into his bed at night to escape the shadows on her wall. For years he'd kept his hands off her, and when he hadn't, she hadn't stayed in her own room, had she? In many cultures, a girl of ten or twelve, untainted by womanhood, was considered to be at her best.

His alter ego, poor old inoffensive Albert Forester, had been accused of rape and worse. He'd been in town when both of those Woody Creek girls were murdered. Amber had recognised old Albert Forester. She'd bailed him up down at the bridge one night and told him she'd get him. Women were better equipped for war than men. Get on the wrong side of one of them and they'll get you any way they can. She damn near got him that first time.

He'd been camping in a hut on McPherson's land, sharing it with a lanky redheaded lad the night he'd found a slim-bladed knife beneath his bedroll. A good Sheffield steel carving knife. He'd washed the blood off it down at the creek, thinking it had been used on a bunny. Knew now what she'd used it on.

They'd charged him the second time: with murder and rape of a minor. He was no murderer, and, as it turned out, that Duffy girl hadn't been raped. Put him away for corrupting a minor; like their grandmother before them, any one of those Duffy girls could have corrupted a saint.

One of the flying pages was headed for the street. He retrieved it before it spread its news, then walked his lawn collecting the rest. He found the page with the photograph and studied it beneath full sun. Something of the woman she'd become was in her face, the eyes. Wished he'd discontinued his voluntary work at the asylum earlier — or never begun it.

Later, his copy of the *Melbourne Truth* burned, he consoled himself with the knowledge that it was not the type of paper most in his street might read, and that the article had not been on the front page. All things pass.

The *Melbourne Sun*, a family newspaper, was delivered six days a week to Archie's door, and to fifty per cent of his neighbours' doors. And there he was on the cover of Monday's edition. Few might recognise the ancient old codger getting into his brand new Holden. Many would recognise his name, in bold print beneath the photograph: *Archibald Foote, a retired Hawthorn doctor . . .*

Live fast, die young and leave a good-looking corpse. That's what he used to say to Tru. He'd lived fast, but by the look of that photograph, his corpse wouldn't look so good. He read of his 'elderly' wife that morning. Tru wouldn't appreciate that. He read of his granddaughters, his great-granddaughters — an interesting enough tale, had he been able to disassociate himself from the old bastard that paper accused. He couldn't; nor would his neighbours, his cousins, members of his concert group, neighbourhood women who popped in with pies and biscuits — and how many more?

He saw how many more, also on the front page: 432,021 copies of the *Melbourne Sun* were sold each day.

The gaining of his father's house had given Archie immense personal satisfaction. Dining with young cousins he'd been introduced to as the family scallywag had filled some basic need for family. No more dinner invitations. No more concert group. No more chess on Monday mornings either. The retired chap, two doors down, who he'd enjoyed thrashing at the game, cut him dead at his front gate.

No more tasty apple pies. At three thirty, a young neighbour who had brought a pie to his door only last Friday, hurried her clutch of schoolchildren by.

The following morning, when he walked out to his letterbox

to retrieve his latest collection of bills, two bastards sprang from behind the hedge, cameras clicking.

Archie had ridden with the hounds once or twice. As he scuttled for cover that morning, he knew how a bailed-up fox felt just before its guts were ripped out.

'Never darken this door again,' his father's ghost whispered.

'Your sins will come home to roost one day, Archibald,' his mother's ghost wailed.

'Some you win and some you lose,' he told her nagging ghost, and he took up his car keys and drove down to the bank to clean out the account, apart from two and sixpence. Archie Foote had never been a loser, or not for long.

That afternoon, he packed what he couldn't live without, what he wouldn't want to live without, and, in the dark of evening, loaded cases and cartons into his car.

Failing eyes don't appreciate being called on to drive at night. He didn't force the issue. Went to bed early and slept well until just before dawn, when he dressed in suit and tie, locked the front door, closed his father's gate and drove away, gleefully leaning on his car's horn, blasting that street from one end to the next with an off-key and elongated beep, blasting until his two hands were required to make a right-hand turn.

The streets were his own that morning, apart from milkmen and their patient nags, an early truck or two. He skirted around the city, leaning on his car horn again as he drove by bluestone prison walls. Then away, the open road before him, the city behind, the sun not yet risen over it.

Or each continent and island, dawn leads another day.
The voice of prayer is silent, the strain of praise away.
Oh, the sun it is a wakening, in the eastern sky,
and hour by hour it's making, thy wonders seen on high.

The Sun will always Rise in the morning . . .

He'd sung that one in his youth for his parents' guests. They'd been proud of his voice back then. Not so proud later, when he'd sung bawdy songs at his mother's piano. He could remember them all, every word of every song he'd ever known, and he sang them all while his foot increased its pressure on the accelerator, one song following the next, words not thought about in years sliding easily to his tongue.

A man's memory is a remarkable tool. His hadn't faded. His voice wasn't all it used to be; he was the first to admit that. He didn't like the way it quavered on the high notes. But nothing is forever, not youth nor beauty, not money nor eyesight. Only the sun is forever. Somewhere, at any given time, it was rising. He'd watched it rise over oceans, over mountains, over jungles, always offering a new day, a new beginning for Archie Foote.

The car purred on, eating up the miles, delighted to be out on the open road. He'd been promising it such a trip for weeks. Short trips around the city were no good for new motors.

At eight o'clock he was halfway between Willama and Woody Creek. And where better for an innocent man to run than back to the town of his accuser, where for three weeks he'd played the caring doctor? Whose side of the story were they likely to believe? Kindly old Dr Foote's or his crazed, murdering daughter's. It was no contest.

He'd renew his acquaintance with Jennifer, with his grandson, get to know his granddaughters, and torment Tru into the grave.

He laughed, lifted his head and sang again. And why not? He had money in his pocket, petrol in his car — and by the time he went blind, he'd get free medical treatment.

Oh the Sun always rises in the morning
And sets each evening in the western sky . . .

You can dodge the truth forever, if you work at it. You can run from intolerable situations, escape tenacious women.

You can't dodge Old Man Kangaroo when he's intent on crossing the road to get to greener grass on the other side. There's not a thing you can do about Old Man Kangaroo.

THE MERRY WIDOW'S HAT

Norman's wireless had found a space in the rear corner of Gertrude's kitchen. Gertrude enjoyed listening to the six o'clock news. She made a point of sitting down to dinner at six. The local news usually consisted of saleyard reports and the price obtained for fat lambs. That night, the announcer spoke of a horrendous road accident fifteen miles south of Willama. The elderly driver, who had been travelling alone, was pronounced dead on arrival at the Willama hospital.

The ten o'clock broadcast stated that the car, a Holden, had been registered to a retired Melbourne doctor. Gertrude didn't hear that broadcast. Early to bed, early to rise makes a man healthy, wealthy and wise — she was healthy. And widowed for the second time to the same man, so the local police officer told her at nine the following morning. They'd found the driver's name on his licence, though an official identification was still required.

She'd do it. 'Give me ten minutes.'

She dressed in her black suit, in her black and white striped blouse, rolled on her only pair of stockings, wiped dust from her black shoes, and took her merry widow's hat from its box on top of the wardrobe. It was black, with a scrap of veil and a cheeky red feather standing tall. Vern had bought it for her in Melbourne twenty years ago. She wore it to Willama that morning, not convinced that the dead man was Archie until they drew back that sheet.

Even death had been kind to Archie Foote. There was hardly a mark on him. The impact had broken his neck. He'd always had a skinny neck — and a hard head.

'It's him,' she said. She didn't touch him. 'He'll have two scars on his scalp: one over his left ear and one on the rear of his crown.'

She'd stitched both of them. Hadn't made much of a job of the first — just a fool of a weeping girl back then. She'd put too many stitches in the second while he'd played possum on a cell bed. Tried to tickle the possum out of him with her stitching — but not a flinch out of the sod, not a whimper.

The scars were still there.

She didn't say goodbye, and had no intention of burying him. 'He's got family in Melbourne. I don't know where. They'll no doubt bury him.'

Walked away without a backward glance. Only the red feather waved goodbye to Archie Foote.

Car accidents were no longer newsworthy in the city; a death might receive a line or two. Archibald Gerald Foote received a two-inch column on page three, along with mention of his daughter's recent accusation.

Not that a soul in Woody Creek believed a word of Amber Morrison's lies.

'He was a lovely, decent old man,' Mrs Vevers said. 'He sat with our Linda all night when she had that disease. We would have lost her, like we lost Tom, if not for old Doctor Foote.'

'His lying daughter deserves hanging, not letting out — or wasting our taxes keeping her in there,' the people said. 'They hanged that prostitute for murdering a bookie.'

Doctor Archibald Foote received two columns in Friday's *Willama Gazette*. They wrote about the retired doctor who had laboured untiringly during the influenza epidemic of '47, but made no mention of his daughter's accusations.

Gertrude received more than the usual stares when she rode into town that Friday, clad in her uniform of drill trousers and boots, her hair tucked beneath her old felt hat.

'I don't know how he ever married her. He was such a fine old gentleman.'

Always one of the world's great mysteries — how dead men are never the bastards they've been in life.

Not a good year, 1951. There was a bad epidemic of polio in New South Wales, which led to fear of strangers bringing disease into town. There was a bad accident at Davies's bush mill in June. Lenny Hall worked out there, and the young chap who had been killed had started there the same week as Lenny. His death was followed by the senior Mick Boyle's — suddenly — then old mother Lewis followed him — not so suddenly.

Archie started the rot. Within ten days, there'd been three deaths in Woody Creek.

Vern Hooper and his lamp-post daughter drove up for Mick Boyle's funeral. Lorna caught the train home that night, leaving Vern and his car out at the farm, in the care of Rick Thompson, the farm manager.

Vern spent more time than necessary in town, but had sense enough not to crawl back to Gertrude one last time. He wanted to. Stopped himself where the road forked and drove on out to the farm. Harry ran into him at the post office. Vern asked if everyone was well down there. Harry told him they were, and asked about Jim and Jimmy, which cut their conversation short.

'The boy's well,' Vern said and left without checking his mail.

Elsie became a grandmother in September. Joey sent

photographs of his son and Elsie howled for two days. A new baby in Bundaberg, Queensland, might just as well have been in London. She couldn't get up there to mother it.

Cara Jeanette turned seven on the third day of October. Jimmy turned ten two months to the day later.

Then Christmas, and, for the first time in over eighty years, Christmas dinner wasn't served in Gertrude's kitchen. The tables and chairs were set up in the yard; Elsie's mob had grown too large.

They were all there, seated around the table, cracking walnuts, slapping at mosquitoes, when they heard the motorbike. There were a few around town. Most went on by. This one came put-puttering down the track. Gertrude and Harry left the table. They didn't recognise Ray beneath his riding glasses and leather helmet. They didn't recognise the bulk of him when he dismounted. Four years to the day since they'd sighted him. Four years can change the shape of a man.

Jenny had once likened his eyes to those of a lost lamb. His riding goggles removed, Ray's eyes were more crazed horse, wide, shaking, showing too much white as they searched the yard for Jenny. She'd gone indoors to watch through the bedroom hatch.

Smell of hot petrol, of the bike's exhaust, in Gertrude's yard. Then she and Harry smelled more than petrol and exhaust. Thirteen pair of eyes watched Ray unbuckle his riding jacket. It wasn't his waist that had thickened up. Like a caesarean birth, he eased a well-grown baby from beneath the jacket. And Gertrude yelled for towels — as she might have at a birth. Elsie ran inside to the wardrobe, ran out with the towels in time to see Ray dig another one out of his saddlebag. It was alive. It had the wail of the newborn. Let Elsie get within smelling distance of a newborn and she'd mother it. She claimed that tiny baby, wrapped it and ran for home.

'What'th he doing with babieth?' asked Margot, standing beside Jenny.

Georgie was behind her, the taller of the three. She'd turn twelve next March. 'Probably buried their mother in our garden,' she said.

Gertrude carried the larger baby across the paddock. Elsie had a bathroom and they'd need it. Harry took charge of Ray. He rolled him a smoke then led him across the paddock. The kids tailed them, Harry's seven and Jenny's two.

Dinner plates stacked high on the table, pudding plates, mugs, empty saucepans on the hob. Jenny washed them, was still up to her elbows in dishwater when the girls came back.

'There'th thomething wrong with the big one,' Margot said.

'You should see Ray, Jenny. He's got one of Harry's navy blue singlets on with pyjama pants. That's all they could find to fit him. He's sitting in the kitchen, shaking. He can't even talk, can't pick up his mug of tea. Granny said to get her brandy.'

They ran back across the paddock with the brandy, and didn't return until ten, Gertrude with them.

'Stay out of the shed if you don't want to run into him, darlin'. Harry's thrown a mattress down in the corner for him. It's just for tonight. We'd do as much for a stranger on Christmas Day.'

No need for Jenny to stay away from the shed. Ray's clothes must have been dry enough by dawn. They heard his bike start up. He hadn't taken his babies.

A lost day, Boxing Day of '51. Gertrude wanted to contact the constable. 'Lord only knows what happened to the mother of those babies,' she said. Elsie wanted to wait for a day or two. Georgie thought she knew what had happened to the mother, and, by the look of Ray when he'd arrived, she could have been right.

'Wait till tomorrow, Mum,' Elsie said.

Distance denied her her grandson. She gave him love by proxy that Boxing Day, and by the end of it, had named the babies: Lynette and David.

'Their mother will have gone to the police,' Gertrude said. 'They'll be searching the countryside for them. We have to let someone know where they are.'

'I'll go in in the morning,' Harry said.

The bike returned that night, near eleven. No light showing at Elsie's house, but Jenny was burning the midnight oil. She opened the door to him. He'd brought a bulging wheat bag, bulging enough to have the mother in it — maybe not heavy enough.

'You can't stay, Ray. Those kids need their mother.'

'Sh-sh-she w-w-won't look after 'em,' he said.

He stood in the doorway, blinking into the light. She stood with her back to the table, looking into the dark.

The bag placed down, he took her wedding photograph from it, offered it. She didn't want it. He stepped inside and placed it on the cane couch, then took a wad of pound notes from his pocket and offered them. She turned away, needing Gertrude, needing Harry, needing to get him out.

Gertrude came, dressing-gown-clad, her long plait hanging. 'Make a cup of tea, darlin'. See if there's a bit of cake left.' Patience personified, Gertrude. 'Put your money away and sit down, Ray.'

He put his money on the table and took a packet of cigarettes from his pocket.

'If you want to smoke, you'll have to do it outside.' Law-maker, Gertrude.

Too fast, he obeyed her law, slid the cigarette back into its packet, packet in his pocket, and sat.

'Your little girl is a bright wee mite but your boy needs special care. We can't give it to him. There's places in the city —'

'H-he's m-m-mine.'

He's mine.

A wind-up chimp will play the drums until its cogs rust, its spring snaps or its drumsticks wear out. It's not haunted by secrets. It has no memories. Jenny had been playing the wind-up chimp, functioning, refusing to think, wearing herself out with labour, going to bed when she could no longer stand.

He's mine.

Those words hit the wind-up chimp's main spring, and something snapped.

Is it your first, Mr King?

She'd aborted his first, and his second. He brought them back to haunt her.

Shook her head and poured boiling water over tea-leaves, then set the pot on the hob to draw for a minute. Old clock on the mantelpiece ticking towards midnight. Her mind travelled to her days here when she'd thought Gertrude was dying. So sure of herself then, strong . . .

'What age is your boy?' Gertrude asked.

'He c-came O-O-O-October twelve m-months ago. D-Donald H-H-Henry. G-g-girl's R-Raelene. She came l-last N-N-November.'

Jenny poured tea into three mugs, listening to his struggle for words. Could never get any information out of him in Armadale. Gertrude was better at it than she'd been.

'He's fourteen months, Ray,' Gertrude said. 'He should be walking.'

'H-h-h-he's g-g-getting b-better.'

They drank tea with him — or Gertrude drank tea with him. Jenny stayed on her feet, watching him, listening to him, thinking; remembering him sleeping on the couch when she'd thought Granny was dying, how she'd been pleased he'd been on the couch those nights.

He had no one, no friends. He had a factory job, half a house — where he wasn't wanted. And two babies.

He's mine.

'I'll make up a bed up on the couch, Granny. It's too late to do anything tonight.'

'J-J-Jenny?'

Shook her head and went to the bedroom for a pillow, a blanket.

*

Not a lot of sleeping done that night. Gertrude's bedsprings complained; Ray spent the night in the yard, no doubt leaving a trail of butts; and by dawn, Jenny wished she could join him out there. Hadn't had a smoke for close on four years. Hadn't wanted a smoke. That night she did.

Early birds chirping; a few dancing on the roof when Gertrude's springs complained for the last time and she rose. They shared the bedroom: Jenny up the north end, Granny down the southern end. Jenny kept to her bed, not wanting to deal with him yet. Maybe she dozed. Woke to the sound of an axe on wood. She rose and peered out through the hatch. He was at the wood heap, cutting, stacking, stove-sized wood.

She made the porridge. Didn't offer him a bowl. Offered him two slices of toast, no stew to put on them, no butter either. Jam, honey. He ate the first slice dry, added honey to the second slice, and watched her every movement.

The money he'd left on the table last night had been moved to the dresser. Jenny picked it up and placed it beside his plate.

'Get yourself a room at the hotel,' she said.

Eyes of a whipped pup meeting her own. She looked away, knowing she had to get rid of those eyes.

'There's no room down here for us, Ray. You have to go.'

He left at nine and returned at two, with a bedroll, butter, sausages, minced steak and a large loaf of bread. She cooked his minced steak. Uncooked, it would go off fast in this weather. She cooked his sausages that night, different sausages. Gertrude commented on them.

'W-W-Willama,' he said, attempting to dip melted butter from the bowl.

He wouldn't go.

On the third day, he rode out to Davies's bush mill and rode home with a job. He didn't tell them. Lenny told them; he worked for Davies too.

They tried to get rid of him. Harry tried. They tried to speak to him about Donny. A floppy little boy, he looked like Ray, same shaped head, similar features, big-boned, though not an ounce of fat on those bones and nothing in his eyes. Raelene had less meat on her bones but a head of black ringlets. She was nothing like Ray.

Jenny changed her tiny wet backside on the fourth day and wondered if God was offering her a chance to make restitution. And what if he was, and what if she didn't take that chance?

Crazy. Wanted nothing to do with Ray.

But argued for him.

'He's got no one, Granny.'

Or his little girl had no one. Little girls needed someone to care enough to weave them into this crazy patchwork of life.

'I'll raise Raelene up here, Ray,' she said on the seventh day. 'I won't raise Donny. Granny says he'll be in napkins when he's thirty. Go home. There are places in Melbourne that will take care of him.'

'He's m-mine, J-Jenny.'

Hated those words. Hated him saying her name. Pitied his eyes.

'We've got no room here!'

'I'll b-b-build on. I've g-got m-money.'

She let it slide. Didn't know why. Guilt? Pity? Restitution for her sins? More rooms maybe. Or maybe she was Norman's daughter. He'd taken Amber back. He hadn't shared her room, or not at first. She'd cooked and cleaned for him.

'What are you going to do about him, darlin'?'

'I don't know, Granny.'

'Elsie's got no room for those babies.'

'I know.'

Harry and Lenny carried the old green cot across the paddock. Jenny carried Raelene. Ray carried poor little Donny. They set the cot up at the bottom end of the kitchen; the old pram found a space in Gertrude's bedroom, beside Jenny's bed. Ray, the lodger, slept in the shed.

A crowded house, a crowded kitchen, five now seated each night around the battered kitchen table.

'What do you want to do, darlin'?'

'I don't know. I'm . . . floating, Granny.'

Lorna's Defeat

Back in '42, when Vern learned of Jim's involvement with the Morrison tramp, he'd made a new will. Both Lorna and Margaret had been confident he'd name them joint beneficiaries — until they'd opened his will, the contents of which had sent Lorna to bed with a three-day migraine. The farm, the entire estate, along with his daughters, were to be passed on to Vern's half-brother, Howard Hooper. When Howard passed on in '45, a new will was made. Margaret and Lorna were convinced Vern had realised their true value. Lorna had run the sawmill, if from a distance, had kept his books. She'd driven him to Willama to make the new will — which left his all to his nephew, Ian, son of Howard Hooper.

That was the day Lorna had decided to get Jim's boy.

And she'd got him. She'd orchestrated their escape from Woody Creek, had stood at her father's side when the neglect charges were made. He'd been reliant on her in the city. She'd driven him to his city solicitor's office week after week during the legitimising of James's birth. She'd driven him there when the new will disposing of the Hooper fortune was to be signed.

With the aid of a steaming kettle, she and Margaret had opened it, and the first name they'd seen was Ian Hooper's. Vern had named him guardian of boy and estate until *the before-mentioned James Morrison Hooper reaches his majority. Should the said child predecease his cousin, my nephew, Ian Howard Hooper* . . .

Should the boy predecease his halfwit cousin, the halfwit would inherit Lorna, Margaret and the estate. Children died every day! She had achieved nothing. And it was not to be tolerated.

'After all we've done for him, Margaret.'

'How could he, Lorna?'

'How dare he, Margaret?'

Since '41, Vern had been living on borrowed time. By 1951, he was failing daily — and pining for Woody Creek, according to Margaret.

When Lorna learned of the passing of the senior Mick Boyle, a neighbour for thirty years, she'd offered to drive the car to Woody Creek and leave Vern for a month in the care of the farm manager and his wife. She'd taken the train home. Control of Vern's estate her objective, she'd come to the conclusion that whoever controlled Jim's boy would control the estate, and in order to legally adopt her nephew, she would require a husband — and had no time to waste in finding one.

An envelope addressed to her maternal uncle, Henry Langdon, of Thames Ditton, England, and Lorna put pen to paper.

My dear Uncle Henry,

I hope this letter finds you and Aunt Leticia in good health, as it leaves me. I cannot say the same of my father. Being confident in the knowledge that the following will be seen by your own eyes only, I now agree with statements made by you during my sojourn in Thames Ditton that it would be in my better interests if I were to wed. Thus, I make this appeal to you, my only male relative, to choose for me an Englishman of refinement and good breeding, view matrimony.

Taking into consideration my father's age and current health

issues, this request should be met at your earliest convenience.
Your loving niece, Lorna Hooper

Time being at a premium, Lorna was waiting at the post office at nine, where the letter was adorned with airmail stickers. It flew away on a hot summer's day to land in England's chilly winter.

Henry Langdon had raised no offspring to inherit his fifteenth-century manor house and grounds. Lorna, the only daughter of his older sister, was his closest blood relative. Aware of her age, as desperate as Vern for an heir, he wasted no time in procuring her a mate.

On a pleasant morning in late March of '51, Lorna waited at the dock to meet her prospective husband. Her mail-order mate was not all Lorna had been hoping for. He measured all of five foot five and a half when shod — in shoes the size of her nephew's. *Cherubic* was the word that sprang to the mind of most when first their eyes fell on little Bernard. Pink skin, a bald pate, a circle of red-gold fuzz at ear level, and eyes that, when he finally dared to lift them, revealed themselves to be . . . golden.

'A rough crossing?' Lorna finally broke her clamped-lipped silence.

Not so rough as the landing. Bernard did not find his voice until they were seated in a restaurant, at which time Lorna decided he was an over-educated, pint-sized pommy bore.

Shopping via mail order is never as satisfactory as personal shopping; Lorna had run up against the same problem when ordering her size eleven shoes from a catalogue. However, the time spent in composing acidic letters and the posting back of unsatisfactory merchandise was not always worth the effort expended. She decided to don these shoes as soon as possible and break them in to her liking.

*

A man with no common sense requires a good education; a man of refined tastes with no money to support them requires a rich wife. When the proposition had been put to Bernard, he'd accepted gladly. A long sea voyage could only add to life's experiences, and at the end of the trip . . . well, if he did not feel some attraction to his intended, there was always the return voyage to dear old England.

He had not correctly interpreted the delight in Henry Langdon's eye when he'd presented him with a one-way ticket to the colonies. Bernard saw the dazzling blue of Australia's sky, felt the warmth of the land and he desired it. He looked at the skyscraper lines of his intended and desired only a fast boat home.

Oddly enough, neither Henry, nor Leticia, Bernard's sister, replied to the desperate telegram sent five minutes after Lorna Hooper drove away.

THE INTENDED IS UNTENABLE STOP PLEASE SEND FARE STOP

Nor did they reply to his second telegram, sent the following day: PLEASE WIRE FARE STOP INTOLERABLE SITUATION HERE STOP MUST RETURN IMMEDIATELY STOP

A five-page pleading letter also remained unanswered.

By April, his cash reserves dwindling, Bernard was forced to downgrade his accommodation. He took a small room in a fourth-rate hotel, where the food was poor and the company worse, and in its bleak surrounds he began slipping into depression. He lost track of time, of dates, of appointments with his intended. Failed to meet her at theatres, arrived late at restaurants.

As he had minimal access to the hotel telephone, his intended offered her home number so he might call each morning at ten to verify the place and time of their assignations. He placed a call to her residence at ten one April morning. The gentle voice of an unknown party convinced him he had dialled a wrong number — until the acerbic tones of his intended came down the line, demanding privacy before giving him instructions on trams, church, and the time of their appointment with the parson who would seal his fate.

He caught the right tram, but, taken by a plump little personage with platinum hair, he missed his stop. The wee woman got off at the next stop, Bernard behind her. She glanced at him. He glanced at her astonishing breasts.

'I am, I fear, lost,' he said. 'I am to meet . . . an acquaintance at . . .' he named the church.

The dear wee thing smiled, her chubby little face dimpling so prettily. She directed him with a lifted arm, and how delightful that plump little arm after his intended's black-clad tentacles; how delicate that hand after the hawk's talons.

'It's quite a short walk. You will see the spire clearly from the next street,' she said.

With no excuse to dally longer, Bernard continued on his way, turning though for one final glance, as did she; then another glance, as did she, before she disappeared into a side street like a plump sprite into a glade of greenery.

He found the church, late, where he suffered the barbs of his intended's tongue and the parson's badly concealed snigger.

Later, depression engulfing him, he sat in his third-floor room staring at a page of script his intended had ordered him to copy in his own hand and to have in the mail before noon. She'd supplied a sheet of writing paper and a stamped envelope addressed to *Mr Vernon Hooper*. He was an artist, but today his hand was too unsteady to take up a pen. For two hours he'd sat sweating over the formal request for her hand in marriage — and much more. And he could not do it. He would not wed her.

He slid her original into the envelope, put it into his breast pocket and considered the long jump to the pavement. The distance may be enough. His intended's letter would make a fair enough suicide note — to those who knew her. Although a broken leg or back would make him a sitting duck . . .

He left the hotel and took a tram to St Kilda beach, which offered a less painful means to end his sorrows. The southern oceans were known to be full of man-eating sharks. Was being eaten alive by one man-eater worse than another?

The day was warm. The ocean looked cold.

Perhaps he might throw himself on her mercy, explain his desire . . . his lack of desire . . . suggest they delay the wedding . . . or wed in England. Once on home soil, he might . . .

His watch, rarely wound, told him it was near one. Lorna was to collect him from his hotel at two.

A godly man, Bernard. Needing guidance, he caught a tram to the city and a second back to the street where the sniggering parson's church stood. The man-eater lived nearby, but if she was prowling the waters near his hotel, her home waters may offer sanctuary.

Numbers never his forte, he left the tram at the wrong stop, overshooting his objective. Nothing for it but to follow the tramlines back. He'd crossed over two streets and was approaching a third when he saw his intended's black vehicle make a right-hand turn out of a green glade and into the path of an oncoming tram. He froze, expected salvation with no need of the sniggering parson. She evaded the tram and drove on, and he scuttled towards that greenery now turning gold. Surely not her habitat? He'd visualised black bitumen and concrete, a street bereft of trees. He'd seen red, hard-faced houses standing behind hard brick fences. Instead, English trees shaded green lawns, aging houses sheltered behind flowering shrubs. A pretty street.

He was stooping to gather a leaf touched by the artistry of autumn when he saw the wee one, locked away from him behind tall metal gates. Like a sinner locked out of paradise, he stood beside a tree from where he might watch her gather a bouquet of flowers.

He stood too long. She turned.

'Hello,' she said, approaching the gate and peering between the bars. 'I thought it was you. Are you lost again?'

Her sweet face dimpled at him; his own dimpled back.

'I am seriously astray, I fear,' he said.

'You look all hot and bothered.'

Perhaps not hot, but surely bothered. She asked if she might fetch him a glass of water. And thus, Bernard entered in through the gates of paradise to sit in a grape-vine-sheltered arbour where the wee one brought him cool water. And sat with him.

He spoke of the street, of the English trees. He told her he'd left those same trees naked in dear old England. She asked what had brought him to Australian shores. He told her of a relative who may or may not reside in this very street. She commented on a shrinking world.

Perhaps he took too long in emptying his glass. She told him her father had eaten early and would be looking for his afternoon tea, and excused herself to attend to him. He had been dismissed, but he sat on, watching the delicious rounds of her buttocks disappear indoors. Certainly, he should leave, but having found sanctuary, he could not force his legs to stand.

And perhaps she was pleased he had not. She returned to the arbour with a tea tray, two cups, two slices of cream sponge.

'You must give my salutations to your cook,' he said.

'It's quite some time since we've had a cook,' she said.

Margaret watched her little redheaded visitor make love to her sponge with his mouth, her large eyes moistened at his obvious appreciation of her labour. He looked up and caught her eye. She blinked, three times, rapidly, then rose to fetch him another slice.

When she returned, he spoke of his sister's cook, with the family for thirty years; and she spoke of her childhood, of her mother who had made similarly light sponges. And when his plate was empty, she almost reached out to wipe a dab of cream from his chin. Of course, she didn't. A gesture only towards her own chin, a smile, and he dimpled and wiped the cream away.

He sat for half an hour. They exchanged Christian names. He sat for an hour and she asked for how long he would remain in Australia.

He told her he had come to attend his distant relative's wedding. She said she loved weddings, and asked if it was to be at the church he'd been looking for that day. He admitted it was to have been there; however, he feared the groom had absconded. She told him of her girlhood friend, Sissy, who had been left, virtually, at the altar, and her protruding eyes moistened at the distant memory.

Margaret knew few of her neighbours, other than those with sons her nephew's age. She asked the family name of the relative.

'Hooper,' he said.

'Another Hooper? Would you know the street number?'

Bernard had no memory for numbers. He'd had on ongoing battle with adding, dividing, balancing numbers for most of his life. But the envelope he had not posted, the letter he had not copied, was on his person. He removed it and glanced at the street number written there. Thirty-three. For some time, his eye had been drawn to two matching brass threes screwed to the brick supports of a front porch, aware, on some level, that they meant something. Aghast, he sprang to his feet. He'd been drinking tea in the grey shark's home waters, and that shark, not finding her sprat where it was meant to be, would return.

Margaret walked with him to the gate where she offered her hand. He could not deny himself one touch of her softness. The small hand between his, he looked into blue eyes a sprat may drown in.

'You are raising your nephew, sweet Maggie?' he asked.

She frowned, but didn't deny his words.

'Be warned,' he said. 'She has designs on him.'

'Perhaps you should sit a while longer. You don't look at all well.'

'Lorna,' he said. 'She has designs on your nephew.'

'Your colour is concerning me, Bernard.'

'How sweet is the voice of pity.' He released her hand. 'The nephew holds the key to the family's fortune. Be warned, sweet Maggie.'

And he got away, but not with his envelope. Whether by design or accident, it fell to the footpath to lie beside the russet of an autumn leaf.

Margaret picked it up. She recognised Lorna's distinctive black copperplate script. The envelope was not sealed. Of course she helped herself to its contents — and found a page of Lorna's personalised writing paper addressed to *Mr Vernon Hooper.*

It was a request for Lorna's hand in marriage; a request that a new will be drawn up before the wedding day; a request that he, Bernard, and his wife be allowed to provide a normal family environment for Vern's grandson, that the before-mentioned grandson would retain the Hooper name after the adoption.

The Balwyn house will become the sole property of . . . Margaret read.

The letter also assured Vern that his younger daughter would be given a home for life.

'As the kitchen maid!' Margaret said. 'Bernard! Bernard!'

Margaret was not dressed for the street. She was wearing a house frock, house shoes, no hat or gloves, but she was on the street and running.

'Bernard!' He'd reached the corner. 'Bernard!'

He turned.

She was pink-faced and quite out of breath when she caught him, literally caught him, took his arm and swung him around to face her. 'This must be discussed.'

He allowed her to lead him to a corner café, to a battered table in the corner, where, her back to the wall, she ordered tea for two and two vanilla slices, then realised she had no money.

'You'll have to pay, Bernard . . .'

'For my last supper, eaten in the company of an angel, I will pay willingly, sweet Maggie,' he said.

The family dormouse, Margaret, the family maid. As a girl she had dreamt a girl's romantic dreams of love; had, on two brief occasions, convinced herself she'd found love, but never had a man named her angel. Never in her forty years of life had she been in the company of a man or woman who had not immediately taken the dominant role. And such a sweet little man, such a gentle soul — caught up in Lorna's infamy.

Margaret's one goal in life had been to become a mother to her darling boy. Lorna would provide *a normal family environment* — God save a street urchin from that!

And God save Margaret. If not this little man, Lorna would find another willing to do her bidding. Unless . . .

Here, on the table, were explicit instructions on how Margaret might achieve her heart's desire. Could she? Dare she?

The tea and vanilla slices arrived before she spoke again. Bernard had taken a small bite.

'I don't quite know how to put this . . .' He waited. 'If you came all the way from England to . . . I mean, you did come here to marry . . . My goodness.'

She looked down at her plate, picked up the vanilla slice and bit, needing to fill her mouth. Barely tasted it, washed it down with tea and wiped her lips.

'I don't know why you'd agree to such a thing, but if you were . . . were agreeable to . . . to changing horses mid-race . . . I mean, you and I could . . . We have her letter to follow.'

'And the gates of paradise shall swing wide to me, my sweet, sweet Maggie.'

And in that dingy little corner café, Bernard made a knee and kissed her hand.

All is fair in love and war and the inheritance of property — not that Margaret was interested in the property. She wanted to be a mother. And, when all was said and done, she wouldn't be the first in the world to steal her sister's intended.

*

At three thirty, the little couple collected James from school and rode a tram to the local library, where they were offered pen and ink. While James browsed amongst the books, Bernard made a copy of Lorna's letter, with a few minor variances. Where the original said *Lorna,* he wrote *Margaret.* Lorna's wording relating to the adoption of James could not be improved on, nor could the paragraph regarding the Balwyn house becoming the sole property of Margaret, nor the final paragraph, other than the alteration of one sister's name for the other:

> *As it is unlikely that Lorna will appreciate her sister's altered situation, thus, until the arrangements have been finalised, it is imperative that any meeting between us should remain confidential, and be arranged at my hotel at your earliest convenience.*

Bernard signed it, printed the name of his hotel, his room number, then sealed it in Lorna's supplied, stamped, addressed envelope.

'Perhaps we shouldn't,' Margaret said, and an arrow pierced Bernard's heart. 'Shouldn't post it in that envelope,' she added. 'Lorna's handwriting is very distinctive.'

Bernard took the tram back to his hotel at four. Margaret returned home with her darling boy, where, blushing, she handed the folded page to Vern, and later called a taxi.

Vern found his prospective son-in-law short on inches and common sense — and perhaps a perfect match for Margaret. Unbeknown to Lorna, Vern's final will and testament was written, signed, sealed, locked safe in the solicitor's vault, and his solicitor instructed to get to work on the adoption papers. Only a formality; the boy's mother had relinquished him in '47. As had Jim — more or less.

On the third Wednesday in May of 1951, while the grey shark mourned the sprat that had got away by disappearing from his fourth-rate hotel, a smiling little couple met out front of the

Melbourne registry office, where the deed was done. After a fine dinner and two glasses of wine — for courage — they caught a tram to Balwyn to break the news to Lorna.

Vern and his grandson spent that week at the holiday house in Frankston, which was as well. Balwyn was not a pleasant place to be. Lorna's bitter gall rained down upon the newlyweds, submerging them. However, negotiating the raging torrent drew the odd little couple closer — by day. By night, Margaret slept in her virginal pink and white room and Bernard slept in the studio. Until the Monday night when he, venturing late to Margaret's door, knocked, and was invited to enter. A courtly gentleman, Bernard, he took her hand to his lips. The lifted arm, the gaping armhole of her gown, the exposed portion of one astonishing breast, led to . . . a surprising fringe benefit . . .

The vociferous tirade from the third party was water off two merry ducks' backs when they exited that not so virginal bedroom the following morning.

An arranged marriage, a marriage of convenience, call it what you will, but for Margaret, it was a breaking free. She had her final blooming in '51. How she delighted in her married name. No more the Miss Hooper who had missed out; she was a wife. And, before her dear boy's tenth birthday, the courts made her a mother, made Bernard a father.

'Just try to say Mummy, my darling boy. The first time is always the hardest.'

Jenny was his mother, though she'd always been just Jenny. Michael and Peter called their mothers 'Mummy' or 'Mum'.

The first time was the hardest, but he'd got his tongue around it, because Aunty Maggie wanted him to. He couldn't call Bernard 'Daddy'. He had one of those. He'd seen him two times.

'I've had three mothers and three fathers,' he told Michael one afternoon.

'People can't have three.'

'I did. Mum, didn't I have three mothers and fathers?'

'I'm your mummy now, your only mummy forever and ever more,' Margaret said.

REVELATION

*O*n 6 February 1952, King George VI died, and Vern Hooper took a massive stroke — brought on, perhaps, by the knowledge that a whippersnapper of a girl would now be Queen of England.

For ten days he lay paralysed and unable to speak — in a vegetive state, the doctors told his daughters.

Vegetables don't hear. They don't think. That term annoyed Vern. He'd never been fond of vegetables. He knew he was supposed to stop breathing and be done with it, but, uncertain of what he might find in the hereafter, and of who might be waiting for him, he wasn't over-eager to give up sipping on oxygen, to give up thinking either, or give up wishing he'd crawled back to Gertrude one final time.

Cool hands on that woman. Always cool. He wanted to feel their touch again. If Margaret had told her he was taking his time about dying, she might get down to give him absolution.

Margaret sat with him daily. She didn't care if vegetables could hear or not. She spoke about Queen Elizabeth, and how lovely it was to have such a pretty young woman on the throne. Lorna scoffed and prodded him with a talon to see if he was dead. She spoke to the nursing staff but not to him.

And what was the world coming to when a young wife and mother could become Queen of bloody England? Vern had been born during the reign of Queen Victoria. She'd still been squatting on the throne when he'd wed — and that poe-faced old bugger should have been enough to put him off marrying a pommy. It hadn't. Lorna Langdon had been worth five hundred pounds a year to him, and he'd needed that five hundred the year he'd wed. Hoped she wasn't waiting up there for him. Like her daughter, that one, she'd be waiting to cut him to shreds with her tongue.

Three times he'd vowed to love, honour and Christ only knows what else. He'd taken those vows for money twice and for his reputation once. Only his last, only Joanne, had given him a son. Always too much of her in that boy. She'd been addicted to doctors when he'd wed her, had spent a fortune on doctors during their marriage, and in the end had died on the operating table.

He'd done his best to stay out of the doctors' clutches, and for much of his life had succeeded. They had him now.

Another dose of oxygen sipped and his mind turned to the fortune he'd paid out to doctors since Jim had been brought home. The desire to live had to be born into a man, along with the will to keep going, no matter how hard the road he walked, just to keep limping along it to the next corner. Who knew what was around the next corner.

He got me a grandson. A man has to be thankful for that, Vern thought. Blood, and the continuity of the blood line, was all there was when it came to the end. A man begot his son, and his son begot a son, and one day Jimmy would do his own begetting. That's all that counted in the end, the begetting.

Vern had never worked his way much beyond all of the begetting in the Bible. Maybe he should have persevered. He'd had too many demands on his time, and by the time he hadn't, the small print had buggered up his eyes. Anyway, there had to be more to being judged a decent man than making a knee to a bloke who had so little faith in his flock, he'd hidden his face from them for two thousand years.

I've lived a decent life, more or less, Vern thought. I've done no real harm to anyone — disregarding that hot pants little bitch — but no grandson of mine was going to grow up a bastard.

Never give an inch if you're in the right, lad. Fight to the death if you're in the right, old Pop Hooper used to say.

Vern had lived life by his grandfather's set of rules, and, whether upstairs or down, he'd be waiting to shake his hand. Jesus mightn't — if he was up there. Vern sucked in another breath, just in case *He* was up there waiting to throw the book at him.

It was just putting off the inevitable though. Jimmy was safe. The will was in order.

Lorna wouldn't like it. A man ought to consider himself lucky that he wouldn't be around to see how much she didn't like it. A dominating bugger of a woman that one. She'd ruled Margaret for most of her life; had attempted to rule him since he'd handed over his car keys. Dominating women needed to be kept down or they'd take over the bloody world.

Someone was nearby. He could feel them. He hoped it was Gertrude. Hoped Margaret had told her. Craved the touch of her hands. Just one last time. Craved her mouth. He'd give up his final breath to her kiss. Loved that independent bugger of a woman.

I should have gone against you, you mean old pommy bugger. I should have married her. What a dynasty of Hoopers we might have bred between us. It's your fault I ended up with . . . what I ended up with . . .

An eye for an eye. That hot pants little half-dago bitch had taken his son so he'd taken hers.

Old Pop Hooper used to be big on *An eye for an eye.* He used to say it was in the Bible. Anyway, if Jesus was up there compiling his list, then the saving of a grandson ought to be on the plus side not the minus.

He'll be the first good-looking Hooper. A pity I won't see him grow. Margaret is doing a damn fine job with him. A good mother, a good daughter too — if not mine.

Wouldn't it be a lark if he got upstairs, where all questions were finally answered, and found out he'd been wrong all along about Margaret? She had the Hoopers' staying power. She had their desire to win.

I could have done a lot worse.

A breath sighed out and he thought about Gertrude and what she used to say about her time in India, how the folk there had looked on a river as one of their gods. He liked rivers, liked the idea of a river god, just flowing on down to the ocean, being picked up as rain, and flowing on down again. It seemed more logical than a bearded old bloke threatening hellfire and brimstone.

Gertrude used to say the Indians believed that folk didn't die, they just left one life and came right back to have another go at getting it right. 'I'm coming back as a man next time around,' she'd said. 'And with any sort of luck, you'll come back as a woman.'

Bloody hell! That was it. That's what hell was!

The revelation took Vern's breath away, though no one noticed until a nurse came in later to take his temperature at eleven ten on Monday, 17 February.

When the telephone rang in Balwyn, Margaret was at the clothes line, hanging Vern's oversized pyjama pants. Lorna took the call from the hospital. Five hours passed before Vern's matching pyjama shirt, maroon with a blue stripe, was hung. Never again would Margaret wash her father's pyjamas. She wiped a tear.

Still, one must look on the bright side; one must be pleased for him that he'd gone so easily. Many strong men lingered on in their beds for months, and how he would have loathed that, she thought.

She picked up her laundry basket, her peg bag, and took the longer path around the garden to her laundry. The perfume of damp earth, wet leaves and mowed lawn was intoxicating after the rain. She loved her garden, her house, its position, adored it, but an hour ago — fifteen minutes after Lorna had taken to her bed with a migraine — Margaret had called two estate agents, asking each to give her a valuation on the house. Before she'd come out to the clothes line, a chap from Fletcher & Parker had returned her call, eager to arrange a time.

The house was situated in a quiet street where ancient elms grew tall, spreading their greenery over the road and high brick fence. Vern had bought the property for a veritable song, as he'd bought several other properties during the depression. In '48, when they'd moved in, Vern's sister-in-law had lived next door. She'd passed on five months ago and her house had sold for an astonishing figure. Balwyn was now considered a prime residential address.

Margaret hadn't seen Vern's latest will, but she wasn't expecting any surprises. Ian Hooper, her cousin, would be the executor. He'd been so supportive since Vern's stroke, and again today. He'd offered to drive out and let Jim know. The funeral, of course, would be in Woody Creek.

It saddened her that her beautiful boy could not attend his dear grandpa's funeral, but it was out of the question. He'd taken the news well. She'd prepared him when they'd learnt the serious nature of the stroke.

'Grandpa is sleeping at the hospital, waiting for the angels to come and carry him home to heaven,' she'd said. 'How pleased he'll be to be with Grandmother Joanne. She's been waiting for him for such a long, long time.'

'What did she die of, Mum?'

'She became very ill when your father was younger than you, darling. The doctors tried very hard to make her better.'

One death raises memory of others. He'd asked how his other family had died.

She flinched each time he mentioned his former family, flinched from the lie she'd told him during their time at the city hotel — a difficult time, and at the time, according to Vern, the Morrison girl *had* been at death's door.

'I believe it was a very nasty pneumonic influenza.'

'I had it, but I didn't die.'

'You were so precious to your grandpa, he drove you all the way to Melbourne where he found the best doctors. Do you remember the doctor who came to the hotel?'

He remembered. 'Did . . . did my other granny die of it too?'

'We must try to be very quiet today, darling. Aunt Lorna has one of her headaches and is sleeping.'

'Can I ride my bike down to Michael's?'

Far better he be at play today with rowdy boys than asking questions she found difficult to answer.

'Ride on the footpath,' she'd said.

She stood with her laundry basket, surveying her garden. The old farm rose had a few buds; they'd be open by Friday. Her father had loved that rose. She'd take a bunch of its blooms with her on Friday.

Most of his rose cuttings had done well in Melbourne, though their flowers were not as vibrant in colour as they had been in Woody Creek. Different soil. Different weather.

She glanced at the sky, cloud-covered this morning but only blue overhead now and the sun with a sting in it. A typical Melbourne day: intermittent showers all morning, but a fine afternoon — a little like Margaret's own life. There had been so much rain in her early morning, but such a wonderful afternoon.

She'd come late to motherhood, though since the day she'd first held Jim's boy in her arms, she'd known God had meant him for her own. He had Jim's long limbs, his wide mouth and something of the Hooper jaw. There was much of the mother in his face, her eyes, her fine features, but had he been the green child of a Martian, Margaret would have adored him. A long-buried instinct to mother had emerged to fill her, to flood her life with joy.

Lorna cared for the boy as she may have cared for any hard-fought-for possession. She'd been born with Vern's desire to control, and had near lost control when the call came from the hospital.

Never had Margaret known her sister to express any real emotion. She abhorred Margaret's tears, disapproved of her laughter, but, Lord, how she'd smiled the morning she'd returned home from her petrol-buying excursion with the singlet-clad, towel-wrapped boy. She'd presented him to Vern like some sporting trophy.

What a day that had been, a fearful day. Within minutes, they'd been on the road to Willama. The hospital bursting at the seams, Doctor Frazer had suggested they take the child home. Lorna had suggested Melbourne.

Children are quick to sicken and as quick to recover. How he'd screamed for the squalor from which they'd saved him. Her lie had been born of desperation and lack of sleep.

'Jenny has gone to live with the angels,' she'd said. 'You're going to live with Aunty Maggie and Grandpa now.'

They'd moved from the hotel to the Frankston holiday house, where, for days at a time, she'd been left to manage him alone. She'd walked him down to the beach when he was strong enough, and he'd told her how he and Jenny had taken their shoes off and how the waves had chased their feet up the sand. Margaret had taken her shoes off, then his, and he'd allowed her to hold his hand while they'd played chasey with the waves.

She'd claimed him when he was five months old, the day she'd saved him from a hornet out front of Blunt's shop. During their weeks in Frankston, he'd claimed her.

Keeping her head low, Margaret crept by Lorna's bedroom window. The blinds were pulled. Lorna was unable to tolerate the light when she had a migraine. The laundry basket and peg bag placed down, Margaret stood a moment looking at the studio. She'd told the estate agent that it had previously been utilised as living quarters for servants; that, with little money spent, it could be made into comfortable living quarters for a couple, which should add more value to the property.

'Lord,' she whispered, clapping her hands to her cheeks, chastising herself for her mercenary thought. Of course she mourned her father. She'd wept when the hospital called. During this past week, she'd sat daily at his bedside, not wanting him to die alone. He had, and there was nothing to be done about it, and now she must look to the future.

And what a future.

A moss-covered brick path led down to the studio, overhung by trees; a treacherous path after rain. She placed her feet carefully, tapped gently on the closed door then opened it. She didn't enter. The smell of paint and turpentine permeated the air within.

'Lorna out yet?' the artist asked, glancing up from his palette.

'Not yet. Hopefully she'll feel better tomorrow.'

She watched Bernard slash a blue blob with a brush full of black. What on earth would emerge from that daubing, she did not know. He was a modern artist. She didn't understand modern art.

'A pity you couldn't bury him down here,' Bernard said.

Margaret hadn't been back to Woody Creek since '47 and was not looking forward to running into the Morrison girl, of having her make a scene at the grave side.

'It's what he wished. We will follow his wishes to the letter.'

'I don't envy you.'

'No. It's a long trip.'

'I was thinking of Lorna,' he said.

'Oh. She'll be fine on Friday.' She stood watching the brush slosh white on black, then slide down, drawing a spiralling tail of blueish-grey. 'The will won't be read until after the funeral,' she said.

Lorna lay on her brown spinster bed, staring dry-eyed at the ceiling, a nest of fire ants feasting on her brain. She hadn't seen the will. She was afraid she'd handed those cretins the sword with which to smite her.

GUARD OF HONOUR

*P*ut a red north wind behind a fire in a eucalypt forest and there's hell on earth. The state burned again in February of '52; Woody Creek lost fifty acres of timber out behind the slaughter yards. A few of those blackened trees would die; most would be sprouting in a month or two, seeds at their feet would stir. That's the way it was with the eucalypt, the way it had always been, the young sucking nutrients from the ashes of their forebears, and, with them out of the way, finding space to grow. That was life: the old making way for the new.

The smell of burning still hung in the air on the Friday of Vern Hooper's funeral. No sound of axe or tractor that day; not a logging truck moving on the road. The mills stood silent for Vern.

The shops closed their doors at three thirty, and a crowd gathered out front of the Methodist church. They were all there for Vern: every mill worker in town, every retired mill worker, and most of the tree fellers. News was exchanged while they waited for four o'clock.

The town was abuzz with news: the fire — the Duffy boys most blamed for setting it; and the closure of Vern's mill. The place hadn't been updated since the war; much of the equipment was antiquated. Six weeks before Vern was flattened by his final stroke,

Mervyn Martin, one of the mill hands, had lost half of his right hand. A month later, the mill boss received notice that Vern was getting out of the sawmilling game. Vern's accountant had driven up yesterday to pay off the last of the crew, and to hand out large bonuses to those who had been with him for years.

'Say what you like about him, he was a decent old bastard.'

'A hard boss but a fair man was old Vern.'

'As long as you knew he was the boss.'

George Macdonald had upgraded his mill in '51, doubling its size and output. He'd taken on three of Vern's men. Davies's bush-mill equipment was pre-pre-war, but he took on two more men, and had his eye on some of Vern's better equipment. Simpson, who had got Mick Boyle's mill up and running during the war years, took on two workers and sacked one useless city bugger.

The city chap who rented Vern's house was at the church, more concerned about losing the house than losing his landlord. He'd been made aware of the situation with that house before signing the lease, and with Vern dead, the house went to his son, who may not want to renew the lease.

'There'll be a few empty houses up here in a week or two. Billy Dobson is packing it in,' someone said.

Billy and his wife were heading for the city. Billy's brother, already down there, building Holden cars, said the work was no more repetitive and a damn sight less dangerous than mill work, and with overtime a man could make a fortune.

'We're losing too many of the young chaps to the city. This town will die without its young blood,' the old men said.

Another of the young married chaps who had served his time in the war had got a loan through the RSL to build in Willama. He was working at the cannery. They had a butter factory down there, a flour mill. Willama offered choices. They had a high school, a technical school. Nothing up here. Nothing but mills and a few jobs farm labouring.

*

Gertrude watched that coffin carried into church, a rough-made red gum, which was something of a dying tradition, only offered now to the old blokes, to the most honoured amongst the old blokes. Back when Moe Kelly had planted the dead, most of the mill men had been buried in red gum.

The Hooper family must have entered through a rear door. They were already seated in a front pew when Gertrude found a seat in the back row. No one had sighted Margaret since '47. She created a lot of interest. Not so Lorna. They'd seen her at old Mick Boyle's funeral. There were three chaps sitting with the girls; one would be Ian, Howard Hooper's son. He had the look of a Hooper about him, though not the height. The old chap was Vern's accountant. It was the third of them, a grey-headed chap, Gertrude couldn't identify. No sign of Jim. She'd hoped to have a word to him.

The service wasn't long. At four thirty, eight strong men carried Vern out, Lorna walking behind the coffin, Margaret behind her, blubbering on her cousin, the accountant and the grey-headed chap following them — grey headed and walking with a limp.

It was Jim, lean, pale, his hair silver grey. She tried to catch his eye, but he didn't look left or right.

Half of the town and most of their kids were outside to see Vern carried between two long lines of mill men who had formed a guard of honour, suited mill men, but each one holding an axe high and giving him a last 'Hooray'. It moved Gertrude. Vern would have enjoyed their axe salute.

He would have enjoyed his last ride on Mick Boyle's dray. An aging Clydesdale took him on a sedate tour of the town, the Hooper cars following behind him, the cousin driving the girls and Jim. Always a driver, Jim. He'd been driving since he was twelve years old. Not today.

Someone must have been down at Vern's mill. His mill hooter started up, a terrible, mournful sound, a swan calling for its dead mate, and that hooter more meaningful to Gertrude than the parson's words. It got her tears flowing, which annoyed her. After what he'd done, he didn't deserve her tears. Damn them, and damn her for the fool of a stupid old woman that she was becoming.

The hooter was still going when the dray turned out of Cemetery Road, a trail of cars now following it.

There was a time when folk had walked behind the coffin. Gertrude walked, needing that time alone to gather herself for the final goodbye.

She shed a tear or two more when the hooter silenced, when they dropped Vern deep into the earth. Then Simpson's hooter started up: a hard-on-the-ears siren; ten seconds later Macdonald's, a high-pitched howl joined in. Folk plugged their ear canals with fingers as they walked away. Gertrude plugged her own and looked around for Jim. He was surrounded.

Hot, his back, his head. Jim rubbed his head, felt the prickle of too short hair. It offered no protection from the sun.

Lorna had ordered he be made viable for the day. They'd been charging his batteries again, coming for him while he was still half asleep, crucifying him on a table, even to the crown of thorns, metal thorns. They'd been swapping his upper denture for a long-handled rubber mouthguard, then flicking the switch.

He could remember the night electricity was turned on in this town, how it had lit Woody Creek up like a Christmas tree. That's how he saw himself, strapped down and glowing — imagined seeing himself. He saw nothing. Had no memory of it afterwards, other than the taste of rubber and the smell of overheated cogs.

It made him pliable, if not viable. For a few days he became a blank white page anyone could write on. He felt smoothed out, his agony smoothed out, made wearable, bearable. At times he even got to see the world in colour.

Today was in colour. The greens looked greener, the flowers on the coffin looked like the bouquet of roses he'd given to Jen. *The last rose of summer* . . .

A lot of dark suits here. Too hot for a dark suit. He'd been half-way up here today before he'd known he was wearing a suit. He'd been sitting in the church before he'd realised why he was wearing it.

Ashes to ashes, dust to dust.

Someone must have told him his father was dead, that they were taking him back to Woody Creek. He might remember them telling him tomorrow, or the next day. His battery only held a charge for a few days. Too many wheels and cogs inside his head that never stopped turning.

He'd been to a lot of funerals, watched a lot of good men go into those holes. He'd dug the holes — back when he'd had two legs.

He'd known this town too — back when he'd had two legs, known all of those faces.

He'd known that fat woman coming at him, trying to kiss him. Too short. He held his precarious balance and shook her hand. Knew who she was. Knew it as well as he knew his own name. Tomorrow he might remember her name — if he bothered to remembered today.

She had enough fat on her to have survived over there for a thousand days. The bloke with her would have survived on his gut for as long. Jim flexed his hand and wondering what that bloke might look like whittled down to skin and bone. Then someone else offered his hand. Jim took it, shook it like a man. His father might have been proud of him . . . had he not been the reason for the shaking of hands.

He couldn't feel his father's death. Maybe tomorrow. Maybe not. Maybe he'd miss him tomorrow. Maybe not. The hole was deep enough.

The holes he'd dug over there hadn't been so deep. No coffins over there. No shrouds to waste on dead men. Died like flies. Here today and gone tomorrow. The yabbering little yellow bastards had cut their numbers down. Couldn't feed their own army. Hadn't tried to feed their prisoners. Cut the heads off a few to cut them down to size. He hadn't lost his head, only his leg.

A tall skinny bloke with a mop of carrot hair taking his hand, pumping it. Knew him. Remembered him. Cards, playing cards.

He mentioned Jimmy. 'We thought you might have brought him up to your dad's funeral, Jim.'

Funerals were no place for kids. Funerals give kids nightmares. He'd stood amongst these same tombstones when they dropped his mother down that dark hole, then they sent him back to his school masters.

School. Up here. Miss Rose. Miss Rose had red hair. He searched for red, for the one name he could put his tongue to.

Not here.

Jen wasn't here. He never forgot her name. When he woke up with the taste of rubber in his mouth and wet pyjamas, he searched his smoking cogs until he found her name hiding in there beside his own. Jen and Jim.

She'd married someone he'd gone to school with. He'd known his name yesterday, or the day before.

That was the worst of their blank page. No names written on it. They always came back, with that crumpled-up agony.

Dry throat. Burning head, the sun setting fire to the back of his jacket.

There was a river up here. Plenty of water up here. No, not a river, never been big enough to be a river. A creek, marking the boundary line of . . . that house with mushrooms growing in the dining room. He could see it, smell that clump of indoor mushrooms. Whose house? He knew. Always had.

He'd remember that name tomorrow — if he remembered the mushrooms — if he wanted to remember them tomorrow.

An old chap, his arm in a sling, apologising for not shaking his hand, shaking it with his unbandage hand.

Jim stared at the bandage. They would have killed for those white bandages over there. They'd had nothing. Blood and guts, dysentery and suppuration, bags of bones buried in shallow graves . . .

'Good to see you, Jim,' a youngish woman said.

People, tall, short, old, young, big hands, small hands. He shook them, and his hand ached and his arm ached and his head burned.

'I'll see you around at the pub,' a stocky bloke said.

He'd been to school with him! Built like Nobby, all chest and not a lot of height. Lucky Nobby, bought a ticket home by a lucky shot though the knee. Not so lucky Paddy. Blown to bits. Bull? What happened to Bull?

'We're leaving now, Jim.'

Ian, his cousin. His name, the Hooper name was welded into the cogs. Always around, always had been, would be. Ian and Margaret. They came, at two, on Sundays. Lorna didn't come on Sundays. His father hadn't come.

Where's your pride, boy?

Over there with my leg, Pops.

He'd been pleased to see him, at that other hospital, back when he'd had two legs and no teeth. Ian and Margaret, hospital visitors way back then . . .

And Sissy. Sissy Morrison. They'd brought her in to sit beside his bed when he'd . . . he'd smashed his father's car, knocked his teeth out — coming home from Monk's!

Monk's house! It was Monk's house that had the mushrooms growing beside the wall in the dining room. Monk's cellar, cool on days like this. Always cool.

I've loved you since I was four years old

'Monk's,' Jim said.

'I think the girls want to get going, Jim. I doubt they'll agree to going out there.'

'Are they still up here?'

'The Monks. Not for years. Your father bought their land.'

'Jen and Jimmy,' he said.

'Bernard is looking after Jimmy today.'

Bernard. That's who she'd married, who he'd been at school with . . . Bernard, Bernard . . . Bernie Macdonald! Bernie and Macka Macdonald! That stocky bloke.

See you around at the pub.

No. No. She'd got the train out of town the night before they could tie her up to him. Left him standing at the altar and gone to Melbourne.

'Where's Bernard?' Jim asked.

'He's at home, dear. Come along,' Margaret said. 'It's been a long day for all of us.'

'Are we dropping by the hotel?' Ian asked. He was wearing a suit. He was hot.

'Lorna won't go there. We'll have a cup of tea in Willama,' Margaret said. 'What an atrocious day it's been. I do hope it's cooler in Melbourne.'

'Are you going around to the wake, Mrs Foote?' Maisy asked.

Gertrude shook her head.

'They did him proud.'

'He would have been pleased with the last of it.'

'They didn't bring Jimmy?' Maisy said.

Gertrude didn't bother replying to that. She'd known that little boy's future the day Vern had set eyes on those miniature double-jointed thumbs. Play your cards right, she'd told Jenny when she'd brought Jimmy home from Sydney. She'd played them wrong.

She glanced towards the crowd still clustered around the Hoopers, saw the back of Lorna's head. Didn't want to see the front of that woman. No sign of Margaret. She'd be in the centre of the crush. Didn't want to see her either. She could have given Maisy a call to let her know Vern was dying.

'I would have got down there somehow to say goodbye,' Gertrude said, to Maisy or to herself.

'He wouldn't have known you, Mrs Foote.'

'He would have known me. I'll walk home, love. It will do me good.'

Maisy had driven her into town. She drove her home and turned her motor off when they got there.

'What does she plan to do about Ray, Mrs Foote?'

'Thanks for your help today.' Gertrude was out.

'If they're back together, with Vern dead she might have some chance of getting Jimmy back.'

Gertrude didn't reply. That little boy wouldn't come back, maybe wouldn't want to come back.

'Thanks again, love.'

WORM IN THE APPLE

*R*ay had stood with Davies's men in that guard of honour holding his axe. He went to the wake. The beer free until closing time, the bar was packed solid, Freddy Bowen, the publican, his wife and son, run off their feet. The mill workers guard of honour had been a custom for years, as was raising a glass to a fallen workmate. Somewhere along the line it had become the custom for the mill boss to shout that beer. Vern, long-term mill man and boss, was paying today, and never a man to do anything by half-measure.

A few in town believed February's stifling temperatures had dictated the late hour of Vern's funeral. It had nothing to do with the weather. Lorna and Vern's accountant had chosen the time. A town full of mill workers could put away a lot of beer in an hour.

Suit-clad mill workers stood elbow to elbow with the mayor, the bank manager and town toffs today, most of those toffs farmers. They were Woody Creek's new elite. They sent their kids to boarding schools; their wives bought their fancy suits and hats in Melbourne.

Ray King's dark grey wedding suit had been purchased in Melbourne. It was well cut. He wore it well. A few from out of town eyed him, wondering who he was, most of them women.

No woman in the bar, but their voices infiltrated. The backside of the bar opened into the dining room, and from Ray's vantage point he saw tables piled with cakes and sandwiches, fancy-clad farmers' wives rubbing elbows with mill wives — or not quite rubbing elbows. The toffs' wives had taken over the far corner, forming their own clique. There must have been four-dozen women in there, plus a handful of the town wowsers drinking tea. The barroom hum of massed male humanity didn't compete well with the higher-pitched female voices. And they were still arriving with their plates of cakes. Each time the passage door opened, there was expectation on a few faces — still hoping one of the Hoopers would put in an appearance.

They'd be well out of town by now. At times, Ray considered getting on his bike and riding away. He had no place in this town, wasn't wanted here, wasn't needed here. He needed them, or his kids needed Jenny.

Glass in his left hand, he looked towards the Macdonald pack. George was no drinker. The town joke, George Macdonald, he ordered pots of raspberry cordial. Built like an ape, he must have been close to Vern's age, but still fronted up at his mill each day. Hands on him like stunted mallee roots, worn that way by raw timber. He hadn't been born to the timber game.

Ray had. Son of Big Henry King, he had brawn, thick wrists, ham hands — not yet seasoned by timber. If he hung around long enough, they'd get seasoned — if Jenny let him hang around long enough. That's what he'd done at old Phoebe's: just hung around and made himself useful until she'd stopped telling him to go.

A dangerous trade, the timber industry: logs rolled, trees fell, branches snapped, saws cut where they weren't supposed to cut. A few of the drinkers held pots with hands missing fingers. Compo paid by the knuckle. A thumb was worth a packet. A death on the job set the widow up for life. This town looked after widows and kids.

Ray lifted his head as someone — Tom Palmer — called for glasses to be raised to one of the world's gentlemen. Ray had been at school with Tom Palmer's sons.

'He and a few more carried this town through the depression,' Tom said.

They drank to Vern Hooper. Ray hadn't been here through much of the depression, but he raised his glass along with the rest, raised it to the man who had brought around a load of sawdust to cover up Big Henry's pool of blood.

Seeing that red-gum coffin, hearing the parson preach, had stripped the years back today, had taken him back to Big Henry's funeral. A different church — Big Henry had called himself a Catholic. Ray called himself a Catholic. Had tried to baptise his son a Catholic, but the priest wouldn't do it. The Catholic Church didn't recognise kids born of adultery.

His son. For six months, he'd had a future prime minister in that crib. Flo's mother had taken that dream away, and the doctor she'd brought to the house.

'Retard,' they'd said. 'Put him away.'

Flo hadn't wanted to put Donny away, not then, not until later. She'd been big with the next one before she'd started on the idea. Nothing wrong with the second one. It had come out head first. Flo wouldn't look after it. Her mother had come to help; two weeks she'd spent in the sleep-out; two weeks nagging him to put Donny away. Maybe he'd thrown her out. She'd told the cops he'd thrown her out. Maybe he had.

A roar of laughter rose in the bar and Ray turned to its source: the Macdonald twins, clad in their army uniforms. They'd been out of the army since they came home from Korea. Still playing dress-ups. He hated those bastards. He had gone there looking for work, looking for old George. One of the twins had been in the office.

'N-n-not taking on men right n-now, Ray,' the bastard had said.

They'd mocked his stutter in the classroom, and when he'd taken on one, he'd taken on two. He might have taken that one on, had Joss Palmer not reached out to shake his hand.

'Try Davies, Ray,' he'd said. 'He's looking for men.'

Joss Palmer, son of Tom: they both worked for Macdonald. Joss had wed one of the Macdonald girls. Weasel Lewis had got work with Macdonald. He'd wed Joss Palmer's sister. Every bastard working at that mill was tied up somehow to Macdonald or Palmer. Between them, they had this town boxed up like one of those crossword puzzles young Georgie sat filling in, each word woven into another. The whole town was connected up, even Charlie White, the grocer. His daughter had wed Alfred Timms whose sister had wed a Thompson. Thompsons connected to Nelsons, Nelsons to Lewises, and back to Palmer/Macdonald.

Ray didn't fit into the crossword. Born flawed, he was incapable of joining.

Harry Hall didn't fit in either. A blow-in from Melbourne, Harry had wed scrawny little Elsie, a darkie connected to no one. Their kids might join them in one day; they were white enough. In this town though, they'd never be more than one of those grey squares, where a wrong word had been pencilled in and erased by a wet finger.

An elongated, rusty-headed fringe dweller, Harry Hall. Employed by George Macdonald for his driving skill back when few in Woody Creek could handle a loaded truck. He'd talk to anyone, migrant or mayor, talk politics or atom bombs, confident in the knowledge that he had the words waiting on his tongue. His suit trousers had seen more wear than his coat. He didn't own a pair of shoes, but his working boots had been polished for Vern Hooper.

Ray's shoes were new, his white shirt was brand new, his wedding suit had cost him three weeks' pay back in '46. It didn't change who he was. He was less than Harry Hall; less than Shaky Lewis, who was putting away more than his fair share of free beer.

'He got a good turnout, Ray,' Harry said.

Ray nodded.

In his youth he'd sought friendship, had followed new friends like a hulking cur pup, its tail wagging, eager for a pat on the head. Too often he'd been kicked in the guts and run home yelping — only to be kicked in the bum by his nasty bitch of a mother. He'd learnt early to accept his position in the scheme of things.

His hand, seeking purpose, reached for his glass. Empty. Freddy's wife had returned to the women; his son, attempting to help out, pulled beers that were half froth.

'Freddy. There's blokes choking of thirst down here, mate,' Harry called. From his trouser pocket, he removed a tin of tobacco, the small packet of Tally-Ho papers half buried in the weed. Ray watched him pinch a few brown threads, watched deft fingers roll a slim smoke faster than most could get a ready-rolled out of a packet. Ray got one out, lit it.

'That little moustachioed bugger,' Harry said to Lenny.

'Tony?'

Harry nodded. 'He bailed me up as I was getting out of the truck. I think he was jabbering about marrying Joany.'

'She told Mum a week ago he'd asked her to marry him.'

'I don't know how she understands a word he says.'

Woody Creek had taken in its share of those left homeless, landless, by the war. Pommy ex-servicemen had brought their wives and kids out on the first boats and not a soul had kicked up a fuss about them. Nor had they about the next lot: blue-eyed blonds, their countries of origin somewhere near the Baltic Sea. A few of them had brought women and kids. These last years, the Immigration Department, running short of blue-eyed blonds, had started shipping in dagoes, a younger bunch, and not a woman or a kid amongst them. A lot in town were kicking up a fuss about them. Some of those swarthy little buggers were darker-skinned than

Harry's darkest, and it was universally known in Woody Creek that they all carried knives and would slit your throat and rape your daughters as quick as look at you.

A pack of them worked for the Forestry Commission. Harry had two teenage daughters, Joany and Maudy. They'd brought a couple of those Italian boys home.

'What did you tell him?' Lenny asked.

'To ask me again when he'd learnt the lingo.'

Weasel Lewis had a distinctive snigger. The Macdonald twins didn't snigger; they howled like a pair of dingoes.

'What's the joke?' Harry asked.

'Your neighbour could give you a few tips — on the lingo, like,' Weasel sniggered.

Harry wished he'd bitten his tongue.

It didn't take much to start rumours in Woody Creek, not if your name was Jenny Morrison, not if you hadn't been sighted in town for five years. Folk still drove down, or sent their kids down on bikes, to buy eggs, fresh vegetables in season. That old cane pram, pressed back into service as Raelene's crib, had been sighted by a few. A few had asked Harry if Jenny's latest was half dago.

He glanced at Ray, hoping he thought Weasel was referring to Gertrude, who got on well with a Latvian woman who'd also recently come to town. Ray was looking at the women in the dining area. Harry hoped he hadn't heard.

No sign of the Hooper women or Jim. Harry had shaken Jim's hand out at the cemetery. If he'd remembered him, he hadn't made it obvious. Too many wanting to shake his hand and Jim looking as if he wanted to be anywhere else but there.

'Five minutes, lads,' Freddy said.

Lenny pushed his glass across the bar. Ray emptied his glass and turned to leave.

'We ought to get going too,' Harry said.

He was rolling a smoke for the road, his back to the Macdonald pack; didn't see what happened or how. Heard the thump, felt the rain of beer, saw an empty glass crash to the bar, shatter.

No one saw it coming.

Like his glass, Weasel Lewis had taken wing. Landed on his bum between the funeral shoes, his landing separating the Macdonald twins.

Identical, Bernie and Macka Macdonald, no necks, broad in the shoulder, barrel-chested, as bald as their father with not a lot more height. They stood, arms swinging at their sides, Ray between them, flexing his fingers. When his fragile cords of self-control snapped, they snapped clean. Ice in his head; no thought there but to smash what was before him. Which one?

'He's half your bloody size, you st-stuttering bastard,' a twin said.

Decision made. Ray nailed him with a sledgehammer left to the mouth. Turned to take care of the other one, but the second bald-headed bastard was back-pedalling.

Every eye in the bar fixed on Big Henry King's son for an instant, seeing the man, the height of him, the breadth of his shoulders, his thick butter-yellow hair, his strong, straight teeth. He was no Rock Hudson, but Woody Creek wasn't Hollywood.

Tom Palmer opened the door for him. Freddy Bowen watched one of the Macdonald twins spit two teeth to the bar-room floor. Three or four women peered over the bar to see what had gone on, Maisy amongst them.

'I'll be able to tell you apart,' she said, as the twin who wasn't bleeding kicked the door shut behind Ray King.

Old timber pub, standing on that corner too long, the glass in its termite-riddled window frames, mocking that overgrown stuttering kid who'd come to that pub two and three times a day for his father's billy of free beer.

His bike mocked him before roaring into life. Old now, bruised, its paint peeling, it roared its rage through town.

He didn't turn down the forest road. He lived on Gertrude's land under sufferance, and no one knew it as well as he, so he rode on, over the bridge, and out towards Three Pines, pushing that bike faster than it wanted to go. Rode until the ice in his brain thawed, then he turned around and rode home to her.

She was sitting at the table, feeding mush into his boy who wasn't a boy. She glanced up, saw him at the door. He stood watching his boy stare at the lamp. A flickering, dancing flame behind its glass chimney tonight, barely competing yet with the outside light.

An imp in the flame, Gertrude would say. She'd lift that chimney and use her scissors on the wick. She'd fix it. She wasn't in her kitchen tonight, so it danced.

The two girls were setting the table, flitting around the light, one looking like a part of the flickering flame, her long red hair picking up the light, dancing like fire; the other, pale, pudgy, a thick-bodied white moth caught in that other one's flame.

They'd both be burnt by this town.

Jenny scraped the last from the bowl and fed it into Donny, wiped his face, then carried him to his cot. Two hours ago Gertrude had gone to her room to take off her funeral outfit. Almost seven, and she was sound asleep, lying face down across her bed, still dressed for the funeral, her legs stocking-clad. Jenny hated Vern Hooper as she hated no other, but could understand Gertrude's pain. Until these last years, he'd been at her side. She understood the escape of sleep; a soothing place to be when life doled out too much pain. She didn't wake her.

Pots waiting on the hob could wait a little longer. The onion sauce had turned to glue. She added a dash of milk, gave it a stir and replaced the lid. A lump of corned beef was safer in the pot than out. She moved the pot well off the heat, then reached for a packet of cigarettes. Every day, Ray left a packet on the mantelpiece for her. She didn't thank him for them, but she smoked them.

The girls had gone over to Elsie's to listen to *Dad and Dave*, a radio show Gertrude considered a waste of battery power. She made the rules. The girls obeyed her rules.

No sign of Ray. He'd be sitting outside somewhere, chain-smoking. Not in the shed. If they were intent on burning money, they could burn it in the yard, Gertrude said. If he wanted to drink, he could do it somewhere other than on her land, she'd said. He'd been drinking at Vern's wake. Jenny had smelt it when he'd come to the door. He hadn't come inside.

She walked down the side of the house, keeping her eye out for him, cut through the vegetable garden, then down to the orchard — orchard by reputation: a bunch of old trees with one or two seedlings allowed to grow tall enough to prove their worth. Two young apple seedlings had been allowed their space but had not yet grown an apple. The old tree, already gnarled when Jenny was young, had split in the winds of last August. It hadn't died. Its remaining branches were loaded; maybe its final attempt to seed the world with the sweetest apples ever grown. The sky darkening, the bravest stars were already peering down as she walked by the fig tree. So much foliage on it, its fruit was hidden — from her, if not from the birds. She lit a cigarette behind the fig tree and drew the smoke deep, hiding there thinking — always thinking.

She'd made a mess of her life, but she only had one, and this was the one she had. She had to sort it out. She'd never sleep with Ray again, but she was his wife. She could get out of that marriage, but it would cost money to get out, and what for?

She drew the last from the cigarette then tossed the butt, making her own shooting star. Followed its light — not as wise as the Three Wise Men. It led her to the lopsided apple tree, where she killed the ember, grinding it deep into the earth.

Loved starry nights. As a kid, she'd believed the stars fell to earth each morning when God folded away his sky blanket. She'd searched the dust for their twinkle. Thought she'd found one that day on the railway line — the day Vern and Jim had found her there. Had sighted a twinkle of blue and run to claim her fallen prize — just a piece of broken glass. That's life. You think you'll finally hold a star in your hand and you end up holding something capable of cutting.

All bled out now. And her stomach grumbling hungry. Plenty of apples — not that Granny's apples should ever be eaten in the dark. They were full of grubs. Always had been.

Joey had introduced her to Granny's apples; not withered like the apples Norman had bought from Mrs Crone. She could remember her first bite; still see Joey, perched up that tree, a cheeky brown-eyed elf amid green foliage, picking apples so Granny could make chutney. And hear him too.

'What's worse than finding a grub in your apple, Jenny?'

'Not finding it,' Jenny, the child, had replied smartly.

'Finding half a grub, 'cause you chewed up the other half,' Joey had giggled.

'I swallowed it whole,' she told the old apple tree, and lit another cigarette.

The girls must have woken Gertrude when they came in. The rattle of pots roused Jenny from the orchard.

'Why didn't you wake me up?' Gertrude said.

'Why did you go to sleep?' Jenny countered.

No need to find an answer to either question. They knew the answers. Two of a kind, Jenny and Gertrude. No blood joining them; something much stronger than blood had welded those two.

'Your onion sauce has gone gluey.'

'A bit of milk will fix it.'

They worked together, keeping clear of the other's elbows. A dangerous place a crowded kitchen when two women are tossing pots around. Gertrude lifted the lump of corned beef to a plate. The smell of meat drew Ray in from wherever he'd been.

'B-big funeral,' he said.

'I haven't seen one bigger since Moe Kelly,' Gertrude said.

Ray walked down to the rear of the kitchen to stand beside the old green cot and watch Donny sleep. He looked perfect when he was sleeping.

Through the years, Gertrude had spoken a dozen times about building on a couple of rooms. If Ray and his babies were staying, something had to be done. That old cot took up too much space. Jenny wanted more rooms, and a bathroom. Ray had offered to pay for a couple of bedrooms.

Gertrude slicing beef, serving it to five plates.

'Don't give me any,' Jenny said.

'You'll eat what you get and like it.'

'I don't like it.'

'It's good for the blood.'

She'd be eighty-three this year. She'd never divorced Archie Foote. He'd never divorced her. Maybe she'd been his shield against his many women — and Gertrude's against Vern Hooper.

'I was dreaming I was back in India,' Gertrude said. 'How does the human brain come up with the crazy dreams it dreams?'

'What was it about, Granny?' Georgie asked.

'I was on a train with Archie, and I was hiding a baby in my sewing basket. I knew it was Vern, and I knew Archie wouldn't let me keep him if he found out.' She placed a dollop of mashed potato onto each plate, scraped the last scrape from the saucepan. 'They've got this belief over there that when we die, we come back as a newborn. I told Vern once that he deserved to come back as a woman and I'd come back as the man.'

'If they come back straightaway, he'll be too old for you when you come back,' Georgie said.

'And he'll look like Lorna,' Jenny said.

Laughter as five plates were passed around the table,

interchangeable plates, apart from Ray's. He had two slices of meat. Gertrude made no allowances for fussy eaters — she'd served him silverbeet, carrot rings and not enough potatoes. In Armadale he would have scraped the carrots and greens from his plate. He ate what was served to him in Gertrude's kitchen. In Armadale he'd pitched his soiled clothes into a corner. He put them into the dirty clothes basket up here.

'It's a beautiful bit of meat,' Gertrude said.

'T-t-tender.'

They spoke. The girls spoke. Jenny's mind travelled, travelled in circles as she watched him mix his silverbeet with the onion sauce. In Armadale, he would have been cutting more meat by now, spreading bread, making himself a sandwich with a slab of corned beef. It was on the dresser, covered by an upturned basin, still accessible.

Wondered if he'd brought his roadkill home to Florence May Dawson, if she'd sliced up his livers, fried them, boiled his tripe in milk and onions, cooked him mountains of potatoes. She'd been a nineteen-year-old girl when Raelene was born, eighteen when she'd had Donny, seventeen when he'd got her pregnant.

He'd told them no more than her name, that she'd gone home to her mother and left him with the kids. The wheat bag he'd brought with him that night had contained his clothing, the kids' clothing, and two unopened envelopes. One had contained Raelene's birth certificate. Raelene Florence, they'd named her, and what a god-awful name to saddle that pretty little mite with. She should have been . . . Lynette.

Babies grew on you. She wanted to raise Raelene. Wasn't certain why, other than some convoluted idea that if she unravelled the tangled threads of that little girl's life, she might untangle her own. Wasn't sure why she'd allowed Ray to stay, other than if he went, Raelene would have to go.

And life was easier with him than without. Last week, he'd paid the water carrier to fill the rainwater tank and suggested they buy another one. She wanted another tank. He'd found a new vocation for Granny's old tin trunk when they'd moved it out of the kitchen to make room for Donny's cot. It lived outside the door now and was filled each morning with wood by Ray.

Maybe there has to come a time in every life when you stop wanting what you can't have and you settle for a trunk full of wood, a tank full of water, a jar full of money, two more rooms — and a kerosene refrigerator. He'd ordered one from Fultons. It should arrive next week.

BLOOD MONEY

*B*ack in '22 when Vern Hooper had bought his first car, Wilama had been forty miles of unsealed road away. By 1952, a bare twenty-nine miles separated the two towns. Neither one had picked up its foundations and moved. The Mission Bridge, promised since the affluent twenties, had its official opening in January of '52, and would have been opened sooner if the sealing of the stock-route road had been completed on time. That back road had always offered a man on horseback a faster means of getting between towns. It took the diagonal; and, as any one of Harry Hall's kids would tell you, taking the diagonal through Joe Flanagan's paddocks cut a quarter off the distance to school.

Give a cow an acre field of clover and she'll still reach over the fence to find something better. Give a man or woman thirty-minute access to doctors, dentists and hospital, plus unlimited petrol to drive there, and a week or two later they'll be demanding access to higher education for their kids.

The council bought a school bus. The garage man, who had five kids of his own, kept it in reasonable repair. When kids returned to school in '52, seventeen Woody Creek students made the daily round trip to high, technical and Catholic schools.

The bus seated thirty. To recoup a little of their expenditure, the council decreed that adults could fill the spare seats. They charged them five bob for the return trip and a bob each for kids over the age of three. It started a stampede of shoppers. Willama had Coles and Woolworths stores, offered a choice of three or four grocers, butcher's shops on every corner, shops selling nothing but fresh fruit and vegetables. Within a week, shoppers were required to book seats.

Mrs Crone was the first to complain, then the butcher. Charlie White's takings were down. He was on the town council. He raised the subject at a meeting, where it was decided that too much money was being spent outside of town. By April, only adults with doctor's or dentist's appointments, and those with folk in the hospital, were allowed to ride the bus, and the price went up to seven and six per adult and two shillings each for kids over three.

Georgie rode that bus each morning. Teddy and Maudy Hall rode with her; Teddy only catching it because Harry forced him to. Mechanics didn't need an education. He wanted to fix cars, drive cars. Like Joey, Teddy had his growth spurt early. Unlike Joey, he hadn't stopped growing at five foot six. He was fourteen, and stretching fast towards Harry's height. He hadn't inherited his father's colouring. He had Elsie's dark eyes and hair and a suggestion of her darker complexion. He'd be a good-looking boy once he grew into his face. Maudy, a year Teddy's senior, wasn't a lot taller than Elsie. She had her dark hair and Harry's blue eyes. Georgie, now twelve, had long outgrown Jenny and was reaching for Gertrude's height. She was well developed for her years, looked fifteen, and caught the eye of many. Margot, still chubby, an immature thirteen, had not yet made it to high school. Sixth-grade students had to sit an entrance exam and she hadn't passed.

In May, Jenny waited at the bus stop with the kids, Donny flat on his back in a fancy stroller. She had a doctor's appointment at nine thirty.

Three times in her life she'd been to Willama, twice to the

hospital. Little can be seen from a hospital ward. At fourteen, she'd stood on stage at the Willama theatre at night. She'd seen the theatre and that's all. This morning, as the bus made its slow way through unfamiliar streets, Jenny's face was turned to the window. There were hotels on every corner, an entire block of brand new houses, a flour mill, big modern garages with yards full of cars, then an entire block of shops. Was it any wonder Maisy did her shopping down here?

The bus turned right and pulled into the kerb out front of the Catholic college. She'd heard about that college all her life. Norman had considered sending Sissy there, as a boarder. He'd never offered Jenny the option. She wouldn't have argued.

The driver helped lift the stroller down while kids jostled to get off.

'Be here at three thirty,' the driver said. 'I can't hang around.'

She'd be back. All she had to do was take Donny to the doctor then go to the bank.

Maisy had given her directions on how to get to Doctor Frazer's rooms. She'd offered to drive her down. It would have been easier, but would have meant having lunch with one of Maisy's daughters and Jenny wasn't ready for that much interrogation.

Steps up to the doctor's rooms. There's only one way to get a loaded stroller up steps, backwards, the door held open with an elbow, then a lot of heaving. She got him in, and he didn't like the company, and she didn't blame him. The waiting room was packed solid with coughing kids, harassed mothers, old women and one solitary old man — the only spare chair used to prop his walking stick. She offered him the stick, and sat, plugged Donny's wail with his dummy.

The woman on her right turned to her, rattling something in a tiny jar. 'Me gallstones,' she said. 'To think I had them rolling around inside me. I had it done in Melbourne. Doctor Wilson sent me down to a lovely chap.'

Two doctors on duty: Wilson and Frazer. Jenny was seeing

Doctor Frazer. He'd dragged Jimmy out of her with forceps, and, according to Gertrude, had saved her life and Elsie's in '47.

Chairs emptied, and filled, kids coughed, mothers wiped runny noses, Donny sang his dirge around his dummy, and Jenny watched her watch's hands creep around to ten. So much for an appointment at nine thirty.

Ten minutes past eleven before her name was called. It had never felt like her name, felt less like it in this place, but as no other Mrs King rose, she manoeuvred the stroller through a door and down a passage behind a balding man Norman had once referred to as a callow youth. Doctor Frazer was no longer youthful.

He sat on his own chair, signalled towards the patient's chair. She wasn't the patient so she stood.

'I'd like the name of a children's specialist in Melbourne, please.'

'What seems to be the problem?'

'He's retarded.'

'Sit,' he said.

She didn't want to sit. Just in and out, with the name of someone who might convince Ray his son wasn't suddenly going to stand up, walk and talk.

'A big boy,' he said. 'What age is he?'

'Eighteen months.'

He came from behind his desk to study Donny, to lift his arms, legs, comment again on his size.

'His father is big.'

He listened to his heart, his lungs, then he sat again, asked if the boy could hold a biscuit, roll over.

'He drinks, he sleeps, he . . . sings.' Granny had named his throaty dirge singing.

'Are you well in yourself, Mrs King?'

'I'm here to get the name of someone who might convince his father that his son isn't well.'

'Bring him down to see me.'

'I've tried that.'

'Who was the delivering doctor?'

'He was born in Melbourne.'

'Was his condition explained to you and your husband at the hospital?'

She wasn't here to tell him her life story, but gave a condensed version. 'I was separated from my husband for five years. Donny is his son.'

Donny spat the dummy. She popped it back in, the doctor watching her, waiting for more. He had a room full of people out there, no doubt with appointments. He was already running an hour and a half late.

'All I know about his birth is that he was born backwards. My grandmother was a midwife. She thinks the cord could have been around his neck and starved his brain of oxygen. My husband says he's getting better and he's not.'

'You're back with your husband?'

She sighed. 'More or less.'

'If he won't come down here to see me, how do you expect to get him down to speak to a Melbourne specialist?'

'He's from Melbourne. If I go with him, he'll go.'

'Pop on the scales for me,' he said.

'I'm eight stone.'

'We'll allow the scales to be the judge of that.'

She stood on his scales, and she was a bare seven stone three. Not satisfied with her weight, he wanted her blood, wanted to know what she ate, if she was planning to have more children.

'No.'

'Are you using a contraceptive?'

'No. I'm not back with him in that way.'

He told her he'd look into chaps who specialised in retardation and post her a referral. He wrote her a script for iron tablets and told her to return a month from today, told her to eat more meat, to eat liver at least once a week, and for that he was rewarded with a smile. He didn't understand her smile, but remembered it.

'Do you do any singing these days, Mrs King?'

The question surprised her. She shook her head.

'My wife and I heard you at a concert, sometime before the war.'

She nodded and turned the stroller towards the door. He rose to open it and she got away. Almost.

'I read recently that there are plans afoot to release your mother,' he said.

'I choose not to think about her. Thank you for your help.'

Still four hours to fill and Donny wet, and when he wet, he wet. She changed him in the doctor's laneway, plugged his whinge, lit a cigarette and walked down to the corner where she turned west towards the town centre.

Her bank account was at the National, which, according to Maisy, was a greyish-white stone building on the corner just up from Coles. She had over four hundred pounds in that account: Norman's three hundred and forty-seven pound investment, plus interest on it, and her own fifty-two pounds squirrelled away during her months singing at the jazz club. She planned to withdraw a hundred of it. Ray, Harry and his boys were building two rooms out the back of Granny's house: a bedroom for Ray and a laundry-cum-bathroom for Jenny. Ray was paying for the building materials, Granny had paid for a second water tank, a big one. Jenny would pay for a bathtub, new wash troughs and pipes to connect them up to the new tank.

She found the Commonwealth Bank, also on a corner, the State Bank a few doors away, and finally the National, where Maisy had said she'd find it, on the corner not far from Coles. Jimmy had loved going to Coles . . .

She wasn't down here today to think about Jimmy or Coles. She was here for Donny and for her bathroom.

More steps leading up to the bank, wider steps and three of them. She dragged the stroller up, through two sets of heavy brown doors and into a brown and gloomy area. Donny whined. She plugged it, and looked around for withdrawal forms. They hadn't altered in the years since she'd last used the account. She filled one in, signed it Jennifer Morrison Hooper King, the name in her bankbook. No one waiting at the teller's cage, she passed the book through the slot beneath the wire screen — and wondered how Laurie had robbed banks. No way through that screen — unless he'd carried wire cutters.

'There should be a bit of interest to go in it,' she said. 'I haven't been in for two years.'

He took her book down to the rear of the bank and she waited alone there, looking around, peering in through the wire. Distrustful institutions, banks. Were they in '39? Was Laurie still out there somewhere, still stealing? He'd been twenty-six when she was fifteen. Did he still look like Clark Gable? Was he back in jail?

Minutes passed. Hoped Maisy hadn't made a mistake when she'd paid in the cheque for Norman's money. It was written in her book so it must have been in the bank's ledgers. Wondered how much interest the bank had paid her for two years. At least four pounds a year. She'd have eight or ten pounds extra.

The teller was back. He needed identification. Did she have a driver's licence?

Been there, done that. She'd come prepared. She had her child endowment book, Jimmy's birth certificate and her own. She had Charlie's letter of identification, written in '47. *Charles J. White, Justice of the Peace.*

'The account was opened in Sydney, back during the war. I had it transferred from Sydney to Melbourne in October of '44,' she said, passing documents through the slot. 'I lost my old bankbook in '47 and was given a new book.'

He gathered her identification and disappeared again down to the back room.

Two wire cages side by side. Only one teller working, and two customers now waiting behind her. Why couldn't life get easy? Everything was too hard. Banks, doctors, Donny.

And he was back.

'Is there a problem?'

'No problem, Mrs King. Our records show that a large amount of money was paid into the Melbourne branch some time back. We're making a phone call to Melbourne now. If you'd like to step aside for a moment?'

She stepped aside, and the woman behind her looked at her as if she was a bank robber. Look, no water pistol.

A bawling baby. 'Shush,' she soothed. 'We won't be much longer.'

It had to be some problem with Norman's money, and without it she'd only have the fifty-two. Money had always spelt security. Did she want to spend that little security on a bathtub and pipes?

Her back to the wall, she watched the teller hand over two pounds to the woman, watched him take a calico bag full of money from a male.

Then a door opened behind her. 'Mrs Morrison Hooper King?'

'Yes.'

'The account hasn't been used for some time.'

'I explained all that to the teller. A cheque for three hundred and seventy-four pounds was paid into it in April of 1950.'

The cry of a newborn in a small area is noisy; Donny had eighteen-month-old lungs and, according to Doctor Frazer, they were healthy. His bellow may have convinced the bank manager to give up Jenny's money. A minute later, book, banknotes and identification stuffed into her handbag, the bank manager opened his doors for her, helped lift the stroller down his steps, eager to be rid of the noise.

She plugged it, lit a cigarette and removed ten ten-pound notes from her book before glancing at the figures to see how much interest they'd paid for the use of her money. And she was a bank robber.

'They're mad,' she said.

Their total was crazy: 2,675/16/9.

She turned to go back, to tell them they'd made a mistake.

Couldn't take Donny in there. He was bellowing like Flanagan's bull. Plugged his bellow and held the dummy in. He bellowed around it while she stared at those figures.

Itchy-foot had left her his money!

Solicitors can't get a person's bank account number, or can they? Granny had given it to them. She'd known about that bankbook since the cheque for Norman's money had come in the mail. She would have told me.

Then she saw the date. That two thousand pounds had been paid in on 12 December 1947. Itchy-foot had been alive in December of '47.

Cringed into the wall, knowing where that money had come from. It was the cringe she'd been carrying with her for five years. It was the hollow in her heart, the tremble in her head, and nowhere to hide from it down here. Exposed on a busy street; what she'd done exposed in that bankbook. She'd sold Jimmy for two thousand pounds. She'd sold him like Granny sold cockerels at Christmas time.

'Are you all right, dear?' the woman with the jar of gallstones asked.

She wasn't all right. She wanted the wall to crumble, crush her, bury her. She'd sold him, traded her beautiful boy for . . .

'Your baby is crying, dear.'

He wasn't her baby and it wasn't a cry. And Granny hadn't given Vern Hooper her bank account number, not before April 1950. Ray. He'd been one of the devils, fighting over her soul, at the hospital. She'd signed . . . their papers.

He's mine.

He was yours and now he's mine.

The money was paid in in Melbourne. Ray hadn't burnt her old bankbook. He'd given it to Vern.

'You need to sit down before you fall down, dear.'

'I'm sorry,' she said. Sorry for living. Sorry for . . .

'There's a café over the road. I'll walk over there with you, dear.'

Had to shut Donny up. Had to think. She reached into the hessian shopping bag hung on the stroller's handle, grasped a bottle. Condensed milk and water — what she'd fed Jimmy on the train to Sydney.

Stop with Jimmy!

Dragged the bottle out too fast. Dropped it. Napkin-wrapped, it bounced. The woman picked it up. Jenny got the teat into that bellowing mouth. Donny gagged, swallowed, then sucked. He didn't grab for the bottle. Lay on his back and sucked.

Silence then.

'The café is just down past Coles.'

Everything was just past Coles. Everyone knew Coles.

Or Jim? Of course it was Jim. He'd paid her for services rendered. That day in Sydney when he'd opened the account, he'd told her to add Hooper to the Morrison name, that he'd get the army paymaster to pay money into the account. He'd written that number down to give to the paymaster. Of course it was Jim. He had his own money.

Thank God she hadn't gone to the funeral, hadn't made a fool of herself. Thank God.

'My cousin has a retarded girl,' the woman with the gallstones said.

Jenny lifted her eyes to the woman's face, surprised she knew Donny wasn't normal. He looked normal when he was sucking, when he was sleeping. Granny and Elsie had known the first night they'd handled him. Doctor Frazer saw it in an instant. Ray could see it too. He saw what he wanted to see and he didn't want to see that.

He's mine.

'What age is he, dear?'

'Eighteen months.'

'My cousin's girl is one of those mongoloids. What happened with your boy?'

'He's my husband's, not mine.'

That altered the woman's attitude, her tone. 'You've taken a lot on. They can be very hard to manage once they start running around. My cousin's girl is eleven and, my word, does she keep her on the run.'

Jenny's mind was elsewhere. Far better that it be Jim who had paid that money in, she thought. If not for Ray, those rooms would never have been started. If not for Ray, the new tank would never have been ordered. Far better it be Jim. His ring was loose on her finger, and no wonder. Seven stone three. Take it off, she thought. Pitch it, and get him out of your head. Can't. Ray thinks it's his ring.

She took the stroller's handles and pushed on. They crossed the road together and walked by Coles, the woman with the gallstones discussing her cousin's girl, Jenny breathing in that old essence of Melbourne wafting out through the store's wide-open doors. Didn't want to breathe it, didn't want to think about Melbourne.

'They've got a nice big ladies' room, right down the far end,' the women directed, holding the restaurant door open.

'Thank you,' Jenny said.

Got away from her, pushed on down to the ladies' room and changed Donny's backside, stuffed the wet napkin into a rubber-lined drawstring bag, washed her face, combed her hair, and found a bottle of Bex tablets. Her hand a cup, she swallowed a tablet, then checked the time. Late enough for lunch. Donny might sleep for a while. She tucked him in tight then returned to the dining area.

A row of cubicles had been built against the café wall. She slid into one that might hold six eaters. A clean ashtray on the table beside the salt, pepper, sugar — four necessities to most diners. She lit a cigarette and opened her bankbook. So much money. Two thousand, six hundred and seventy-five pounds, sixteen shillings and ninepence. So much.

'It was always going to happen,' Granny had said. 'He'll be safe with Jim.'

Always going to happen.

She could remember little of that first year of no Jimmy, just hating Vern Hooper, just wanting to smash him. She could remember chasing his car, smashing his windscreen because she couldn't smash him, remembered making him run into a tree.

He'd thrown something at her that day, spun something at her through the window. Cigarette packet?

She looked at the interest paid into her account. *June interest*. Four lots of June interest. Three lots of forty-odd pounds and one lot of fifty-two. And there'd be more next month. Even the interest was riches.

Blood money. Jimmy's blood. She could never spend it.

Beautiful boy, beautiful baby sitting on Jim's chest in that park in Sydney, Jimmy wearing his daddy's army hat. Like a coloured photograph she carried always in an inner album.

A week, that's all they'd had together. One week of playing daddies and mummies in the room over Myrtle's parlour, Number Five, their home. A happy home. He'd said he'd loved her in that room, he'd made love to her. And she'd loved him, loved everything about him.

And he'd paid her off.

LEAF LITTER

*T*he bus trip home was faster than the trip down, or it seemed that way to Jenny. Georgie and the Hall kids took the short cut across the paddocks, but you can't lift a loaded stroller over fences, or propel it along narrow tracks worn between trees.

Half a dozen workmen were erecting new light poles out front of Macdonald's mill. She walked around their heavy machinery, wishing they'd erect their poles out the forest road.

Two new houses had been built in Henry King's corner. His old shack gone now — and no older than Granny's house. A new pumping station, built behind McPherson's land, pumped water to the town. Joe Flanagan had town water and electricity. So near and yet so far from Granny's land.

Only last week Harry had spoken to Flanagan, about the laying of pipes and poles across his land. The miserable old coot didn't want anyone or anything on his land. He'd set his half-starved dogs onto the kids — until they'd started carrying treats. Joe's dogs waited for them each morning in the wood paddock, greeting the kids with wagging tails. Jenny smiled as she walked, thinking there was probably enough money in that bank account to make miserable old Joe wag his tail.

She walked on, keeping the stroller's wheels well clear of the gravel, knowing every grain of sand, every tree trunk and rotting log, every cawing crow and crawling ant, walking fast, wondering at Jim's motive — other than the obvious, the pay-off. What good could be done now by knowing? It could change nothing. But it was like an infection, that money. She kept fighting it off and it kept coming back at her.

She'd been fighting off the flu the day they'd taken Jimmy. Vern Hooper sitting in the police car. *We know about that filthy abortion business.* She could hear those words now, see his winner-takes-all face.

Pick up your money. Use it to get some order into your life. He'd said that the day she'd broken his windscreen. What had he tossed at her? Not like him to throw an empty cigarette packet from a car window.

The track leading off the forest road to Gertrude's gate had always been steep. Jenny's mind not centred on the stroller or its contents, it overbalanced, tilted to the side, almost tipped out its load. But she'd been pushing prams too long. Familiar with their idiosyncrasies, she righted it and continued on to the boundary gate, opened it and pushed the stroller through. About to close it when her inner album flashed up a photograph of Vern's smashed windscreen, of something flying by her, a flash of blue.

Pick up your money.

Pick it up from where?

She left the gate, walked back to where she'd stood that day, then stepped off the track to where a mulch of leaf litter, green twigs and dead wood covered the forest floor. She picked up a small branch and used it to scrape at the litter. Colonies of insects down there, all going about their business; webs of white fungus doing their best to return fallen timber to the earth. She exposed a rotting cigarette packet, predominantly red, one of Ray's. Buried it for the insects and mould to work on.

How much leaf litter fell each year? How long did it take for gum leaves to rot back to earth?

She wandered deeper into the trees, scraping here and there with her shoe, searching for a needle in a haystack and not knowing if it was Granny's darning needle or Amber's fine needle for embroidery she was looking for.

And what use anyway?

Proof.

Proof of what?

Proof that the money hadn't been paid for a week of prostitute services. Proof that that week had meant as much to Jim as it had to her.

And what was she going to do if she found her proof?

Nothing.

Only Margot in the kitchen, and Raelene sleeping. Like an abused kitten, fallen on its feet into a good home, all she did was purr — or gurgle.

'Where's Granny?'

'She went over to Mum'th. Joany got an engagement ring from that Tony dago.'

Margot still called Elsie *Mum*. Easier for her to say than Elsie. The engagement ring wasn't news, nor was the baby in Joany's belly.

Jenny hauled Donny up and out of the stroller and laid him on a blanket on the floor to change his messy backside, grateful he hadn't soiled while she was out. When he was clean again, she propped him on pillows and turned on the wireless. Music soothed him.

'Where's Granny gone?' she asked him. Never any response from Donny.

Margot was riffling through the shopping. No one went to Willama and came home with empty bags. She found a parcel of bras and pants from Coles.

'I told you to only buy me white panth.'

'They didn't have white in your size,' Jenny said.

'You were thupposed to be going to the doctor, not thopping. You're not allowed to go on the buth to go thopping.'

'There's no law saying I can't shop after I've seen the doctor,' Jenny said. Heard, smelled, burnt milk, and swung around. 'I've told you to stand and watch when you're boiling milk.'

'I wath watching it.'

'You can't watch milk from a distance.'

'I wathn't at a distanth before you came in with hith thtink.'

Never worth the effort of arguing with Margot. She'd argue that black was white, wear the other party down with illogicality, have them gasping for air — or for a smoke. Jenny cleaned the mess from the stove while Margot scoffed at Georgie's bras. Envied them maybe. She had the build of an undeveloped eleven year old — eleven going on fifty when she played cards. Recently, she'd become addicted to Joany's and Maudy's *True Romance* magazines. Granny told her they were rubbish, that she shouldn't be reading them. Rubbish or not, they'd got Margot reading.

And no sooner was the stove clean than she moved her saucepan of milk back over the central hotplate.

'Get that off the stove, Margot!'

'It hath to be boiling when you pour it.'

She had a germ fetish. Blame Georgie for that; blame high school, and science, and invisible bugs, made visible by Itchy-foot's microscope. It would pass. With Margot, all things passed in time. Her desire to feed Donny his bottle when Ray was around had passed, as had her obsession with yellow. She was going through her white period now. Germs were easier to see on white.

'Where's Georgie?' Jenny asked.

'How would I know?'

Margot watched her milk, and caught it as it threatened a second eruption. She made cocoa in her personal mug and took it over to drink at Elsie's. Harry didn't buy cocoa for his lot. Like a swarm of locusts, Harry's kids, they ate him out of house and home. Lenny and Ronnie were both working; Joany would be moving out of town in a week or two.

Jenny walked around the table to Donny. He was singing his dirge, which was easier on the ears than his whine. Ray interpreted dirge and whine as hunger. He liked feeding him, liked watching him do the one thing he could do. Fed him too much, and every Weet-Bix, every piece of chocolate, every bottle, turned to fat.

'Joany got her ring,' Georgie said as she entered. 'It's a diamond with fancy silver bits at the sides.' She found and unwrapped sausages. 'How rare,' she said. 'Sausages for dinner.'

'Willama sausages,' Jenny said.

'Ah, Willama sausages — a world of difference — or twenty-nine miles.'

A green kerosene refrigerator now stood where the sewing machine had lived for years, near the window. Gertrude didn't trust it, didn't like the idea of a tank of kerosene and a burning wick in her kitchen while she slept. The sewing machine had been moved into the lean-to, only until the new rooms were habitable.

'Keep your eye on Donny for me for five minutes, love. I ought to pop over to Elsie's.'

Jenny's intent when she stepped outside was to cross the paddock and offer her congratulations. But what for? For contracting to produce a baby every year until menopause? She looked across the paddock as she lit a cigarette, then turned on her heel and walked west, up the track, squawking chooks following her, expecting to be fed. They turned back. She continued on to the boundary gate, where she leaned a while, blowing smoke. Out that gate then to scrape again at leaf litter.

With evening approaching, the smell of rotting leaves was pungent. She wandered, scraping with her shoe, blowing smoke until the heat of the butt burned her fingers and she was forced to drop it. Killed its spark with her heel, ground it in deep, then, with her shoe, scraped leaf litter to cover it. Granny's law. She couldn't stop

Jenny and Ray from polluting their lungs, but she could stop them polluting her land.

Granny's law exposed a faded blue triangle.

Jenny fell to her knees, wiping away leaves and compacted soil, and the triangle became a rectangle of blue, swollen by moisture, mouldy, insect-eaten. It was her old bankbook. Her proof.

'You bastard! You pair of evil bastards!'

Squatting there, she tried to open it. The years and the elements had sealed that account.

'You bastards.'

Stood then, wiped the cover carefully against the bark of a sapling, then, determined to separate the rotting pages, she did, and for her effort found a segment of mouldy page bleeding blue figures: 1/17/6; 15/-; 10/-; 2/10/0. Immobile as the trees surrounding her, she stared at blurred memories of Sydney. That one was money from overtime at the factory. That one was from the club.

Tried to turn the page. Tried too hard and the rotting paper came apart in her hand. That's all there was: half a page of bleeding figures and the smell of mushrooms. And proof that Jim hadn't paid her off.

Like a bruise on her soul that wouldn't heal, Jim Hooper, and holding that bankbook made that bruising bleed anew, made her howl, because he knew there wasn't enough money in the world to buy Jimmy, or to buy her. He'd loved her. Once upon a time, in a faraway land, he'd loved her.

Tears running, shoulders heaving, she howled, her head against a tree, holding onto that tree. She was a crazy woman, and she didn't care, because life was one crazy mixed-up nightmare and only crazy people could survive it.

Davies's mill truck stopped her tears. He dropped Ray and Lenny off out front of Elsie's house. And she had to go home and start dinner.

Wiped her face on her petticoat, sniffed tears, and told herself Vern Hooper was dead and buried, that his daughters were bitter old maids, that wherever Jimmy was he was with his daddy, that he had a good life because he had Jim.

She had Ray. And she wasn't going to Melbourne with him, staying at a hotel with him, taking Donny to a specialist who would only tell her what she already knew. And she wasn't going to feel guilty about not sleeping with Ray either. He was a lodger. She looked after his kids, and he paid her to do it — like she'd paid old Mrs Firth to look after her kids when she'd sung at the jazz club.

And the next time Amy and John McPherson nagged her to sing at one of their concerts, she would. And she'd make herself something beautiful to wear too, and she'd be who she was and stop trying to be who she wasn't.

Squatting then, she scraped a hole with a sharp stick, scraped it deep enough, wide enough, to bury that book, to bury Sydney and childish dreams. Not Jimmy. One day she'd see him again; five, ten, twenty years from now she'd see him and know him, and he'd know her. One day.

THE ROOT OF EVIL

*F*ire in January, floods in winter — a crazy land, Australia, but you name a mineral, a metal, and somewhere in this vast continent, man had found it. Gold in the colony's early days. Convicts had dug and hauled coal a hundred and fifty years ago; and there was enough left to last another hundred and fifty years. Australia had hills of iron ore. Now at a site in South Australia — Radium Hill, they'd found deposits of uranium. Very valuable stuff in '52, vital to those wanting to make better bombs. Britain wanted it. They made their own atomic bomb that year.

No intention of testing it on home soil though. There were a few useless islands off the coast of Western Australia, and few inhabitants near enough to suffer any effects from the blast.

Through June, July and August of '52, Margaret and Bernard suffered Lorna's blasts, cringed from her detonations. In that gentile, tree-lined Balwyn street, the walls trembled and Margaret trembled — until September, when Lorna again boarded a boat for England. God help her uncle Henry, who Lorna had entrusted to select her mail-order husband. With luck, her boat wouldn't make it to port. On 3 October, the Brits blew up the Monte Bello Islands, and who knew what might happen when that atomic energy hit the immovable wall of Lorna.

Perhaps radioactive fallout caused the madness in Balwyn. There was waltzing up and down the passages, hilarious laughter in bed. Happy days, gloriously happy days.

The papers transferring the Balwyn house to its new owner had been signed some weeks ago. Margaret and Bernard had found their dream home in Cheltenham, by the seaside; a small house, with no spare room for Lorna. They'd purchased a house for her in Kew: middle-aged, tall-roofed, indestructible; its garden, in the main, grey cement, with a cactus or two to offer atmosphere.

'For years she's spoken of gaining her independence, Bernard. She'll be delighted.'

They did their best for her, once she was gone. They furnished her house with the heavier pieces from the Balwyn house, hung the Hooper relatives in her hall, parked Vern's car in her garage.

For themselves, they took delivery of a green Holden, also ordered some weeks earlier. Bernard was licensed to drive, but incapable of doing so with any degree of safety. He was an artist, more prone to searching for inspiration than watching road traffic. Margaret had gained her licence as a girl in Woody Creek, but with Lorna always in the driver's seat, she'd had little opportunity to practise the skill — until Bernard ran them onto a footpath one afternoon, dented the new car's green fender and his head.

While the fender was being straightened, Margaret took a few refresher lessons, and thereafter Bernard sat at her side, free to ponder the beauty of God's great universe.

The removalist's van came in late October. Ian Hooper, Margaret's faithful cousin, drove the Holden and its occupants to their new address, his wife following in their own car. They were no more fond of Lorna than most and swore never to divulge the new address.

James was required to change schools before the final exams.

He was a bright boy and at a stage of his life when making new friends came easily. Margaret bought him a brand new racing bike; the beach was a few streets away; Aunty Lorna thousands of miles away. He loved his happy new home.

Bernard's art thrived there. The smell of paint and turpentine permeated every room, but he painted an ocean scene, which, if one looked at it on an angle and squinted, almost resembled an ocean. Margaret planted a garden, determined to create her own Eden by the sea. Happy months, hopeful months.

All mail was directed to their accountant's office, collection of which necessitated a weekly train trip to the city, where the little couple lunched with their accountant and made decisions over a glass of wine. No letter or card arrived from Lorna, but in December they received an airmail letter addressed in a spidery hand.

'Leticia,' Bernard said, recognising his older sister's script, and on the train home he read aloud of his brother-in-law's death, of Lorna hiking in Scotland.

'She didn't attend his funeral,' Bernard said.

'The distance, perhaps,' Margaret said.

Bernard doubted it had much to do with distance. When last Lorna had spoken to Bernard, it had been to name him a pile of imported rat turds.

'Wouldn't it be wonderful if she decided to remain with her aunt?' Margaret said.

'Have pity, sweet Maggie.'

He felt pity for the families of 180 souls lost in a horror train crash in London — *an express train from Scotland, collided with a London suburban train* . . .

'Good lord! What if Lorna was on that train?' Margaret said.

'My word, yes,' he nodded, his tone not expressing the correct concern.

*

In December, Bernard painted *Lorna's Return*: a grey mushroom cloud, the fires of hell reaching up with ghoulish fingers of flame. There wasn't a violent bone in Bernard's little body, but that painting was violent, and quite wonderful. Margaret praised it, and displayed it in their narrow hallway.

Days disappearing too quickly. Only ten more shopping days to Christmas. Only seven more shopping days . . .

'We are running out of time, Bernard. It must be done.' Lorna's return trip had been booked prior to her leaving.

Margaret fetched pen and pad, and the couple sat subdued at the table, staring at a blank page and unable to fill it. She had to be informed of her altered living arrangements, and before she boarded the boat. They'd ascertained how long it took an airmail letter to reach its destination, give or take a day or two; had decided the letter should not reach her more than a week before her boat departed, which may save Leticia a little of the blast, and certainly the smoke would have cleared before the boat docked in Melbourne.

'The trip home will give her time to appreciate what we've done for her.'

'God grant it be so, sweet Maggie.'

It took the entire afternoon and five drafts, the pen passed from one to the other, each word questioned, accepted or rejected.

My dear sister,
How sad for you to lose your dear uncle. I hope you have come
to terms with his loss and that it is some consolation that you
had seen him shortly before his passing.

A line or two was filled in hoping that Leticia was well and also coming to terms with her loss, then the pen got down to business.

You will have noticed the enclosed photograph. The house
is yours, dear, for your lifetime. We have ascertained that the
neighbours on the right are a pleasant couple, with adult

*children, and that you are well sheltered from the house on the
left.*

*The estate will pay into your account a quarterly allow-
ance, which will increase with the cost of living. Bernard and
I both feel that you are long overdue for your independence,
which I'm certain you will agree you deserve. We also feel sure
that you will be impressed with both the position of your property and the furnishings.*

*You will find the key to the front door of No 43 beneath
a black rock situated in the rockery near your back door. All
other keys are inside, on the dining room table. The pantry and
refrigerator are well stocked.*

We wish you a safe and pleasant journey home.

Love, Margaret and Bernard and James

The couple spent some time choosing which photograph to
enclose. They read the letter aloud, wondered if they should have
mentioned selling the Balwyn property, but as they hadn't included
their new address, perhaps visualising them where she'd left them
might be easier at this stage.

A sweating January; a fiery sun burning Margaret's garden of Eden
where little thrived. Bernard painted *January*, a chaos of grey on
grey on grey.

Come February, they were counting the days, then the hours,
Bernard hopelessly turning the pages of his newspapers searching for ocean disasters. Icebergs all melted. Perhaps a Russian
submarine . . .

Her boat docked on the eleventh day of February. On the thirteenth, Vern's black Ford drove into their yard and Lorna unloaded
her luggage.

They tried to bar the doorway.

'As you can see, dear, it's a very small house.'

'You *will* comply with the terms of my father's will; a will you and your pile of pommy horse droppings coerced a dying man into signing.'

Bernard gave up his bedroom studio. Lorna cleared it of canvases, threw them into Margaret's struggling garden, the paint on two still wet. Margaret and Bernard retrieved them, picked off leaves and twigs, shook off grit, stood them against the walls of their bedroom.

James rode his bike further afield. Stayed away longer.

'You have your own house, Lorna. You must go home, dear.'

'Look to the will, you devious, bug-eyed cretin.'

In May, Bernard and Margaret put the Cheltenham house in the hands of an agent and moved down to the beach house in Frankston, the emptying of their dream home into storage achieved while Lorna was in hospital. She'd taken on a truck driver, or his truck, fractured her skull, broken her spindly ankle, a rib had punctured her lung. They made no visit to the hospital, sent no get well card, directed their accountant, and the estate agent, to keep their whereabouts under lock and key.

Beach houses are not meant to be occupied in late autumn. No telephone, the kitchen was archaic, the furniture dank and moth-eaten. A stop gap, just for a week or two until the agent found a suitable house well distanced from the city. No school for James; not worth enrolling him for a week or two.

They were not aware that Lorna had been released from hospital. She arrived in a taxi, hobbled down the drive on a crutch, her scalp shaven, a beret covering the many stitches.

'Who?'

'How?'

Their accountant's receptionist had given them up in Cheltenham. She'd since been given her marching orders.

James gave up his bed to sleep on a moth-eaten couch. The following day he spoke again of his maternal grandmother's house, of Jenny. Margaret had hoped he'd forgotten Woody Creek and his other family.

Two weeks of hell before their new property, sixty miles from the city, was available. The accountant saw to the moving of the stored Cheltenham furniture and Bernard's paintings. The little family made their escape in the night, James's racing bike in the car's trunk — not quite in it. They lost it somewhere between Frankston and their new address.

'Never mind, darling. We'll buy you a new bike.'

They were safe from vilification until August of '53, when Bernard displayed three of his art works at a city gallery. They sold *Lorna's Return*, renamed *Holocaust*: Britain's nuclear devices were big news, and coming soon to the mainland. They sold *Storm*, a sombre work, which, in Margaret's opinion, had been somewhat assisted by its near brush with death in the Cheltenham garden. Bernard was delighted with his brief mention in *The Age*; and with his photograph and half-page spread in the local paper. And of course Margaret was delighted for him — may not have been so delighted had she known Lorna was again in collusion with the investigator who had dug up the dirt on the Morrison girl.

She came again, her hair grown through, spiky and grey.

The constant disruptions, the changing of schools, was playing havoc with James's grades — and the quality of his companions.

Then Jim disappeared off the face of the earth. Since Margaret had inherited responsibility for her brother, she'd had him moved to a pleasant place in the hills. Bernard, so recently on a high, fell into one of his depressions. Margaret, frazzled by decisions, wanted to join him and couldn't. Decisions had to be made. The tenant wanted to purchase the Woody Creek house. He'd made a good offer. She wanted it sold, wanted to cut all ties with that town, but couldn't contact Jim to ask if he wanted to sell it. Knew that selling it wouldn't cut the ties with that town anyway. The farm, which Vern had stipulated must never be sold, would tie her forever to the place.

Then James went missing. For twenty-four hours they didn't know if he was alive or dead. Margaret was convinced Jim had taken him, or the Morrison girl — or both. The police were called in. They found him and his so-called friends halfway to Melbourne; may not have found him had one of the boys not punctured his back tyre.

Back in '48, Vern had put his grandson's name down at several of the better private schools. The advisory pages of Margaret's favourite magazine stated that boys of his age required strong male figures to guide them. Bernard was a perfect companion for her, but by no stretch of the imagination could he be described as a strong male figure.

Carey Grammar agreed to take him midterm, and once more her dear boy changed school. Sadly, he was pleased to go.

'The school is in Kew, Lorna, only a short tram ride from your house,' Margaret informed her sister. 'James could spend an occasional weekend with you.'

A scoff said it all.

Having been raised in the era when housekeepers dealt with the merchants, when servants served, Lorna was ill equipped to live independently. The threat of weekends with her nephew made her cling more possessively to her guest room.

The accountant suggested he advertise for a live-in companion who might cook and clean for Lorna at Kew in return for free board.

'Do what you think best,' Margaret said.

The accountant spoke of the Woody Creek tenant's offer.

'Do what you think best,' Margaret said.

The accountant moved Mrs Matilda Muir into the Kew house's guest room. A well-spoken and sprightly little widow, she had worked as a domestic before her marriage.

Two nuclear devices detonated at Emu Field, Woomera, were fireworks beneath a midday sun compared to Lorna's explosion when she discovered Mrs Matilda Muir was a Jehovah's Witness.

'God help us, Bernard.'

'He has forsaken us, sweet Maggie.'

Margaret turned from God to her horoscope, which suggested a new direction. Lorna's house, being so close to her darling boy's school, would be so much more convenient. They packed the car while Lorna was at church — or flung items into its trunk and rear seat. The long drive on a Sunday was harrowing, the roads unfamiliar, but why fear disaster when one is escaping catastrophe? And dear, comforting Mrs Muir waiting to greet them, to sit them down with a cup of tea. Such a gentle, sweet-natured woman — and they'd thought to subject her to Lorna?

For a time they were safe in the grey shark's home waters; so safe, Margaret started planning her boy's birthday party. Each December, since '48, she had created splendid parties for groups of small boys. She telephoned Michael's and Peter's mothers in Balwyn; Graham's mother in Cheltenham.

'How surprised he'll be, Bernard.'

The surprise was for Margaret. When she drove with Bernard to the school on Friday with written invitations for James's new friends, he told her Alan's father was coming down to take them to the cricket for their birthdays.

'I've already invited several of your little friends, darling.'

'I'd rather go to the cricket with Alan, Mum,' he said.

Driven to tears by his rejection, driven frantic by chaotic peak-hour traffic, driven off the road by a brewery horse, Margaret and the Holden mounted a gutter and attempted to enter a house via its brick wall. Thankfully, the wall was only half a block from Lorna's house. She and Bernard walked home suffering little worse than bruises. The Holden was towed away.

Party invitations cancelled, night had fallen over the city when the couple, bathed and clad for bed, Bernard in green silk pyjamas, Margaret with nipples showing through the clinging fabric of her brief pink gown and negligee, sat down to tea and ham and mustard sandwiches.

Lorna entered via the rear door with her small travelling case. 'Cover yourself, you harlot.'

Margaret's incredible and unsupported breasts trembling, her nipples making a hasty retreat, she stood and placed her sandwich down.

'No,' she said. 'No, no, no, Lorna. We have been such good companions for so long. We have worked together for a common objective, supported each other in our times of trial, but you have become . . . obsessive, Lorna. And it must stop.'

Lorna reached for a ham sandwich. She hadn't been eating well.

'Can't you see there is no sense to this obsession of yours? I am a married woman. I want to live with my husband and son, as a family. Surely we can come to some compromise? Mrs Muir is a dear and good woman, a fine cook and housekeeper.'

Lorna reply was more snort than scoff. Her mouth was full.

'Bernard and I will return home in the morning. You *must* remain here. Of course, you'll be welcome to join us for Christmas. We'd have it no other way.' She looked towards the passage, where Bernard had scuttled on seeing the grey shark's return. 'We want Lorna to have a place in our lives, don't we, Bernard?'

He heard her; he didn't reply. His back to the wall, he was watching that pile of sandwiches shrink.

'We have been more than generous to you, Lorna. We have gone far beyond the terms of Father's will.'

The shoulder strap of Margaret's gown had slipped, her breast was attempting to escape.

'You're no better than that Morrison harlot, flaunting your wares.'

Lorna's normal speaking voice could have been mistaken for a male's: deep, slow, a professor's lecture to his class of cretins. Emotion raised it tonight, and raised her arm to smite the harlot. Instead, she smote the plate of sandwiches to the floor, and Bernard's small mouth opened, closed, like a cod out of water.

Margaret adjusted her strap. 'You have a malevolent nature, Lorna, and if I have become devious in my dealings with you these last years, then certainly I learned all I know from you. Don't you dare deny that you were planning to do exactly what I have done. Bernard and I copied your letter verbatim, and I have kept it to prove your . . . your . . . perfidiousness. Had you wed Bernard, I would have been put out, or put upon by you for the remainder of my days.'

'You inherited all you know from your lying slut of a mother.'

Again Lorna's arm rose. In their youth, a slap had swiftly silenced Margaret's hysteria. Margaret saw the blow coming and parried it with her own raised arm.

'You saw that, Mrs Muir?' The little woman had crept out of her room to stand at Bernard's side. 'Ring the law, Mrs Muir. One way or the other, we will have this . . . this hostility out of our house tonight.'

'You threaten me with the law!' Lorna shrieked. 'You, who coerced a dying man into leaving his estate in the hands of two nameless bastards! You're no Hooper, and my father always knew it.'

'Coerced?' Margaret's plump little hands went to her impressive buttock humps, her gown gaping. 'Coerced? He was delighted, you evil witch of a woman. Jim said it better than I, but if I never set eyes on you until I'm on my deathbed, it will be too soon.'

Margaret was magnificent and quite capable of handling the situation. Bernard backed away. For the first time in months, he felt a painting coming on. His paints . . . had Margaret packed his paints?

'You've got more in common with the Morrison trollop than a lack of morals.'

'I vowed never to tell you this. Why do you think Father took you with him when he travelled? Because you were his favourite? Oh, no, no, no, you were not. One of the last things he asked of me was that I keep his grandson out of your clutches. Those were his words. Don't allow her to ruin him like she ruined your brother, he said to me.'

Bernard recalled sighting Margaret carrying two stretched canvases out to the car. Had she carried them in? In his mind's eye he could see a masterpiece: his Maggie framed by the doorway, sandwiches spread at her fluffy pink slipper-clad feet, the contents of Lorna's teacup dripping from her chin, staining her negligee, moistening it enough to cling.

Until that night, he had not seen Margaret's claws. They were exposed tonight and capable of drawing blood.

He glanced at Mrs Muir, who appeared to be praying for peace. 'Canvases,' he said. 'Did you sight them, Mrs Muir?'

She had her finger on the pulse of this house. She found his paintbox, his canvases. The last he heard of the altercation was his sweet Maggie's voice.

'My marriage enabled Father to die in the knowledge that you would have no hand in the raising of James. Had you wed Bernard, I would have raised that little boy alone.'

The smoke cleared by midnight, perhaps earlier. Paint-smeared but satisfied, the bedcover paint-smeared, Bernard emerged from his work as Margaret entered requiring her bed. He removed his paraphernalia, leaned his painting against the wall then stood back, pleased with the triangles of white bread and black rye, the pink ham stretched between two hands, one large, its talon nails dripping blood, the other dimpled, a pale, virginal hand, with sharp claws.

The painting had not dried sufficiently to transport, but Margaret ordered a taxi for eight the next morning. The painting travelled home on his and Mrs Muir's laps. Margaret sat with the driver.

Lorna arrived at five that afternoon. Bernard hid in his studio.

Margaret took a phone call from the mother of Alan, James's new schoolfriend. They were planning a camping trip over Christmas, and Alan would so much enjoy having James spend his Christmas with them. Say no, and she would subject that dear boy to six weeks of unrelieved Lorna. Say yes, and a bitter, lonely Christmas loomed before Margaret.

She took the woman's number and told her she'd discuss it with James's father. The phone returned to its hook, she ran to her bedroom, flung herself down on the bed and cried. All she'd wanted was her darling boy, and slowly but surely she was losing him. All she'd needed was the Balwyn house and enough money to live on. The wording of that letter to Vern should have been altered, giving Lorna control of the estate. She would have thrived on the responsibility, made decisions with a wave of her hand. She was a woman who needed to control and Vern's will had stripped her of control. Her only power now was her presence and her evil tongue.

The telephone rang again. No one answered its call and the exchange gave up — for five minutes, then it began again. Bernard would chose not to hear it. Lorna, who had an appalling phone manner, had been asked not to answer it. Someone had to silence the thing.

It was the accountant, with the news that Rick Thompson, Vern's farm manager for thirty years, had dropped dead in the paddock. Where were they going to find a man to replace him? And the funeral — the Hooper family must be represented there.

FASTER YEARS

Rick Thompson's funeral was big news in Woody Creek, or Margaret Hooper turning up for it with a husband instead of her sister was big news. The Hooper women had been inseparable for forty years.

The service wasn't as well attended as it ought to be. With Christmas only days away, people had other things on their minds, and the day was a scorcher.

Charlie White had other things on his mind. Born on 21 December 1873, he'd celebrated his eightieth birthday the day before the funeral, celebrated it alone. Hilda, his one offspring, hadn't remembered it — or not until Glenda, her daughter, called from Sydney mid-afternoon and reversed the charges.

'Happy birthday, Grandfather,' she'd said. 'Can you put Mother on please?'

Three words for him and she'd spoken to her mother for half an hour, and every penny being sucked down that telephone line by their blabbering would come out of Charlie's cheque account. And when Hilda finally put that phone down, she'd started on him again to sell the shop and buy a business in Sydney. He'd told her the telephone company would go broke if she moved. She called him a miserable old coot, begrudging her a five-minute talk to his only granddaughter. He told her it was closer to twenty-five minutes, that he'd had his stopwatch on her.

'Happy birthday, Dad,' she'd said and walked out.

He paid her a man's wage, paid her for a forty-hour week, and was lucky if she worked twenty-five. He'd educated his granddaughter at one of the better Melbourne ladies' colleges, which had made her so much better than every other bugger in town, she wouldn't set foot in it. Which he'd told her mother last night.

'I bought your husband a brand new car,' he'd said.

'You bought it for yourself,' she'd said.

'It's in his name, isn't it.'

'Only because the constable won't give you a licence.'

She could argue like her mother had, didn't do it as nicely though, liked rubbing it in that he couldn't get a licence and she'd got one. Not that it stopped him from driving the car — or not since the new copper had been in town. He didn't drive it far: picked up a few goods from the station; delivered a few orders on Friday mornings.

'You'll get the lot when I'm dead,' he'd said.

'You'll be standing behind that counter for the next twenty years and I'll be standing beside you.'

'Go to Sydney if you want to go to Sydney. I'm not stopping you.'

'What are we supposed to live on!'

'Not me for a bloody change,' he'd said and walked out, ridden around to the pub for his dinner and a few beers to calm him — a few too many beers. He hadn't gone home either; he'd spent the night on an old easy chair in the shop's storeroom.

She hadn't come into work today and he'd been run off his feet. A man of eighty with a serious hangover should have been sitting on his backside nursing his hangover, having folk run around after him. He was dead on his feet by two o'clock. He didn't go to Rick Thompson's funeral, didn't get to see Margaret Hooper and her husband. He heard about them. For the rest of the afternoon he heard about them.

He didn't get away from the store until six, and when he leaned his bike against the veranda post, his car wasn't where it ought to have been, nor was his trailer.

No one in his kitchen. And their room was bare.

Ate a tin of preserved peaches for dinner, forked them from the can while walking his house looking for what was missing. A lot was missing. The crystal cabinet, along with its contents. Jean's jewellery.

His bed was still there.

He walked out to the yard, still forking up peach halves. He needed that car. Couldn't report it missing. He needed Jean's jewellery too. He liked looking at it at night, her ghost at his side, discussing where they'd bought each piece.

They'd taken her ghost with them — or she'd hitched a ride to keep an eye on her treasures.

'Not to worry,' he said. 'I'll be seeing you in the flesh soon, Jeany.'

That night Charlie fell into a bed to die in comfort, and was disappointed he was still alive when he woke the following morning.

He was still alive come January. He didn't look as neat, nor did the shop. The customers missed Hilda. She'd kept them abreast of the news.

'Have you heard from Hilda and Arthur?' they asked.

'Who?' Charlie replied to one and all.

'I dare say you're missing her.'

He was missing Jean's ghost. She'd always been flitting around that house somewhere. Just an empty house now, and Charlie didn't want to be in it.

Mick Boyle the younger, who now delivered the orders, moved Charlie's bed and kitchen table down to the storeroom. At night,

Charlie locked his doors and fell into his bed. He woke wearing his apron some mornings, then worked all day in it.

He was still alive come February. His diet of tinned peaches had eroded the little fat he'd had and started working on muscle. He looked shrunken, strained, stained, unshaven, but was too damn tired to give a bugger what he looked like, too damn tired to ride home for a bath and a change of clothes, too damn tired to climb ladders, stack shelves, set mouse traps.

'Have you heard from Hilda and Arthur, Mr White?'

'Who?'

Mice chewed holes in his cornflakes packets, held race meetings on his long counter, left their calling cards on every shelf; and when irate customers returned damaged goods and threatened to go elsewhere, Charlie was too damn tired to be polite.

'It's a long bloody walk to Willama,' he said.

He may have given up and died; he may have locked his doors and remained in that bed until he rotted. One thought kept him going. His will. *To Hilda Jean Timms, my only daughter and sole beneficiary, I leave my all.* If he'd had muscle enough left, he might have ridden his bike to Willama and changed that will. He didn't have muscle enough to push that bike out to the cemetery to visit Jean's tombstone.

He was asleep on his feet the day Georgie Morrison and her limpet sister walked in, both clad in high-school uniform.

'Sleeping on the job, Charlie?' Georgie greeted him.

'Just resting my eyes, Rusty,' he said, allowing his eyes to rest on that mane of copper hair tied back in a heavy ponytail. He'd had a soft spot for Georgie since the day he'd seen her drive a pair of embroidery scissors into Vern Hooper's thigh.

She took a list and a pound note from her pocket. 'Are you growing a beard?'

'Saves wasting razor blades,' he said, fingering a ten-day growth of stubble.

He filled her order, wrote down each item, totalled it. She didn't hand over her pound note but pointed to his figures.

'It's eighteen and ninepence, not seventeen and ninepence.'

He eyed her. 'You're adding it up upside down, and what are you complaining about? It's your way.'

She shrugged and Charlie checked his figures. Upside down or not, she'd got it right.

'Time to get myself new glasses,' he said, or to clean the ones he was wearing.

'Are you older than Granny or younger, Charlie?'

'I'm a hundred and ten, and it's none of your business,' he said.

She dropped the change into her pocket, loaded her string bags and walked out, her sister at her elbow.

'Hey,' he called. Margot kept walking. Georgie turned. 'You're not looking for a job, are you?'

'I would be if I was old enough.'

'How old are you?'

'Fourteen in March.'

'Too young for me,' he said.

'Are you looking for a shop assistant or a wife, Charlie?'

She stood there smiling at him, the weight of her shopping pulling on her right arm. Her mother had been a beauty. This one was something more than beautiful — and one of the few who ever smiled at him.

'I could work on Saturdays and after school,' she added.

'I need someone full-time, Rusty.'

Her shopping placed down, her hand went to her pocket to finger coins as her eyes took inventory of the shop, its chaos, of Charlie in his soiled collarless shirt, his formerly white apron now a fair match for his greasy white hair.

'The school is taking us down to see the Queen on Monday. I could start next Tuesday.'

'It's not March on Tuesday,' he said.

'It's near enough though. Can I?'

*

In February of '54, schoolkids from all over the country were transported to large centres so they might catch a glimpse of royalty. Margot, going on fifteen and measuring a bare four foot ten inches, stood in the front row out front of a fancy civic centre, put up in a hurry to impress Queen Lizzie. Georgie, five foot eight, stood in the back row with the boys. She'd remember that day for the rest of her life, not because of the new civic centre, the Queen or Philip, but because of the long bus ride to get there and the brief glimpse of a world outside of school and Woody Creek. And because that day would forever be marked in her memory as her final day of childhood.

The following morning, instead of catching the bus, she rode Norman's bike into town and sat on Charlie's doorstep until he opened his doors. Jenny and Granny had told her to go to school. Maybe she would tomorrow.

Didn't know if she wanted to work or not. She wanted . . . things. She wanted . . . separation from Margot. Wanted money that wasn't Ray's. Wanted her own bed. Wanted to go to Sydney and find her father, to see if he did look like Clark Gable. She wanted everything, and working for Charlie might start a bit of that everything happening.

That was the year the town got to know Georgie Morrison, the year the good ladies grew accustomed to her knocking on their back doors to take their orders. And if a few of the old brigade didn't like the idea of dealing with one of Jenny Morrison's illegitimate brats, they missed out on having their cartons of groceries delivered by Mick Boyle on Fridays.

A fast year, 1954: athletes ran faster, planes flew faster, Christmas came around faster.

In '55, New South Wales abolished the six o'clock closing of hotels. Their doors could now remain open until ten. Border town hotels along the Murray did well; old bridges, built in the slower days of the horse and gig, rocked with the traffic, all going the same way at six and the other way after ten. Road deaths increased. Most were alcohol related.

In March 1956, tax was increased on cars, smokes, grog and petrol. In July, poker machines were legalised in New South Wales. Someone had to pay for the Olympic Games, and who better to hit than the working man. It had been learnt long ago that he couldn't survive without his car, smokes, grog and petrol, that he liked to gamble. And why not try his luck on the pokies if he had a few bob left over at the weekend? The working man became the government's goat that year; poker machine clubs their milking sheds, where the government milked them dry.

The news wasn't all bad. Salk vaccine was introduced in July and immunisation programs were underway to wipe out polio, a disease feared for decades. Television came to Melbourne that year, just in time for the Olympic Games.

Georgie read about the November extravaganza. She read about television, about Dawn Fraser and Murray Rose, John Landy's record-breaking run. Charlie read about the share market — or didn't read it. His eyes were bad. She read it to him between customers. She'd known nothing about stocks and shares. He had piles of them. She stripped his bed each Saturday, rode home with a bundle of sheets and shirts, pillow slips and aprons to boil up in the copper and in exchange Charlie bought her small packets of shares so she could watch how money grew.

They got on well, Georgie and old Charlie. He'd always been somewhere in the background of her life. Maybe she'd found her father figure. He'd found a granddaughter who smiled at him and invited him home for meals. He sat with Gertrude, speaking to her about Jean and the old days, of epidemics they'd lived through, of those who had been lost in childhood, those of their age group who hadn't made old bones.

*

Gertrude still laced on her boots in the mornings and unlaced them at night. Elsie still searched out those white give-away hair roots, still painted them away with a toothbrush dipped in dye. Chooks still had to be fed, eggs had to be sorted, apricots had to be made into jam, but when it was done, Gertrude was content to sit longer.

Raelene commenced school in January of '57. Georgie transported her in, on the child's seat Jenny had once ridden in, fitted again to Norman's bike. At three each school day, Jenny collected her from the school gates and Raelene rode home more comfortably seated behind Jenny's new bike.

Donny? At seven, he had the advancement of a fourteen-month-old baby and was the size of a ten year old — an overweight ten year old — and had started taking fits. They'd bought him a single bed. He rolled out of it. Gertrude suggested a mattress on the floor. No use talking to Ray about it. He kept on tucking him into the cot at night, hauling him out of it the next morning. A solid cot, its bars made of iron, big enough in another lifetime for two little girls. Donny filled it.

Jenny read books on retardation, became an expert on the degrees of feeble-mindedness. Some kids never learned to feed themselves. Some managed simple tasks with supervision. Donny knew where his mouth was, had learnt to hold his feeding bottle. He could hold a biscuit, find his mouth with it, stuff the lot into his mouth and gag on it too. He recognised his colourful Donald Duck bowl and related it to food. His hands wanted that food, but add the third element of spoon and the relationship between bowl and mouth was too distant for him to grasp.

Hours, hours and more hours Jenny spent with him the year Raelene started school. Achieved nothing. He could roll about on the floor. He could stand alone; once stood, even step if she held his hands. She needed him to walk. As a two year old he'd been too heavy to haul around. At four he'd grown out of the stroller. They'd replaced it with a wheelchair.

Donny liked going for walks. Liked watching the chooks in the yard. Liked the wireless. Liked staring at the lamplight. He wasn't toilet-trained. Would never be toilet-trained. She lined his morning napkins with heavy layers of toilet paper, which worked if she watched what he ate. Ray watched him at weekends, and fed him chocolate.

He was a good father. There was no denying that. Gertrude, born to sweep up lost souls and nurse them back to health, had accepted Ray into her pack. Maybe all he'd ever needed was acceptance. They'd heard him laugh once or twice.

Two tall rooms now sheltered Gertrude's hut from southern winds. Ray and Donny slept in the western-facing room. The second room was Jenny's laundry-cum-bathroom. Pipes from the large tank fed water to wash troughs, bath and chip heater. Pipes running beneath the floorboards carried waste water out to a gutter that ran down to the orchard. The old copper had been moved from the shed. It stood in the open, close to the washhouse door. A hose from the tank filled it. The girls shared the lean-to bed. Jenny shared Gertrude's room; Raelene shared Jenny's bed. A segmented house, a segmented family, but with Gertrude at the helm, it worked. And apart from Donny, life was . . . At times, life was good.

Jenny didn't wear Ray's wedding ring but she was Mrs King, Raelene King's mother. She wore Ray's friendship ring beside Jim's. She sang at the concerts. In Armadale, Ray hadn't wanted her to sing. He didn't go to the concerts. He'd be going to the school concert this year; Raelene would be in it. A born pixie, that one. A pretty, dark-eyed kid, head of dark curls — an easy baby, if not such an easy child.

Ray loved her — and was ruining her — he came home from work every night with a bag of lollies in his pocket. Gertrude told him he'd rot her teeth, but if he didn't have that bag of lollies in his pocket, Raelene didn't love him. He needed that love. He carried her with him into town on Saturday mornings, on his bike; she never came home empty-handed.

'Look what I got, Mummy.'

Jenny had never been 'Mummy', other than for that week in Sydney . . .

Shush, you'll wake Mummy.

Too young to be a mummy at eighteen, she was more than old enough now. She'd turn thirty-four this year. Wasn't certain how she'd got there, but she had — against all odds, old Charlie might say.

Age forced acceptance of many things. It forced understanding too. She found a bare smidgen of understanding for Amber while changing Donny's napkins. There was no joy to be had in caring for a child you didn't care about. She did her best. That was all anyone could do.

Maybe she loved Raelene. She loved making her pretty clothes to wear; she tried to love her, tried to curb her wilfulness too.

Wondered if Myrtle loved Cara. Wondered if a baby born to another forever belonged to that other.

SPUTNIK

On 3 October 1957, Cara Norris had her thirteenth birthday; one day before the Russians put their satellite into space. Sputnik, the newspapers named it, and tonight they'd said on the radio that it may be visible to the naked eye in the southern skies. Myrtle Norris, out stargazing with her husband and daughter, said her short neck had not been designed to look skyward. She gave up on Sputnik and went inside. Cara and her father didn't give up.

Myrtle wanted to sell the boarding house and buy a nice little house somewhere else. Robert and Cara didn't. Gran Norris had a nice little house and she wanted them to live with her. Myrtle, Robert and Cara were in full agreement about not wanting that. Gran had a bad hip, a bad back, bad neighbours, bad sons and bad grandchildren who never visited her. There wasn't much about Gran Norris that wasn't bad. She said a boarding house was a bad environment in which to raise 'that girl'.

Always 'that girl' to Gran. Had she ever said her name? Myrtle rarely said her name; she called her 'pet'. Robert called her 'poppet'. Sarah called her Caro, as did a few of the girls at school. Most of her teachers called her Cara. The headmistress had called her

Miss Norris today and told her that such bad behaviour in a young lady was not acceptable.

Cara sighed and turned to look at the house her parents wanted to sell. She loved Amberley. She'd learnt her numbers from the boarding-house doors, had learnt to read Myrtle's many signs before she'd started school. Since she was six years old she'd been running upstairs to deliver phone messages written on Myrtle's special message paper — and reading them before doing her deliveries.

'What would I do without you to save my legs?' Myrtle used to say.

'You'd have to pin notes on Bowser's collar.'

Poor old Bowser had lost most of his fluff. He no longer barked and wagged his tail, but still spent his nights guarding her bed. Robert still brought him to life on days when the sun was shining in through the parlour window at just the right angle and painting its coloured patterns on the wall. He made the best shadow puppets, and Cara's favourite was Bowser. When she looked at her father's hands, of course they looked like hands, fingers raised or bent, but when she looked at the wall, she saw Bowser chasing dragons through a green, blue, pink and gold jungle.

The boarding house had been full up with people when she was small, the lodgers' kitchen like a cage full of hens, all clucking and cackling for their dinner. They had six lodgers now, all upstairs: Miss Robertson, Mrs Collins, the two Miss Keatings, Miss Jones and Mrs Gladstone, all too old to cluck and cackle in the lodgers' kitchen. They were the reason Cara couldn't have a real dog. Pups were boisterous, Robert said, and with so many old ladies coming in and out of the gate, one would surely let him out onto the busy road.

Sarah North, from over the road, had been given a puppy one Christmas. It got out the gate and was run over. Her mother had got her another one, which they kept prisoner on a chain. He'd grown into a crazy dog. Cara wouldn't go anywhere near Sarah's backyard — not that she'd ever be likely to go anywhere near Sarah North ever again, not after today.

She turned to her father, wanting to ask him something. He was searching the sky with his binoculars. She watched him for minutes, uncertain of how to start, or even if she should start.

Until today, she and Sarah had been best friends; until lunchtime, when Sarah had whispered something to Elaine. You always know when people are whispering about you. Cara had known, even before Elaine told Lena and Lena told Cara at afternoon recess.

She'd gone up to Sarah as they were going back into class. 'If you want to tell lies about me, then say them to my face instead of whispering behind my back,' she'd said.

Sarah said it to her face, right in her face, so Cara pushed her — not hard, but Sarah wasn't expecting it and she'd tripped on the step and skinned her elbow against the brick wall, really skinned it, which was why Cara had to go to the headmistress, which was worse than embarrassing because Robert taught English to the senior kids at the same school.

'Can I ask you something, Daddy?'

'That sounds ominous, poppet.'

'It's just about why I pushed Sarah.'

'I thought she was your best friend.'

'Well, she's not any more. She told Elaine that you weren't my proper father.'

Stars in the night sky blurring. Silence in the street, or in Robert's ears. For years Myrtle had feared this night. The silence continued too long. He had to find the right words and find them fast.

'Don't tell me they got you and Sarah mixed up at the hospital? I always thought she looked a bit like me.'

'It's not something to joke about. Why would she say that?'

'Because she's a silly goose and she was angry about something else. Tomorrow she'll be whispering to you about Elaine. Here, you have a look for a while. My eyes are too old.'

He passed the binoculars to her. She took them, but didn't look at the sky.

'Why are you and Mummy so old?'

'Old? Us? We're still spring chickens.'

'You're nearly sixty. Sarah North's father is thirty-six.'

She'd asked that question before. He'd never answered it, and didn't answer tonight. She placed the binoculars to her eyes and looked up.

'The stars keep wriggling,' she said, and the binoculars were on her lap. 'Sarah said she heard Mrs Rowe talking to her mother about how you were away at the war when I was born, so you couldn't be my proper father. And she said that Mummy must have had a boyfriend, and that he must have been one of the lodgers or the minister or something because she never went anywhere except to church.'

'Don't tell me you're the milkman's daughter?'

'You always do that.'

'What do I always do?'

'Make a joke of everything. You always do it. Are you my proper father?'

'There has never been a more proper father than I. I'm very, very proper. I'm probably the properest father I know.'

'There is no such word as "properest". Were you away at the war when I was born?'

'You know I was. You were ten months old when I first saw you, and you were the most beautiful baby ever born. You're just looking for compliments.'

'I mean, how long were you away before I was born? I know how long a baby takes . . .'

'Are you that old? I don't even know that. How long do they take?'

'Stop being silly. I'm not laughing at you.'

Robert took the binoculars and again placed them to his eyes. 'If we went through life trying to work out what silly people meant when they whispered about us, then we'd be as silly as they, wouldn't we? You are my very own, my one and only, beautiful daughter. Mummy and I are older than most of the other parents because by the time you were born we'd given up hope of having our own baby, then God blessed us by sending his most beautiful star down from heaven and it landed right in Mummy's arms.'

'Time has a way of concealing details, of blurring memories,' he'd said to Myrtle six weeks ago when she'd spoken again of selling Amberley. Time blurred, but didn't erase.

Through the years they'd had a few moments of fear. In '47 they'd come close to selling and moving to New Zealand when a chap knocked twice on their door asking about a Jennifer Morrison. Had Robert's mother been a well woman, they may have made the move, but the chap hadn't returned and they'd forgotten about selling.

Until Myrtle had given in and allowed Cara to have her hair cut short, like Sarah. Curls released from their weight had become a crinkled cap. Several times they'd caught Miss Robertson staring at the cap of gold. She'd made no comment.

Myrtle had. 'She's the image of Jenny with her hair like that.'

'It will grow,' he'd said. 'Miss Robertson is retiring at the end of the year and going home to England.'

Miss Robertson had retired and gone to England for ten weeks. Not finding the land she'd left thirty years ago, she'd returned to their door. Amberley had been her home. What could they do but take her in?

Done with stargazing, Cara safe in the bathroom, Robert relayed the earlier conversation to Myrtle.

'If Mrs Rowe has been gossiping to Sarah's mother, she's been gossiping to others,' he said.

'New Zealand, Robert. We'll stay with my brother until we find a house.'

'I don't want to place an ocean between me and Mum. Melbourne perhaps,' he said.

'It's too close.'

Not so close. A good five hundred miles south. And on a school oval five hundred miles south, a mob of raucous schoolboys and one of their young masters were doing more skylarking than stargazing.

One of those boys stood head and shoulders above his schoolmaster and most of his mates — not as tall as Jim and Vern, but tall enough to be nicknamed Lofty. His mother called him 'darling'. Aunt Lorna called him James. No one called him Jimmy — not that it worried him much what anyone called him. Viewing life from his lofty perspective allowed him to distance himself from much of it.

He went home some weekends. His mother and Aunt Lorna were civil. Mrs Muir was like a gentle old granny in the kitchen. He didn't see a lot of Bernard who spent his life in a tin shed he named the studio. Pops, he called him; could never force his tongue to call him Dad. Jimmy had a real father, who, as a kid he'd believed to be dead — until they'd visited him at a hospital one Christmas. The war had damaged him, they said. There'd been more to what was wrong with his father than war damage. He wasn't in the hospital now. No one knew where he was — and they didn't look for him either.

Jimmy could remember Australia being at war, and when it ended. He could remember the words of war: *Enemy lines, counter-attacks.* As a little kid, he'd thought it was some sort of team game, with two captains who drew lines, put up long counters, then across those long counters the goodies fought the baddies with bayonets.

In the movies, the goodies and the baddies remained a constant. In real life, there was no constant. In real life, alliances altered every day. Until Bernard came along, Lorna and Margaret had fought on the same side. After Bernard, Lorna had become public enemy number one. As had the Russians, who had been allies during the war, lost millions of their people to the war. They were the bad guys now, the reds, the communists, while the Germans, responsible for the war, were immigrating to Australia. The Japs, such bad guys America had dropped two atomic bombs on them, were no longer considered the bad guys — or not by some.

Yanks were the perennial good guys, big on God, freedom and equality, though still lynching a few Negroes in the southern states — and pouring millions of dollars into perfecting better bombs to drop on the Russians, which would probably mean the end of the world, because Russia also had the bomb, and if America dropped one on them, they'd drop one on America. Like kids in the schoolyard: you hit me and I'll get you back double.

And what was so bad about communism? He'd asked his mother once and all she'd said was that they were godless people.

Until Jenny and everyone had died, he'd probably been a communist. He'd never been inside a church, never been baptised. His grandfather might have been a communist. He hadn't gone to church, though towards the end of his life he'd liked to sit and look at the family names written in the big Bible — Hooper family names, not Morrison. Some days his grandfather would allow the book to fall open, then run his finger down a page looking for a message from God. Once, long ago, Jimmy had asked him where God lived. He'd pointed up to a cloudy sky.

No clouds up there tonight. Jimmy smiled, imagining a Russian rocket ship ramming into heaven, imagining the newspaper headlines: GOD ASSASSINATED BY THE REDS.

He'd pretty much given up believing God was up there since his grandfather had died. Try as he might, he couldn't imagine a pair of feathered wings big enough to hold up his grandfather's weight.

He'd pretty much given up believing that smoking would stunt his growth too. He'd smoked all he could get during his fourteenth and fifteenth years. It had been too late by then to stunt him but he'd hoped it might halt his growth. It hadn't.

He'd lost faith in the government. Only last week one of the teachers read an article to the class about radioactive fallout from atomic bombs, and the danger it presented to mankind, yet Menzies was still allowing Britain to tests bombs in Australia.

All traces of radioactivity are expected to pass from Australian territory a day or two after the tests, the newspapers said. What territory was it going to pass into after it passed out of Australia? Did anyone think about that? It had to go somewhere; or did it just float off into space and poison the Martians?

He looked up, searching the sky for falling Martians. And he saw Sputnik! It had to be Sputnik. Just a tiny star moving across the sky too slowly to be the light from a plane.

'There it is, sir,' he said, his finger pointing.

'Trust Lofty,' Alan said. 'He's got an unfair advantage.'

Schoolmates, schoolmasters, were the only constant in Jimmy's life; they'd remain a constant for another year — then what? So many people he'd already known and lost; so many houses he'd lived in. He could remember each one: Myrtie's in Sydney, Granny's little dark house, Balwyn, Cheltenham. For a time, change had been the one true constant in his life.

They'd stopped moving since he'd been away at school. Some sort of truce had been signed. Lorna had become a constant at her desk in the sitting room, telephone at her elbow, snarling instructions to solicitor and accountant. No more lunches with the accountant for Margaret and Bernard; they took long holidays instead, little Mrs Muir left at home to feed and water Lorna.

'Georgie thhould be home,' Margot said.

'It's not nine yet.'

'The'th alwayth going out thomewhere.'

'She said you could go with her.'

'Ath if,' Margot said.

'Walk in with me to meet her. We might see Sputnik once we're out of the trees.'

'How can you thee one tiny little thtar in that thky?'

'It's like a rust-riddled tin dish placed over the world tonight, the sun peeking through a million holes,' Jenny said. 'Fancy the Russians beating the Americans up there.'

'Who careth.'

Margot had more important things on her mind than Sputnik. She'd heard something today that she was busting to tell Georgie, who should have been home by now. Georgie was always going out somewhere. She played table tennis at the town hall. She went square dancing there. Getting too big for her boots, that's what she was doing.

Last Sunday, she'd told Margot to stop calling Ray 'Daddy Ray'. 'For God's sake, Margot, you sound like mad Blanche with your Daddy Ray.' They'd seen that Marlon Brando movie together. She hadn't told Raelene not to call him Daddy Ray, had she?

'Are you coming for a walk?' Jenny asked.

'Ath if, I thaid.'

'Suit yourself,' Jenny said and she walked alone up the track.

Georgie had started that 'suit yourself'. Now everyone said it, even Raelene. More like they suited themselves.

Like today. Maudy was getting married to a Molliston bloke, and Maisy had driven her and Elsie down to Willama to buy material for her wedding dress, and talked Granny into going with them to get herself something pretty to wear to the wedding. Margot had wanted to go too. She loved going to Willama. But she couldn't go because someone had to stay home with Donny while Jenny rode in to get Raelene from school.

Granny couldn't even look after him. How was Margot expected to?

'Just watch him,' Jenny had said. 'I'll only be fifteen minutes.'

'What am I thupposed to do if he taketh a fit? Anyway, what'th to thtop Raelene walking home? I had to.'

'You didn't have to until you were ten years old. You either keep your eye on Donny or you help me get him into his chair and push him into town,' Jenny had said.

Margot chose the second option.

They were at Blunt's, Donny's chair parked out front while they picked out a zipper for Georgie's bridesmaid's dress — no one had asked Margot to be a bridesmaid — when a woman came into the shop and screamed, 'If that isn't Jenny Hooper, then I'll go hopping to hell!'

'Lila Jones?' Jenny said. 'What are you doing up here?'

'Lila Roberts, I'll have you know. My new hubby lives up here.' She'd married Billy Roberts, a truckie.

'We worked together in Sydney during the war,' Jenny explained to Miss Blunt. Then she introduced Margot.

'I remember you as a bulge in your mother's belly,' Lila said.

'Margot is eighteen,' Jenny said, and blushed. Miss Blunt might not have seen the blush but Margot did. 'Jimmy was the baby I had with me in Sydney. He's living with his father now,' Jenny said too fast, then chose her zip fast, paid for it and got out of that shop. Lila followed her out.

'He's yours too? What's wrong with him?' Lila said when she saw Donny.

'He's my husband's. He's got a little girl too, I have to pick her up from school.'

'I thought he got killed in the war — your boy's, Jimmy's, father?'

'He was in a prison camp. I married Ray before Jim came home.'

'My parents should have been shot for letting me marry my first.' She'd walked with them to the school, filling in the years since the war. 'Norma died, two years after the war. She got cancer. Barbara is married with two kids. So what happened to you?'

'I was in Melbourne for a while after I remarried.'

'I mean — you know.' And she winked. 'Sydney. After you left the factory.'

'I came home.'

Raelene was waiting at the gate and not happy about walking home.

'I had to walk in and out becauth of you,' Margot said.

'You're big. I'm little,' Raelene said.

Lila pushed Donny's chair for a block or two; Jenny took over the handles at the forest road fork.

'How far out are you?' Lila asked.

'Another mile or so.'

'No wonder you're skinny, pushing his weight around. I'll drive down and see you tomorrow,' Lila said.

'I live with my grandmother, Lila. She's elderly. I've got my hands full with Donny. I'll ride in early tomorrow and we'll catch up.'

Something had gone on in Sydney: Jenny's blush, Lila's '*bulge in the belly*' reference. Margot wasn't dumb. You can learn a lot from *True Romance* magazines, and she was Maisy's granddaughter, a born gossip.

No friends to share her gossip with, apart from Brian and Josie Hall. She gossiped about Georgie to Brian and Josie, about her high heels and lipstick, which she only wore so the boys would look at her. Girls like Georgie got themselves into trouble all the time in the magazine stories; not that the magazines told the interesting bits, the how. They had a girl walking down a dark lane and coming home pregnant.

Margot knew the seed bit; the male bit that went in. Jenny had bought a book about it a few years back. Most of it was about rabbits. Margot preferred people stories.

She'd read an old-fashioned one tonight about the sailing ship days, and a girl called Dianna who was on a boat with her family and the boat hit a reef and sank. Everybody died except Dianna and Roger, her stepfather, who had almost drowned in trying to save his wife and the other children, so Dianna, who was a champion swimmer, had to save him. There was an uninhabited island not far away, and she'd got him to it. No dark lanes on that island; plenty of beaches and coconuts and bananas and fish. Eventually a ship came to save them, but by then Dianna had a baby so they couldn't go home. They ended up turning the island into a banana plantation and they got rich.

She had another favourite, about a girl named Mary who was orphaned when her mother and father and all of her family were burnt to death in a house fire. Mary was in hospital for weeks, disfigured by burns until the son of a rich uncle found her and paid thousands of pounds to a famous doctor in Switzerland to remove every one of her terrible scars. While she was wrapped up in bandages, the rich uncle's son fell in love with her, not knowing she was beautiful beneath the bandages. He'd fallen in love with her beautiful mind, he said. As it turned out, he wasn't her real cousin. The rich uncle had adopted him, and when he died, his son got all of his money.

Margot was writing her own true romance story, which she'd named *Love in the Ashes*. Georgie and Granny were out, and Donny knocked the Coleman lantern over and the two back rooms exploded in flame. There was a blustering wind, and it blew the flames into the old part of the house where Jenny and Raelene were asleep. Ray was out somewhere. When he came home, he found Margot wandering through the ashes. 'We'll go back to Armadale where the bad memories won't reach us,' he said. He'd lost his stutter. The shock had cured it. They had to stay for the funerals. *Three coffins were lined up in the church that day.* That night, they were waiting at the station for the train, Granny and Elsie waving to them, when Georgie came running out of the dark, yelling, 'Wait for me! I'm coming with you.' *The train was already moving. Georgie was left standing there.* And serve her right too.

Georgie was standing in the middle of the road with her bike, looking skyward, when Jenny approached.

'Can you see it?' Jenny asked.

'Nope. Just wondering if there's anyone up there looking down and wondering if there's anyone down here looking up.'

'Who knows?' Jenny said.

'Anything seems possible at night, doesn't it?'

'What do you want to be possible?'

'Everything that isn't,' Georgie said. 'Want a dink?'

Sixteen years separated them. A lot of living separated them. Two of a kind, Jenny and Georgie, not much separated them that night, Georgie riding the pedals, Jenny on the seat, holding on, laughing like a kid.

No More Amberley

November 1957. Dear diary, something is going on between Mummy and Daddy, which they're keeping secret from me. And Mummy keeps spoiling me. I just looked at this diary in the newsagent's and she bought it for me. I didn't really want it, but now I've got it I suppose I have to use it.

She's let two of the downstairs rooms too, and she said years ago that she wasn't ever going to let them. And Daddy's mind is somewhere else. I told him on the way home from school that I'd got ten out of ten for an English test and he sort of looked straight through me as if he didn't even hear me. Maybe Gran Norris is dying or something, and we're going to move in with her.

Sarah North's grandmother is dying of cancer, which I found out today, which is why Sarah has been nasty to everyone, not just to me . . .

Eight lodgers, then eleven. Two girls in Number Five, and there had never been anyone in Number Five, which was right above the parlour and had always been used as a storeroom. Now every time you sat in the parlour you could hear footsteps overhead. One of the downstairs new lodgers drove a car, and there were two cars and Robert's new trailer parked in the backyard and no room to play basketball.

One night at dinner, the phone rang, and Robert stood for fifteen minutes speaking to a man about wages and furnished rooms while his dinner got cold.

'Who was that, Daddy?'

'We've employed a man and his wife to manage the boarding house, poppet.'

'Where are you going to fit them?'

'We'll be moving after Christmas,' Myrtle said.

'I'm not moving to Gran's.'

'No, you're not,' Robert said. 'I've applied for three positions in Victoria.'

'Gran may be coming with us,' Myrtle said.

'Then I'm not,' Cara said.

December 1957. I nicked off to the city with Sarah today and we went to a picture show. It was almost dark when we got home and I got lectured for hours about Sarah being a bad influence, and how it's a good thing that we're leaving if Sarah is going to lead me into such stupidity. It wasn't even Sarah's idea, and I told them so. I am not going to Victoria. I'm not moving from here . . .

It's still December and I don't care what date it is. Instead of putting up the Christmas tree near the parlour window, they're piling boxes up there. Boxes and boxes and boxes of everything, which the wife of the man who is supposed be going to manage the boarding house nearly fell into. She's fat and so is he, and he smells of cigarettes, and I don't want them living in our private rooms . . .

'You lied to that man, Mummy. Daddy didn't get a transfer. He applied for the job.'

'A vice-principal's job, pet. He never would have been the vice-principal if he stayed at his old school. Now please go through your books and decide which ones you want to take with you.'

'Why did you lie to that man?'

'You've always known that we'd move one day. You've heard us discussing it since you were a tiny girl.'

'Yes, but we never did it.'

'Just think, now you can have a real Bowser.'

'I don't want a dog if I can't show it to my friends. I'm not going, Mummy.'

'You'll make new friends.'

'I don't want new friends. I want my old friends.'

She had to go, and to a town she'd never even heard of, Traralgon, which she hated the sound of. They tried to make Gran Norris go with them but she dug her heels in, thank God, told them they knew what they could do with Traralgon, that she'd lived alone for most of her life and she'd die alone, deserted again by her firstborn.

They spent Christmas Day with her and Uncle John and his family, then came home, fixed the trailer to the car and started loading boxes. The day after Boxing Day, they drove away from Amberley, the loaded trailer rattling behind them, Cara howling in the back seat, boxes beside her, boxes at her feet.

She didn't speak until they stopped at the Dog on the Tuckerbox town, where she had to speak because she was starving and they would have bought her something she didn't want to eat if she hadn't spoken. Then they got back into the car and drove to Albury, to the house of some man Robert had known during the war. He had a big garage. They left the loaded trailer in it and went to a hotel for the night. Cara had to sleep in the same room as Myrtle and Robert, and she'd never, ever shared their room, or not since she could remember.

'One of you snored all night,' she said. 'I'm not sleeping in your room again.'

'You didn't complain when we borrowed Uncle John's caravan,' Robert said.

'That was holidays and Sarah was with me, and everybody does silly things when they're on holidays, then they go home. We won't be going home, and I want to go home,' she howled.

She howled for an hour, and didn't even have anywhere to do it in private. She had to lock herself in the hotel bathroom, and people kept wanting to get in. She couldn't even go for a walk because she didn't know where to walk.

They stayed two nights at that hotel, and on their last night had dinner at Robert's friend's house. All of their kids were there, all of them older than Cara, except for one who had been born after the war. It was like there was a war space between the kids in that family, which Cara fitted perfectly into.

Boring mile after boring mile the next day, and a worse hotel because Robert wanted to drive through the city early, before there was any traffic around. They left at daylight, got lost about six times before they got to the other side. And when they got there, Cara wished they'd stayed lost. The house looked like two match-boxes joined by a tin roof.

'If that's your idea of a nice little house then it's not mine.'

She wouldn't get out of the car. They left her sitting while they unloaded boxes and introduced themselves to the neighbours.

The sun forced her inside, and it was as hot inside as out, and the house stank of paint, and there was nothing but boxes in it, and the shop that was supposed to deliver the furniture before noon didn't come until four, and the horrible stuff they brought in looked as if it had been ordered out of a catalogue, which it had. Nothing looked right. Nothing smelled right. Nothing fitted. They carried in a steel-legged kitchen table and four green vinyl chairs with metal legs. They carried in a bookshelf, and couldn't find a wall to put it against. It ended up in the passage, which didn't leave enough room for two people to pass. Nothing belonged and Cara didn't belong.

And the shops? It was like a wild west town, tacked up in a hurry. There was nowhere for the eyes to rest, nothing beautiful for them to rest on.

January of 1958 was the worst, the loneliest, the hottest, most atrocious, most despicable, most unreal month of Cara's life, and she couldn't even curse Traralgon in her diary because she refused to unpack her boxes, and Robert, who was losing patience with her, told her she'd live with those boxes until she unpacked them.

The day she started at the high school, where she was introduced to the kids as the new vice-principal's daughter, had to be ten times worse than the worst day of her life. Kids hate schoolteachers, so they hated her. She heard two girls mimicking the way she spoke, and she couldn't help how she spoke. It was her mother's fault for teaching her to speak like that. Everything was her mother's fault.

'Tell me why we had to leave Sydney, Mummy.'

'We've always planned to leave, pet.'

'Why? You hate this house as much as I do.'

Unable to deny Cara's words, Myrtle's big soft eyes turned to a lettuce she'd paid too much for and couldn't find an edible leaf on. She wanted to cry for Amberley, for her little greengrocer on the corner, for her own kitchen. She missed the lodgers, missed the traffic on the street, missed Sarah North's barking dog.

'We'll make some phone calls when we get settled and see if we can find Bowser,' Robert said.

'I'm too old to bribe with puppies.'

'We know it's difficult for you, poppet, but imagine how good it will be for Mummy once we settle in. For the first time in years, she'll have time for herself.'

'To do what, Daddy? There's nothing to do here.'

'It's not a bad little town. We have to give it a chance,' Myrtle said, slicing onion, giving her eyes an excuse to weep.

'Tell me what happened in Sydney that caused you to suddenly decide to leave. Something must have happened. Did you get the sack for something?'

'I applied for a promotion.'

'Something bad happened up there and we've come down here to hide. What are we hiding from?'

'Go to your room and unpack your boxes,' Robert said.

'My room is in Sydney, and I'm never unpacking, or not until you take me home. This is the rottenest town, and the rottenest house in the entire world and I hate it.'

'You mean the most rotten, perhaps, poppet?'

'Stop calling me poppet! And I mean the shittiest town in the entire universe!'

'Go to your room!' Myrtle said.

'Stop calling it my room. It's not my room.'

'Then go to the room at the end of the passage, brat, and unpack your boxes. We've had enough of your tongue for today.'

She went, and slammed the stupid door almost off its hinges. Stupid cream door, stupid flat walls, stupid ceilings a tall man could almost hit his head on. She didn't unpack her boxes. She lay face down on her new bed and howled.

It was as if an atomic bomb had gone off beneath her family and blown everything that was good away, and they wouldn't even tell her who had dropped the bomb. It was like they were refugees from World War Three, immigrants in their own country. And you could smell the stink of that bomb in the air — or the stink from the place where they made electricity.

For three weeks she drove to school with the vice-principal and barely spoke to him. For three weeks she barely spoke to Myrtle or to her teachers, or to anyone else.

Then Rosie Taylor came running into the school toilets howling while Cara was hiding in there. That was the day she found out Sarah North had been responsible for dropping that atomic bomb on her family.

*

28 February 1958. Dear diary, I haven't written a word for months because you were packed into a box, which you were safer in than out of, because life has been so rotten I probably would have filled all of your pages with swear words.

I've got something huge to tell you. Rosie Taylor is adopted and so are her two brothers and they didn't even know it. Their cousin, who was having a war at school with Rosie's brother, told everyone, and her brother, who is sixteen, tackled his parents about it and they admitted that it was true. None of the kids are even related.

And I bet all of the money I've got in the bank that I'm adopted, and Mrs Rowe knew about it, and that's why we left Amberley to come to this rotten place, because they were scared I'd find out.

If Rosie's brother could tackle his parents, so could she. She waited until Sunday dinner, until the roast was served and her parents were sitting down, then she looked Myrtle in the eye and said it.

'Mrs Rowe knew I'm adopted, didn't she?'

Their eyes and actions told her the truth even if their mouths didn't. They both stopped eating, looked at each other, then quickly down at their meals.

'You are not adopted, Cara,' Myrtle said.

'I don't care if I am. I just want to know.'

Robert went to their bedroom and returned with Cara's birth certificate. He handed it to her. Their names were on it.

'How would I know if the adoption people put your names on it when they gave me to you?'

'It's your original birth certificate.'

Maybe it was, but a piece of paper meant nothing because being adopted explained everything. It explained why Gran Norris liked Uncle John's kids better than she liked Cara; it explained why she was taller than her female cousins, when Myrtle and Robert were shorter even than Aunty Beth and Uncle John. It explained why she was the only one in the entire Norris family with fair hair and blue eyes. Big, cornflower-blue eyes, curly golden blonde hair that glinted with copper highlights when the sun caught it.

Every single thing about her was different. Myrtle's hands were plump, her fingers tapering to points, her fingernails small perfectly shaped almonds. Robert's hands were broad, his fingers short. Cara's fingers were long and shapeless, square-topped; her fingernails were the weakest, most shapeless, atrociously ugly fingernails anyone in the world had ever been cursed with. Every single thing about her was different — hands, legs, the shape of her face. Why had she never noticed that before?

In Sydney, there hadn't been time to notice anything. In Victoria there was nothing but time.

March 1958. I just played tennis, just thrashed a fourth-form girl off the court, and it was so good. Mum bought me a new tennis skirt. I wish Sarah North could see it. We used to play tennis at home and she always wanted one of those skirts. Rosie Taylor doesn't play. She said that only snobs join tennis clubs. I can't stand her sometimes but she's the only friend I've got. I'm going to write and ask Sarah to ask her mother exactly what Mrs Rowe knows about me, except I can't right now because Mrs Collins wrote to Mum and told her that old Mrs North died.

April 1958. There's this boy everyone calls Deano — because he looks a bit like Jimmy Dean, sort of sneers like him, pouts, tries to walk like him. Anyway, he's a friend of Kevin Cooper, who everyone used to call Chicken Coop, until he bought a car. Anyway, Coop is a friend of Rosie's brother and all of them were hanging out at the milk bar yesterday, playing the jukebox, when Rosie and I went in to get a milkshake, and Coop started mucking around with Rosie, like wanting her to rock and roll with him, and then Deano asked me if I could rock. Rosie and

I practise together at her place, so we danced with them. She's liked Coop for ages, and before we went home, she said we'd sit with them at the pictures on Saturday, which is like a sort of first date, I suppose.

GONE WITH THE WINTER

Gertrude was two months away from her eighty-ninth birthday when the posters for *National Velvet* went up out front of the town hall. Jenny and the girls were going.

'Get a bottle of dye while you're in town, darlin',' Gertrude said. 'I'm going with you.'

'You told me movies were ratbag things when I wanted you to go with me to *Gone With The Wind*,' Jenny said.

'Then it's past time I found out if I was right or wrong, isn't it, and this one is about horses not wars.'

They watched that movie on an evening when winds buffeted the town, threatening to blow the power lines down and end the show. The movie didn't end until it ended, and Gertrude didn't want to move when it did. Lenny drove them home, and the night too cold to go to their beds, they sat by the stove, Gertrude talking about the movie and that beautiful horse.

'Man's magic,' she said. 'It's like I know that little girl. What was her name again?'

'Elizabeth Taylor,' Jenny said. 'You would have loved Scarlett in *Gone With The Wind*.'

'I always thought it was a good title,' Gertrude said. 'Everything gets blown away with the wind; everyone I ever knew, the world I knew, got blown away. My mum and dad wouldn't know what they'd struck if they came back to earth today. Human nature and the weather are the only things that don't ever change. We had these same howling winds the week my dad died. I swore it was his land mourning for him.'

Almost one o'clock. They should have been in bed, but so little of their time was spent together, just the two, so they sat on, listening to the wind, speaking of many things.

'The older you get the less sleep you need,' Gertrude said. 'There was a time when I was ready for my bed when the sun went down.' Then out of the blue, she added, 'Don't you go mourning for me when I go, will you?'

'Talk like that and I'm going to bed.'

'No, you're not. You're going to sit there and listen to me. All I want to hear in that church is your beautiful voice singing me off to my rest. You remember that.'

'You still look sixty-five — on a foggy morning. You'll outlive me, Granny.'

'That would have sounded nicer if you'd left out the foggy morning bit, and I want your promise that you'll sing that one you sang at your father's funeral.'

'What do you want with hymns? You've never been to church in your life — apart from funerals.'

'Some of the old hymns are the best part of religion — and you can finish off with *Wish Me Luck As You Wave Me Goodbye*. And no tears. You shed one tear over me and I'll come back and haunt you.'

'I don't believe in ghosts.'

'You'll believe in me. I'll walk my land all night and make terrible noises at the window hatch.'

'I'll blame it on the screeching owls — and I'm going to bed.'

*

In June of '58, Georgie found a Duckworth in the newspaper's death columns. '*Charles Duckworth,*' she read aloud. '*Loved father of Reginald, brother of . . .*'

'It's your great-uncle Charles,' Gertrude said, and with the aid of her magnifying glass she read the names of his siblings, most followed by *deceased.* Only three Duckworths still with the living: Millicent, Wilber and Olive.

'Your sister's name is there,' she told Jenny. '*Loved uncle of Cecelia.*'

'Sissy, who needed two chairs to sit on?' Georgie asked.

'My only blood granddaughter,' Gertrude said. 'It says here that he died at home.'

'Sugar diabetes,' Jenny said.

'It doesn't say that.'

'If Sissy's been housekeeping for him, he's been living on toffee and jam sandwiches.'

'You wicked girl. He was your uncle. You should send a card.'

'He was Norman's uncle, not mine, Granny.'

'She still sends Maisy a Christmas card, you know,' Gertrude said. 'She's never sent me one.'

'That would be like sending one to the town slut,' Jenny said.

'I've told you not to use that expression.'

'She said it first.'

'You were raised as sisters. You share the same memories if nothing else.'

'She's welcome to them. She's nothing to me, and never was — or not since I turned eleven.'

'If you look at it like that, then I'm not your grandmother.'

'I hate to tell you, but you've left it a bit too late to wriggle out of that one.'

'It's a funny old world, isn't it?' Gertrude said. 'How some families breed like rabbits and others die out. The only blood I'll leave behind is Sissy — and Jimmy, in a roundabout way.'

'How will it be in Jimmy if it'th not in me and Georgie?' Margot asked.

'Vern was my half-cousin, darlin'. I was born a Hooper.'

Charles Duckworth had been born in the same year as Gertrude. Maybe his death was to blame, maybe *National Velvet*. In early July, Jenny caught Gertrude attempting to saddle her horse.

'What do you think you're doing?'

'What does it look like I'm doing? The old coot has forgotten what a saddle is.'

'You're not getting on his back, Granny.'

'I look sixty-five on a foggy morning. It's foggy. Now give me a hand and stop treating me like an old woman.'

'He's old and he's fat and lazy. Leave him alone.'

'He needs the exercise and so do I.'

'And I'm exercising my right to stop you from killing yourself.'

'Elsie still does as she's told. I'll call her over to help me.'

'Where do you want to go?'

'To choose some new wallpaper, if you must know.'

'I'll choose your wallpaper.'

'I'm not letting you choose it again. I want something with colour in it not prison bars. Now are you going to help me or do I yell out for Elsie?'

Gertrude hadn't been on that horse's back in two years, but she got up, and without too much effort, and old Nugget was too fat and tired to bother shaking her off. Jenny walked ahead of them to the boundary gate, opened it and left it open. She watched them up to the road, watched until they disappeared around the bend.

They returned two hours later, Gertrude looking pleased with herself and old Nugget looking more alive than usual.

Three days later, Harry picked up her wallpaper: brilliant blue cornflowers for the bedroom; a cream paper, embossed with self stripes and flowers, guaranteed by Robert Fulton to be washable, for the kitchen; and pale green paper with a large bamboo pattern for the lean-to, which turned that room into a jungle, but offered the delusion that the walls might hold up for a year or two more.

Gertrude's cornflower walls were concussive when the eyes opened to them each morning, but the kitchen looked lighter, cleaner, and led Gertrude's eyes towards the ceilings. Hardly ceiling, just strips of lightweight timber and kalsomined newspaper, layer upon layer of newspaper, eighty years of sagging newspaper.

'I should have got Harry and the boys to put up decent ceilings in here while they were lining the new rooms,' Gertrude said. 'I might get them onto it.'

'There's eighty years of dust underneath that paper. We'd have to move everything outside.'

'Not eighty. I helped my dad put it up when Amber was two months old.'

'Sixty then.'

'She can't be sixty.'

'She's over sixty. I'm thirty-four. She was twenty-eight when I was born.'

'How did you get to be thirty-four? It seems like yesterday.'

Ray bought a tin of white paint. Jenny and Georgie painted the kitchen ceiling. It showed up the sags, but it looked clean.

It was the following day, the empty paint tin still outside the door, beside the wood trunk. Jenny didn't know the date. She was sitting on the trunk, stealing a smoke, one eye watching Gertrude, who only last night had totalled up the amount of money Jenny and Ray wasted on cigarettes each year. It was well after four o'clock. She'd been into town to pick up Raelene. It was a Wednesday, a dull day, more rain on the way, Gertrude's maroon cardigan the only patch of colour in a wintry landscape.

She'd never altered her way of dressing, never wore a coat. Always and forever, she'd milked her goats in that corner with no more than a woollen cardigan to keep out the cold. The day Jenny learned where milk came from, Gertrude had been sitting in the corner of the goat paddock on a packing-case stool, the same or an identical bucket between her knees.

A splash of white where there ought not to have been a splash of white that Wednesday. She'd spilt the milk.

Then she fell, slowly, easily, to the side, one arm raised, a wave to those she was leaving, or to those she was greeting.

Running. Pitching the burning cigarette. Screaming for Elsie, and Elsie running from her back door. And nothing they could do when they got there. Nothing bar sit in the cold dirt of that goat paddock, cradling Gertrude between them and screaming, screaming for someone, screaming for anyone.

Only Elsie to cling to when they carried Gertrude from her land. Just clinging and bawling, clinging until Harry came, when Elsie turned to cling to him, to bawl on him. Only Georgie then for Jenny. Margot bawling for attention at Elsie's house, Raelene bawling at Jenny's heels until Ray came home, came home hungry to a dark house. He lit the lamp. He filled the bowl with kerosene. He stoked the firebox.

'She had a g-good i-i-i-nnings, Jenny,' he said. 'Eighty-n-n-nine's a good age.'

Didn't want to hear about good innings, good ages. Walked away from him, blindly, to Granny's empty bed, to bawl into her pillow. Georgie came to lie with her. Ray fed the kids, noisy kids. Raelene wanted Mummy, wanted to go to bed with Mummy. No more room in that bed. At nine, Ray took her to his bed.

He went to work the next morning, and if Daddy could go to work, Raelene could go to school. No one would take her to school. She punished them for that.

A long day, Thursday, long day of the empty kitchen, which wasn't empty. Full up with Donny's whining; and the napkin Ray had pinned on him before he'd left for work was unlined. Smell of Donny's napkin filling that kitchen. Someone had to clean him.

Jenny bawled while she cleaned up his mess. Georgie ran from the odour to the garden to pull weeds and howl in the rain. Hell in that kitchen. Margot yelling at Raelene. Raelene yelling at Margot. Donny singing his dirge. Couldn't run anywhere. Rain pouring down to the yard, dancing in muddy puddles.

You can't pull weeds in a downpour. Georgie came inside. She lit the lamp at four. Donny slid around to watch the flame's flickering dance. It altered the pitch of his dirge. She walked to the wireless and turned the volume higher, to drown the sound.

Margot seated at the table, flipping through *True Romance* magazines. Raelene wanting a jam sandwich, stamping her feet for a sandwich, until Georgie took bread from the tin and cut two slices. She was spreading them when that song came on the wireless, a beautiful song until yesterday.

I wake up in the morning and I wonder why everything still seems the same . . .

Georgie left the bread on the table and ran to pull more weeds.

Don't they know it's the end of the world . . .?

Raelene yelling for her sandwich. Margot yelling at Raelene to shut up her yelling. Jenny's back to them, her two hands gripping Gertrude's mantelpiece, that song digging its fingernails into raw nerves.

She couldn't sing tomorrow. She couldn't go to that church tomorrow. She couldn't see Granny go into a wet hole in the ground tomorrow.

Couldn't.

Her eyes swollen with weeping, her back to the table, she didn't see it happen. Heard the squealing complaint of old wood, the *thunk!* Saw the light in the room alter. Turned to see Raelene dancing back, *True Romance* magazine in her hand, Margot half-risen from the chair, Granny's old table tilting, lamp on its side, rolling.

Saw it all in a split second, a split second stretched long. Saw the lamp crash to the floor, its glass chimney shatter, kerosene spill. Then too fast, longer shadows playing on cream-papered walls as blue flames tasted aged floorboards, found them good, and raced headlong to taste the cane couch.

For the first time in twenty-four hours Jenny stopped bawling to react. Picked up the lamp and pitched it out the door. Tried to stamp out blue flames while Margot and Raelene stood together beside the lean-to curtain, screaming in unison for a change.

Granny's black coat hanging where it had always hung, behind the door. Ripped it from its nail, swiped at the flames with it, flung it over the flames, stamped on it. All done without conscious thought. Just done; and as fast as they'd been born, the blue flames died.

Time then to notice her hand, burnt by the lamp. She walked to the refrigerator, opened its door to placed her palm on ice.

Georgie entered. 'What's going on in here?'

Jenny turned, expecting Granny. It was her voice, her tone, her question.

'Margot did it,' Raelene said.

'You did it, you little liar.'

Old table, as old as Gertrude, one of its legs known to be unreliable. Georgie kicked it back to its rightful position. Jenny picked up the overcoat, looked for scorching. Wool didn't burn easily. Shook it, brushed it, hung it back on its bent nail.

'You're three times her age. Act it, Margot,' Georgie said.

'Well, thee'th a liar. The wath the one that knocked the table leg.'

'Because you pushed me into it,' Raelene yelled.

Georgie swept up the shattered glass. Jenny went around to the back rooms for the Coleman lantern. No wick in that light; its mantle offered a stronger, whiter light. Gertrude wouldn't have it in her kitchen. It didn't drink familiar kerosene, but shellite, a form of petrol, pumped to the mantle under pressure. She shook it, testing the depth of fluid in the bowl. As ever, it needed filling.

Across to the shed then, tears all gone now. The light would be gone soon. She was pouring shellite from the bottle when she heard movement in the rafters.

Big-eyed barn owl looking down at her. It had been years since they'd had a barn owl. Granny had encouraged owls. They'd kept the shed's mouse population under control.

The human mind is a crazy thing. It can choose to believe what it wants to believe, or needs to believe at the time. Jenny knew who was perched up there. She knew who had knocked that table leg, had started that fire. Knew why she'd done it too. Never once in her life had Granny broken a promise.

'I know you,' Jenny told the barn owl. 'And you can haunt me as much as you like, I'll cry if I want to.'

THE FLOOD

Gertrude Maria Foote was buried on a Friday. The world wept for her. By the following Tuesday her paddocks were waterlogged by the world's tears, the forest road was a muddy bog. In town, the sides of the roads became lakes as street gutters overflowed. Her bike useless in the mud, on Tuesday morning, Georgie took the short cut across Flanagan's paddocks, Raelene on her back, pleased to be going to school.

Granny used to say she'd shared a back fence with old Joe Flanagan for sixty years and the only time he'd ever knocked on her door was the night young Joe had been born. Young Joe, no longer young, and as miserable as old Joe, had two young dogs who kept most from his land. Never Georgie. She tossed them scraps of sausage, and as their predecessors, they followed her along the track worn through Joe's paddocks, hoping for more.

Charlie was pleased to see her back. He didn't mention Gertrude, didn't ask after Jenny. He'd been at the funeral.

There were few shoppers about. Georgie swept dusty corners, wiped dust from packets, wiped down the long counter, knew there'd be little gain in mopping floors. The few who came in brought half the street in with them.

Maisy came in, wanting to talk, Georgie escaped to the store-room, to cut bread, open cans — one of baked beans and one of beetroot. By the time she'd made two bean and beetroot sand-wiches, Maisy had given up.

Georgie took her sandwich and her mug of tea out to the veranda, where she sat on the doorstep watching the dance of the rain. Woody Creek was too flat. Its fine red soil would grow any-thing, but it didn't know what to do with a glut of water given fast. There was little road visible in front of the police station.

They'd had four policemen since Denham. The last one had barely unloaded his furniture before his wife loaded it again. The new bloke was young and unmarried: Constable Jack Thompson, a country boy, Maisy said, born and raised in Molliston. There was hope that one of the local girls might catch him and encourage him to stay. Plenty of unmarried girls to choose from in Woody Creek — not enough young men to go around, or not enough Australian men. Boys left high school and went to the city to work in banks; left the technical school to take apprenticeships in Wil-lama. They didn't come back. Not a lot to come back for.

Leanne Dobson had married a Latvian bloke. A Duffy girl had gone against family tradition to marry one of three Italian brothers who grew tomatoes out on Three Pines Road. A few said she was probably on with the lot of them. Lena Fulton, who had lost her husband in the war, had married Jorge, an Albanian, who may not have been as old as he looked, but still looked twice her age.

Georgie knew this town. She knew who to give credit to and who to refuse; knew the Abbots looked like the Dobsons because their grandmothers had been sisters; that Joe Flanagan had a Chinaman great-grandfather on his grandmother's side, which was why all Flanagans were born with chips on their shoulders. Charlie spent a lot of time passing on the town's history; he had a willing student in Georgie.

Most in town called him a mean old coot. Most swore he'd kicked his only daughter out of his house. Maybe he had. He never heard from her. Georgie never saw Charlie's mean side. He paid her an adult male's wage, bought her small lots of shares each Christmas, each birthday, or whenever she suggested she was due for annual holidays. She'd never had a holiday. Nowhere to go anyway.

His eyes were bad. She read the papers to him, the share-market prices, celebrating with him when the price crept up, commiserating when the value dropped. They had much in common, Georgie and her employer.

Her mind was far away when the new cop slammed his front door and ran through the rain to his car. He backed out too fast, the car slewing to the side, and Georgie stood, expecting him to end up in the water-concealed open gutter. He hadn't been here long enough to become familiar with Woody Creek's greasy mud. But he got two wheels onto bitumen, then, siren wailing, he drove towards Blunt's crossing, spraying mud and water.

'Someone's had an accident,' she reported to Charlie, who had wandered out to the call of the siren, a spoon in one hand, the half-full bean can in the other. Like Granny, he didn't approve of waste — though a few customers might suffer for those beans. Old men's muscles weren't all they could be.

'Which way did he go?'

'Towards Blunt's, and in a hell of a hurry.'

As was Lenny Hall, who came down that same road and pulled up out front of Charlie's, two of his tyres remaining safe on bitumen. With rain pelting in from the south, he opened his protected window. 'Mum said to get you and Raelene, Georgie.' He looked pale, tight-mouthed.

It was Jenny. She'd gone down to Willama with Lila Roberts to order Granny a tombstone with an owl on it.

'They've had an accident?'

He nodded, and her heart died. 'At the mill,' he said.

Ray. And her heart slammed into her lungs. Not Jenny.

She ran to the ute, mug still half full of tea in her hand, Charlie left standing, holding his can of baked beans.

No raincoat, no umbrella, rain pelting down, she ran through the mud of the school yard to knock on her old classroom door. 'There's been a mill accident,' she said to the auburn-haired woman who Jenny had known as Miss Rose, who Georgie knew as Mrs McPherson, who Maisy called Amy.

They buttoned Raelene into her rain cape, and Georgie, Raelene on her back, returned to the ute. Away then, Lenny's tyres slewing. He got them to Elsie's house.

Georgie made her way to the tiny kitchen. Donny taking up too much space in it; Margot at the table, using up more space; Elsie at the stove. No room for Georgie there. She left Elsie spreading a jam sandwich for Raelene after trying to talk her into Vegemite. Raelene had a sweet tooth.

Front door open, Georgie stood watching Macdonald's new tractor roar by, a bare twenty feet away. It shook the house. Their truck was behind it, its tray loaded with mill men heading out the road towards Davies's mill. One by one, trucks and utes came from town, then the council grader came, scooping mud, piling it up to the sides of the road. One of the Macdonald twins' black utes itching to pass it. Simpson's truck behind him, also loaded with men.

How bad?

Very bad.

George Macdonald had set up that bush mill. He'd walked away from it during the early days of the Great Depression. Davies had bought it sometime before the war. Set up in the midst of the raw product of city fences, termite-proof stumps for city houses, railway sleepers, bridge supports, the mill was three miles on from Gertrude's land, out along a gravelled road — and there'd be nothing left of that road come nightfall.

'We weren't working,' Lenny said, joining Georgie in the doorway. 'Just batten down the hatches, Davies said. That's all we were doing. The creek's broken its banks out there. The mill will be under water by tomorrow.'

He rolled a cigarette as slim as one of Harry's, lit it and blew smoke at the rain. Not Harry's son, but he was all Harry in other than appearance. Little of his Aboriginal forebears in Lenny. A blue-eyed, blond-headed white-feller's son, Lenny Hall.

'He would have died outright, Georgie. The log stack rolled, just out of the blue. Nothing anyone could do. No time to yell. I can see it every time I close my eyes, like in slow motion, over and over and over. Just one, then that whole bloody pile of logs rolling down on him. I'm getting out of it. That's two that's died out there since I started.'

Georgie nodded, watched the road.

Jenny got home near four o'clock, light almost gone, rain pelting down again.

She'd been to the school to get Raelene. Amy McPherson had told her there'd been another accident out at Davies's mill. Only one reason Raelene would have been taken home early. Jenny knew the reason.

She'd come as she'd left, via Flanagan's, Lila not prepared to hazard her car in the forest road bog. She was dripping wet, her shoes mud-covered. Her eyes were dry.

'How?' was all she said.

'A log stack rolled,' Lenny said. 'We weren't even working, Jen, just battening down the hatches.'

'Come in out of the rain, lovey,' Elsie said.

Jenny looked at her shoes, half of Joe Flanagan's wood paddock stuck to their soles.

'I won't take my shoes off twice, thanks, Else.' She turned to Lenny. 'Could you haul Donny over for me?' she said, and started back across the paddock, one thought only on her mind. Donny. Or maybe two. *I should have slept with him. I could have. He wasn't even forty.*

Donny . . .

Wiped mud from her shoes on tussocks of grass, as she may have any other day. Lenny came behind her, Donny over his shoulder, Georgie behind him, Raelene on her back. First thing first: the stove. Out.

Donny on the floor, near the wireless. Raelene wanting Jenny to take her Red Riding hood cape off, not Georgie. And Margot came in, her *ahzeeing* wail reaching a crescendo.

Hell was Raelene's foot stamping on cold bare boards, Donny's ongoing dirge, Margot's wail — and that bloody chimney dripping rain onto a cold stove, pooling in the back corner of the hob.

I could have slept with him. It wouldn't have killed me . . .

Stop. Get the stove burning. The wood trunk was full.

No more Ray to keep it full.

Donny.

Full stop! Don't think about that now!

A dark day; the kitchen a freezing pit. Donny didn't like the dark. Georgie turning the wireless on; crazy dame singing a crazy song: *Ying tong iddle I po.* Donny didn't care. Georgie cared. She changed the station while Jenny placed a saucepan on the hob to catch the trickle of water, mopped up the pool, then reached for an empty Weet-Bix packet, shredded it and poked the cardboard into the firebox to encourage not quite cold embers into life. Squatted before it then, blowing on the embers.

Smoke. Where there's smoke there's fire, Granny used to say.

It was too soon. It was less than a week since . . .

Not the same. Nothing like the same.

Georgie, preparing to light the lamp, changed her mind and flung the door wide. She had a nose like a bloodhound, could smell Donny's soiled napkins at the instant of their soiling. No doubt biscuit-filled today, bottle-filled during the hours Jenny had been away, then the lot shaken up by his ride across the paddock on Lenny's shoulder. He'd released his load, and far better the winter wind blow in through that open door.

Jenny changed him on the floor, on her knees, still clad in her raincoat, an open newspaper beside her, a toilet roll. She washed him with perfumed soap, powdered him — not for the powder's medicinal qualities but its perfume — then out to the lav with a newspaper parcel, around to the washhouse with the napkin to drop it into a bucket. Half-filled the bucket from a tap, poured in a dash of bleach, a shake of powder. Soaped her hands then, and admitted to those hands, to the soap, that she couldn't do it alone. Wiped the hands on a rag of towel.

'I can't,' she told Ray's bedroom door. 'I'm sorry.'

Then out to a heavier downpour. 'I can't,' she told the rain.

'Get inside,' Granny yelled. It could have been Granny's voice — Georgie's beautiful head leaning out through the lean-to's window hatch.

'Close that, love,' Jenny said.

She walked around to the door. Didn't go inside; went to the old tank to wash her hands again. Always a bar of soap kept in a saucer on the tank stand, always and forever. A new bar had been placed there by Granny less than a week ago. Wet soap today, swimming in its saucer, turning to jelly but eager to lather. She stood there a long time, wasting water, washing her hands of Donny.

It had to be done.

Plenty of water in that tank to waste. Both tanks had been over-flowing to the chooks' yard for days. Little river of water; Chook Creek running fast towards the lower ground of Rooster Lake.

'Get out of the rain, Jen,' Georgie repeated.

'I can't do it, love. Not without Ray, I can't.'

'He's not your responsibility, Jen.'

Nor was Raelene, but she wanted Jenny to take her shoes and Red Riding Hood cape off. Jenny came inside. She took Raelene's shoes off, put her bunny slippers on, hung her rain cape beside Granny's black overcoat, barely scorched by its brush with flame.

Flames licking in the firebox, the shopping put away, Willama sausages placed in a plastic bag in the fridge. The greatest invention since the wheel, plastic bags; every one that came into the house was cherished by Jenny. Used bags were washed, hung on the clothes line to dry. What she wouldn't have given for a few plastic bags in Armadale when he'd come home with his load of roadkill.

No one taking any notice of Margot's *ahzeeing*, she was punctuating it now with accusation. 'You don't even care he'th dead.'

'Shut up with that, Margot.'

No one had told Raelene her daddy was dead. No one knew if he was. Had to get him out from beneath that log stack. It would do no good telling Raelene tonight. Had to get through this night, and deal with her tomorrow.

Georgie piled wood into the firebox, adjusted the flue. Jenny was outside again. She'd bought a large bottle of bleach in Willama. Used a lot of bleach on Donny's napkins.

'I want my cape on,' Raelene said.

'She'll be back in a minute.'

'I want her to come inside now.'

Altogether too much noise.

'Be patient, Raelene, and shut up that *ahzeeing*, Margot. You're driving me mad.'

'He'th dead, and she'th jutht doing the wathing.'

'Who's dead?' Raelene asked.

'You don't care one bit,' Margot howled.

Cared enough to put Raelene's rain cape on, her shoes on, to let her out the door. Better out there than in here.

She cared about the noise. Cared a lot about that. She cared that someone was lying dead under a pile of logs — although would have cared more had it been Lenny under those logs, or Harry. That was the truth. You can't get away from the truth.

Ray's packet of Relaxatabs was on the mantelpiece with Jenny's cigarettes. He'd had trouble sleeping with the light burning for Donny. He'd swallowed two of those tablets every night. She opened the packet. Only two left.

. . . warden threw a party in the county jail . . .

She liked that song. Turned to Donny. Maybe he liked it. His head was against the wireless cabinet, soaking up the beat. Wondered if he thought he was singing. Granny used to say he was.

Wondered if he thought anything.

'It'th too loud.'

'You've got legs. Use them.'

'*Let's rock, everybody, let's rock,*' Georgie sang as she pushed the two tablets from their sealing plastic then reached for a mug, for a knife. She stood beside the stove grinding the white pills to powder with the knife's handle before pouring a dash of water from the kettle into the mug, stirring with the knife blade.

Margot turned the volume down; Donny fell to his back, competing well now with the wireless.

. . . was dancing to the jailhouse rock . . .

Feeding bottle on the dresser; Raelene's bunny mug hung on its cup hook; Margot's private glass was in the corner of the second shelf. Georgie meted out the liquid Relaxatabs to glass, bottle, bunny mug — equal shares for bottle and glass, a smaller share for the bunny mug — a good dash of green cordial into each, then water from Granny's stone bottle.

'*The warden threw a party in the county jail,*' she sang off-key. Maybe she'd inherited her father's voice. She hadn't inherited Jenny's.

Donny wasn't fussy. He'd suck on anything. The dirge silenced.

Jenny came in with Raelene, who snatched up her bunny mug, emptied it while Jenny removed her belted raincoat, shook it, hung it to drip behind the door, removed Raelene's cape, and Raelene wanted biscuits. Georgie gave her two. Margot didn't want a biscuit or her cordial.

'Drink it or I will,' Georgie said.

'He'th out there thquashed under a log.'

'Shut up, Margot, and drink.'

Donny, punishing an empty bottle, banging it on the floor. Georgie reached for Margot's private glass. Margot snatched it.

Her germ fetish hadn't improved with age. She ran through the rain with it. She'd get more sympathy from Elsie.

'How am I going to get him out there to bed? I can't do it, love,' Jenny said.

'No one expects you to, Jen.'

Raelene wanted Jenny to pick her up. Jenny sat and took her on her lap. Georgie walked to the wireless and turned it off, claimed Donny's feeding bottle, tinted green by cordial. Wondered what he weighed. She'd never lifted him. She took his hands and hauled him to his feet. He stood. A fat boy-baby, napkin- and sweater-clad. He could walk if someone held his hands. He liked to walk. She walked him to the table, then, as had Lenny, she got her shoulder down to his middle and heaved, unsure she could lift him until he lifted. Out to the rain then, fast.

'You'll break your back!' Jenny said, rising, sliding Raelene down, but Georgie was running through the rain towards Ray's bedroom. 'It's too early to get him down. He'll be awake at dawn.'

Maybe he would. Maybe he wouldn't.

Margot's germ fetish didn't extend to beds. Georgie found her sprawled across Ray's, *ahzeeing* into his pillow.

'Get off there, Margot, or he'll land on top of you.'

Jenny was behind her. 'We won't be able to get him out of the cot in the morning, Margot. He'll have to sleep there. Get up!'

She didn't move.

Donny was breaking Georgie's back. She dropped him into the cot. It shuddered as it took his weight, the floor beneath it shuddered, but he was in bed. They straightened his limbs, lit his Coleman lantern, tossed the quilt over him.

'How are we going to get him out in the morning?'

'Tip him out,' Georgie said, and they returned to the warmth of the kitchen, to watch Raelene's foot-stamping dance.

'I want my daddy. Why won't my daddy come home?'

Day already given up its light, she knew he should have been home by now with her lollies.

Jenny picked her up, sat with her, rocking, patting her face. Georgie sat watching, waiting for her portion of the pill to do its work. It did. They carried her to bed at five thirty, Jenny assuming she'd worn herself out with her crying.

They made a cup of tea and stood together in the open doorway, warming their hand on the mugs, sipping scalding tea and watching the road; the only noise, the splat-splat of water into the big boiler, the drip-drip into a smaller saucepan, and the steady rain falling on the roof.

'I hope someone milked the goats,' Jenny said.

Harry would be out at Davies's Mill. Elsie and Ronnie could milk. Lenny couldn't. Ronnie worked for a farmer, camped out during weeknights. They'd brought him home when Granny died. They wouldn't bring him home for Ray.

No one had fed the chooks. Most were free to forage. The cockerels were penned, and the rooster. They'd survive a night without dinner.

No movement on the road. No movement of chooks or goats. Old horse standing out in the rain, still waiting for Granny to come home.

'There'll be no light left soon for them to see what they're doing.'

'They'll use their car lights,' Georgie said.

Or stop what they were doing and leave him out there in the rain.

A quarter to six, and nothing. Six o'clock before they heard the distant rumble, then the siren. The council grader led the way into town, the police car's intermittent siren behind it. In the doorway, identically shaped hands linked, gripped, Georgie's the larger of the two, Jenny's grip stronger. Statue still they stood as Macdonald's truck went by, then a black ute, then Simpson's truck, saturated men standing on its tray. Many vehicles, many wet men, Macdonald's tractor bringing up the rear. A slow-moving but noisy funeral cortege. They stood holding hands until the intermittent siren wail became distant, until the tractor's motor faded.

Then nothing. Then pitch darkness. Closed the door on the darkness and lit the lamp, piled more wood into the stove.

At seven, Georgie made a fresh cup of tea. She cut two thick slices of bread and toasted them against the embers, plastered them with butter and honey. Two plates on two hobs, two mugs of tea.

'Pass me my cigarettes, love.'

'They'll kill you. Eat your toast,' Granny's voice said.

How had that happened? When had it happened? She didn't lecture on the burning of money like Granny had lectured. She passed the cigarettes, the matches. 'You eat your toast first.' Didn't want her to crack. No more Relaxatabs. Scared she'd crack.

'It doesn't seem right. I should be crying for him, not eating toast.'

'The world can only end once a week,' Georgie said.

Jenny looked at that girl who should never have been born, who, had things gone right in Melbourne, would never have been born, and she thanked God, or fate, or happenchance, that things had gone so wrong. Loved her. Loved her good sense. Loved her heart, her soul — just loved her. If not for Georgie, she wouldn't have bothered living when the Hoopers took Jimmy.

Her hair looked darker tonight, the ends curled by too-frequent wetting. She looked younger, seemed older. Her eyes lost their green by lamplight, darkened. Too much behind them to read tonight. Weariness, worry, determination.

Laurie's eyes had worn that same expression during those last days in Geelong. *When it's over, it's over, sweetheart.*

'When it's over, it's over, Georgie. When you've got no options left, then there's no option.'

'You've got no options, Jen.'

'I know. It's got to be done, it's just —'

'Say it out loud, Jen. Make the statement now, and stick to it.'

The rain came back to thunder on the low roof and a new

stream of water spilled to the stove. Without needing to move from her chair, Jenny reached for an enamel bowl, placed it. Tinkling of raindrops adding the high notes to the chorus of the drip-drop-splat.

'You look more like Laurie than ever tonight.'

'What was he like?'

'The image of you.'

'I know that. I mean as a bloke.'

Jenny lit a cigarette, attempting to remember what he'd been like to that mixed-up kid who had run away to Melbourne. Only one word came to her tongue. 'Kind.'

'I bet the people he robbed didn't think so.'

'He was kind to me. I didn't know what he did, love. He'd leave me some place for a few days and come back with his pockets full of money and his arms full of parcels, and he'd sit smiling while I opened them.' She drew on the cigarette. 'I was only a kid, unworldly; one minute sitting in the schoolroom, the next having Margot, the next living with a rich man who drove cars. I didn't do much thinking, not at first. Having Margot messed up my head for a lot of years.'

'Did he know you were having me?'

'He called you King George the first.'

'That's why you saddled me with Georgina?'

'I told Granny to register you as Georgie. She turned it into Georgina.'

'Did you love him?'

'I didn't know what love of a man was, not then. He was kind, he was playful at times. I'd look at him sometimes and he'd look so old and worried, then the next day he'd be laughing and he'd look sixteen. I trusted him, love. Trust means a lot to me.'

'Did you ever trust Ray again — after Armadale?'

'Tonight isn't the night to be remembering the bad things. He was as messed up as me, and I could have done more for him.'

'You looked after Donny for him.'

Silence then. A minute, two minutes, they sat looking at the flue, growing red with heat.

'How did you . . . I mean, if you were so unworldly, how did you end up having Margot so young, and with the Macdonald twins of all people?'

'It's old history, and better buried.'

Just the drips then, the splatter-splat, the pling-pling-pling; just the waves of rain on that low tin roof.

'I thought I'd be burying you when Lenny drove up to the shop to get me,' Georgie said. 'Charlie and I were outside. When the cop took off with his wailing siren, we knew there must have been an accident. I thought Lila Roberts had hit a truck.' She shrugged. 'When Lenny said mill accident, the wave of relief almost knocked me over.'

'If I lost you, I'd curl up in a corner and die,' Jenny said.

'I look awful when I blush, but ditto.'

Jenny lit another cigarette. 'I went to a ball in a moth-eaten ballgown I'd dyed the prettiest shade of blue, and I thought I was Cinderella. I sang with the band, and dreamed of being famous and never wearing anything other than beautiful gowns for the rest of my life. Then I went out to the lav. Amber followed me, and ripped my skirt away from the bodice. I told her a few home truths, told Norman a few. He locked me in my bedroom so I climbed out the window. I was going to come down to Granny, but I was too scared to walk through the bush in the dark so I sat on the oval fence, listening to the music. The twins crept up on me. I should have screamed, but I wasn't scared of them; told them they stank like polecats and to go home and soak their heads in a phenol bath. They raped me on old Cecelia Duckworth's tombstone, one after the other.'

Georgie watched her, waiting for more. Jenny said no more.

'Does Margot know?'

'Not unless Maisy told her, and she wouldn't.'

'Were they jailed?'

'They were for a while, but later. I didn't tell anyone — not at the time. I came down here and wiped it out of my head, went to school, sat for a scholarship to a boarding school in Bendigo.

'I thought Margot was wind when she started moving, then Dora Palmer told me her sister, Irene, was having a baby and how she'd got that way. That's when I told Granny. She told Norman. I thought he'd come down and make it all right. He didn't come near me.' Cigarette burning away, Jenny crushed the butt. 'He and Amber got together with Maisy and George and decided to marry me off to one of the twins, for my good name's sake. Once Margot was out of me and I was still alive, I said I would. Anything I asked for, Norman gave me. He wanted to make the problem go away.

'So it did. I stowed away in the good's van to Melbourne.'

'And had me?'

'Laurie ran me down in his car — in someone's car. I sprained my ankle. He drove me around to my penfriend's house, but she'd moved, so he took me to his house — which wasn't his house, though I didn't know it. I told him I was nineteen and he gave me a job house-cleaning. For three weeks that's all I did. If I hadn't told him I was nineteen, he wouldn't have touched me. If they hadn't tried to marry me off, I would have stayed here and signed Margot away. I regret a lot in my life, but never Laurie and never having you. If things had worked out differently, I might have had time to grow up enough to love him.'

'Did you ever love Ray?'

'Don't make me answer that.'

'Are you going to sing at his funeral?'

'He wouldn't expect me to.'

'You're better than half of the singers you hear on the wireless.'

'I was on the wireless a few months before the ball. I won five pounds, back when five pounds was a fortune. I've still got it too.'

'In the bank?'

'Behind the photograph of me and Jimmy and Jim. When

we were living on pancakes in Melbourne I almost spent it.' She removed Ray's friendship ring, then her wedding ring and offered the latter. 'It's not Ray's. I spent his on food. Does that answer your question?'

Georgie took the ring. The engraving was still unworn. *Jen and Jim, 1942.*

'Jim Hooper's?'

'Ray never knew,' Jenny said. 'Tonight I'm thanking God he never knew it — and this isn't doing my head one scrap of good. Get the cards out, love.'

Elsie and Harry came over at eight. They found them sitting at the table playing Canasta, never a good game for two. Georgie dealt them in. That night had to be filled, and is there a better night-filler than a game of cards?

'I'll have a look at that chimney in the morning,' Harry said. 'If it stops raining.'

'We'll have more than drips inside in a day or two,' Jenny said. 'The ground can't take up any more water.'

'We won't go under,' Harry said.

'Granny made sure of that,' Jenny said. 'She used to tell us that the water never made its attack front on, that her front paddocks were higher. It always circled around her land, then, when she took her eye off it, it attacked from the rear like one of Flanagan's dogs.'

Too much competition from the thundering rain for conversation; the four players looking up at the buckled ceiling, expecting it to give way.

'Reminds me of the first night I played cards down here, Else,' Harry said.

'You reckoned Mum's dripping chimney was better than some of the music on the wireless,' Elsie said.

Georgie heard no music in those drips. To her, they sounded like Ray's stutter. 'T-t-time to l-l-leave,' it said. 'T-t-t-time to g-g-go.'

'I'll have to get Donny down to Melbourne,' Jenny said. 'I can't manage him without Ray.'

'You'll keep Raelene?'

'I'm the only mother she's known.'

'How did she take it?'

'Tomorrow will be soon enough for her to know.'

Harry spoke of insurance. Jenny lifted a hand, Norman's sign for 'enough'. She didn't want any more blood money on her conscience.

'When are you thinking of taking Donny down?' Harry asked.

'After the funeral. Ray would want him there. I'll ring Doctor Frazer and see if the ambulance is likely to be going down to Melbourne.'

Georgie swept in the cards, shuffled, then dealt another hand. They played Canasta until that day was gone and a new day begun, until the rain eased off enough for Elsie and Harry to make a break for home.

A DIFFERENT CHURCH

*L*ess than a week since Gertrude's funeral, though nothing was the same. Ray's service would be held at the Catholic church. He'd be buried in the Catholic section of the cemetery.

A display of black clothing had been unnecessary at Gertrude's funeral. Grief had been etched into their faces, worn in their eyes that day. Black was necessary for Ray's funeral, and a hat. Jenny removed the red feather from Gertrude's merry widow hat. She pressed her old black suit coat, made in Armadale, pressed her black sweater. Like Gertrude, she and Georgie were comfortable in slacks. They owned black slacks. Georgie owned no hat. She found a grey paisley scarf. Heads had to be covered in the Catholic church.

Margot was the problem. She wanted to wear black for Ray but owned nothing black. You can't see germs on black.

'No one will see what we're wearing under our raincoats,' Jenny reasoned.

Margot had never been reasonable. 'My coat'th cream, and I'm not wearing it.'

'Suit yourself,' Georgie said.

Margot suited herself. She wore Gertrude's old black coat, the wide-brimmed felt hat Gertrude had worn to town for twenty years, lace-up shoes with Ray's black socks. She looked ridiculous but she walked off across the paddock.

They clad Raelene in her rain cape; Donny in Georgie's old blue raincoat, a foot too long, but he'd be strapped into his wheelchair.

Davies had paid for the undertaker's black wagon to pick them up, drive them home. Lenny hauled Donny across the paddock to the car. Davies should have sent a tractor down to get them — the road was in a bad way.

They got there.

What was there to say about Ray King, the boy who had walked away from this town before his twelfth birthday and returned as a man? No one knew him. His wife didn't know him.

Donny sang his dirge, Georgie bribed him silent with chocolate drops, bribed Raelene to sit still with chocolate drops, wiped chocolate drool, chocolate hands, while the organist played and the priest spoke about a reliable worker, a good husband and father.

Davies's mill men carried him outside to the rain. Not many had honoured Ray in life; enough mill men honoured him in death, gave him his last 'hooray', the Macdonald twins amongst them.

No doubt there was water in the six-foot hole they dropped Ray into, but it was done, and the mourners hurried away beneath umbrellas — away to the hotel where Davies was turning on free beer for half an hour, with biscuits and tea for the ladies.

Widows were expected to put in an appearance. Two or three folk offered Jenny a lift to the hotel. She didn't feel like a widow.

'Thanks, but I'll get the kids home,' she replied to each offer.

The Macdonald twins left the cemetery, elbow to elbow behind Jenny's group. Small feet, short legs, narrow backsides, bulky chests, massive shoulders, triangular heads set on those shoulders, wide jaws, pointed bald domes, their father's eyebrows sheltering pale eyes from the rain.

They dodged Jenny's eye, but eyed her daughters: the redhead pushing the wheelchair; Margot walking beside her, her black coat dragging in the mud, the too-large black hat weighing her down — like a kid playing dress-ups.

Donny's wheelchair bogged on the far side of the gate. Macka walked left around it to his ute. Bernie was parked to the right. He had to walk by them, or paddle through a lake of brown water. Or give them a hand.

He didn't ask. The widow wouldn't have heard him had he asked. She hadn't looked at him since the day she'd ground a double-header ice-cream into his ear. He lifted both chair and boy up to the bitumen.

Georgie thanked him. He nodded and walked on to his ute, parked tail to nose with the undertaker's black wagon. He opened his door and glanced at Jenny, now waiting beside the mud-covered wagon. No sign of the undertaker's offsider no doubt hoping the family had gone around to the wake.

Bernie closed his door. 'Can I get him home for you?' he said.

Georgie dealt with Bernie and his twin at Charlie's. She sold them cigarettes. Couldn't tell them apart unless she was close enough to see Macka's gap, or his false teeth when he bothered to put them in. She eyed Bernie, then his ute tyres, more capable of handling the bog of the forest road than that wagon. Bernie had already proved he could handle Donny.

'Thanks,' she said.

There was no argument to be made against common sense. Jenny didn't argue. She walked down Cemetery Road towards the town. Raelene didn't want her to walk. She bawled.

'Go with her or get in, Raelene,' Georgie said. 'Get in, Margot.'

Neither one got in. Donny did. Bernie hauled him from his chair as if he was nothing, then tossed the chair up to the loading area. Georgie got in, with Raelene.

'We're thupposed to go in the undertaker'th car,' Margot whined.

'Get in the back.' Georgie said, knowing Margot wouldn't want to walk two miles, Granny's hat dripping, muddy coat-tails hobbling her. She scrambled up with the wheelchair and Bernie drove them home.

Getting Donny out was easier than getting him in, until his feet hit the mud. Gertrude's yard looked like melted chocolate. He sat down to eat it. Margot jumped down and ran inside, her coat-tails dragging.

The beer only free for half an hour, Bernie wasted no time in hauling that lump of a boy out of the mud. He tossed him over his shoulder and followed Margot's coat-tails.

It was the first time he'd been inside that house in twenty years. It looked worse than he remembered, which had been bad enough. He dumped his load on the floor and was leaving when the red-head came in with the wheelchair, the dago kid riding it. Stepped back, out of her way. Watched her poke wood into the stove, set three flatirons over the central hotplate. Time had stood still in this place.

Glanced at the dago kid, who wanted a biscuit and didn't get one. And she had to be half dago, even if Maisy swore black and blue that Ray King had turned up with her in one of his saddle-bags. There was no question as to who that lump of a boy belonged to.

Then a younger, plumper version of Jessica, his sister, came from behind a curtain, her coat and hat off. He'd seen a good bit of that kid when she was eight or nine, had seen her around since, though not close up. She was his kid — or Macka's — not that she was a kid. He knew how old she was, knew how old he'd been when he'd made her — or Macka had made her. She had to be nineteen.

'You're the dead spit of Jessie,' he said.

Margot gave him a look that might freeze the devil, then disappeared back behind the curtain.

He had to get out of here. Time was getting away. He didn't leave. He watched the redhead pull muddy shoes from the boy's fat feet, peel off muddy socks, fight the muddy coat off.

'He takes a bit of handling,' he said.

His kid replied from behind the curtain. 'Daddy Ray could handle him. If you'd given him a job when he athked, he wouldn't be dead now.'

Bernie swallowed and stepped back to the doorway. Drizzling rain had grown heavy. He remained under cover. Watched the redhead fill a baby's bottle with green cordial, watched her lie that lump of a boy down, place the bottle into his hands, watched him find his mouth with the teat. That kid had to be eight or ten years old.

'Thanks for your help,' Georgie said.

Rain or not, Bernie had been dismissed.

He walked back to his ute. Its windscreen fogged by its wet load, he opened the corner windows, started the motor, but sat there staring at wet chooks huddling together beneath the walnut tree. How the hell did anyone survive down here?

They wouldn't in a day or two. The creek was as high as it had been in '52, and, according to the midday news, more water was coming down tonight.

He slipped the gearstick into reverse, turned the ute around and ploughed back up the track; wished he'd taken the redhead's advice and dropped them off out front of Hall's when his tyres lost their purchase on the rise up to the road. He backed up, slapped the stick into first, took a run at it and kept on going.

Passed the widow where the road forked, probably sprayed her with mud. She hated his guts. Nothing he could do about that.

Two fast free beers didn't quench his thirst, nor erase the sound of that girl's 'Daddy Ray'. He hadn't known she'd called the big, stuttering bastard 'daddy'. He tossed down another beer.

I was prepared to do the right thing by her mother. I was at the bloody church choking in my collar and tie. It's not my fault.

That tie was choking him today and he wasn't wearing one.

The free beer turned off. A few were leaving.

'I'm off,' Macka said.

'You've been off for years, you bastard,' Bernie replied. He wasn't leaving. He ordered another beer and paid for it, his thirst unquenchable tonight.

Daddy bloody stuttering Ray bloody King, he thought. That girl was a Macdonald through and through. Something should have been done about her.

Sometime after six he drove home to a house full of light and a wireless blaring. George was as deaf as a post. The motor turned off, Bernie sat on, lit a smoke and stared at the house. A roaring fire would be burning in the lounge room, a meal bubbling in a modern kitchen. Warm in there, no leaks in that roof.

Bloody flatirons, he thought. He hadn't known that folk still used those things for their intended purpose. Maisy used one as a doorstop.

'Daddy bloody stuttering Ray,' he muttered while a blood-sucking bat clawed at his throat. He clawed at his throat and stared at a barrowload of wood waiting dry beneath the front veranda, handy to open fire. No open fire down there. No carpet on the floor. No bloody lino on the floor. A saturated wood heap. Mud from arsehole to breakfast time . . .

Had he not had six or eight beers under his belt, he may not have done what he'd done; loaded that barrow of cut wood into his cabin and driven for a second time out along the forest road. So she'd spit in his eye; so what? Mill widows and their kids were looked after in Woody Creek. He was looking after Daddy Ray's kids, that's all, and maybe whatever was choking him would let go after Daddy Ray's widow spat in his eye.

He wasn't drunk enough to attempt a second drive down Gertrude's track. He parked out front of Hall's house.

Saw Lila Roberts' car parked there, and what the hell was she doing down there, and how the bloody hell had she got down there on bald tyres? Not game to go home, maybe. The widow the only woman in town who might give her a bed? Lila Roberts liked beer better than tea; liked men better than women. Men liked her. Women didn't. She knew the widow, had stood with her at the grave side. She'd known her in Sydney, so she'd said. Most of the blokes reckoned anyone could have Lila. Maybe they could. He hadn't had her. Macka would have liked to have her.

He loaded his arms with wood and walked down Hall's drive, fought two gates open, dropped a lump of wood, and, as he stooped to retrieve the first, dropped two more. 'Daddy bloody stuttering Ray.' Guilt and jealousy in a man unaccustomed to feeling either emotion are hard to handle. Bernie wasn't handling it drunk any better than he had sober.

With no hand to knock, he used his boot on the door. Lila opened it. The widow now ironing with those flatirons, the dago kid staring at him, the lump of a boy eating the wireless, redhead packing a red case. No sign of Margot.

'I brought you down a bit of dry wood,' he said. It was pretty obvious what he'd brought down. 'Where do you want it?'

'I could think of a few places,' Lila said. 'They could be splintery.'

'Drop it on the hearth,' Georgie said. 'Thanks.'

He dropped his load and stood dusting his hands 'The creek's broken her banks this side of the bridge. There's a torrent running through the culvert.'

'It went down the last time,' Georgie said.

Jenny placed one iron on the stove and chose another, spat on it to test its heat, or maybe the spit was meant for his eye. He stepped back, expecting her to grind the iron into his ear. She took it to the table and continued her ironing.

'They've got bad flooding upstream,' he said.

'It was on the news. Thanks for the wood,' Georgie said, again dismissing him.

'I've got another armful in the ute.'

The second armful dropped beside the first, he stood on, waiting for his kid — or Macka's — to materialise. She didn't, and they wanted to shut the door.

'If there's anything you need down here, just give someone a yell.'

As he backed from the room, Georgie, looking at his shoulders, looking at Donny, thought, another night of Donny, more stinking napkins. She'd stuffed him with chocolate drops at the funeral.

She glanced at Jenny, knowing she wouldn't give anyone a yell, not if she was drowning beneath napkins, sinking in a quicksand of stinking napkins. Knowing she'd pay the garage man ten pounds to drive Donny down to the hospital in the morning. Georgie had great respect for money. And what difference would one night make — other than two less dirty napkins and ten pounds?

Bernie Macdonald was closing the door.

'Just a tick, Bernie. I don't suppose you could give us a lift down to the hospital with Donny?'

'No worries,' he said, stepping fast back indoors.

And the blood-sucking bat let go its hold on his throat.

THE LEAVING

Margot's world was black or white. The various shades of grey confused her; she chose not to see them. She loved and she hated, and in the blink of an eye one could become the other. She'd loved Ray. He'd loved Donny, so she'd loved Donny, from a distance.

Georgie belonged to her. They'd shared a cot before they'd shared a bed. They'd spent their days together until Jenny came home from Sydney and brought Jimmy with her. After that, Georgie had played with Jimmy. Once he was gone, Margot had got Georgie back, or she had until she'd started working for Charlie and grown too big for her boots.

A mess of twelve-year-old's emotions and nineteen-year-old's desires Margot Macdonald Morrison, bewildered by a world she'd never quite found her place in; a world where nothing was ever the way she wanted it to be, where no one stayed the same.

Like Brian Hall. He'd always been her best friend, always taken her side, played cards on her team. He swapped sides the night of Ray's funeral.

Along with the Halls, she'd seen Bernie Macdonald carrying wood across the paddock. Had seen him haul Donny over to

473

his ute, watched Georgie toss the red case into the loading area, then Donny's wheelchair. Jenny, Georgie, Donny and Raelene had squeezed into the ute's cabin. Margot hadn't asked why; hadn't asked where they were going. Everyone knew the floods were going to be bad, that Granny's house could be flooded if the creek kept rising. Maybe Jenny was moving into town to stay with Maisy or Lila.

Nine o'clock when the ute came back, no Jenny, Donny or Raelene in it. Georgie told Margot that Doctor Frazer was sending Donny down to a home for retarded kids in Melbourne; that Jenny and Raelene were staying the night at a Willama hotel and going down with him in the morning.

'The'th putting him away?' Margot accused.

'Where were you when his pants needed changing?' Georgie asked.

'I'm not hith mother.'

'Neither is Jenny, and stop sounding like a silly bitch, Marsie,' Brian said.

'Don't you dare call me that!'

'Well, you are if you think Jenny can handle him without Ray.'

Margot ran to Elsie's bedroom to howl. The bedroom was cold and no one cared that she was howling in there, so she came out to the kitchen to do it. And found them playing Canasta: Georgie, Lenny and Brian against Josie, Elsie and Harry.

'No one athked me if I wanted to play,' Margot accused.

Elsie rose from her chair. 'Take my place, lovey.'

Georgie went home when the game ended; Margot tailed her across the paddock, stepping where she stepped. She followed her to the lean-to bed. Georgie got out and got into Jenny's. The night was cold; Margot didn't want to sleep in a freezing bed by herself. She followed her, and Georgie moved back to the lean-to bed. They played musical beds until midnight, until Georgie took blankets and pillow to the cane couch. A hard bed, but barely room for one on it.

*

Dark clouds kept daylight at bay on the morning after Ray's funeral. The rooster forgot to wake his hens, and when he stepped down from his perch to crow, he got his feet wet. Blaming Georgie for Rooster Lake, he flew at her when she opened his pen door.

'If you weren't so old, I'd fry you, you mad mongrel,' she said backing off.

He had her on the run and danced at her again, high-stepping, his wings spread, and he lost his footing and took a dive. It shocked the fight out of him. He emerged from brown water squawking like a hen. And well he may. She'd already opened the cockerels' pen, releasing fifteen youthful rivals.

A sly, creeping flood, sneaking in via Flanagan's. His wood paddock was a lake. Unable to take the short cut to work, Georgie went via the forest road, and was confronted by a stream fifty or so feet back from where the road joined up with Three Pines Road. The culvert must have been blocked, or unable to cope with the glut of water. She took her shoes off, rolled up the legs of her slacks and paddled through freezing water.

All her life, Georgie had heard tales of flood, only tales, told at night around the stove. She was experiencing the reality now, and finding it interesting how the water showed up the levels of Woody Creek. Three Pines Road was high and dry, or high and dry to the bridge, as was the stock-route road. They'd built it up before they'd sealed it. By the look of the water backed up against it, not much of Joe Flanagan's land would be above the water line by nightfall. A few of his fences already stood in brown lakes. Someone with a good eye for levels had chosen high ground for the town centre.

'I had to paddle out,' she explained, perched on Charlie's counter, brushing her feet before pulling on socks and boots, before rolling down the legs of her slacks.

'She's broken her banks down behind Dobson's,' he said.

'Has the town ever gone under, Charlie?'

'Not in my lifetime.'

Rain, rain and more rain that day, and the news all bad.

'Three Pines Road is cut a mile this side of Bryant's old place. I drove in through a foot of water.'

Paul Jenner now owned Bryant's land. He'd built a new brick house on it three months ago. Maybe he'd built it high enough.

'Monk's old place is surrounded.'

Hooper's new manager, from Cobram, lived in the old mansion. They'd put the share-cropper chap and his five kids out. No one in town knew the new manager, or cared if he got his feet wet. His wife was a stuck-up bitch.

Crops were drowning. Nothing to be done about that. Those with stock had time to do something. All day, cattle and sheep were on the move through town, all heading out along Cemetery Road to land well distanced from the creek. A busy morning that one.

Not so for the timber men. Like the forest that fed them, the mill workers enjoyed a decent flood. A batch of flood babies would be born in nine months' time.

Bernie and Macka had no good reason to remain in their beds, no woman to share them. They paid for the little they got in Melbourne, when they could get down there. No good reason to get out of their twin beds either. The pub didn't open its doors until ten thirty. Nowhere else to go.

Plenty of empty rooms in Maisy's house; two grown men had no good reason to share. Maisy had tried hard to separate them at fourteen. They'd half-killed each other in attempting to settle the matter of which one should move out. Neither one had.

They'd half-killed each other at eighteen over which one should be the groom and which the best man. A pack of cards had given Bernie the right to be left standing at the altar. Jenny dealt those cards, and hadn't spoken to either twin since — until last night.

Bernie had hauled that kid into the hospital, then stood around waiting for the doctor to turn up, hoping he didn't turn up, so he could offer to drive her to Melbourne and go to the football while he was down there. The doctor turned up.

'Anything you need, just give me a yell,' he'd said as he was leaving.

And she'd spoken to him. 'Thanks for your help,' she'd said.

They had a history. Righto, so it wasn't a good history. He wasn't much in the looks department. There was no denying that — not when you had a mirror image looking back at you from the second bed — but after stuttering bloody Ray King, he mightn't look such a bad prospect.

That ugly bastard in the next bed could still read his mind.

'Davies and the old girl were talking about starting up a fund for her while you were pissing around after her last night,' Macka said.

'You ought to see the house they're living in,' Bernie said. 'It's like taking a step back in time.'

'It'll be floating downstream in a day or two.'

The house was there when Georgie paddled home that night. By Saturday, there was water beneath the new rooms. On Sunday morning, she rolled her feet out of bed and into water. Only at the back end of the lean-to. The kitchen was still dry — or it was until four, when Harry and Teddy came over to move the furniture out to the back rooms, to carry the refrigerator across the paddock. The sewing machine went with it. Metal rusted.

Georgie had gathered the family treasures, which were few. Only Jenny's shoe box of letters and the old purse and brooch, only the framed mug shot of the water-pistol bandit, which she should have pitched out years ago. Hadn't then, couldn't now. She placed it into the shoe box, the shoe box into Itchy-foot's carton of notebooks, which had come six months after his death, and which Granny hadn't allowed her to read. She was old enough now — not that she'd get a chance to read anything at Elsie's. Uncontrolled bedlam over there, and Maudy was getting married in three weeks' time.

The water kept coming, working its way across the goat paddock. John McPherson came in his rubber boots, with his camera, to photograph Granny's house standing in a lake. The goats were moved into the top paddock with the horse. White chooks covered Gertrude's old cart; a few, seeking higher ground, had found perches in the walnut tree.

A hundred yards of water to paddle through on Monday morning, fast-flowing water. She wouldn't be paddling back. Bought a sleeping bag and inflatable mattress from Fultons.

'You've got a lodger for the duration, Charlie,' she said.

He shouted her dinner at the pub, then walked her home to his empty house. Not so empty with Georgie in it.

GOING TO THE MOVIES

*L*orna Hooper well remembered Woody Creek's last major flood, or recalled the delight of spending the school holidays at school rather than on a waterlogged farm. Always an avid reader, Lorna, she read *The Age* from cover to cover. Ray King's death had gained a small mention on page five, only in connection with the flood. *Tragedy dogs family of mill worker.*

Lorna cut the item from the paper; not to keep, but to destroy before her nephew saw it. The boy should have been moved from that den of iniquity before his memories had set in stone.

On a Saturday morning in August, Lorna was in Bourke Street, Melbourne, walking towards Swanston, her nephew at her side, when she sighted the Morrison tramp holding the hand of a black-headed child. Lorna threw her spindly ankles into reverse and made a sharp right-hand turn. With a tongue that rarely missed an opportunity to spit insults, this was out of character, as was her entering the premises of G.J. Coles, where she was forced to take refuge — driven to slumming by that tramp. She might not have recognised the boy alone; however, if she sighted him at Lorna's side, she would surely recognise him.

'What are we buying, Aunt?'

A laughing, tormenting fool of a youth, altogether too much of the mother in him. The Hooper features had become lost — other than his mouth, height, hands. His adult voice was not his father's nor his grandfather's. He'd been influenced by his schoolmasters and that imported pile of pommy sh– poop he called Pops, which Lorna converted to P.O.P.S.

Confronted by a counter of sweets, she propped. She was partial to aniseed rings; handed her nephew two shillings and tapped on the glass display case with a fingernail of iron to explain what he should spend her money on. Returned to the doorway, leaving him to deal with the painted-faced whore behind the counter.

She didn't exit the store, but peered out, as cagey as a black rat peering from its hole in a cat house — and sighted her again, standing before Coles's window, no doubt admiring the wares. A back step into cover, until he came with the bag of sweets. The Morrison tramp and child disappeared, Lorna exited the store and turned towards Elizabeth Street.

'You're twisted, Aunt. You're going the wrong way.'

She ignored him. He followed until she stopped in a jeweller's recessed doorway to snort at a display of rings, or their reminder that she had once considered donning a wedding ring.

'Want to buy me a nose ring?' he asked.

Her lifted finger may have meant 'sit' or 'heel'. He did neither, but looked at his watch.

'We'll miss the start.'

'Step lively then,' she said.

They had three hours to fill while that pile of pommy sh— poop kept a doctor's appointment, or so it had been said. Always a good walker, Lorna stepped lively to Elizabeth Street, followed it to Lonsdale, turned right, and by the longer route gained her objective. And was late. The movie had commenced.

A fool of a movie, it did not engage her mind. She sat ramrod straight, convinced the Morrison tramp was seated directly behind her, until the screen's action offered sufficient light to scan that row of seats.

For two hours she sat, her mind not in the theatre but with P.O.P.S. and his bug-eyed cretin wife. They were hatching more infamy. She knew it, but as yet could not pinpoint it. She had won a major war; had gained control of the estate, more or less. She made the decisions, accounted for every penny spent, had proved she was more than a match for the three morons she cohabited with.

Jimmy was more than a match for his aunt. He allowed her her moves, when he was in the mood to play. His mother had asked him to keep her occupied today, which was no punishment in the city. He loved Melbourne, loved the old theatres. They brought back memories of Jenny.

He could remember her hair. There was much about her he remembered, though not her face. He could remember her presence in the smell of sausages frying. His mother never bought sausages. At times, when he was in the mood, he bought his own. Mrs Muir fried them for him. He ate them as Jenny had in Armadale, rolled up in bread with tomato sauce or chutney. Shop-bought sauce didn't hold the flavour of Jenny. Some brands of shop-bought chutney did.

He loved his mother. She never did anything not to love. Still treated him like a six year old, but he could forgive that.

He couldn't categorise Lorna's treatment. To her, he was neither child nor adult — perhaps a prize dog she believed she was training for the Royal Show. He tolerated his grooming, tolerated her. His mother had told him they had to tolerate her, because of his grandfather's will. Mrs Muir had learnt to tolerate Lorna's 'Muir!'

He'd sat through a lot of movies at Lorna's side — romance, war, comedy. She'd watch anything, as would he. It was the theatres he loved, the smell of massed humanity in the dark, the not knowing who might be seated behind in the dark.

He'd seen an old Fred Astaire and Ginger Rogers movie on television a month or two back and had known he'd watched that movie with Jenny, that they hadn't taken the tram home that day. He'd got a wipe-out wave of memory of riding on the back of a wooden dray, a giant horse lifting its tail and splattering manure.

In Armadale, Jenny had swept up horse manure to put in her compost bin. She used to say that a horse had left her a present for her garden.

He knew she'd had frizzy hair. It had tickled his face when she'd kissed him goodnight. There were no photographs of her, nor of anyone from the other side of his family. His mother had heaps of Hooper photographs, even one of his Hooper great-grandparents. After watching Fred and Ginger, he'd sat for half the night turning the pages of old albums, sifting through boxes of photographs. Without photographs, it's the faces you lose.

He remembered her singing on stage in a Snow White costume; remembered the doctor who they'd met that time at the hospital had been in that play. At school, they tried to get him to sing. He could, but felt a fool doing it. Wondered at times if that old doctor had been some sort of relative. He'd sung a duet with Snow White.

Colours could jog the memory. A certain green, and he was back in that dark old kitchen, and Granny was there, with her weird hairpins holding her long plait high. A certain shade of red hair, even a brand new penny and Georgie was pushing him around the Armadale backyard on his trike.

Trees were memory shakers; rainbows too. They took him to a house with a magic window, just for a brief, non-graspable instant.

Dreams he could grasp. He dreamed often of walking down a Melbourne street and seeing Jenny walking too fast ahead, or turning into a dark theatre. In his dream he'd run after her on leaden legs, run down the aisles, knowing she was in there, smelling the scent of Jenny's hair, like lemons. In the dreams, he never found her, but when he first awakened, he could, for the briefest of split seconds, remember her face.

She was dead. They were all dead, had died of some terrible flu epidemic he'd almost died of. And what was the use of straining to remember the dead?

He loved his mother; felt older than her, had for years. He never felt older than Lorna. She was a family antique, like his great-grandmother's chair in the sitting room, which he wasn't allowed to sit on. It was totally useless but too old to throw out.

THE LICENCE

What goes up must come down. When water stops rising it starts to recede. It took weeks for the land to dry. Scummy green water still lay in low corners when Maudy married her Molliston man and left town to live happily ever after. With Maudy's bed now empty, Georgie was obligated to return home.

Gertrude's floors were mud-covered. Her wallpaper had disintegrated to the high-water line, buckled and gone mouldy to shoulder height. There was a stench of rotting grass and dead fish about her house, but it was shovelled out, hosed out, scrubbed out, and when it dried, the furniture was moved back where it belonged.

For a time, stranded carp fought for air in stagnant Rooster Lake. They gave up the fight and the chooks picked their bones clean. The mad old rooster had gone west, and no doubt a few of his harem. The young survived; the cockerels, previously penned for the Christmas trade, had learnt to fly. They were birds; their ancestors had flown. Harry and his boys penned them. They crowed their protest for days before settling down to grow fat on forgotten golden grain. The goats were back in their paddock. Pliable beasts, goats, accepting of change.

The week after Maudy's wedding Georgie moved back across

the paddock. Margot remained with Elsie. Maudy had left her a two-foot-tall pile of *True Romance* magazines.

Jenny and Raelene didn't come home, and in early August, Georgie found out why.

Dear Georgie,

You might remember Veronica, Mrs Andrews, a neighbour I used to sew for when we first moved to Armadale. She's a nursing sister, and now runs a health farm in Frankston. I'm working for her, as a receptionist, or trainee receptionist, so I doubt I'll be home for a while.

We see Donny every Sunday. Maybe he knows us. I still feel guilty about leaving him there, but he's clean and cared for and I know I had to do it.

Now, some motherly advice. You're young enough, have brains enough, to do anything you want to do with your life, and no chance to do anything up there other than waste your god-given brain standing behind Charlie's counter. He's not your responsibility any more than Donny was mine.

Margot has always been happier with Elsie, and she's got her grandmother up there. You've got no reason to stay, as I've got no reason to go back. You said once that you wanted everything that wasn't to be possible. It could be down here. You're young enough to go back to school. There are night schools down here. Give Charlie notice and come down. I miss you . . .

Maybe she would, in a week or two. She had things to do on her first Sunday at home. She boiled up a saucepan of glue and set to work pasting newspaper around the lower sections of the kitchen walls. A hotchpotch of old news, upside down and right side up news. She'd begun the second layer when two cars drove into the yard: Bernie Macdonald's ute and the cop car. Georgie met her visitors at the gate, as Gertrude had always met her visitors. There was a stranger with them.

'Arthur Hogan,' he said. 'Maisy is my mother-in-law. She asked me to have a look at the house — if it's all right with you.'

'What's up?'

'Mum and a few are thinking about doing some improvements,' Bernie said.

'Go for your life.'

Georgie resumed her pasting, and fifteen minutes later Margot came across the paddock to see what they were doing.

'When is your mum due back?' the cop asked her.

Margot shrugged and walked by him.

'I dare say you're missing her,' he said.

'Ath if,' she replied as she disappeared into the kitchen.

He stood in the doorway, watching Georgie paste sheets of newspaper until she glanced up from her work and caught him staring. Arthur Hogan was walking around the roof.

'I hope he doesn't come through.'

'He's checking for leaks. Bernie was saying you've got a few.'

'It's the chimney, or the bricks it's sitting on. Harry fixed it — until the next time.'

A heavy iron chimney, rusty, but solidly built, put together with large rivets, spent its life attempting to drag itself free from the roof. Harry had put wooden props against it this time, had poked a bit of concrete between its brick foundations. Hogan suggested there could be heat enough in that chimney to burn the props, then he came inside to hammer on walls, study upside-down news.

'They've used decent enough timber in the frame of these front rooms. That little lean-to has been chucked together.' He pointed to Jenny's tin-plate plaque still hanging on a nail over Gertrude's door. *Ejected 2.8.1869.* 'Is that fair dinkum?'

'It's a private joke,' Georgie said.

'When's your mother due back?' Bernie asked.

'When Donny settles in,' Georgie said.

The cop carried in a carton of groceries before he left. Davies had sent them down.

'Tell him thanks,' Georgie said.

'Your little sister doing all right without your mum?'

'She's older than she looks.'

Chubby Margot, not much more than a child's height. She'd always been chubby, her chest measurement not much more than her waist. Elsie's cooking was adding to her weight.

The men left, Georgie continued pasting, Margot sorted through the carton of groceries. Butter, two packets of cereal, a packet of tea, a tin of apricot jam.

'Ath if we need that,' she said.

'How would he know what we need?'

'They juth came down here to have a good thtickybeak.'

'They came down to fix the chimney.'

'Harry already fixthed it.'

'Until next time.'

Georgie sighed and thought of Frankston, visualised Armadale, visualised St Kilda beach. Apart from Ray, she'd loved living in Melbourne. Missed Jenny.

'Brian hateth me now.'

'Tell him you're devastated.'

Wanted to go to Frankston. Couldn't, or not until she found someone to take her place at Charlie's.

He'd enjoyed the flood, or enjoyed living in his house with her. He'd told her she could stay on there. She'd never lived in a house where hot water came out of pipes, where she could have a hot shower every morning. Wanted . . . wanted more than Granny's house.

Margot was always happier with Elsie.

Margot wouldn't be happy anywhere.

'He hateth you too. He thaid you're too big for your booth.'

Sighed. Wanted to pitch that glue and run.

'Tell him I'm devastated, Margot.'

They were sisters and they didn't speak the same language and thank god Margot didn't like baked beans. She went back to Elsie's when Georgie opened a can. Georgie sat, spooning them out, like Charlie, spilling drips onto the pages of one of Archie Foote's diaries.

His handwriting was small, and in places he'd added a paragraph of mirror writing — the hot stuff more honest though. She read the afternoon away.

As did Margot. She read a story that changed her life. It was about an English girl, Penelope Wood, an orphan who had come to live with her aunt and uncle on a cattle station in Australia, where Tommy, a black boy, worked for her uncle. They fell in love, but the uncle and aunty were too stuck up to let them get married. Then, one night, Tommy climbed in through Penelope's bedroom window to tell her he'd won a scholarship to an English university.

That wasn't all that happened. The story didn't say exactly what did happen, but it said enough for Margot's imagination to fill in the gaps. *His hand crept like a dark shadow over the cream silk of her gown's bodice, as his lips found her mouth . . .*

Over and over again, Margot read those lines. How could words in a magazine make her ache for something she didn't understand? She lay on Maudy's bed, her own hand playing the dark shadow.

Six days a week, the train came in at ten, or there about. The mail was sorted by eleven. Georgie picked up the shop mail and a letter for Jenny, an official letter in a long brown envelope. Jenny had told her to open all mail. Mill men were insured against accident. She opened it, expecting it to be about Ray. It was about Ray, but not about his insurance.

'Hell,' she said. 'Hell.'

Two pages, the first typewritten only, a few lines. The second page was handwritten.

Dear Mrs King,
My name is Florence Keating. My husband and I saw in the
paper a while back that Ray was dead . . .

Her reading was interrupted by the cop demanding the keys to Charlie's old ute.

Two years ago, Charlie bought a '47 Ford ute from the garage man. He only drove it to the station to pick up a few goods, and on Fridays when he did the deliveries; rarely used more than one gear.

He'd made the mistake of complaining about his eyesight to Emma Fulton, who had come in with a legal document requiring her signature to be witnessed by a Justice of the Peace. Charlie, an always accessible JP, complained to everyone about his eyes, had been for years. Constable Thompson overheard him that morning.

'You shouldn't be driving, Mr White,' he said.

'My long distance is all right.'

'What's your year of birth?'

'None of your business.'

'I've just made it my business. Can I see your licence?'

'Can't help you with that,' Charlie said.

'Failing to produce a licence when requested to do so is a chargeable offence. Your licence, please, Mr White.'

'You can't see what I haven't got to show, can you? The coot before the coot before you wouldn't give me one.'

Thompson demanded the ute keys.

Georgie slid the letter back into its envelope and walked to Charlie's side. 'We'll have a pile of stock at the station,' she said.

The cop turned to her. 'Can you drive?'

'I've moved it.'

'I'll take you for a run now if you've got time, kill two birds with the one stone. I need to talk to you.'

*

Georgie was the reason Jack Thompson had gone into the shop, or her grandmother was. He'd done more than his fair share of eyeing Georgie Morrison. Not a man in Woody Creek between sixteen and sixty didn't eye her. She was tall and shaped the way a woman ought to be shaped, and on top of that she was gorgeous.

The driving lesson took some time. There was more to handling a '47 Ford ute than sitting behind the wheel and finding a gear that would move the thing back or forward. Jack Thompson took the wheel. They picked up Charlie's goods from the station, he helped carry the cartons into the storeroom, then drove the ute over the road to his own yard and down behind his house, just in case Charlie had spare keys.

Georgie and Charlie stood in the doorway watching him, Charlie cursing him — until he came back and made Georgie an offer she couldn't refuse.

'I could give you a lesson or two — that's if you're interested?'

That was how it started, how everything started, on that final Monday in August. Like the cogs inside Granny's old clock, still ticking on the mantelpiece, one turned and moved the others, and the old hands jerked forward, each action leading irreversibly to another.

TIME'S SOVEREIGNTY

Dear Jen,

I will come down, but not for a week or two. Would you believe, the new cop offered to give me driving lessons — after he'd confiscated Charlie's ute keys — which hasn't put Charlie in a happy state of mind. Remember how Granny used to say that when trouble came to Woody Creek, it came in cycles? It's been coming since the train got in this morning.

I picked up a letter for you, which I'm enclosing. It's from a solicitor and I don't like the sound of it.

Next: the new cop asked me to let you and your sister know that there's going to be some sort of hearing soon in Melbourne about Amber. He says there's a good chance that she'll be let out this time. I've told Maisy to let Sissy know.

Speaking of Maisy — not sure if this is a problem or not, but Maisy and a few others have got a fundraising committee going for you and Ray's kids. They want to do something about Granny's house. It needs it. Its wall linings were more or less washed away by the floods. Arthur Hogan has been down looking at the house. Maisy says he'd be in charge of things. Harry says Arthur built Elsie's house and that he's a qualified builder so he'd probably improve it. He's got some sort of idea to move two rooms from someplace and attach them to the two back rooms. He seemed a bit impressed by the age of Granny's front rooms, said that they were as solid as a rock — and the lean-to wasn't. He'd have to wreck it. They need your say-so to go ahead, just a signed note giving them permission.

Now, for the high note. I've been working my way through Itchy-foot's diaries and, if you can wade through the crude stuff, and there's a lot of it, they're interesting reading. I've found a bit about Juliana, which you may not want to read in its entirety, but she was married to a rich old Italian banker when she was seventeen years old. Archie met her on a cruise ship and got her pregnant. Her old banker paid for her to stay in Australia to have you. She was supposed to leave you at an orphanage and go home.

I know Granny always said he was an evil old coot, and no doubt he was!!! But he was a poet too. I've found dozens of poems scattered through his books, about all sorts of things. As I find them, I'm copying them in an exercise book for you. You'll enjoy some of them. I'm enclosing two: one he wrote in February of '51, only weeks before he died. It's sort of sad. The other one I reckon it could be about you. It was written in '34 when you were ten or eleven. Everything is dated. It's like he's documented his life, or the last thirty years of it.

Okay, off the high note and back to the low.

I'll have to move in with Elsie while they're building, or back into Charlie's house, which would be preferable, but with Maudy gone, Elsie is trying to mother me. And it's probably not a good idea to let Charlie get any more dependent on me than he is if I'm planning to desert him.

Righto, I'm off to bed — while I've got my own bed to be off to.

Love, Georgie

Reading one of Georgie's letters was like sitting with her by the stove late at night. Jenny almost reached for a biro to keep the conversation going. Just a glance at the solicitor's . . . He was working for a Florence and Clarence Keating.

'Keating?' She turned to the next page, handwritten.

Dear Mrs King,

My name is Florence Keating. My husband and I saw in the paper a while back that Ray was dead, and that he still had the two children with him when he died. He might have told you about me. My name was Florence Dawson when I lived with him.

This is very hard for me to write, knowing what most people think of a mother who leaves her children, but there were all sorts of reasons why I did.

The doctors told me when Donald was born that he had a bit of brain damage. He was a big baby and he was born backwards with the cord twisted around his neck. I was told not to have another one for a few years, but Raelene got started right away. I wasn't myself for the whole time I was carrying her, and after she was born I ended up having a total nervous breakdown. My mother had to come and look after me and the children. She never got on with Ray, not after she found out he was already married.

He was drinking. You probably know how dangerous he got when he was drinking. Flora Parker told me you'd left him for the same reason. He broke Mum's arm and we had to go to the hospital. I only left the children with Ray for two nights, but when we went back with the police, he'd gone with both of them. The police said they'd find him, but they never did. Mum said they weren't interested because I wasn't married to him.

I've been married to Clarrie for three years now. We haven't got any children. My doctor says that having had the two children so close and both of them big babies, it could have done

something to my insides. I've never got Raelene out of my mind.
I did try my best to look after both of them.

I know you've been a mother to her and to Donald, and we
wouldn't ever try to cut you out of their lives, but Clarrie and
I want to raise Raelene.

I hope after you read this that you won't look too unkindly
on me and that you'll understand a bit of what my situation
was at the time.

I'd be a good mother to her and Clarrie would be a good
father. He's got a foreman's job at a factory and he brings home
a decent wage. We built a nice house six months ago. She'd have
her own room. The school is quite close by.

Clarrie and I would like to meet you and talk face to face.
We've got a car. We can come up there, or you can come out
here, or if you'd rather, we could meet at the solicitor's office.
Yours faithfully,
Florence Keating

Just when you think it's over, it starts again. Jenny felt sick in the
stomach. Raelene had never heard of Florence Dawson.

The handwritten page placed face down, she glanced at the poems
Georgie had enclosed, uninterested . . . until she started reading.

GIRL [1934]

I know you, girl.
Feet in the dust, eye in the sky,
watching the eagle fly,
wondering why
he flies so free.

You dare to dream, my girl.
They're free.
You pick them from the roadside like dandelions.

and weave your daisy chains
of dreams.

I have lived where you play, my beauty.
I've followed the flight of the eagle,
my eyes upon the sky.
Dreams, as the dandelions, die.
Now wilted daisy chains
bind my feet
to the dust.

TIME'S SOVEREIGNTY ['51]

Old dreaming, mother fantasy
Dissembler of all boundary
The earth, the sky, the open sea
The world, my one true destiny
I swung on the rim of old rainbows, stole moon-dust to paint
*   a dawn sky*
Filled up my pockets with embryo stars, stole from a cherubim's
*   eye.*
I soared in the clouds with the eagle, at one with his supreme
*   nobility.*
Then time's arrow stilled my flight,
And a dark place stole my light
Now hell invades each day's totality
For the tyrant god Reality,
Hid well beneath the masonry of cold red-brick conformity,
He outlawed my sweet fantasy and placed a ban on dreaming.
It's lost.
It's gone.
In vain I stalk the boundaries of my life and strive to raise a
*   dreaming*
From an ever-widening gulch of yawing dislocation and despair

There's nothing there.
No more to suck on fate, nor breathe its draught of chance.
No more on borrowed wings to soar on high above the earth's
    cold floor.
Oh, hear my cry.
No more.
No more.
Oh, gift to me Aladdin's lamp and polish cloth,
Wove of the evening spiders, spinning in the banks of mist at
    river's end
That I may raise that ancient genie into life
And beg of he my promised wishes three.
Wish one: return deep dreaming.
Wish two: come home sweet dreaming.
And thrice my plea is dreaming.
Oh, fill this void with dreaming.
Cast out reality.
For fantasy alone can free time's prisoner of machinery
A rusting clock. No tock-tick-tock
Its main spring snapped
Old hands spread wide
From nine to three
The crucifix.
The final plea.

Grim tale, time's cruel sovereignty.

Jenny sat unmoving, disbelieving those words were from the pen of Archie Foote, her sire, Granny's crazy quack with itchy feet. For minutes she sat, one hand cupping her mouth, holding inside her the knowledge that there, on that table was irrefutable proof that she was of his seed. She wrote poems, similar poems with no rhythm and little rhyme, just a spilling of words, inner words that came from some well of truth within.

It was weird, and weirdly moving, like she was peering in through a secret window and seeing Archie Foote exposed, his varied personas removed and placed away. No jazz club singer jacket, no doctor suit, no kindly grandfather's blue tie to match his eyes, not behind that window. Just an old, old man, maybe a lonely old man, aware of his wasted years, aware that his lifetime party would soon be over and that he'd left no one behind to miss him when he was gone.

Only her.

Jennifer.

She hadn't missed or mourned him, had rarely thought about him. When Granny had heard he was dead, she'd taken her cheeky hat out of its box . . .

He'd drugged her, had aborted her first baby . . .

Jenny shook her head, attempting to remove a thought before it surfaced. But it was there, would always be there. She'd aborted two of Ray's babies, and until she'd lost Jimmy, had felt no guilt. A tree sprung from a seed may not produce identical fruit to the parent tree, but they are usually akin to it.

She liked to tell herself she was the daughter of Juliana, the tenacious woman. Granny had always said she'd had staying power, and good recoil.

'You've got the recoil of a rubber band,' she'd say. 'You, my girl, can be as obstinate as a mule.'

Obstinate? Who was Granny to name anyone obstinate? She'd wanted to burn Archie's diaries the day they'd arrived. 'That man never put anything on paper that was fit to read.'

Not Granny's to burn, though Jenny had done little more than flip through a couple, in the dark of the bedroom. Since '52, since the Foote family's solicitor had posted them to *Jennifer Morrison, Woody Creek*, those diaries had lived in a carton on top of Granny's wardrobe. It had taken Georgie to bring them out into the light of day, to find . . . maybe to find the inner man.

And Juliana, seventeen-year-old bride . . .

I have to go home, Jenny thought. I have to read those diaries. I have to get some distance between Raelene and Florence Keating too.

Her mother. Her blood.

Ray's seed.

'God! Where does it end?'

GREEN PLUMS

Joany Hall gave birth to a son after two girls. Tony, her husband, worked for Dave Foster fifteen miles out along Three Pines Road, and on a Saturday afternoon in September, Elsie, Harry, Brian and Josie drove out to visit the new arrival. They didn't ask Margot to go with them. Brian and Josie now referred to her as that 'pain in the arse'. They'd asked Teddy to go. He didn't. Lenny and Ronnie were going to the Willama dance and he wanted to go with them. They didn't want him. They were meeting girls at the dance, and the last time they'd taken Teddy he'd got into a brawl outside the dance hall.

Ten minutes after Lenny and Ronnie drove off, Jack Thompson arrived to take Georgie for a driving lesson.

Envy gnaws like a rat at a sack of grain, and, once in, it despoils. By eight o'clock, and still no sign of Georgie, envy was consuming Margot's entrails. Teddy wouldn't let her listen to Pick-A-Box, and she couldn't even go over the paddock to listen to it on Granny's wireless because Georgie didn't want to get the battery charged. She said the wireless reminded her of Donny.

At five past eight, Margot fought Teddy for the station, shoved him, pulled his hair. He caught her wrists and held them while she struggled.

'You're hurting me. I'm telling Harry on you.'

Early in life, Harry's boys had learnt to never lay a finger on the girls. Teddy wasn't hurting her, only controlling that snarly little bitch and enjoying watching her struggle. He was a year older than Margot. They'd suckled together for a brief period before he'd been weaned to a cup, which may have coloured his attitude towards her. He couldn't stand her.

She kicked him and he released her wrists, grasped her around the waist and carried her out the back door.

'Go home, you pain in the bum. You put my teeth on edge.'

'It'th my home here ath well ath yourth.'

And the snarly little bitch came back. He gave in. She changed the station, and sat damn near on top of the wireless to listen. So he stopped her listening.

'Is Georgie going out with that copper?'

Margot turned the volume higher. 'Thut up, will you.'

'Well, is she?'

'He'th giving her a driving lethon. Now thut up.'

'That's what she tells you.'

Margot didn't reply, didn't say another word until the bloke took the money instead of the box and missed out on getting a new car.

'Why doesn't he take her for a lesson in the daylight?'

'He workth.'

She sat beside the wireless until the show ended, then she rose and walked to the back door. Still no lights at Granny's house, and why did he take her for driving lessons in the dark? Margot stood watching the house, imagining Georgie kissing Jack Thompson over there in the dark — *his hand like a dark shadow* . . .

'Is she home?' Teddy was behind her.

'I can't thee, can I.'

He changed the station over to the wrestling, and she left the house, high-stepping along the track through the goat paddock, scared of snakes, of cobwebs, but wanting to creep up on Georgie and catch her kissing the copper.

A torch beam lit her feet.

'Coppers don't teach people to drive.'

'Well, he ith.'

'If you think driving lessons is all he's giving her, you've got rocks in your head.'

'I'm devathtated,' she said.

No car in the yard. She opened the door and he turned the torch off.

'Turn it on, will you?'

'Try saying please for once in your life,' he said.

'I want to light the lamp . . . pleath.'

He turned it on and focused its beam on her face. 'Do you know what he's doing to her, Marsie?'

Brian and Josie used to call her Marsie, never Teddy. He called her a snarly bitch. He'd liked putting her outside though; liked the feel of her against him. It had stirred him up.

'Want to know what he's doing, Marsie?'

The torch beam died and he grabbed her, aimed his face at her face, worked his way around to her mouth, got a grip on it and hung on.

A first kiss is soul-shaking to a twenty-year-old youth. He ran from it.

'I'm telling Elthie and Harry on you,' Margot yelled after him.

Gone, with his torch, and Margot left to feel along the mantelpiece for a box of matches . . . left to feel . . .

Her heartbeat was a throbbing drum in her breast . . .

Margot was throbbing, but not in her breast.

Teddy's hormones raging, he walked into town, looking for the copper's car, thinking of his brothers dancing with girls in Willama, or parked with them, kissing them, probably doing more than kissing them, like that copper was probably doing more than giving Georgie driving lessons. They'd been gone for two hours.

Teddy had been in love with Georgie since she'd turned twelve and he wanted to smash that pie-faced copper's head in.

He shouldn't have done what he'd done. He sweated over what he'd done, relived it, but stayed away from the house until Harry and Elsie came home.

When he did go home, he couldn't sleep. Margot slept in Maudy's room, a wall away. Tossed, turned, was awake when Lenny and Ronnie came in. Tossed until dawn, when he got on his bike and rode. He stayed away until nightfall, Georgie was sitting in the kitchen, Elsie serving up one of her curries. No one looked at him as if he was a leper.

Margot came in. He sat, waiting for that little bitch to open her mouth. Barely tasted his meal, his heart lurching every time she opened her mouth.

She didn't dob.

All week she stayed out of his way, or he stayed out of her way. Then the following Saturday, Lenny was playing football out of town, Ronnie, Brian and Josie went with him to watch the game, the copper turned up to take Georgie for her lesson, and Elsie, Harry and Margot wanted to play cards, wanted Teddy to make up the four.

He let them nag him into suffering one game. Harry and Elsie always played on the same team, which left him to partner the snarly bitch. And they won. They thrashed them. He liked winning. He sat on in the kitchen when Harry and Elsie went to bed, watching Margot play a game of Patience, pleased when she didn't win.

'How come you didn't dob on me?'

'I will nex_t time,' she said.

'Want there to be a next time, do you?'

'You thut up, Teddy Hall, or I will dob now.'

*

Elsie never could get enough of babies. The following Saturday, Harry and Elsie drove again out to visit Joany. Jack Thompson came by for Georgie, and Ronnie and Lenny left for the Willama dance. Teddy waited until they were well gone, then he turned the wireless to his favourite station, and waited for Margot to change it to Pick-A-Box.

She did at eight. And he grabbed her around the waist, pulled her with him to a chair and held her on his lap. Her backside rubbing up against him drove him back to having another go at her mouth. She didn't yell, didn't scratch his eyes out, didn't say a word when he pushed her from him and went out to the kitchen to get a drink, and imagine what the copper was doing to Georgie.

The bloke with the box refused to take Bob Dyer's money and ended up with a packet of washing powder.

'Thtupid fool,' Margot said. She turned the wireless off.

He walked in, turned it back on and changed the station, eyeing her as the loser might be eyeing his packet of washing powder.

'Get out of my sight,' he said.

'I don't have to.'

'I'll make you.'

He came at her. She stood her ground. He grabbed her, got a grip on her mouth. She was too short for him. Georgie would have been tall enough. Georgie had something under her sweater that he'd feel against him too. If Margot had anything beneath her bulky sweater, it was against his lower rib bones, but he sucked on her mouth and she pushed whatever was under her sweater into him, and maybe there were little green plums there. He kissed her, rubbed against her until he was busting out of his pants and he had to run.

Teddy was a mechanic, apprenticed to the garage man. Working on cars got his addled brain together during the day, held it together all week. Not at night. He'd start off imagining Georgie's breasts rubbing against him, and end up feeling Margot's little green plums. He tried to imagine kissing Georgie's lipsticked mouth. No imagination necessary when he thought of Margot's dry little mouth.

He'd got rid of her though. She moved back across the paddock that week; the rebuilding delayed for a month or two — Arthur Hogan was in a city hospital with a smashed hand.

She stayed home on Saturday night, listening to her own wireless. Harry had brought their battery in to be charged up. Teddy couldn't stand Pick-A-Box. He hated the hope of it, the dashed hope. Harry and Elsie never missed it, and when Bob Dyer's voice came on, Teddy took off outside.

Georgie and her copper were at the pictures. They'd given Brian and Josie a lift into town.

He stood staring across the paddock, considering a ride into town and letting the air out of the copper's car tyres. Or maybe he'd walk, cut through Flanagan's.

He made it as far as the orchard. The light from the old kitchen window was like a beacon on a black night, lit by wreckers to draw ships onto rocky shores. It drew Teddy towards the rocks, or to the window.

Margot was sitting at the table, turning the pages of a magazine while Bob Dyer howled, 'The money or the box'. He was offering a thousand pounds. No question what Teddy would have done. He'd take the money and run.

He liked watching her lick those dry lips, smile, living her life through the people on that show. She had nothing else. Harry had had enough of her, as had Elsie, though she wouldn't admit it. Teddy hadn't. He walked around to the door and let himself in.

'What do you want?'

'I want to hear if he takes the thousand.'

'You could have knocked,' she said.

'Like you do when you come over there.'

'Shut up and lithen then.'

Bob Dyer upped the price to one thousand, five hundred, and the bloke took it, and missed out on a can of baked beans. And that's the way it ought to be. You take what you can get your hands on.

He got his hands on her, tilted her chair back. Its front legs off the floor, she grabbed at the chair as he reached for the lamp and turned the wick low.

'Yell out for Mum, Marsie?'

Wick spluttering. Flame fighting for a while to live. Margot fighting to get off that chair. Then dark.

It all came down to accessibility in the end. Margot was accessible, and why had she moved back across the paddock if not to make herself accessible?

The back of the chair between them, he got a hand up under the front of her sweater and found his way up the rolls of pudge to those little green plums. Got his fingers down her petticoat to the soft silky cup of her bra. Not skin. Warm like skin, but his fingers wanted skin, and he got two inside her bra, and found a plum stalk.

Maybe she turned her head to protest. He gave her no time to speak, got a grip on her mouth and sucked while his four fingers found their way into that cup. Got the plum in his hand then, rubbing, kissing, until rubbing and kissing wasn't enough.

The chair dropped back to its four legs, he pulled her to her feet, pulled her sweater up, off, and pitched it; lifted her onto the table. High enough for him then; he licked that goat's-milk-and-cocoa-tasting little mouth, fought her bra clips open, her petticoat straps down. And he had both of them to play with, to lick and suck on.

Sweet, sweet Jesus, he'd opened the box and struck gold.

Ripped his own sweater off, his singlet off, opened his fly, and that little bitch panting for his mouth — and maybe more. She whined when he opened up her knees and got between them, rubbed his naked heat against her pudgy thigh, rubbing until he had to run — and where had he pitched his sweater?

He drew away from her to find it, and she whined and her hands made a grab for him. He hated that whine above all else. All his life, he'd hated it. Not tonight. He went back to suck the whine out of her.

'Are you going to dob, Marsie?'

Not a word out of her, but one of her arms was around his neck, stopping him from . . . from stopping, and, far beyond fear of consequences, he went for the goalposts. She could have stopped him when he pulled her pants down, when he dropped his own around his ankles. She didn't. He might have kicked that goal on Gertrude's kitchen table had either one of them known what they were doing. They didn't.

He had to get her down. Plenty of beds in this place. Try finding a bed with a pair of trousers tangled around your boots, when thrown off-balance by raging hormones, with utopia wrapped around you. He tried to shake one boot free, she slid, and *pow!* He blew the roof off. Blew his roof off.

'Bugger fuck,' he said as he fell to his backside, Margot on top of him. 'Bugger shit fuck.'

Maybe she came to her senses. She scrambled free.

It wasn't ending like that. He wasn't letting it end like that.

He took his boots off, pulled his trousers off. Located her by her breathing, her movement. She'd pulled her petticoat up, had one arm through its strap. He stubbed his toe on a chair leg, but he got her into the lean-to, sat her on the bed, got her skirt off, her petticoat off, then pushed her down and got down on her, every part of her pudge touching a part of him, his right hand exploring what was touching, his tongue exploring inside her mouth, a panting hot little mouth, soft with wanting what he was giving her. Holding him, even helping him to get inside her.

Margot was nineteen, had been reading *True Romance* magazines for five years. Tonight she was experiencing the bits the magazines didn't print. She'd always known about the male bit going inside. The sex book had talked a lot about the mating habits of rabbits, but had said nothing about things exploding in the female rabbit even before the male got in. None of the *True Romance* magazines had written anything about that. *Earth-shattering*, one of them had said, or *waves crashing against the shore*, or *stars bursting in the sky*. That's what it was like: earth-shattering, waves, Guy Fawkes-night fireworks at the same time, over and over and over, until the whole world was rocked by an exploding volcano that spewed out red-hot lava and buried her alive.

She couldn't move. He lay on top, panting into Georgie's pillow, lay for a long time, crushing her. And she didn't want him to move.

He did when he got his breath. He untangled himself and she lay as he'd left her, on her back, limbs spread. Thought he'd get dressed and go home. He didn't. He came back.

'Are you dead or something, Marsie?'

Maybe she was. Maybe she'd died and was floating in heaven.

'Where do you keep the matches?'

No words in her. Nothing. Just so beautiful. She was so beautiful.

He found his trousers, found matches in his pocket, and came back to the lean-to where he struck one. She had to move then to shade her eyes from the glare.

'I thought I'd killed you. Are you all right?'

'Put it out.'

'You look like one of those old-fashioned paintings of nudes lying there.'

'Put it out, I thaid.'

The spoilt bitch came back with that lisp. He'd always hated it. Wanted to touch that flesh and blood nude though. Wanted to get on that bed and do it all over again. Too late. The pictures came out at eleven. Fifteen minutes to, if the old clock was right.

He returned to the kitchen to find the rest of his clothes, and hers. He tossed a bundle to the bed.

'The pictures will be over. Georgie will be home soon.'

'That clock'th fatht,' she said.

'How fast?'

'It thaid quarter patht when Pick-A-Box thtarted.'

They did it again.

'Don't tell anyone,' he warned.

'Don't you either.'

'You'll have to do something about that bedspread,' he said.

And he got dressed, and he left.

Only the smell of his sweat then, and that other smell. Stupid magazines.

She rose. The lean-to bed was Georgie's. She lit the lamp and found out what Teddy had meant about the bedcover. The magazines hadn't told her what would happen to faded green chenille bedspreads either. She removed it, rolled, and pushed it deep into the wardrobe, straightened the blankets, the pillow.

Georgie would notice the missing bedspread.

Not if Margot was in her bed, she wouldn't.

An experienced girl might have smelt a rat when she came in ten minutes later and found her bed occupied. At eighteen, Georgie had evaded a few aimed kisses, most of them aimed by Jack Thompson, but was by no means experienced. She smelled fly spray and guessed Margot had found a spider in Granny's bedroom. Margot didn't spray spiders. She drowned them in spray.

Granny's bed was the more comfortable of the two beds on offer, its mattress, the one they'd brought home from Armadale. Georgie slid into it and slept like a log.

TRAGEDY DOGS WOODY CREEK FAMILY

A working bee to rehouse the family of the late Raymond King, killed in a horrifying mill accident in July, is being organised by Mrs Maisy Macdonald. The King residence, one of the first homes built in Woody Creek, will require considerable restoration, Mrs Macdonald said. Donations can be forwarded to the address below. Tradesmen willing to donate their time are asked to contact . . .

The newspaper cutting, pinned to Maisy's calendar in July, was yellowing, curling at the edges. The *Willama Gazette* had given her rehousing project three columns, had given her address and phone number. That paper had a wide circulation. For a week her telephone had run hot. Fifty per cent of the calls had been genuine. The second fifty per cent had been from women wanting to speak to someone about their own tragedy or from sickos who liked breathing heavily. Maisy had enjoyed telling them where to go. She'd received a lot of letters, fifty per cent of which had contained donations, a few had come from tradesmen offering their help.

Giving out her address was a mistake. In hindsight, she knew she should have said donations could be sent care of the post office. Since August, bits and pieces of furniture had started arriving on her doorstep. A month on, and every stick of unwanted junk in a thirty-mile radius was stacked beneath her verandas. She'd barely mentioned furniture to the *Willama Gazette* chap. 'Building materials will be most welcome,' she'd said. 'Any good furniture won't go astray.'

There are varying degrees of good. Her own idea of good was two or three years old. The depression had made hoarders of her generation; they'd saved their junk for a rainy day. The rains had come and gone, Ray King was near forgotten, Jenny had shaken the dust of Woody Creek off her feet, and Maisy couldn't get out her front door.

Dawn, her unwed daughter, spent time clearing a pathway through the junk. Maisy spent time sorting it, and taking the worst of it to the tip. George, now well into his eighties, spent much of his time kicking it out of his way.

It should have been gone by now, or the renovations at least started. Paul Jenner had offered his old house, Lonny Bryant's old house. The newer section was in reasonable repair. Arthur and his men had already disconnected two rooms and a small front porch; had removed windows and door from the back rooms. All work had stopped since Arthur had his accident.

There was a second news item pinned to Maisy's calendar.

WILLAMA BUILDER SUSTAINS SERIOUS ACCIDENT
The working bee to rehouse the family of the late Raymond King, killed in a horrifying mill accident in July, was delayed when Arthur Hogan, Willama carpenter, was rushed to Melbourne where surgeons are fighting tonight to save his hand.

The *Willama Gazette* had made more of Arthur's injury than it was, but a second trickle of donations had come in, along with a moth-eaten couch and two easy chairs.

Every man in town pledged his support when the rehousing committee was formed, but life had a way of getting in the way. One of Pat Carter's boys died in a car accident in Sydney. Then Charlie White tripped over in his storeroom and broke his arm. And Maisy started having women's troubles.

Breeding ten kids in ten years hadn't done her insides a lot of good, and Doctor Frazer said she had to do something about it. He made the appointment in Melbourne. Dawn tossed a coin to see which twin would drive her down there. Macka won. Dawn was going with them. Bernie got the booby prize. Someone had to stay home to keep an eye on George.

'She should have struck while the iron was hot,' George said.

A flying carton emphasised his words. It disintegrated. Pots flew; pots deemed useful by Maisy.

'She would have got rid of it weeks ago if your useless bloody son-in-law hadn't smashed his hand. And stop kicking shit around, or I'll stop picking it up.'

Bernie retrieved the set of saucepans and the caved-in carton as his father picked up a three-legged chair and pitched it at the fence. The chair had possessed four legs yesterday.

His mother had elected herself president and treasurer of the housing committee, so Bernie elected himself her deputy and called a meeting at the pub. They totalled up the available cash; opened the collection tins placed for weeks on shop counters. A few felt weighty, most of the weight was in pennies.

'Mum's going to be down there for two or three weeks,' Bernie reported. 'Hogan's hand will be out of action for months. What about you, Clive? Can you do it?'

Clive Lewis, referred to, when he wasn't around, as Shaky, had joined the committee because of the free beer. He'd been a builder before the grog got him.

'Nothing to it,' Shaky replied.

He was usually steady, even coherent, by nightfall, though you can't build a house by lantern light.

'Righto then. We do it next weekend.'

They had enough money. Maisy had started the fund off with a cheque for fifty quid. Freddy Bowen added a twenty, a few folk had put in a tenner. Most of the envelopes from out of town were lucky to contain ten-bob notes but they'd got a few decent cheques. A hardware store in Willama had delivered eight sheets of asbestos, the corners missing from a few. Another had donated three big tins of paint. A blow-in from Melbourne, who'd bought ten acres of creek frontage out past Davies's sawmill, where he was setting up a camping ground, had donated bricks for the chimney, delivered to the site, or to the road out front of Hall's. And thanks to the blow-in, they could need one of the Willama electricians. Melbourne campers might like roughing it, but they preferred to do their roughing with all mod cons. The blow-in, worth millions, was paying to have electric poles put in. They'd pass by Gertrude's front fence.

There are days in every man's life when he would have been better off staying in bed. Saturday, 20 September was such a day for Bernie Macdonald. It was Grand Final day, and his team was playing Macka's, and bloody Macka was staying down in Melbourne to go to the game — and he'd probably paid for an all-night last night. And there was Bernie, standing bum high in grass, watching his new log buggy hooked up to Bryant's front rooms.

Harry was behind the wheel. He got the load moving, moving at a snail's pace, riding on logs they'd wired and chained to the floor supports, logs that cut twin gutters through grass to the fence line.

It took half an hour to get those rooms out to the road, where they started their slow skid towards town, leaving twin gutters behind them. Log skids aren't wheels. They were too slow for Bernie. He drove on ahead to check on the crew at the site.

No sign of Shaky Lewis. He was supposed to be supervising the levelling, the spreading of sheep dip — Woody Creek's first defence against termites.

'Those bloody rooms are not far behind me!' Bernie said.

They were a good hour behind him. They'd reached the bridge and could go no further, the railings too narrow for the load. Bernie left his ute on the far side and walked over.

'Why didn't someone think about that bloody bridge?'

'Ask your mother and Arthur bloody Hogan,' Weasel Lewis replied.

'Nobody bloody expects you to think about anything, you dumb bastard,' Bernie said, and joined Joss Palmer and Harry who had the measuring tape out.

'If we get rid of that veranda thing, she'd squeeze through,' Joss said.

'Otherwise it's the bridge railing,' Harry said.

They stood rolling smokes while Weasel bitched. A car pulled up behind Bernie's ute. The driver sat for a time, watching interested enough, until a third vehicle joined the queue, then the two drivers walked across to see what was holding them up.

'She's too narrow,' Harry said.

'You'll have to back her up,' a farmer said. 'I can't hang around here all day.'

A house on log skids can only go one way. They considered the front porch/veranda, but knock it off and half the roof could go with it. That hadn't been in Hogan's plan.

The farmer tested a bridge railing with his boot. With little effort, it fell overboard and he damn near went with it. Harry watched the railing sink, bob up, turn itself around and float off downstream.

'She's still running swift,' he said, giving a post an experimental kick. It followed the railing.

A dozen boots kicking, and Harry stepped back up to the cabin. The truck and its load continued forward, men walking ahead, kicking posts and railing. That bridge had been in need of repairs for years.

The turn into the forest road took some doing. A tree had to come down. Plenty of experienced tree fellers in the group.

Away again, the logs gouging their twin gutters through Gertrude's top paddock, sliding across long grass in a straight line.

By ten thirty, Lonny Bryant's front bedroom, a portion of his passage, a decent-sized sitting room and his little front veranda had been manoeuvred into place, against Gertrude's eastern kitchen wall.

The troublesome iron chimney was down, along with its sinking foundations. The back of the stove sat flush against Bryant's room.

'What was Arthur going to do about that stove?' someone asked.

'A bit of asbestos will fix it,' Bernie said.

With still no sign of Shaky, he sent crews up to fix the fences they'd had to take down, while he drove back into town to get his builder, Harry behind him in the log buggy.

Shaky lived behind the pub. Bernie found him supporting one of its veranda posts, waiting for the bar-room door to open.

'We're waiting on you down there, Clive.'

Too early for Shaky to get his tongue working. He opened his mouth to say he was on his way, and exposed two canines glinting like pearls in a diseased oyster.

And that's the trouble with living in a bloody country town all your life, Bernie thought. You watch your heroes rot and your enemies prosper.

Few remembered who Shaky had been. Bernie remembered him as the only local ever to play first-class football in the Melbourne league. As kids, he and Macka used to piss off from their boarding school to watch him play. He'd been a champion until he'd buggered his knee, had been an average drinker until his wife pissed off with his kids.

Bernie belted on the pub door until Freddy came, trouser-clad, bare-chested, bare feet.

'We need him down there, Freddy. Fix him fast and put it on my tab. I'll be back.'

Shaky gone in for his fix, Bernie headed around to Lena Fulton's. Jorge, her Albanian, could lay bricks. Bryant's lounge room would need a chimney.

He was driving by the mill when Harry walked out, rolling a smoke. Bernie stopped. He could save him a walk back. He hated admitting it, but that rusty-headed, skeletal bastard had a head on his shoulders. He had four sons too, one of them a bloody good footballer. Three daughters too, two wed and one breeding. The bastard had a reason to get out of bed in the morning. And what did Bernie have? Bugger all, that's what he had — except for an illegitimate kid.

That was another trouble with living in a bloody country town. You grew old there; woke up one day knowing that you'd reached the halfway mark of your life and had nothing to show for it.

They drove back to the site, Shaky shaking, the Albanian jabbering. Harry took charge of the Albanian, led him over to the pile of bricks and offered him a wheelbarrow. Bernie took Shaky on a guided tour of the roofs and told him to work out some way of joining them. Shaky tossed his hands in the air and went inside to poke a broom handle across the stove and into Lonny Bryant's wall.

'We'll shove a sheet of asbestos behind it,' Bernie said.

'Burn them in their beds,' Shaky said.

'Not much loss, Shaky,' Weasel Lewis sniggered.

No one called him Shaky to his face. And another Lewis shouldn't have been down here. Everyone knew what was likely to happen if you got two of them in the same room. There was ten or fifteen years between uncle and nephew and a good height difference. Weasel might have made a good jockey, had he ridden a horse.

Shaky backhanded him. Weasel, looking for a way out, went through to the lean-to. No way out of there, until Shaky pitched him halfway through the back wall. It had to come down anyway.

Weasel was wed to Irene, Joss Palmer's sister. Joss got between the combatants.

'We're supposed to be constructing down here, not destructing.'

Weasel extricated himself from the wall; armed himself with a piece of it, which he swung at his uncle's head. Bernie needed his builder. He bulldozed the smaller Lewis through a side wall.

Twenty-odd men saw the lean-to roof begin its fall. Twenty-odd men dodged. Two didn't.

Bernie rose from beneath a sheet of corrugated iron. They dragged Weasel out; he swore he'd broken his back and went home, walked and twenty-odd men wished they could go with him.

Not Shaky. He was feeling better. He stepped over and on the fallen roof to peer into the washhouse-cum-bathroom, to walk through Ray's and Donny's bedroom.

'Make this one into their kitchen,' he said.

'They lose a bedroom.'

'Turn the bathroom into a bedroom and build them a new bathroom, where the bit we knocked down was.'

'They'd be walking through their bathroom to get to the kitchen.'

'Toss up a wall.'

That was the plan they went with, more or less.

The stumping of the new rooms was well underway when Freddy Bowen drove in with a keg of beer and a box of sandwiches supplied by the ladies of the building committee.

Many hands make light work and too many cooks spoil the broth. Gertrude's little stove, carried out into the light of day, now stood beside Norman's wireless. Harry connected up the battery. Lenny connected the aerial to the chicken-wire fence, and they tuned in as the Magpies and the Demons lined up for war.

And the bloody delivery truck from Willama chose to turn up. Bernie was the deputy treasurer. He held the purse strings. He missed the first kick.

At half-time, Freddy Bowen came down to collect his empty barrel and drop one off which was full, plus another pile of sandwiches and cake. Cake suggested tea to some. Elsie and Josie supplied the tea, and hung around a while to watch from a distance. Margot watched from a safer distance, watched Teddy, who watched her watch him.

The Albanian, occupied in building a fancy fireplace and chimney, approached the group. He used a combination of tongues, picked up in concentration camps, refugee camps, timber camps. Christ only knew how Lena understood him.

'Piss off and build your chimney,' Bernie said. 'Lay bricks.'

'No much de bleeka,' the Albanian said.

The footy had started again.

'Piss off, and get yourself a beer, you jabbering bastard of a man.'

'Da booza uberflieben. No much de bleeka. Is vay Ozdralia, ya?'

'You're in bloody Australia. Talk bloody Australian, or don't talk.'

'Upya vit morser, kinda poovta,' Jorge said, and he raised his hat and went home.

Poovta didn't require a lot of translation. Jorge's departure broke up the barracking group. Shaky returned to the job of wedding Gertrude's original roof — a skillion and near flat — to Bryant's tall gable, taller now, they'd stumped it high, and to the newer rooms, a lower gable.

He ripped out Gertrude's ceiling to see what was beneath it. It took five minutes for the dust cloud to settle.

'Rip the iron off her,' he instructed. 'And someone cut that bloody rose bush back.'

No one knew what he was doing, but he kept on doing it.

Once they'd found a wall beneath that climbing rose, someone cut a hole in it, about level with Gertrude's existing window hatch, which they'd ripped off to let in a bit of light. A couple of Bryant's old windows should fit those gaps.

Collingwood was ahead when some bugger knocked the aerial down with a sheet of asbestos. Lenny found it, connected it, and the game continued.

The bathroom was taking shape. The bathtub, cement troughs, water pipes once worshipped by Jenny were out in the yard. They'd knocked a hole through the south side of Ray's bedroom, big enough to fit the old iron chimney Harry had hoped to get rid of. Someone should have been watching the Albanian. He'd created a fireplace fit for a tsar, and ran out of bricks before the sitting-room chimney was four foot high.

Gertrude's kitchen was no more. It had no roof. They'd ripped up its floorboards. Found two shells beneath it.

'What the bloody hell are sea shells doing there?'

'Washed in from the ocean in the bloody floods.'

Collingwood won.

Macka would have been at that game. He'd be celebrating tonight. Should consider himself lucky he wasn't at the building site. Bernie may have knocked the rest of his teeth out. He turned the wireless off, unable to take more punishment.

The hammering, the sawing, masonite falling, men's cursing, continued until mosquitoes started biting and the sun sank down behind the walnut tree.

The new kitchen's new window gaps looked directly into the setting sun. Plenty of light in that room. No windows in any of those gaps yet. That was for tomorrow. Still a lot to do tomorrow. The electrician was coming at eight.

'Can you take your boys out to Bryant's old place in the morning, Harry, knock their old chimney down?' Bernie said. 'We need a ton more bricks. The Albanian lives near you, Joss. Kidnap him if you have to.'

Bernie was the last to leave. He lit a smoke and walked the walk. Never before had so much muddling activity by so many achieved so little in such a big way. It wasn't quite what he'd visualised when he'd driven down this morning, or what Arthur had visualised. Not a lot turns out the way you think it will.

'Bloody Collingwood.'

RAILWAY STATIONS

Nothing ever turned out the way Jenny expected it to. She'd expected to be home before six, but the way the tram was moving, she'd be lucky to catch the six-ten train, and it would be packed solid.

Finding her way out to Box Hill south on public transport had taken hours. Shouldn't have called in to visit Donny. He didn't know her. He didn't miss her. Should have asked someone at the home to call her a taxi. Hadn't. She'd thought she could do it on trams, but the tram hadn't gone far enough, and waiting out in the sticks for a bus was like waiting for grass to grow — in a drought. Raelene was almost asleep on her feet.

Florence Keating hadn't been what Jenny was expecting. She was so normal, pleasant; more nervous than Jenny, and the living, breathing image of Raelene.

And what the hell was she supposed to do now? Tell Raelene she wasn't her mother? How was she supposed to go about that? She was the only mother that little girl had ever known.

Wished someone had told her sooner that Amber wasn't her own mother. Not knowing who she was had messed up her life.

Give me a child to the age of seven and I will show you the man — someone once said. Raelene was seven. She'd had her Daddy Ray for seven years. He'd made her what she was. Demanding at times, but a perfect kid when she had no competition.

She'd been the centre of attention at Florence's house.

Florence and Clarrie Keating. He was a nice bloke. They were a nice couple. Jenny had gone out there today not wanting to like them. On the train into town, she'd planned to tell them that she'd fight them for Raelene — as she should have fought for Jimmy. On the way home, she was arguing both sides. And getting nowhere.

She hadn't known Ray had taken those kids. Maybe he hadn't, but Florence seemed honest, and, knowing Ray, he probably had.

The guilt she felt about leaving Donny at the home had dissipated over afternoon tea. If Florence wanted Raelene, then Donny too became her responsibility. She'd never felt like his mother, had never wanted to be his mother. Pitied him — as she'd pitied his father.

The Keatings owned a beautiful little house, brand new, or they'd own it in some future year. Clarrie was an ex-serviceman. He'd got a loan to build it. They'd started a garden, had a big backyard, a big black dog with a laughing face. Jenny, who'd never had much to do with dogs, even liked their dog, a gentle lolloping Labrador.

She looked at her watch. They'd be at the station in perfect time to strike the football crowd. She'd chosen the wrong day for her afternoon tea party. It would have been all right if they hadn't spent half an hour waiting for a bus to take them to the tram, then another twenty minutes waiting for the tram.

Raelene, chin down, was almost asleep, the doll she'd held onto for three hours sliding. Jenny caught it, removed it gently from Raelene's grasp, then drew that curly head against her. Finding a comfortable pillow, Raelene's eyes closed, and, carefully, Jenny placed the doll into her bag.

The Keatings had bought her that doll — not a big doll, but it wouldn't have been cheap.

Vern had bought Jimmy with a tip truck . . .

Shook her head, shook Jimmy away, and turned her mind back to Florence.

Florence had written twice; the solicitor had written a more threatening letter before Jenny made that first phone call, from the health farm, advised to make it by Veronica.

'You can't ignore solicitor's letters. Keep it out of the courts if you can, kiddo,' she'd said. 'Agree to meet with the Keatings, let Raelene meet them, and see where it goes from there.'

Should have met them at the solicitor's office while Raelene was at school. It might have been different to meeting them in their own home, meeting their dog.

It wouldn't have been. What you saw was what you got with Florence. She was so open — as Jenny had never been — except to Georgie and Veronica.

'I was a fool of a girl,' Florence had said. 'I got pregnant with Donald at seventeen. I thought I was in love with Ray at the time. He didn't tell me he was already married, or not until I told him he'd have to marry me.'

She'd said it in front of Clarrie. And he hadn't risen up from the couch, walked out. He'd taken her hand. He loved her. She loved him. It was written all over both of them. Lucky Florence.

If things had been different . . . If I'd married Jim in Sydney . . . If . . .

Florence had spoken about Flora and Geoff Parker too, how Flora had been so helpful with Donald. 'We keep in touch,' she'd said.

'We don't want a court case,' Clarrie had admitted. 'I don't make that sort of money.'

Jenny had Vern's two thousand pounds. She hadn't touched it, would never touch it. She'd touched the interest on it. Maybe that's what she should do. Take Raelene home and make the Keatings' solicitor take her to court.

She hadn't intended to stay in Melbourne, not until the day

she'd caught a tram out to Armadale and knocked on Wilma Fogarty's door — and was greeted like returning royalty, and offered a bed. Wilma had Veronica's phone number. One thing led to another.

Weird how life turns in circles, how people you leave behind keep coming back into your life, as if no move you ever make can cut the thread of who you are. Like Lila turning up in Woody Creek and knowing Jenny had been six months pregnant when she'd left the Sydney factory. Had to lie to her. Told her she'd found a nursing sister who had got rid of it. To some people, you have to lie. Now Florence, turning up out of Ray's past.

And Veronica. The day she'd gone out to Frankston, Veronica had picked her and Raelene up at the station and driven them to the same guesthouse Jenny had stayed at with Laurie. Not a lot had changed there. The dining room was the same, the reception. New desk, new phones, new paint and wallpaper; same trees, just older. It had been like coming the full circle of her life — with the same old red case in hand.

Maybe that's what you have to do: return to the start, knowing where the pitfalls are, and dodge them the second time around. Maybe she was supposed to start out fresh, and this time get it right.

Or break out of the cycle.

So break it. Go home and fight them for Raelene.

She's Ray's. I was his wife. I've raised her.

She's Florence's too. They've got the same hair, the same eyes.

Question: Do I love her enough to fight for her?

Question: Can I love her more than her own blood mother could?

Juliana would have loved me like I loved Jimmy.

Loved him the first time she'd held him, and he'd been the ugliest, most misshapen little bloke ever made. Hadn't seen his misshapen head, his scratches, just felt the love rising in her, overwhelming her.

Never, never, never would she come to terms with losing him. Never. She could tell herself a thousand times that he was with Jim, that he was attending the best school, that he'd end up with Vern's fortune. It didn't help. Nothing helped and never would. She'd wanted to watch him grow into an incredible man and to know that a part of her would continue on in him.

And she had to stop thinking about him.

Glanced out the window. Not far from Spring Street now. She recognised the park. Raelene sound asleep against her. Give her a few minutes more.

No part of herself would continue on in Raelene. A part of Florence and Ray would.

Football revellers everywhere, groups of them walking to the tram, the train.

She always looked for the tallest amongst the groups of boys, though Jimmy would be a young man now, seventeen in December. One day she'd see him, and she'd know him too. He'd have his father's hair, his father's hands.

Good hands for a football player. Did he play? Did he follow one of the Melbourne teams? Was he at the match today? Who would he barrack for?

The Magpies. He'd liked the warbling magpies.

The tram turned into Flinders Street. She woke Raelene when it crossed over Exhibition. 'We're nearly there, love.'

'Where's my dolly?'

'Safe in my bag.'

'I want to hold her.'

'When we get on the train you can hold her.'

They left the tram at Swanston Street and crossed the road to the station. People everywhere, swarms of them at the station, short men and tall, old men and young, groups of raucous boys, a few girls and women. The train would be packed to the rafters.

They were fighting their way through to their platform when Jenny saw a head above the crowd. Her legs wanted to follow. Not tonight. She'd followed too many tall boys, tall men. Always disappointed. And Raelene was attempting to get the doll. She always woke snitchy.

'Leave it, love. You'll spill everything,' Jenny warned, and turned with a segment of the crowd towards her platform.

A tired child is a determined child. Raelene pulled back. 'I want to carry my dolly now.'

'Hold my hand or I'll lose you.'

'No.'

Georgie is mine, Jenny thought. Jimmy was, and ever will be mine. Chips of her heart had broken off and made their way into those kids. Hold my hand, she'd say to either of them and they'd hold her hand, even seek that hand to hold. Walk, she'd say, and they'd walk for miles.

Ray was dead, and Raelene was Florence's daughter, and in the crush of a football crowd at Flinders Street station, Jenny knew what she had to do. She'd meet the Keatings again, but in the city next time, or they could drive down to Frankston. They had a car. She'd do it slow, let Raelene get to know them and they to know her.

'I want to carry my dolly, I said.'

'And I said, when we're sitting down on the train.'

And she saw him, standing on the opposite platform.

Pushed between the crowd blocking her view. And of course it wasn't him.

But it was, and the shorter, thick-set bloke he was standing with looked like . . . it was Nobby. Nobby and Rosemary from the week in Sydney.

Jim.

Call out to him. Jump down and run across the lines.

'*Six ten to Frankston, arriving platform . . .*'

To hell with the six ten to Frankston. She took Raelene's wrist and started back the way they'd come.

'Why are we going backwards?'

'Be a good girl and run for me, Raelie.'

'Why are we going backwards, I said?'

She'd seen too much of Margot, spent too much time arguing with her.

'I have to see someone.'

'That Florence again?'

'Someone I know.'

Or had known once upon a time; someone she'd kissed good-bye on another crowded station.

It was all circles, circles within circles within circles. And people stopping her from getting back to the beginning. Too many going her way, going the other way, and no one going fast enough. And Raelene dragging on her arm, not going anywhere.

Jenny lifted her and pushed her way between massed humanity, found a clear space on the platform and ran.

Couldn't see him when she got there. No train could have come in and gone out, not so fast. He could have been seeing Nobby off. She searched the crowd for his head, wasn't tall enough to see over those hemming her in. She'd never been tall enough without her high heels.

Frankston train on time, pulling in opposite. Always another train to catch. Raelene struggling to get down. Jenny freed her, and Raelene sat down.

Try picking up a bawling, kicking seven year old. Determined seven year olds stay down. Raelene's bellow dispersed the crowd. And Jenny glimpsed the back of his head. She'd know those ears anywhere.

'Jim!'

A few turned to the name. A few turned to stare at an out-of-control brat, to tut-tut at the mother. Florence Keating was her mother.

'Jim!' she called again. This time he turned to his name, and he saw her. Raelene left to kick and bawl her disapproval, Jenny ran.

*

Raelene thought about getting lost. She had one day in Myer's, when Jenny wouldn't buy white sandals at the sale; she'd got really lost and got scared. She scrambled to her feet and ran bawling after Jenny. Saw her grab hold of the tall man's hand.

Grown-ups didn't howl unless their grannies died. Jenny was howling, and talking, and the earrings that had pearls locked inside them like pirate's treasure were bobbing around her face.

Raelene pulled at her arm. 'Mummy, we're missing our train now.'

Jenny didn't care about trains. She had hold of both of the man's hands now, or he had hold of hers, as if they were both trying to stop the other one from getting away.

Trains made sparks at night, like trams did. They were electric, Jenny said. Raelene liked watching those sparks. The train came in, almost went past before it stopped, then everyone was pushing to be first in, and a heap of people came running down the platform.

'Mummy. You're being stupid.'

She was too. She was bawling against the man's coat now, right in close to him, and his big hands were sort of holding her there. One was on her back, holding her close to him, and the other one was holding her head, and his hand was so huge he could hold nearly all of her head in it.

They looked like love actors in a picture show. Everyone was staring at them. Even the people walking away looked back over their shoulders to stare, probably to see if the picture ended up with kissing stuff, like heaps of them did.

Big gentle hand brushing away her tears, and Jenny crying more at the touch of his hand, covering it with her own, locking it to her face. Loved his hands touching her, always had. They could reach deep into her soul and release the one she'd been born to be.

'Jen.'

Crying anew at the sound of her name on his lips, loving his voice, loving the way he said her name. Always had. Just Jen, never

Jenny. And her hands reaching for his face drawing it nearer, as she had that day at the Sydney station in '42. She hadn't cried that day. Too young then to believe in loss, in death. She couldn't stop crying today.

A million questions inside her, ten million words she wanted to say, but knowing, knowing she had all the time left in the world to say every last one of them, and that here, now, words weren't needed.

Just 'Jim.'

'Jen.'

That's all. Jen and Jim. That's all there'd ever been, all they'd ever needed.

And mouths, finally those wanting, aching mouths, one a little salty, reaching up, one a little out of practice, reaching down.

That's all.